THE
DEED

THE DEED

SUSANNAH BEGBIE

hachette
AUSTRALIA

hachette
AUSTRALIA

Published in Australia and New Zealand in 2024
by Hachette Australia
(an imprint of Hachette Australia Pty Limited)
Gadigal Country, Level 17, 207 Kent Street, Sydney, NSW 2000
www.hachette.com.au

Hachette Australia acknowledges and pays our respects to the past, present and future Traditional Owners and Custodians of Country throughout Australia and recognises the continuation of cultural, spiritual and educational practices of Aboriginal and Torres Strait Islander peoples. Our head office is located on the lands of the Gadigal people of the Eora Nation.

Copyright © Susannah Begbie 2024

This book is copyright. Apart from any fair dealing for the purposes of private study, research, criticism or review permitted under the *Copyright Act 1968*, no part may be stored or reproduced by any process without prior written permission. Enquiries should be made to the publisher.

A catalogue record for this book is available from the National Library of Australia

ISBN: 978 0 7336 5079 6 (paperback)

Cover design by Christabella Designs
Author photo courtesy of Kerrie Brewer
Typeset in 11.5/17.5 pt Sabon LT Pro by Bookhouse, Sydney
Printed and bound in Australia by McPherson's Printing Group

MIX
Paper | Supporting responsible forestry
FSC® C001695

The paper this book is printed on is certified against the Forest Stewardship Council® Standards. McPherson's Printing Group holds FSC® chain of custody certification SA-COC-005379. FSC® promotes environmentally responsible, socially beneficial and economically viable management of the world's forests.

FOR MY PARENTS

1

Jenny was woken by her breathing. Short and shallow, barely making it to her lungs. When she sat up the weight was there, a lead ball in the middle of her chest. So she knew. Something was wrong. Badly wrong.

When she stepped outside the light was dawning, a pale, almost translucent blue. She got in the ute and turned the ignition. It was a shame to disrupt the hush, but she had no choice.

He was tired when she visited last. He looked thin, but she couldn't say it. When she left, he was standing in the front yard, Nell by his side. He was strong and tall in the sunlight and Jenny told herself he was fine.

She drove slowly. Carefully. She pulled off the highway onto Coorong Road and crept along Main Street. Coorong was dead at this time of the morning. No cars, no streetlights, no people. Jenny would have enjoyed it without the weight. She took a breath in, like she'd been taught, and slowly let it go. It didn't help. Counsellors knew about anxiety, but they weren't much use when it came to premonitions.

The stock route had a name now. Wangara Road. It was a big name for a few kilometres of gravel. Ellersley took up most of one side, which wasn't saying much. As Jenny's ute rattled over the grid and hit the dirt track, the sun tipped over the ridge. She followed the track to the homestead, spitting up eddies of dust, and killed the ignition a few metres from the house, rolling down to the yard.

Her boots crunched loudly on the gravel. It sounded more like a tip truck emptying than a person walking.

She unlatched the gate and continued warily up the concrete path. The screen door was jammed half open, and thick silence was pouring out of the house.

Jenny clomped up the steps and leaned in.

'Hi Dad, it's me.' It was the first time she'd spoken that morning and it came out croaky. She cleared her throat and tried again. Louder.

'Dad? You here?' Her father scoffed at the idea he was going deaf, but he hated to be caught off guard.

Jenny scraped the screen door wide open and stepped into the porch.

'Dad?' Her voice collapsed in front of her, knocked down flat. She crossed the cracked lino and stood at the hallway entry, not ready to cross the threshold. The air smelled stale and trapped, like any old man's house, but there was something else. Something foul. A hostile presence, telling her to get out. She would have obeyed, would have run, if it were any other house. But it wasn't. It was Ellersley. It was her dad, and she was the only one there. She had to keep going.

Jenny stepped across the metal strip pinning the carpet edge and paused for a moment to let her eyes adjust to the dim. She went slowly, cautiously.

Three steps in she found the crumpled body of her dead father.

2

'Now that's the way to bury your old man.'

Tom Edwards smacked the side of the telly, rattling the dinner plate on top. The fuzzy lines dispersed, leaving one transecting the screen. It was the best he'd get. He could see the people, at least.

'Look at them. The whole bloody tribe must be there.'

He sank into his Jason recliner, wincing. He put the telly on for company during dinner. He couldn't eat much, but it was easier if he was distracted from the bloating.

The program was part way through, but it didn't matter. The documentaries were all the same. That bloody half whisper of some English bloke who thinks he's discovered a lost civilisation.

Tom stabbed a fork into his lamb chop, sawed an edge off and started chewing.

It was all bullshit. Those people weren't lost. They didn't need some foreigner sniffing around them like a hungry dog. They sure as hell didn't need their lives broadcast to the rest of the world.

He extracted a piece of gnawed meat from his mouth, inspected it, and put it back on the plate. Six months ago, he'd butchered this one himself. Now he was hardly fit to swallow it. He couldn't taste it anyway. Nothing had taste now, not even a homegrown hogget.

I should turn the bloody thing off, he thought irritably. But once he was settled with a meal on his lap it was hard work to haul himself up again.

The scene changed; a body wrapped in red cloth, and women dancing and wailing. A whole lot of carry-on. Too much, in Tom's opinion, but at least they were mourning. At least they showed up. It was more than he could say for his tribe.

Where were his kids? A lump growing in their father's belly and his limbs wasting away, and where the hell were they?

He'd been losing strength for a few months, but he hadn't paid much attention. The lump though, the lump was serious. It was growing at a rapid pace. And the weight had been falling off him just as fast. He knew he didn't have long to go. A month, maybe.

And he would bet on his property – the whole ten thousand acres – that when he died there would be no king's robe wrapped around his body. No handwoven mat to keep him safe in his grave. His kids couldn't get it together to chop down a tree, let alone build a coffin to bury him in.

Tom watched as two men lowered the corpse into a shallow pit. It was a serious moment, and Tom meant no disrespect, but he found himself smiling. It wasn't the documentary. It was the thought. It was the most entertaining idea he'd had in a long time.

Tom pulled the side lever on his recliner and rocked himself up. He switched off the TV and took his plate to the kitchen, most of the food still on it.

Maybe it could be done and maybe it couldn't. He'd never know unless he tried. It might prod them hard enough to open their eyes. Even if it didn't, it would give him a laugh, and bloody hell he could do with it.

One month left, or thereabouts, and four children to wake up.

Tom Edwards was going to enjoy himself.

3

He was lying on the bedroom floor in his old-man pyjamas, face down and buckled over, one arm splayed out on the rose-patterned carpet. A trail of blood and shit streaked down his legs, and a tarry stench leapt up at her. Jenny blocked her nostrils and stood her ground. She breathed softly, letting go of the tightness in her chest and waited for the stillness to arrive.

When the stillness came, Jenny didn't have to make the decisions. Somehow a path of action opened before her. She knew where to put her thoughts and her feet; what to do with her hands.

Now, for example, she knew it was time to do a site survey.

A wobbling track of excrement led Jenny down the hall to the bathroom. It was a long way for a dying man to walk. She could see him though, determined not to be caught out. Not even by death. She imagined him stubbornly putting his slippers on and his shoulders back, walking down the hallway to use the toilet like a civilised person. How he got back was a different question altogether. The thought of her father too weak to walk was beyond Jenny's imagining.

The smell was sickening. It was as rotten as roadkill. Worse. It filled her nostrils, becoming stronger and fouler with each step closer to the bathroom. Jenny pulled a man's handkerchief from the pocket of her dress, held it to her nose and pushed open the bathroom door.

He hadn't used the toilet like a civilised person. He had used the bath instead. Splattered black tar was spread far and wide on the wall tiles, the floor, the cracked porcelain. There was a puddle of bright red jellied blood in the bottom of the old claw-foot tub. Jenny looked down at the congealed mass, and then up at the flecked tiles above the bath. She shook her head with wonder. How did it get all the way up there? It didn't quite make the showerhead, but it wasn't far off.

First things first. She tied her hair back from her face, folded the handkerchief into a triangle to cover her nose and mouth, and knotted it behind her head. She tucked her Liberty dress into her large cotton briefs and pushed the window above the handbasin wide open.

The ledge under the mirror held her father's few toiletries. Shaving kit, a black plastic comb, a toothbrush. The end of a tube of toothpaste in a cracked mug. Jenny gathered it together and took it through to the laundry sink.

There was a hose curled up in the geranium bed by the back door. Jenny attached it to the garden tap and turned the pressure right up. Doubling the end of the hose back on itself, she dragged it into the house. Once she was through the bathroom door, she released the kink and water shot out.

She started with the excrement clogging up the bath; rusty bore water shooting into the faeces and red jelly, flushing and flushing until the plughole was no longer blocked.

Pressing her thumb hard on the end of the hose, she directed a high-pressure spray to the walls, starting at the top and washing down, lifting the black splatters off the tiles. When the bulk of the material had been washed away, she kinked the hose and clumped back through the laundry to chuck it outside.

Now for the real work. Jenny didn't mind. Real work was just fine. It had a solid surface, well-defined edges. You knew where you were with work. It was everything else in life that was the problem.

She pulled a bucket down from the shelf and turned the hot tap on. She half-filled it with steaming water and added a generous dose of A-grade hospital bleach. A second bucket with clean water for rinsing, rubber gloves, scrubbing brush and a car sponge and she was ready to go.

Scrubbing was first. Jenny worked methodically with the brush, scouring each tile and the grout in between. Ledges and edges, the mirror, the cistern, the iron claws; nothing was missed.

Her cotton-clad bottom wobbled hard as she scrubbed, but she was unconcerned. There would be no ridicule. The only other person in the house was dead. She covered the same area again with the sponge, and then rinsed it off with hot water and a rag. As she reached the end of the tiles she backed out on her hands and knees into the hallway. She stood up, stretched her back and smiled appreciatively.

'Time for a break, Jen. What do you think?'

She knew there was more to do, but a person couldn't work without a break. It had been an early start that morning, so she had plenty of time.

She untucked her dress and headed down the hallway to the kitchen, making a brief stop at her father's room to straighten him out. The last thing she wanted was her father's body stiffening up in that awkward position. He'd hate it if anyone saw him like that. She rolled him onto his back, stretched out his legs and placed his arms by his sides, patting his chest gently before she left the room.

The kitchen was cool, and the rainwater clear. Jenny leaned back against the bench, glass in hand, and considered the next stage of the job.

It wasn't going to be as satisfying, trying to lift the stains from the carpet. But bleach could give surprising results. She drank her last mouthful, gave the glass a quick rinse and went back to the hallway.

She started at the bathroom end, methodically scanning the carpet for blood and faeces. She applied a diluted bleach solution to each spot, rubbing gently to remove any solid matter. In this way, on her hands and knees, she shuffled towards her father's bedroom. She could feel the pressure growing in her chest and it was getting hard to take a proper breath.

'It's only natural to feel anxious,' she could hear Dr Phil saying to a talk-show guest. 'Death is very stressful.'

But it wasn't death that concerned her. A dead body was fine. The trouble was what came next. Once she had finished cleaning her father there would be nothing left to do. Not a single thing that could reasonably excuse her from calling Christine.

His body was already stiff and cold. It was a good thing she had straightened him out.

Jenny undressed him and laid him gently on a towel. She sponged the loose, dry skin, all the way from his bony forehead to his hooked toes and patted it gently dry. She spoke to him quietly as she worked, and he listened. It had been a long time since he had listened so kindly.

She dressed her father in fresh pyjamas, made his bed with clean sheets, and, with great care, lifted him into it. It wasn't hard to carry him. He was so thin. So light.

She washed the carpet he had been lying on, bundled the soiled clothes and linen into a plastic bag and put it in the hall. She went back in, one last time, to close his eyes, then came out and closed the bedroom door. It was done.

What Jenny most wanted, then, was to leave her father and her family home in peace. To pick up the garbage bag and walk out, closing the screen door behind her. To leave him there in his clean pyjamas, so he could keep on sleeping forever and ever, Amen.

But she knew it wouldn't work. It would come back to bite her sooner or later. Probably sooner, given that it was summer. Bodies don't hold out that long in the heat.

It was a dreadful thing, but the time had come. She had to ring Christine and set the disturbance in motion.

4

'What's dead?' Christine was distracted. Nicholas was due at cricket, and he was complaining because he couldn't find his gear. She put her hand over the mouthpiece and glared at him.

'For goodness' sake, Nicholas, look in your wardrobe. Third shelf. Clean whites. Claudia! *Claudia!* You're coming too, so get down here.'

She tuned in to the phone again. 'Look, Jennifer, this really isn't the best time. Can we talk about it later?'

Not long after she married Stephen Minehan, cardiologist-in-training, Christine had taken to using her siblings' full names. It was more dignified, and besides, those were the names they were baptised with. They should be used. Christine felt the same way about Nicholas and Claudia. The last thing she needed in her household was a 'Nick' or a 'Claudy'. The thought of it made her shudder.

'*Move*, Claudia – I'm not joking. In the car.'

Christine knew how to do volume. It was part of her skill set. She had learned it by bellowing across the paddocks as a child, but it was highly transferable. She could raise a family member from the far corner of their two-storey home with no effort.

Christine put on the dishwasher as she spoke, and a gentle beep was followed by the vigorous sound of water slushing.

'I'm sorry, Jennifer, was that dead or Dad?' She pressed the phone against her ear to seal off the background noise.

'Dad's dead?' Christine paused to listen properly. 'I see. Dad's dead.' She was processing the information. 'Well, that's both words, really, isn't it?'

Christine's response was not immediately sympathetic, but she didn't want to be late. Nicholas's coach was strict about punctuality.

'All right, what have you done so far? Called the police? Dr Briggs? How about David and Sophie?' Christine reached for her handbag, checking for the essentials. Wallet, mobile, lipstick.

Christine paused. 'You've cleaned up a bit? Our father has died, and you have "cleaned up a bit". For goodness' sake, Jennifer. How long have you been there?'

Christine placed her hand over the mouthpiece to snap instructions at her children, both standing helplessly before her. 'In the car, go. We're still going. *Go!*'

'Oh,' she said into the receiver. 'You thought I might do it. All of it, no doubt. From six hundred kilometres away. Yes, I see. Fine. No, Jennifer, you just stay where you are, and I'll get onto it. Jennifer? Are you still there? Hold it together. This is not the time to fall apart. All you have to do is stay there and I'll sort it out.'

Christine hung up, opened her compact mirror and applied a fresh layer of lipstick, considering the day's program as she worked. Alterations were required. Significant alterations. She snapped the mirror shut.

First job – Stephen. He had started doing a Saturday list for procedures. It suited his clientele. Heart attack–prone patients didn't like their work schedules interrupted. Christine punched in the number of his consulting rooms.

'Nicola, it's Christine.' Christine tapped a staccato rhythm on the marble benchtop and waited for Nicola to respond. There was always a delay.

'Yes, of course you should put me through.' The ten-second music loop started, and Christine tapped faster.

'Scrubbed? Fine. Yes, you can take a message. Write this down. My father has died. I will drop Nicholas at cricket now and bring Claudia to the rooms where she will sit in the waiting room until

Stephen finishes in theatre. He will then take Claudia to pick Nicholas up from Jonathon's house where I will arrange for him to go after cricket. I'm going to Ellersley. I'll phone from the road to make further arrangements.' Christine could hear hurried scratching at the end of the phone.

'Have you got that? Fine. Goodbye.'

Nicola was one of Stephen's more annoying receptionists. Snippy and smart. Way too quick with the hold button. She needed to be pulled into line.

The kids were waiting in the car, so Christine kept moving. She dashed up the stairs to her bedroom and packed an overnight bag. Old clothes for work, a suit for the funeral and her toiletries. She carried it down to the garage, switching off lights as she went, and set the security alarm on her way out.

An hour later Nicholas was batting in the practice nets, Claudia was sitting in Stephen's waiting room with her iPad and Christine was on the highway. She had even achieved a three-minute conversation with Stephen between procedures. Now it was time to get to work.

First, she dialled triple zero. She was quite aware this would not be classified as an emergency, but triple zero was the most efficient option. The recorded voice listed the choices of ambulance, fire and police, and Christine paused, hoping for another option. A capable woman, maybe. Now that would be a service worth offering. Perhaps she would suggest it to the NSW Emergency Services.

'Police please.' Although it wasn't exactly what she wanted, Christine was aware of the value of courtesy.

'Good morning, Officer. My name is Christine Minehan, I'm calling from St Ives in Sydney. My father, Thomas Edwards, has passed away. He is at the family property, Ellersley, near Coorong. Currently my older sister, Jennifer, is at the house.

She's understandably distressed and feels unable to make the call herself.'

The officer who answered gave Christine a lecture regarding the use of emergency services, then put her through to the Coorong Police Station. It rang and rang, and Christine was preparing a message when the phone was picked up. Christine shifted from irritated to polite, introduced herself to the Coorong police officer and explained the situation. Officer Greaves was surprisingly helpful. He said he would get out to Ellersley straight away. Christine doubted it, but at least the intention was there.

The tag on her windscreen beeped as she hit the motorway, and she instructed her phone to call the Coorong Medical Practice.

Dr Briggs was old now, but that had its advantages. He took the time to answer Christine's call, and he didn't hesitate in offering to meet the police at Ellersley. The patients could wait, he said. If he was gone long enough some of them might get sick, which would be a nice change.

Christine didn't bother ringing the solicitor. No one at Mindle, Seifort & Sloane would be working on the weekend. Lawyers in the country played golf on Saturdays, or plucked the deadheads off their roses.

The limit changed to 110 and Christine increased speed. Next on her list was David.

David was as hopeless as ever. It had nothing to do with their father's death. Semi-commitment was the way he worked. There was no such thing as 'yes' or 'no' with David. He was the master of maybe. But he agreed to return to Ellersley, at Christine's firm suggestion, which was something. Not just for the funeral, but today, or if that proved impossible, tomorrow.

Christine adjusted the climate control before making the final call. Fury was, if not inevitable, highly likely. Cool air would be required.

Sophie's phone rang out. Once. Twice. Three times. Christine left a message for her to call back and punched the button on her steering wheel to hang up. It was ridiculous to own a phone and never answer it.

Sophie had to start living in the real world. They were the adults now.

5

Jenny knew she was meant to stay at Ellersley. She knew it would look odd, suspicious even, if she left. She knew the police were on their way and she knew what the rules were because Christine had made it quite plain that she had to stay put, but she still couldn't do it.

It was too hard to breathe. She did try. For twelve minutes and thirty-five seconds. She counted on the digital clock on the desk. Then her arms hoisted her up from the wicker chair and her legs walked out before she'd even realised they were moving. She left a note tucked between the flaking frame and the netting of the flyscreen door.

Dear Officer,
I'm sorry I couldn't stay.
Yours sincerely,
Jenny Edwards

It wasn't the right thing to do; she knew that. But it was polite. And it was true.

She broke into a trot as she crossed the yard, the garbage bag banging against her leg. She chucked it on the back, started the ute and made her getaway.

The police would be fine without her. It was probably better she wasn't there. Otherwise, they'd be pawing through the bag of bloody clothes with their plastic gloves, making a mess after she'd tidied everything up so nicely. It was much better for them to inspect the place without her.

It was a lovely, clear run home. There was enough time to drop the bag at the tip and still get back in time for morning tea.

The ute rattled into the drive and Jenny killed the ignition. She hurried up the steps onto the verandah, kicked off her boots and opened the back door. Ten twenty-five. Jenny smiled. She'd made it.

She padded across the kitchen lino and switched the kettle on. Humming quietly she rinsed out the teapot and reached for the plastic canister. Making tea, that was her job now. It had nothing to do with officers or sisters or being told to wait, just *wait*, for who knows how long.

Jenny got her morning mug and a packet of Iced Vovos, and when the tea was poured took her refreshments to the rocking chair in the lounge room. She held the mug between her palms and took a sip. Ah, yes. Yes, indeed. She closed her eyes and rocked gently.

Just as she was drifting off the telephone rang, jolting her eyes open. It gave her a nasty shock. It always did. Such a startling clanging; and it would go on and on until she picked up. That was before Matthew installed the answering machine. It was unsettling to hear his voice announce, 'We are unable to come to the phone right now', but it was so much better than opening a direct line to the unknown.

Jenny let it go to the machine the first time, but Christine's message was sufficiently severe to make her answer on the second.

It was a mixed blessing, hearing that Chris couldn't reach Sophie. On the one hand, it took the focus off Jenny's speedy desertion of the farm. There was the other hand, however. It was holding a dreadful task. Christine was putting Jenny in charge of finding Sophie.

Jenny didn't want to call Sophie. It was bad enough phoning Chris, and she knew Chris would manage just fine. It was different with Sophie, though. She was unpredictable. The best outcome for Jenny would be Sophie not answering. Then she could say she'd tried, and that would be enough. But Sophie might pick up. And if she did, Jenny would have to tell her.

Even though she hadn't spoken to Sophie in months.

Even though her palms were sweating, and her voice was shaking, and she had no words to tell Sophie the news and no words to say after that, either.

6

The shrill ringing dragged Sophie up through layers of consciousness until she was almost awake. She opened her eyelids a crack and squinted at the bright daylight. Ouch. She rolled to face the wall and pulled the sheet over her head.

It had been a big night. Huge. Sophie had had an epiphany. Okay, maybe not an epiphany, but definitely a flash of insight. She was sorting mail at the Newtown Post Office when it hit her like a bolt from the depths of the enormous canvas mailbag. She was done with being a postwoman. It was over. So she stood up, walked through to her bitch of a supervisor and quit.

There was nothing more satisfying than chucking in a shite job. Especially if the boss was mean from day one. Which Beryl was. Do this, do that, not in there, put it here first, then the tray, sort it by blah, blah, blah. She never let up.

There were no breaks, either. Apart from the thirty-minute lunch, which was compulsory, so it didn't count. A break meant a few minutes for a laugh, or a cigarette every now and then. Beryl was not the kind of boss to let that happen.

'No smoking in an Australia Post facility,' Sophie was instructed on her first day. 'If you need to be reminded of the regulations read the Policy and Procedures Manual in the second drawer.'

That was a word-for-word Beryl quote. The woman deserved everything she got.

'You can't just quit!' Beryl was in shock when Sophie told her. Sophie could see her reaching for the second drawer.

'Watch me,' Sophie said.

Beryl had the manual on the bench and was flicking pages like a woman possessed. 'The rules are a minimum of two weeks' notice.'

'Sure they are.' All Sophie's ex-bosses had tried to do this, one way or another.

'Look! It's right here.' Beryl was jabbing a finger at the page.

'What are you going to do?' Sophie was extracting her bag from the regulation locker. 'Call the police?'

'I might.' Beryl's face was going purple. Or red. Either way, it was the colour of furious. 'You can't do this! You just can't. The rules are there for a reason.'

Sophie rummaged in her bag for her cigarettes. 'Are they?' She flipped open her lighter. The blue flame flickered around the end of the cigarette, and it caught, glowing red. Sophie inhaled deeply, blew a smoke ring at Beryl, pushed the door open and left. Finally, she was out of there. So what if it had only been two and a half months? It was sucking the life out of her. She could have lost a decade in there without blinking. It was brilliant to be moving on.

The first time Sophie had a life epiphany she was sixteen years old. Sixteen and eleven months, to be exact. Maybe it was an age crisis. Anyway, one day she decided to go to England. The next she told her dad. Maybe she was trying it on, but he got all proud and sentimental and said at least one of his kids was going to do something with their life. She couldn't pull out then.

He said he didn't mind her leaving high school. He could see she was suffocating, choking on the dust of that old school bus. He said Coorong High wasn't much of a school anyway. It hadn't done the others any good. Besides, it wasn't right for her to be stuck on the farm with only her old man for company. Sophie didn't know what to say to that. They were sitting at the kitchen table, having just finished dinner. Sausages and mash and frozen peas. Her knife and fork were lined up together on her plate, and there was a puddle of tomato sauce near the rim.

The following week he took Sophie to the travel agent in Albury and pulled out his chequebook to pay for the flights. He gave her money to tide her over until she found her feet. Real money. Physical dollars. He said to change it to pounds when she got to Sydney.

It took a while, to find her feet. She told him all about it, for the first year. She phoned Ellersley reverse charges and waited for the coin to drop – at least that's how it sounded – and somehow he was near the phone every time she called. He said there was no shame in working in a pub. A girl had to eat. And pay the rent. And of course she needed clothes. He topped her up every now and then.

They both knew it was temporary, her job at the pub. When Sophie had her first career epiphany – she couldn't remember now exactly what it was – she phoned him straight away to tell him her plans. He loved it. Wanted to hear all about it. He said he always knew she'd succeed. 'Go for it, Soph,' he said. 'Bull by the horns, girl. Go for it.'

But then she found out there was a totally uninspiring amount of training and courses and paperwork and blah, blah, blah. And if she went through all of that *and* got employed, which was no guarantee, she realised she would most likely spend the rest of her life in a grey suit catching the underground to some rubbish job that was more boring than Coorong ever was. She was better off pouring pints.

It was the first career cycle of many. Inspiration, reality check, desperation and back to pouring pints. She made friends who were good for a laugh, and she went out with a nice English bloke, then another and another. She phoned her dad, but less often.

Then one day she was walking to work; it was miserable, cold and dark, and she realised it was only three o'clock in the afternoon. Three o'clock.

Sophie got home from the pub that night and sat on the side of her bed, colder and more miserable still. She called Ellersley for the first time in months. It rang a few times before he picked up the phone and when he said hello Sophie nearly choked up.

'Dad?'

'That you, Soph?'

'Yeah, I've got a cold.' *And I'm sad and lonely and I don't know what to do.*

'How's it going?' He sounded guarded.

'Fine thanks, I don't want anything.' It wasn't great that she had to say this so fast. 'How're you, Dad? Tell me something about the farm.'

'The farm?'

'Tell me about the cattle. Or the rain. Fences, anything.'

'All right then.' And he told her about Ellersley. It was midsummer there. Dry and hot. But he had plenty of water for the stock. Sophie rubbed a painful foot between her cold hands and started to cry. The tears rolled down her face and mixed in with snot, which was disgusting but she let it happen, that's how sad she felt.

It took a while to save up for the flight, but Sophie was determined not to ask for help.

She broke up with her boyfriend the day before she left. She could have done it a month earlier, but he was the type to want sympathy, and twenty-four hours was about as much as she had to offer. She packed her bag like she was going on a summer holiday. She left all her winter things behind. They had farewell drinks at the bar, and she hugged her flatmates and cried.

She did not tell a single person in Australia she was coming home. Not until she had something worth reporting was Sophie's plan. But Christine was never going to let a family member go AWOL for long. She wouldn't rest until she'd tracked Sophie down. It only took her a couple of months.

Sophie had to ring her dad then. She told him yes, she had a job – she didn't say it was in a pub – and yes, she was seeing someone and no, she didn't think it was time to bring him down to meet her old man. But soon, Dad, soon. That's what she said.

The year after she got back, Chris got everyone down to Ellersley for Christmas. Sophie caught the bus down and back – she was only there for half a day. It wasn't any sort of a catch-up, which is why she did it. She didn't have much to say.

One year turned into two, then Sophie stopped counting. She still didn't have anything to take home and show her dad.

She did now, though. After Sophie had packed it in at the post office she took a celebratory ferry across the harbour and had fish and chips and a chilled riesling on the Manly Corso. She watched the rich women with their expensive linen pants and basket handbags, and it came to her. It was time to set up her own business. A boutique on the Corso, why not? She had tons of style. She'd be a self-made woman. Her dad would love it.

When she got home, she had a quiet joint on the patio, and then, still high from the glorious resignation, she headed out. It was a marvellous night. She went high class – a bar with pendant lights and real champagne. She laughed, accepted cocktails and radiated charm. The young professionals didn't know what had hit them.

She hailed a taxi at quarter to five, and when it came to a stop outside her house, she handed over a random bunch of notes, tumbled onto the footpath, and three minutes later she was in bed in a deep, drunken sleep.

Until the phone rang.

The first three calls were from Chris. Sophie rarely answered the phone before midday, and she never took Chris's calls if she could help it, so she sure as hell wasn't answering these.

But Sophie couldn't remember the last time Jenny's name had appeared on her phone. If Jenny phoned, Sophie was absolutely going to pick up.

'Hiya, Jen.' Sophie almost managed to sound cheerful, despite her pounding head.

'Dad's dead. You have to come home.'

Every part of Sophie stopped still.

'Sophie? Did you hear me? Dad's dead.'

Jenny was speaking strangely. Very slowly. She was saying the words distinctly, with great care. As though anyone could miss the meaning of those two words together.

The cicadas ratcheted their buzzing up about five notches, a relentless shriek outside Sophie's window.

'Sophie? Sophie, are you there?' Jenny sounded panicky. 'Are you there?'

But Sophie couldn't speak.

She had nothing to say.

7

Dave was the last one home. He was there by Monday lunchtime, which was a reasonable effort, all things considered. He knew Chris would have his head on the block regardless. He should have ignored her call on Saturday. Let it go straight through to the keeper. But he didn't, so here he was.

Chris wanted him to drop everything and hurry back to Ellersley immediately, but there was no way he could do that. Saturdays were sport. Maybe it was only the under-elevens, but it was his boy. Dave never skipped a match.

And arriving Sunday – bloody hell. Imagine getting there just as the three girls were settling in. There'd be enough oestrogen to fuel a biological war. No way he was going to be part of that.

Sharon had him packed and ready to go on Sunday night. Footy bag in the boot of the Commodore, suit hanging from the window hook. He told her he was in no rush, and she said maybe not, but don't leave it too late. She told him death was a messy business. Better to meet it head-on than be bowled over from behind. She'd know. The shit she'd been through.

She had a soft spot for his old man. Always had. Dave couldn't work it out.

'He's not that bad,' she'd say. 'I've seen worse.'

That was enough for Sharon. 'I've seen worse' and 'We'll get by' covered all contingencies. It was easy to mock a person who only had two things to say about bad times, but she was bloody right. On both counts.

Dave couldn't say if she'd be right now, though. He hadn't shared the financial details of DE Constructions with Sharon for a few years. He told her that was why they had an accountant.

Sharon was conservative when it came to business. Dave respected her for it, but it didn't always reap rewards. Sometimes a bloke had to take a risk. And if he was sitting on a block like Ellersley it barely even counted as a risk.

Anyway, he was in no rush to get there. Better to sleep in his own bed on Sunday night, head down on Monday morning.

But Monday morning's a bloody hard time to leave a project. Everyone needs instruction, and Monday morning's when they need it the most. He was on his way by ten, but then his foreman, Gary, called. The excavator had carved a three-inch notch in the town water supply pipe. Dave had no choice but to turn back.

By the time he got there the water was off, which was a good start, but he still had to co-ordinate plumbers and engineers and whoever else wanted a piece of the action. He had to call Trevor Adams too. Councillor Adams was on edge about the development – he had no grit, that man, no staying power.

All things considered Dave had done well to get on the road by midday. Chris was on the phone before he'd hit the outskirts of town.

'Exactly how far to go? Will you make it by nightfall do you think?' She was narky, even for Chris.

'For goodness' sake, David, even Sophie managed to get here yesterday. We have an appointment with the solicitor at two o'clock.'

Dave felt the sarcasm rise like bile in his throat. *For goodness' sake, David.* Who did she think she was? The Queen of England? Where the bloody hell did she get that accent? And *David*. He was Dave to every other human on the planet – it didn't seem like such a stretch for Chris to join them.

'Go without me,' he said. It made no difference to him.

'Frankly, David, we would have, but he's refusing to read the will until all four of us are present. I'm not at all sure it's legal.'

Dave was rifling through the glove box, trying to find a CD.

'On my way, mate.'

'Well don't dawdle. I'm making a Niçoise salad for lunch. We'll hold over until one, but if you're not here by then we'll eat without you.'

'Yes, ma'am,' Dave said, and hung up.

He loosened his belt a few notches and loaded *Keep the Faith* into the CD player. In Dave's humble opinion it was the best Bon Jovi album ever made. If the bonus live disc was included, it was the best album ever made full stop. He flicked on the cruise control and noted the billboard for Hungry Jack's. Fifty k's. Easy done. No way he was giving up lunch for salad.

Drive-through was the best. Fast. Hot. No one watching to criticise his manners. It felt like a kind of victory when the first drop of sauce hit his shirt. He smeared it on with a napkin and took a swig of Coke.

It made no difference to him if the will was read Monday or Tuesday or any other day. The Edwards will hadn't altered in five generations. Property to the eldest son. Jewellery to the eldest daughter. And a few bits and pieces to fight over, just to keep it traditional. Chris was third in line, so she wasn't likely to get much. She just loved to be in charge. It would seriously piss her off to be held up by a two-bit country lawyer.

It only took an hour and a half to get to the back road now that the highway had been resealed. He nearly missed it. The Commodore handled it, though. The chassis fairly hugged the road. Dave indicated and pulled off the highway. There was tar for a couple of k's but it didn't last long.

Dave slowed down when he hit the dirt, checking out the land either side. There was green everywhere. In December. They must have had plenty of rain.

The Constance property was the exception. Fences nose-dived into the dirt; half-shorn sheep straggling across the paddock. Even in a terrific season it looked like the apocalypse had hit.

The road curved up and over, and the Edwards' mailbox came into view. Dave turned onto the track and rolled over the grid.

The river flats stretched out below him, lush and green; a trail of eucalypts marked the creek. The tractor shed came into view, the corrugated walls gleaming in sharp, vertical lines. His old man must have replaced the tin.

Dave continued around the south end of the cypress hedge, approaching the homestead.

He pulled off the track and nosed in towards the yard. Jen's dual cab was tucked next to the laneway, and a Volvo was parked across enough space for four vehicles.

It was bloody strange, coming back. Extra strange without his father standing in the front yard, shoulders square and arms crossed. It was eight years since he'd been to Ellersley. Dave didn't mean for it to happen that way, but bloody hell, when a bloke has a business and a family and a couple of footy teams to coach – eight years is nothing. If his dad had been a better bloke, they'd have come every year for Christmas. But he wasn't, so they didn't.

Dave switched off the engine and sat in the comfort of the Commodore for a moment longer, enjoying the stale smell of takeaway wrappers, the driver's seat moulded around his back. One fifty-five. There was still a one in it, anyway. He unclicked his seatbelt and braced his hands against the steering wheel, clenching tight. *You'll be right, mate. They're just your sisters. You'll be all right.*

He opened the driver's door and a girl in a miniskirt burst out of the porch. She flew down the front steps, waving her arms and yelling.

'Woohoo! The prodigal son returns! Chris is going to *kill* you the minute you walk through the door, so you'd better give me a hug before it's all over.'

Dave stood up, cracked his neck, and smiled. Sophie grabbed him around the waist and squeezed. Sophie was all right.

'Steady on, mate. Steady.' Dave laughed.

Jenny emerged from the house, and Chris wouldn't be far behind. Somewhere deep in his brain a siren wailed.

This is it, Dave. Game on.

8

It didn't take long for Tom to realise it would have to be a condition of the will. A father's request wouldn't be enough. Even if he was dying. But if their inheritance was at stake, they'd have to give it a shot.

He decided to go with the Coorong solicitor. No need to get Mindle, Seifort & Sloane involved. They'd only try to stop him. But Vince Barton wouldn't be above drafting a will that was out of the ordinary. Especially if Tom made it worth his while. Which he would. If they succeeded, he would pay Vince Barton handsomely for his time. If they failed, he'd give Vince the lot.

Five generations of hard work and smart business – that's what it took to build the Edwards' estate. If his progeny couldn't honour that kind of heritage, they deserved to see Ellersley handed over to a foreigner.

Tom took the precaution of paying a visit to Dr Charles Briggs first. Charlie knew he was dying, and so did Tom, so they got that bit over and done with in no time. Charlie laughed when Tom raised the question of his mental capacity.

'You? Soft in the head? I don't think so.'

But Tom pressed the point. He had to be sure.

Charlie asked him a few questions that could have been answered by a halfwit and then wrote a note in Tom's file.

'Of sound mind is what I'll put. Will that do?'

'That'll do.'

Charlie laughed again. 'You mad old bugger.'

'Don't write that, or we'll have to start over.'

'What do you want with this nonsense, anyway?'

Nosy, Charlie was. Always had been. Lucky he was a doctor; people expected it of him.

'Writing my will.'

'Don't you have one?'

'A new one. Vince'll do it.'

Charlie raised his eyebrows.

'I want you to be an executor. Keep an eye on him.'

'You sure about this?'

'I am.'

Charlie shook his head, but he didn't argue.

'You've certified me sane now, Charlie. You'll have to stand by it.'

Tom stood up, and Charlie came out from behind the desk to shake hands.

'Good to see you, Tom.'

'And you, Charlie.'

'I'll come and see you sometime.'

'Do,' Tom said.

There weren't many he'd invite to Ellersley now, but Charlie was welcome. He'd looked after the Edwards family since Tom and Helena got married. Every man made mistakes, but Charlie had done his best. Tom was sure of that.

Tom paused when he got outside, blinking in the brightness of the day. It was still early. He might as well drop in on Vince while he was in town. No point making another trip if he didn't have to.

The front door of Barton & Sons scraped over the lino, and Tom stepped into the foyer. There was a reception desk at the back wall, and a young bloke with his arm in a sling behind it.

'G'day, Mr Edwards.' The young bloke stood quickly, blushing.

'Ben. What the hell are you doing here?'

He blushed darker. He was a good kid – man, even. Bloody hell they grew up fast.

'My shoulder. It's busted.'

Never one to laze around, Ben Taylor. If he couldn't get out on the farm, he got a desk job. He'd be hating it though.

'Bad luck. It'll be right. Bit of time. Where's your boss?'

'Out.'

He wasn't polished when it came to customer service, but he was honest. And he showed up. It was a bloody good start.

'Tell him to come and see me.'

'Will do, Mr Edwards.'

Tom tipped his hat, opened the door, and stepped into the glare. Business done, time to get home.

9

'Chris is not going to kill you,' Christine said quietly, dropping eggs into boiling water. 'She might feel like it, but she won't do it.'

Christine had been at Ellersley for close to forty-eight hours and she was ready to shoot every person she had met since her arrival. David was high on the hit list.

She had already set the table – cutlery, glasses, serviettes and salt and pepper – but she knew David wouldn't get there in time, so she'd delayed the final steps of lunch preparation.

The ingredients that weren't time sensitive were arranged on four plates. Salad leaves, lightly blanched beans, tuna, potatoes; she would add egg quarters as soon as they were done.

A Niçoise salad was a nice, cool option for such a hot day. Christine had prepared it many times for guests at St Ives, or Whale Beach when they were on holidays. Christine was known for her Niçoise salad. Not at Ellersley, though.

Christine felt resentful, but by now she knew about preparing food when she would prefer to open fire. She'd been cooking for this family since she was eleven years old, not that anyone remembered that.

She'd started with sausages and mash and soggy greens, and gradually worked her way up. Jennifer was fifteen, reading romance novels on the busted trampoline, while David moped around with his volcanic pimples and squawky voice. Their father was angry all the time, looking out at dry paddocks and willy-willies lifting the dust, carrying the topsoil away.

And nobody noticed their mother, their beautiful, kind mother, was disappearing. She was getting buried under that pregnant belly. She was silent and swollen and every day it got worse, and no one did a thing.

Except Christine. She noticed, and she knew something had to be done.

She went to a sleepover at Shannon Burke's house, where there were rosters for everything. Dinner. Shopping. Cleaning. Pets. Bins. Everything.

She got home and started drawing up tables. Everyone laughed. No one more than her dad. No one else followed the roster, but Christine did. She served dinner every night at six o'clock. She cleaned her rostered part of the house each week, so by the end of the month the whole house was done.

The family got fed. Their mum stayed alive. Their home was functional. They made it through that summer of scorching heat, dry paddocks and dust, everywhere the dust. But her dad was still angry, all the time, until Sophie arrived.

Everyone fell in love with her instantly. Their father laughed out loud for the first time in a very long time and crowed, 'We're back! The Edwards are back.'

Christine crumpled up inside, her breathing short and hot, and the tears smarted behind her eyes. She wanted to shout, 'Hey! I've been here all along. Even when you all up and left this family, I stayed right here.' But she didn't.

Instead, she swallowed hard, straightened up and stayed on, despite Sophie's invasion. She cooked, cleaned, and kept the roster running while her mother slimmed down, occasionally smiling at Sophie's single dimple. She held it together while everyone adored the baby and treated Christine, more often than not, as a long-standing family joke.

But they knew, *surely* they knew, it was thanks to Christine's hard work that the Edwards family was fit to welcome a new baby at all.

It was no surprise to Christine that she was the first one to come home. No surprise she was the one to get the meal on the table. And no surprise that she had made the appointment with the solicitor; and then had to reschedule because David wasn't home.

The solicitor. Now, that was a whole other issue.

For reasons Christine could not fathom, their father had not engaged Mindle, Seifort & Sloane, the family firm, to write his final will. Instead, he had employed Mr Vince Barton of Barton & Sons. The local Coorong solicitor, for goodness' sake.

Their appointment with Mr Barton was now at 3.30 pm. He agreed to the later time at Christine's insistence. No doubt he had his own reasons for doing so. He didn't sound like a man who would do it out of the goodness of his heart.

Christine put the plates on the table and paused. She could hear Sophie having a laugh with David outside. Jenny was with them, and soon they would come in for a rollicking family reunion, over another meal prepared by Christine. And apart from the task of dragging her siblings home not a speck of work had been done.

10

'Place is looking good.' Dave was strutting around the kitchen like he owned it. Maybe he did now. Sophie wouldn't have a clue.

'Yes,' Christine said. She was in a crabby mood. 'Jennifer "cleaned it up a bit". Didn't you?' Christine turned to Jenny. Jenny's face went a deep red and she looked at her plate.

'Nice job, Jen.' Dave was halfway down the hall, so he missed the sarcasm in Chris's voice. Sophie could hear him opening doors, checking things out.

'David,' Chris called after him.

'Yeah?'

'We're in the middle of lunch here.' She said it like lunch was a compulsory class.

'Huh?' Dave looked blank for a moment. 'Oh right, sure.'

He came back to the kitchen and sat down. 'Where's the salt?'

It was closest to Jenny, but she didn't move. Chris harrumphed, reached across Jenny, and passed the salt to Dave.

'Be careful, David,' she said. 'Salt causes hypertension.'

Dave rolled his eyes. 'Thanks, Nurse Minehan.'

Sophie laughed, but Chris didn't respond.

'Salt, Soph?' Dave held the shaker out in front of her. Sophie snorted, trying not to spray food out of her mouth.

'Jen? Salt for you?' He was asking for trouble, winding Chris up. Sophie had forgotten how they did this.

'Grow up, David.' Chris had finished by now and she took her plate to the sink. Chris's posture was amazing, like she'd been to finishing school. But she hadn't. She'd only gone to Coorong High, same as the rest of them.

Dave burped loudly and clattered his cutlery down.

'Thanks, Chris,' he said, 'great salad.' Dave hated salad.

Jenny had been quietly, steadily, working through the food on her plate. The lettuce was causing her grief though. Too crunchy was Sophie's guess. The noise could attract attention. Plus, lettuce was awkward. Sometimes it point-blank refused to go inside a person's mouth.

'You right, Jen?' Dave touched her shoulder as he walked past. Jenny nodded, but she didn't say anything.

'Lettuce sucks, doesn't it?' Sophie whispered across the table, and Jen smiled.

Sophie didn't really believe lettuce was the enemy. She liked Niçoise salad. But she'd been too distracted by Chris and Dave's squabbling to eat much of it.

Sophie knew it wasn't going to be a fun-loving family holiday, being back at Ellersley. But at least she'd be entertained.

11

It was going to be an awful time. Jenny barely made it through lunch. There was no way she would be able to stay until the funeral. That's what Chris had decided they should do. The four of them would stay at Ellersley and 'sort things out', then they would have the funeral. Chris had also told Jenny she would have to 'look presentable' at the funeral, as though Jenny made a habit of revealing her underwear in public. She was wearing a dress with flowers on it, and practical working boots. How could pinched shiny shoes with needle-thin heels be more presentable than that?

Chris and Dave had started bickering. Dave had been in the house for approximately five minutes before they were into it. Sophie was wearing skimpy clothes and laughing, so it was only a matter of time before she and Chris were fighting too.

The next thing on their schedule was a meeting with the solicitor. Jenny knew Vince Barton, but only to say hello. He seemed friendly, but he wasn't from Coorong. A person could be as friendly as they liked, but if they weren't local, they weren't local. It was that simple. He wore fancy suits, which Coorong people didn't like. Chris might, though.

As she was getting in the car Jenny made a deal with herself. She would stick it out for the afternoon. She would attend the will reading, but after that, if she was feeling miserable, she would jump in her ute and go home.

12

Vince Barton did not rig the will. He knew no one would believe it, but he did not rig the will. He had been waiting for an opportunity like this for his whole career, his whole life in fact. But it hadn't come. It hadn't even brushed shoulders with him in a crowd. Then, out of the blue, Tom Edwards called.

It was an irregular proposal, to say the least. Vince didn't want to dissuade Tom Edwards from his plan – the potential gain for Vince was mindboggling – but for his own protection he felt he should explain the possible issues with such a will.

Tom was unconcerned. 'Vince, if I'm going to make a will, I'll be the one who decides what's in it,' he said.

Vince even went so far as to suggest Tom get advice from Mindle, Seifort & Sloane. He regretted it the minute it was said, but it didn't matter. Tom wasn't interested.

'I think they've had their fair share of the Edwards' estate,' Tom said, with some level of scorn. 'Why do I want them to tell me what I already know? If I want you to do the job, Vince, that's enough.'

Vince had drafted the will according to Tom Edwards' instructions. Four children, four days, was Tom's thinking. Who was Vince to disagree? He documented their conversations and had Tom confirm they were correct. Tom signed all the documents and Vince hugged them to his chest as he walked to his car.

When he got back to the office, he opened the file and skipped straight to the best part.

DISPOSITION OF ESTATE

(1) I give the sum of $20 000 to Vince Barton of Barton & Sons.

(2) I give the residue of my estate to be divided equally between my four children, Jennifer Ann Edwards, David Hinkley Edwards, Christine Elizabeth Minehan and Sophie Jane Edwards, on condition that they construct my coffin according to the following specifications:

   (a) The coffin must be constructed to Australian Funeral Directors Association Standards;

   (b) The coffin must be a coffin of six sides, with fitted lid;

   (c) The timber from which the coffin must be constructed must be sourced from the Edwards family property, Ellersley;

   (d) The coffin must be constructed using:

      (i) Solid hardwood;

      (ii) Timber to be no more than rough cut at the commencement of the build;

      (iii) Commercially milled timber is not permitted;

   (e) The constructed coffin surface must be finished as follows:

      (i) Sanding – to no less than 120 grit for the body of the coffin and no less than 150 grit for the lid;

      (ii) Finish – natural oil only;

   (f) The construction of the coffin must be completed by my four children, Jennifer Ann Edwards, David Hinkley Edwards, Christine Elizabeth Minehan and Sophie Jane Edwards. All four must participate in building the coffin, and each of my children must physically work on the construction of the coffin;

   (g) The construction of the coffin must be completed within four working days of the reading, in the presence of all four of my children, of this Last Will and Testament.

(3) If the coffin is not completed as specified above, I give my whole estate to Vince Barton of Barton & Sons.

A marvellous will. Marvellous. It was the highlight of Vince's career when Tom Edwards signed this document.

'I beg your pardon, Mr Barton, would you care to repeat those terms?'

Christine Minehan's voice brought him back to the present. She was furious. Vince was grateful for the large mahogany desk separating him from his clients. When it came to physical assault, prevention was key.

The other three were not so intimidating. Jennifer, beige and lumpy as ever, was sitting quite still, pressing her fingers onto her thighs like she was playing a funeral dirge. Sophie was sitting on the arm of Jennifer's chair, all bright eyes and dimples. Like she was at a show, not a solicitor's office. David looked downright unwell.

'Mr Barton?'

Christine had a pink lipstick smudge on her front tooth. A gratifying reminder that she was a country girl, albeit one who had swum a few miles upstream.

'Certainly, Mrs Minehan, I can repeat the reading. "The Last Will and Testament of Thomas Hinkley Edwards –"'

'Oh, for goodness' sake, don't start from the beginning again. What you need to do is explain yourself.'

But after forty long years of self-justification, Vince knew that this time it was not his behaviour that needed explaining. And he wasn't sure he could explain the behaviour of Tom Edwards, even if he wanted to.

People acted strangely when they started to think about family and money at the same time. They made unexpected decisions. They left bundles of surprise for their children to fight over when they passed into rot and decay.

Vince didn't know why, and frankly he didn't care. What he did know was that he had seen it with his own eyes – Tom Edwards, sharp as ever, making decisions with the clarity of a statesman.

If it had been someone else, Vince would have said the testator was mad and the will wouldn't hold. But Tom Edwards knew what he was doing. He had his sanity certified by Dr Charles Briggs. This was not an unequivocal win, as Charles Briggs was now co-executor. But that didn't change the substance of the will.

Tom Edwards had been clear in his instructions, and Vince had been careful in drafting them. Indeed, Vince had taken every precaution to ensure the wording of this will was tight as a drum. Ten thousand acres of prime land is a great motivator.

13

'Well, Mr Barton, you have certainly not heard the end of this. If what you are saying is even legal – which I sincerely doubt – it will be contestable.'

Christine's voice was sharp, but it barely cut through the ringing in Dave's ears.

'Mindle, Seifort & Sloane are the Edwards family solicitors. Please send a copy of this so-called will to their office immediately. You can expect to hear further instructions tomorrow. Goodbye.'

Once Chris had finished talking, she stood up, slung her handbag over her shoulder and marched out to the foyer. Sophie was hot on her heels. Jen paused to thank Vince and then followed the girls out.

There was no reason for him to stay behind, but somehow Dave couldn't leave. He was stunned. Hearing the will had punched the air right out of him. He didn't feel angry, not even upset – not yet – but blank, and a little light-headed.

The coffin building clause was madness, but so what? If there was one thing Tom Edwards had enjoyed, it was setting his kids a near-impossible task. And it was just like him to hand the property over to Vince if they didn't succeed. No surprises there. What staggered Dave was the distribution of the estate if they completed the job.

Four ways. Equally.

Not just the money, or the shares, but Ellersley. Every paddock, every piece of machinery, every fucking blade of grass would be cut into quarters and shared between them. It wasn't right; it wasn't tradition. It wasn't done.

In five generations it hadn't been done. Ellersley went to the eldest son. That was the rule. Except if he pissed off to WA and never came back like Uncle Jock, but that was a special case. A one and only.

Dave hadn't deserted. He hadn't gone interstate. He'd barely driven down the highway. He had a wife and business and nice kids. He was a decent citizen. And there was no younger brother, no Tom, ready to take over this time round.

Vince Barton had been reading straight from the will. He had Charles Briggs along to prove he wasn't making it up. He'd given each of them a copy, so they could check it themselves if they had any doubts.

Dave would take it with him, sure, but it wasn't going to alter the situation.

Christine could get the condition about the coffin-building changed, and she probably would. But that wouldn't come close to the rewrite Dave needed.

After Vince read the part about equal inheritance, Dave barely heard anything else. He could only think about those three quarters. The quarters that belonged to him – had *always* belonged to him – snatched from his grasp. It was like losing possession in extra time and then losing the game. Extra time was a fucking disaster.

14

The sun was scorching hot. Christine stepped onto the footpath and looked at her watch. 4.30 pm. By the time they got back to Ellersley it would be too late to get any business done.

She hoped her siblings had followed her out. She wasn't turning around to check. She pulled her sunglasses from her handbag and pointed the key remote at the Volvo. It unlocked with a beep. She started the engine, fastened her seatbelt and adjusted the climate control.

They didn't take long, but Christine had the next day planned before her siblings had settled in their seats.

1. Contact Mindle, Seifort & Sloane to sort out the will.
2. Call Darby's Funeral Home and arrange a meeting – coffin (a proper one), flowers, stationery, visitors' book etc.
3. Contact the Anglican minister at Coorong – arrange time, date, order of service, hymns. Best speak with him face to face to make sure he wasn't peculiar.
4. Guest list – divide between David and Sophie to notify.
5. Wake – a church hall morning tea would suffice. Inform minister, arrange catering.
6. Extended family – make list, call. She would do this herself. The others would only make a hash of it.
7. House – clearing out and professional clean.
8. External buildings/sheds/farm equipment – inventory for sale.
9. Property evaluation – contact real estate agent. She presumed the others would want to sell. Regardless, the value was important information.

10. Make this 2a – call Stephen and get her family prepared for the week ahead. She would have to speak with Nicholas and Claudia regarding clothes for the funeral. They could fly down and back on the day. There was no point taking more time off school than necessary.

'Seatbelts on,' Christine said, as the others got in. She didn't mean to be officious but the years of transporting children had left their mark.

Sophie snickered and said, 'Yes, Mum.' Dave rolled the passenger seat back and looked out the window in silence. Jenny was still fumbling around for her buckle. Christine waited, tapping her fingers on the steering wheel until Jenny had managed to sort herself out.

It was easy to mock, she thought, but someone had to take charge, and her siblings had never put their hand up for the job. Not once.

So maybe Sophie could leave off the sarcasm. Christine flicked the indicator and checked the rear-vision mirror. Maybe they could all give Christine her due, or at the very least some support. She revved hard and pulled away from the verge. It was time to sort this mess out.

15

Tom had to give the man credit for efficiency. Vince was at Ellersley the morning after Tom had dropped by his office. Bright and early, with his dark eyes glinting as he sized up the house, the sheds, the green paddocks surrounding them. He was so transparent Tom wanted to laugh out loud. His kids would have to work hard to keep Ellersley out of Vince's hands.

Tom had been thinking about the will overnight. Now that he'd decided to add a condition of inheritance, it occurred to him there was no reason to stick with the standard Edwards will. Why not give the whole thing an overhaul? What was there to stop him changing the lot?

He didn't sleep much these days, so he'd had plenty of time to think. For most of the night he lay on top of the bedspread, hands clasped behind his head, watching the shadows move across the plaster ceiling. The sweating came on so fast there was no point getting under the covers. He kept a towel nearby to dry off when he was drenched, and pulled a blanket over his shoulders when the shivering set in. When it all settled down, he'd lie on his back again, eyes open, and get on with planning.

He started with the fundamentals. First up, what was the point of making a will? Tom didn't have to think about it for long. To hand on your legacy. That's what a will was about. Passing the baton to the next runner, so they could build on the work you'd done. To grow it into something bigger, and then, when the time came, hand it to the next in line.

That summed up the past hundred and fifty years for the Edwards family. Each generation building on the work of the one before and handing a better property to the next. More land, more stock, better pastures.

But what did you do when the next generation wasn't up to scratch?

The heir of the Edwards will had always been the eldest son. Until Jock left. Then it fell to Tom, which was for the best. He did what an eldest son should have. Picked up the baton and ran with it. But Dave wouldn't pick up the baton, let alone run. He didn't have a snowflake's chance of running Ellersley. And there was no second son.

If Tom left the land to Dave, Ellersley would go the way of all property when a man was in debt. She would be sold in dribs and drabs to pay off the loan – or maybe only the interest on the loan. She'd be cut up to pay contractors; to meet the mortgage on the family home. Ellersley would go and the debt would stay, and nobody would be any better for it.

So who should be the heir?

The one who deserved it, surely. The one who stood by Tom and his forebears, held strong through lean times and fat times, through seasons and years and decades of life.

By this logic, the prime beneficiary should be Ellersley. He couldn't leave money to a block of land, worse luck, but maybe there was a way to guarantee Ellersley would be looked after.

Tom's face started beading with sweat again. The heat rushed through him, drenching his body, and left as quickly as it came. Cold and shivering wet, he reached for the towel. He dried off, where he could, and huddled under the blanket, waiting for it to pass. When it did he took up where he left off.

Leaving Ellersley to the eldest son wasn't going to do it, that was obvious. It took Tom about thirty seconds to decide the girls weren't up to the task either. But what if he left the property to all four of them? One property, but equal shares. Then he could make some rules about selling the land – a rule that all four have to agree first, or that it can't be sold for ten years – or a whole lot more than ten years. There must be some way of doing that. Tom Edwards wasn't the first man to have a bloody hopeless son.

If he was going to give them equal shares in the property, it made sense to apply the rule to everything else. The farm machinery belonged to Ellersley, so it should be tied to the property, and the shares belonged to Ellersley too, really. If you didn't look after one, you didn't get access to the other. The shares stayed with the property.

So that was it. Equal inheritance. All assets tied to the land and Ellersley preserved for the next generation.

If Vince Barton won the property, that was a different situation. If Vince Barton owned this piece of land, it meant the Edwards were finished, Ellersley was finished and what happened next was of absolutely no interest to Tom. He'd never know about it, anyway.

Thank God, he'd be dead.

16

The will reading wasn't what Jenny expected. It wasn't what any of them expected, except maybe Sophie, but that was only because she had no expectations at all. She was barely listening as far as Jenny could tell. Chris was furious and Dave was ashen-faced and Dr Briggs stood against the wall, looking at the carpet. As though he didn't want to be there at all.

Jenny started the interview counting. Pressing her fingers down, one after the other, keeping it slow and blocking out the rushing in her ears. But when Vince got to the part about the 'Disposition of the Estate', everyone became still. Even Sophie stopped fidgeting. It made Jenny look up, and she heard the words clear as a bell.

'... on condition that they construct my coffin according to the following specifications ...'

This was the point at which the others seemed to check out, but Jenny listened carefully. The specifications were clear. Sensible. It was a tight timeframe, but it was achievable. She would start work as soon as they got home.

17

As the Volvo rolled down the track and the house came into view, sensation returned to Dave's body. He suddenly felt suffocated, trapped.

Who the FUCK did his father think he was? How much – exactly how much – did he want to fuck Dave over? Fucking hell, Dad. Fucking hell.

He tried to open the window, but it was driver operated. He jabbed the button a couple of times without success, then released his seatbelt and leaned forward, loosening his tie, trying to get some air.

The car approached the front yard and slowed down, and Dave swung the passenger door open. He watched the gravel change from a grey blur to sharp, distinct granules and stepped out while the car was still rolling. He slammed the door behind him, checked his mobile and set off up Radio Hill, long legs striding out, moving fast enough to make sure his sisters couldn't follow.

The leather soles of his shoes slipped on the grass, so Dave sought out rocky patches, stony ground to keep some friction underfoot.

He scrabbled up the last few metres of granite outcrop and stood on the highest rock, holding his phone out in all directions to see where he could get a signal.

'Sharon? Sharon, have you got me? Shit, Sharon, I dunno what to do. We are completely fucked.'

The wind was picking up and Dave turned around to have it at his back, cupping his hand over the phone. 'Sharon? Love? You there?'

'Dave . . . can't . . .'

He could only just hear her voice, grainy and indistinct.

'Sharon? Shaz?' He was shouting now, desperate. 'He is a total fucking cunt, and we are fucked.'

'What . . . you . . . Dave . . . ?'

The call ended, and Dave looked at the screen in disbelief. No bars. No reception. No Sharon.

'FUCK!'

18

The slam of the car door startled Sophie. She turned around to see Dave striding off into the paddock. Wow. It was a bit warm for a walk. It's not like she wanted to spend the rest of her life in Chris's car, but she wasn't rushing to get out either. With the AC on it was as cool as a crisper drawer.

After the ignition was turned off the car went from fridge to furnace in about ten seconds. Sophie sprinted across the yard and into the kitchen. It wasn't as cool as Chris's AC, but it was okay. Plus, she was hungry.

The fridge looked full, and no doubt there were some snack ingredients there, but Sophie was having trouble finding them. Maybe she wasn't hungry. Or maybe it was nerves.

She was glad she had worn the miniskirt to the solicitor's office. She nearly didn't, when Chris told her off, but at the last minute she put it on again. She wanted to feel like herself if she was going to hear her father's last words. The mussed hair and lipstick might have been about annoying Christine, but that was the real Sophie too. The point was, Sophie didn't dress up for the hot receptionist. That was luck. Or maybe destiny. Sometimes it was hard to know. Sophie filled a glass with water and looked out the window. She heard the others come into the kitchen but paid no attention to what they were doing. Why would she?

'Are you planning to join us?' Chris's voice was snippy. A platter with vegetable sticks and dips had appeared on the table, and Chris and Jenny were sitting at their places.

'Sophie?'

'What? Oh, sure.'

Sophie sat down and picked up a carrot stick.

Was it wrong to be lovestruck on the day she heard her father's will read out? Were there rules about that? Like a number of hours, or days, that a person had to stay focused on their father's death before thinking about a gorgeous bloke?

He blushed when Christine spoke to him, which Sophie loved. Even better, despite the blush, he kept his cool. He wasn't trying to impress them. He looked like a person who could hold his own. And he had an intelligent glint in his eye – or did she make that bit up? It was hard to say for sure.

Sophie reached out for a piece of cucumber and shoved it into the hummus. One thing she could say was that the meeting with the solicitor went on and on and *on*.

'Don't double dip, Sophie, it's unhygienic.' Chris tapped the back of Sophie's hand and she pulled it back.

It wasn't that Sophie didn't care about her dad's final wishes. Of course she did. But they just kept talking and talking and it wasn't going anywhere. Build a coffin, don't build a coffin. Get the property, don't get the property. Share it equally, give it to the aging solicitor. Do whatever you like, Sophie wanted to say, but let me out of here.

When Chris huffed out of the office, Sophie leapt up and followed her. He was still there, behind that silly desk. He nodded politely at Chris, and then Sophie caught his eye. She smiled way bigger than she'd planned, and though she wasn't totally sure, she thought maybe his eyes crinkled a bit in return. Plus, he blushed again, and that was definitely because of her.

'Sophie? Are you even listening to me?' Christine was reaching for Sophie's plate.

'Oh, right. Sorry, Chris,' she said, and passed it across, cucumber still on it. Hopefully Chris had planned something tastier for dinner.

Sophie didn't need raw vegetables that she couldn't double dip. What she needed was intel on the receptionist. Why the sling? Was it possible he was single, and if so, when would he ask her out?

19

Dave's shirt clung to his back, soaked with sweat. The sun was biting hard. He was hungry too, but there was no way he was going back to the house. It wasn't a need-to-eat sort of hungry anyway. More like a hole in his gut. An eroded gully with cracked mud, drying in the heat. Fucking hell, the heat was relentless.

Dave picked his way down the southern side of the hill, half-jogging, half-slipping on the grass. He needed to get away from Ellersley for a few hours. Get some distance, a bit of perspective. He could take the Commodore for a spin. Head into town and have a couple of drinks at the Newie; loosen up a bit. That was the way to go.

He went around the side of the house and opened the laundry door. There were noises coming from the kitchen. Sophie's laugh; the clatter of a dropped knife. If he was quick, he'd be in and out before they caught sight of him. He tiptoed across to his bedroom and got his gear. Shower, jeans, chambray shirt; R.M. Williams and a slap of Old Spice and he was good to go. He hadn't even got to the pub, and he was feeling better.

He made it to the Commodore unseen, turned the ignition and accelerated, loose gravel spraying out behind him. He put AC/DC on, turned the volume up and started singing.

When he pulled up at the Newie, he aged about fifty years just laying eyes on the place. Peeling paint, splintered rails and a Tooheys Dry sign swinging crooked on its nail – the Newie wasn't what it used to be.

There were a couple of punters on the pokies, and a bloke sitting in one of the booths. Dave asked for a schooner of four-ex and leaned against the bar.

The bloke in the booth had a glass half full, and his attention was fixed on his phone. He had the look of a man about to turn the stock market upside down. Dave snorted. What a dickhead.

The bloke must have heard the snort because he looked up and smiled in recognition.

'Dave Edwards,' he said. 'When the hell did you blow in?'

Dave did a double take. Surely not. The man was bald, for fuck's sake. Completely bald. Apart from that he looked terrific. He was wearing a too-tight shirt, but he was pulling it off. Hard pecs, washboard abs – Dave wished he could say the same for himself. He paid for his beer, sucked in his gut and walked over.

'Marcus bloody Flanagan,' he said. 'I'd ask you the same question.' He put his glass on the table and pulled his phone out. He made a show of switching it off and then reached out a hand. Marcus stood up, and Dave immediately felt better. He'd forgotten how short Marcus was. Back pocket, Dave remembered now. For the Bombers.

'Work, mate.' Marcus sat down again. 'Always work.' He turned his eyes to the pressed-tin ceiling like it was a real hardship, dealing with success. Which he obviously was. You only had to look at his clothes to see that.

'What's work?'

'Property,' he said. 'Property agent. Taken over the family business. It's twenty-four seven, but there's plenty of money in it.'

No shit, Dave thought.

'How about you?' Marcus asked. 'I hear you're bringing Wagga up to speed.'

'Someone's got to do it.' Dave winked, and they both laughed. He was fucked if he was going to give Marcus Flanagan information about DE Constructions going under.

'No, mate, the old man's passed on.' Dave took a swig of beer and, for the first time since coming home, thanked his father. In terms of conversation stoppers, death was in a class of its own.

'Shit, mate, I'm sorry.' Marcus looked sincerely sympathetic, which was a good effort for a real estate agent. It didn't last, though.

'So, Ellersley, hey? Eldest son and all that?' Marcus raised his eyebrows suggestively. 'How big is it? Two? Three thousand?'

'Four, give or take,' Dave said. 'Ten thousand acres.'

'That's a decent-sized property.' Marcus's eyes lit up. 'Don't suppose you're thinking of selling?'

Dave said nothing. Out loud, anyway. In his head it was a different story.

Well, Marcus, I've got a stalled development and a six-point-three-million-dollar debt and no way to fund either. So yeah, I'm thinking of selling. But you can't sell something you don't own, can you?

'You've got a permanent creek, right?' Marcus asked. He was sniffing around like a dog at a rabbit hole. Fucking estate agents. 'And river flats. You'd have to have a few k's of water frontage there. Am I right?'

Dave nodded morosely.

'Plenty of pasture too. Shit, mate, you must be sitting on twenty-five mil.'

Dave shrugged. 'Might be pushing it.'

Twenty-five was pushing it, but fifteen to twenty mil would have been plenty.

Marcus slapped his hand on the table. 'You don't want to talk business now. Your old man's passed.' He flipped open his wallet and handed Dave a card.

'When you're ready,' he said, 'give me a call. I'll look after you.' Marcus stood up and sidled out of the booth. He paused. 'I'm sorry, mate, I really am. He was great, your old man. Fit. Wasn't he?'

Dave nodded despite himself. 'Yeah. He was.'

'Bloody fit.' Marcus pulled his keys from his pocket, swung them around his finger and caught them. 'If we'd let him on the field back then, he would have outrun us all.'

20

'Holy *shit*, Jenny, what *is* this?'

Taking Sophie to Matthew's place probably wasn't such a good idea. Jenny had tried to drop her off on Dean Street, but Sophie said shopping on a Tuesday morning wasn't really her thing. She wanted to spend time with her big sister. Jenny suspected she was just being nosy.

Jenny hadn't wanted to take Sophie into town at all, but she couldn't work out quickly enough how to resist. Sophie had accosted her as she was coming out of the bathroom and wouldn't let Jenny past until she'd agreed to bring her along.

Jenny looked across the shed to Sophie silhouetted in the doorway.

'What's what?'

Sophie raised her eyebrows and threw her arms wide to include the whole shed. 'All of it.'

Jenny was scanning the tool board above the bench, looking for her favourite chisel.

'Oh, just some offcuts. You know, bits and pieces. Can you reach that light switch?'

A couple of seconds later the fluorescent tubes blinked on. Sophie stepped down onto the concrete floor of the shed and looked around.

'No, I *don't* know. I am totally going to get this out of you.'

Jenny kept her eyes on the tool board. Even with Sophie's curiosity sparking questions in all directions, she was finding it easier to stay steady now she was in the shed.

'You could literally fit four cars in here. Maybe more.' Sophie was wandering around the shed, picking up the odd tool, sticking her head under the drop saw to see what it looked like from below.

'Be careful, Soph. Don't switch anything on.'

'Why not? Would it suddenly start? Vvrroom! And there goes your little sister, sawn in half. Would you miss me?'

Jenny was collecting tools and piling them by the doorway. She'd told Sophie on the drive that they were going to pick up tools from Matthew's place. She had hoped that might be enough. But now Jenny saw how unrealistic that was.

Thankfully Matthew was out. Tuesday was his morning with Auntie Bern. Jenny had called in through the screen door anyway, to be sure. Sophie knowing about Matthew's existence was one thing; Sophie meeting Matthew in the flesh was an entirely different matter. It had taken Jenny over five years to let his name loose in the family arena, and when she did it bucked and kicked like there was no tomorrow. She couldn't imagine what would erupt if Matthew himself was brought out.

'Holy crap!'

Sophie had stopped at the long bench against the front wall. Jenny watched her taking in the display. It was worth watching. Sophie was stunned into a moment of actual silence.

There were three small coffins on the front bench. Jenny had finished them the week before. One on order, the others for emergencies. It was important to have at least two in stock, because death is unpredictable.

The problem now was not so much an unpredicted death as an unpredicted coffin requirement. Jenny had known her father was unwell, she just didn't know how to admit it.

Four days – now three and a half – to build a coffin from scratch. They couldn't even use dressed timber. It seemed a shame, given what was available. The coffins on the bench were made of American walnut, blonde ash and a delicate pink ribbon gum. Each of these timbers had been an absolute pleasure to work with. Imagine having access to such species in Albury!

'Oh wow. I mean, seriously, *wow*!'

Sophie's voice reverberated around the shed. She turned to look at Jenny.

'No wonder you didn't want me to come. Did you know Matthew was into this when you got together?'

'Oh no, this isn't his work.' Jenny bent down to rummage under the bench.

'Whose is it then?'

Jenny kept her head down, searching through boxes. She couldn't lie.

'Mine.'

'*Yours?* Tell me that's a joke.'

'It's not a joke.' With a bit more rustling around Jenny found the container she was looking for.

'What are they for? *Who* are they for?'

Jenny picked up a cordless drill and held it out to Sophie. Sophie took the drill and kept on talking.

'I am so getting this whole story out of you by the time we get home. Every detail.'

Jenny thought she'd be able to handle Sophie's questions. She would explain that the coffins were for pets. Which was true. For the most part. There was no need to go into the other side of the business. Most people can sympathise with the burial of a family dog. Stillborn babies and aborted embryos were harder to accept.

21

Apparently, Jennifer and Sophie didn't think there was any work to do. They appeared, ate breakfast and left. Jenny mumbled something about 'picking up a few things' in Albury and they were gone. No cleaning up. No discussion regarding funeral planning or allocation of jobs.

Jennifer at least appeared to have a reason for deserting the premises. Sophie didn't bother to give an excuse. Skipping work was standard practice for her. David was in bed, and who could say how long he'd be there. He'd come home late the night before and stumbled loudly down the hallway. Christine didn't even want to think about how much alcohol he consumed prior to driving home.

It was infuriating. They had come home to bury their father and, once again, Christine was the one at work in the kitchen while everyone else found something more enjoyable to do.

She finished wiping down the bench, straightened her skirt and walked out to the porch. Their father had enclosed it years ago to make a sunroom, the north end serving as an 'office'. There was a grey metal filing cabinet, a desk with the phone and a few pens in a mug. He had shut up and ignored five proper rooms and crammed the office into one end of the porch. It was absurd.

Although it was hot, Christine had dressed in her pinstripe suit and stilettos. She had several visits to make, and she was determined to be professional. This went for phone calls too. There was nothing like wearing business attire to keep the tone of authority in one's voice.

First, she made a spreadsheet. She found names and local phone numbers in a faded White Pages directory lying on the desk. This was a fortunate find because there was no internet. Nor mobile reception. She was working in a time warp.

When the contact details were typed into the spreadsheet, Christine started making calls.

First on the list was Mindle, Seifort & Sloane. They could not have been less helpful if they tried. She was put through to a junior associate who was determined not to let her speak with a partner. Christine gave him some brisk advice on client relations and career advancement, and he found he was able to put her through to Mr Sloane after all.

Mr Sloane believed a fax had come through from Barton & Sons, but it took him some time to locate the document. When he did, he hmm'd a few times but would only say the will was 'unconventional'.

Christine wanted to yell at him, to scream out, 'It's a bloody ridiculous will. You know it and I know it, so fix it!' But Christine didn't yell, and she didn't say 'bloody' to anyone, let alone a partner in a respected legal firm. Instead, she thanked him for his time and requested he communicate with Barton & Sons, with a view to removing the coffin-construction clause immediately.

Regaining composure was at the top of Christine's skill set. It only took a moment and a minor correction to her posture, and she was ready to make the next call.

The Reverend Allen was, if anything, more provoking than Mr Sloane. He spoke with a slow, religious tone that made Christine feel like she was in trouble. Deep, lifelong trouble. He was able to show her the church; but he felt duty-bound to question the wisdom of planning a funeral for this coming Saturday when, although it was none of his business, he had heard there might be some small trouble with the *practicalities* of the burial.

Darby's Funeral Home was closed on a Tuesday. There was no mobile number for emergencies, no receptionist to pass on an urgent message. Closed.

The heat in the porch was uncomfortable, but it was nothing when compared with the effect of the phone calls. Christine dabbed at the perspiration on her forehead and turned to the list on her computer screen.

1. Contact M, S & S – *done* – to sort out the will – *not done*.
2. Call Darby's Funeral Home – *done* – to arrange a meeting – *not done*.
3. Contact minister – *done* – to arrange service – *not done*.

She should have been prepared for this. Trying to complete an administrative task at Ellersley was like operating a printer with a perpetual paper jam.

There was no way for her to progress through items 4 to 6 as they each required answers to items 1 to 3. Even item 2a (call Stephen and arrange her family) was problematic.

Christine scanned down the list. Items 7 to 9 were theoretically possible, but she was disinclined to start any of them. Inside the house it was dark and stuffy, and she resented being the only one on hand to sort through the household items. Outside conditions were just as unappealing. And making an inventory of farm equipment when she didn't know what the machines were was ridiculous.

She sat at the desk, back upright and feet spaced neatly on the cracked linoleum and stared at the unticked list. She wondered if this was how a person went mad.

Perhaps it wasn't the fault of that person at all. Maybe it was the rest of the world that was the problem. A planet grinding to a non-functioning halt, leaving a perfectly sane woman sitting in a stinking hot porch, caught in a life she had worked very hard, for a very long time, not to inhabit.

22

Even divided four ways the Edwards' inheritance was nothing to be sniffed at. Tom had it assessed before finalising the will.

Bill McLaren came out to evaluate the property. They spent the morning studying the boundary maps and then took a drive around the paddocks to have a look at the quality of the soil. Tom knew what would grow, where the worth was. But he didn't know the monetary value.

Three thousand dollars an acre for the river flats. A bit less for the pasture, and less still for the bush, but even the scrubby bits were worth twelve hundred. Bill did a quick calculation looking at the aerial photos and was of the view that Ellersley would bring in twenty million.

Bill was an agent, which had to be taken into account when he started throwing numbers around, but Tom suspected he was about right. The stock and machinery would come to a couple of million. The house and sheds had minimal value. No one was interested in buying someone else's family history, and fair enough. The land was the thing.

The shares had gained steady ground, according to the accountant. Somewhere near one point five million if he sold them tomorrow. Then there was some money in a long-term deposit: a couple of hundred thousand. That would have to be tied to the property as well.

Vince came to Ellersley with an armful of papers and Tom signed on the dotted line. Vince had done his homework. The stakes were too high for him to mess it up.

23

Dave rolled over and squinted his eyes open. Ouch. He closed them again and groaned. He did not feel a hundred per cent. He was barely scraping fifty. Maybe a night at the Newie was not the solution to his problems.

He chucked on a t-shirt and wandered down to the bathroom. It was bloody bright. What was it? Ten? Ten thirty? He took a slash and washed his hands, looking out the window. He couldn't see the sun. Surely it wasn't above the house already.

There was a brisk knock on the door and Dave turned around.

'I'm here,' he said.

'Well make it quick, David, I need to put make-up on.'

'Rightio.' Dave sat on the edge of the bath and stretched his legs out. It wouldn't do Chris any harm to wait a couple of minutes. The world did not revolve around her. It didn't revolve around Dave, either. That had been made abundantly clear.

He took a moment to consider who the world did revolve around, and the only person he could come up with was his father. Look at them all, scurrying around to do his wishes, and him lying dead in a fridge somewhere. It was insane, for the planet to take its bearings from a dead man.

'David?'

'Just a minute.' Rushing a man who was doing a crap was poor form. Dave wasn't on the loo, but Chris didn't know that.

'What are you doing in there?'

Dave flushed the loo and wandered out.

'Tell me you washed your hands.' Chris was standing with her arms crossed. She had her full executive kit on.

'Holy shit, mate, is there a business convention in Coorong?'

'No,' Chris said. 'Nor is there a crappy t-shirt conference, though that would be more likely.'

Dave laughed. Not a bad gag, coming from Chris.

'If you must know, I'm going to inspect the church at Coorong.'

'Right.'

'You could come.' She said it in a semi-welcoming tone. She had to be desperate if she was asking Dave.

'Where are the others?'

'They left after breakfast, and I haven't seen them since. If they can't manage to stay on the premises at a time like this, I'm not sure they deserve to be involved.'

Dave said nothing. It seemed safest. There was no way he was going to inspect a church. He had more important things to do. Like checking in on his multi-million-dollar development. Chris wasn't the only one who had business calls to make. In fact, without the funeral saga, Dave doubted she'd have any business at all. Half her bloody luck.

24

Jenny stacked the tools on the ute tray. She laid sawhorses behind to keep them steady, covered the load with a tarpaulin and tied it down.

They stopped briefly at the servo on the way out of town. It was close to midday, and it was hot. Sophie sat in the passenger's seat, one foot propping the door open, inviting any breeze to come her way, while Jenny filled the tank and went in to pay. When she got back, she handed two ice blocks to Sophie to unwrap while she started the engine.

Sophie would find it harder to ask questions with her mouth full, and on a day like this she'd have to eat the ice block fast if she didn't want to wear it instead.

By the time Sophie had licked up the last icy streaks, she seemed to have lost interest in the interrogation. She chewed on the stick and gazed out the window, smiling. Jenny wasn't sure why, but she wasn't about to break the spell.

It wasn't until they were parked in the shade of the machinery shed that Sophie spoke. She twisted around to check the bumpy tarpaulin and then turned to Jenny.

'Still there,' she said happily, and then paused, like something had just occurred to her.

'Where do we get the wood?'

Jenny unclicked her seatbelt and opened the door.

'I haven't worked it out yet,' she said and stepped down into the dust.

Jenny loosened the truckies' hitch on her side and threw the rope over to Sophie. It sailed over a couple more times, then Jenny untied the final knot and wound it into a figure of eight.

'Maybe Chris took a chainsaw out while we were gone.' Sophie was leaning against the ute, chewing on the frayed end of her icy pole stick. She spat out a splinter and continued, 'She probably chopped down a tree and brought it home in the Volvo.'

Jenny smiled. She let the backboard down with a clang.

'Give me a hand here, Soph.'

Sophie hauled herself up with a sigh and Jenny handed her the drop saw.

'Just inside the gate will do.'

Keeping Sophie involved in the project might be a challenge. She was so easily distracted. She was unloading the ute like she had done more than her share already. Jenny didn't want to deflate Sophie, but sooner or later the whole team would have to face up to the situation. They had three and a half days to complete this project, and the work had barely begun.

25

When the ute was finally unloaded, Jenny agreed it was time for lunch. Sophie wasn't all that hungry, but she did need to check out what the others were up to. Specifically, who would be able to take her to town.

The news was not good. Dave said there was no way he could take the afternoon off. 'Developments like Eastside don't just happen, mate. Someone's got to be in the driver's seat.' Which is exactly what Sophie wanted for him, but he wasn't talking about the Commodore.

'What about Chris?'

'Chris? She left hours ago.'

'Where to?'

'Coorong, I think.'

'What?'

'She said something about a church.'

Sophie would gladly have hung out in a church for half an hour if it meant she could visit the sexy receptionist. Surely, she had not missed her only chance.

'Jen?'

'Hmm?'

'Will you take me?'

Jenny looked up from her Vegemite sandwich. 'Where?'

'Coorong. This afternoon.'

Jenny looked at Sophie as though she were mad and took another bite.

When they'd finished lunch, Dave stood up like a man prepared for battle.

'That's me,' he said, 'time to make some calls.'

'There's no reception,' Sophie said quickly.

'I know how to use a landline.'

Jenny stood and took her plate to the sink.

'Where are you going?' Sophie was starting to feel desperate.

'Outside,' she said, in a way that meant she didn't want company. Sophie heard her murmur a *see you later* to Dave and scrape the screen door open. As Jenny left, there were other noises from outside. An engine turned off and a car door slammed. Sophie looked down the hallway.

Chris was in the porch, kicking off her stilettos.

'Whoa. Steady, mate!'

One of them must have hit Dave. Chris didn't apologise. She stormed down the hall and Sophie slipped behind the kitchen door. She wasn't trying to hide, exactly, but she didn't want to be in Chris's line of fire.

Chris rounded the corner into the kitchen and Sophie opened the fridge and stuck her head in. Probably better than hiding behind the door, but not much.

'Juice?' Sophie grabbed the item nearest to her and held it out to Chris.

'Juice?' Chris said in disbelief. 'No, I don't want juice.'

Sophie stood with her back to the open fridge, holding the juice carton as some sort of protection.

'What I want is a priest,' Chris said. 'Or a church. Or both.' She was standing in her stockings, ticking items off on her fingers. 'How about a funeral home? A decent florist? A competent lawyer, maybe. Or a normal inheritance. That's what I want.'

Obviously, Sophie was not in a position to offer any of these things. Not from the location of the Ellersley kitchen, anyway.

'If you drive me into Coorong, I'll –'

'Where do you think I've come from?' Chris took the carton from Sophie and strode across to the cupboard for a glass.

It wasn't happening, Sophie had to face facts. Tuesday was a no-go in the love department. She seriously hoped there wasn't some other woman with more co-operative siblings visiting Barton & Sons at that minute. And if there was Sophie hoped she was ugly. Or fat. Preferably both.

26

Christine downed her juice and went to her bedroom to change into a suitable outfit for manual work. She had no idea what kind of manual work she would do, but the administrative tasks had gone nowhere and she had to do something.

She pulled an old pair of shorts and a faded blue t-shirt out of the wardrobe. Gardening. She believed she could do that. Not out in the sun, but she could trim the ornamental grapevines. They were wildly overgrown. Or she could remove the spiderwebs from the external walls of the house.

Their father had maintained the farm well, so Jenny reported, but the house and surrounds had been their mother's domain. So typical.

After Sophie was born and their mum had recovered, Christine did these jobs with her. At times her mum would have a rest, sitting on a plastic chair, while Christine continued to work. Christine chatted away, and her mum listened. She laughed with Christine – only ever with – and no one else came out because cutting the grapevines was a pain.

'Chris?'

Christine had a stepladder set up under the eaves of the verandah, and Sophie poked her head out the kitchen door.

'Yes?' Christine was business-like.

'What am I supposed to do?'

Sophie had been avoiding work since the moment she arrived and needed a good talking to, but she spoke so like a child Christine lost the desire to cut her down.

'Did you bring some old clothes?'

'They're all old,' Sophie said, 'apart from my red dress.'

'Come on, then.' Christine chucked her a pair of gardening gloves and climbed the stepladder with a pair of secateurs. She traced a new vine back to the branch and cut it off. She threw it towards Sophie.

'Wheelbarrow.'

'Yes, ma'am,' Sophie said, and Christine gave her a warning glance. Following another vine back to its source, Christine cut it an inch beyond a new bud, and let it fall to the pavers.

Their mother would never have suggested they build a coffin. She would have been horrified at the thought. It was not in her nature to be crass.

'Chris?' Sophie held up a trailing vine, too long for the wheelbarrow. Christine indicated another pair of secateurs.

Their mother didn't swear. She never raised her voice. She was dignified, and elegant, and Christine had no idea how she tolerated being an Edwards when she'd grown up in such refined society. She would have spared Christine from this situation if she could have.

'Wheelbarrow's full,' Sophie said, and Christine looked.

'Press them down,' she said. 'There's enough room for the same again.' Sophie looked doubtful, but she did as she was told.

Christine snipped another vine. She used to be the one at the wheelbarrow, while her mum was in the vines, her voice muffled by the light green leaves. When Christine yelled that she couldn't hear, her mother laughed. It was the best sound in the world.

27

It had been an exhilarating day. Not without its challenges, Vince would admit, but he was more than prepared to meet them.

The reading of the will the evening before, in the presence of the four Edwards children, was a dramatic event, and Vince enjoyed his central role. There was tension, anger, despair and, if Vince's social antennae did not lie, a strange elation from young Sophie. Even the presence of Charles Briggs could not dampen the occasion.

After the meeting he instructed Ben to send the document to Mindle, Seifort & Sloane, and then went home. He enjoyed a bottle of wine and meal for one in front of the TV and had an early night.

It was just as well because he had been on his toes, metaphorically speaking, all day.

As soon as he arrived at Barton & Sons, he collected the will from the reception desk and took it into his office. He made a cup of tea, opened a packet of Mint Slice and sat down.

He observed with satisfaction the dossier lying before him. It was a substantial document. Well researched. Carefully constructed. He touched the paper with pleasure. 'The Last Will and Testament of Thomas Hinkley Edwards'.

Vince flipped through the pages until he reached the condition of inheritance.

It was marvellous. Truly marvellous. Vince dunked a Mint Slice into his tea and sat back in his executive chair.

He was ready and waiting for the call from Mindle, Seifort & Sloane, but they took their time getting in touch. Vince was forced to attend to dull paperwork until late in the afternoon.

He was part way through his afternoon cup of tea when the phone rang. He spilled it. Only a few drops went on the will, lying on the desk before him, but it made him cross.

'Yes?'

'It's Robert Sloane.'

'Thank you, Ben, you may put him through.'

Vince cleared his throat, lowered his voice a tone and answered as though he was dealing with matters too important to be interrupted.

'Vince Barton.'

'Vince? Robert Sloane here.'

'Yes, Robert?'

'I've got this will of Tom Edwards.'

'Yes?'

'Extraordinary document. Never going to stand up, of course.'

'Up to what, Robert?'

'Contestation, Vince. You can't draft a will and be a beneficiary. You should know that.'

'I do, Robert, I do. But Tom Edwards was very clear. He had Charles Briggs certify his mental capacity. I explained the constraints of the law. In fact, as you will see when you read the supporting documents, I referred him to you for further advice.'

Vince could hear Robert Sloane shuffling papers – he hadn't read the document yet.

'Perhaps you would like to call again, when you've had a proper read?'

Robert bluffed, as he always did. 'I've read enough. It's ridiculous. Building a coffin as a condition of inheritance. Contesting the will is the only sensible step.'

Vince had never had the chance to offer Robert Sloane advice, but it didn't hold him back now.

'I'd think twice, Robert, if I were you, about advising your client to contest this will at the present time. It may be that my potential inheritance is overturned, but that is no guarantee the coffin-building condition would be.'

Robert was quiet.

'Four days is all they have to fulfil this condition. It's their one chance at an unencumbered inheritance. Would you advise them to risk it?'

Robert Sloane remained silent. No more bluffing. No putting Vince in his place. Vince had practised this speech many times, but he couldn't have dreamed it would go so well. It was time to wrap it up.

'If that will be all, Robert, I'll say goodbye.'

'Yes, goodbye,' Robert said, trying to speak with a tone of authority. But Vince wasn't fooled. Robert had lost his footing. Vince hung up the phone and tapped a little drum solo on the edge of his desk. He knew it was far from the end of the fight, but it was a promising start.

28

Sophie's eyes flipped open as the sun hit the windowpane. It felt like someone had switched her on. She reached for the pillows scattered on the floor, propped herself up against the bedhead and did the morning inventory. Wednesday. Sunrise. Ellersley. Alone. Bed-wise, at least. Her sisters and brother were on the other side of the door, which, unexpectedly, was good by Sophie.

The irony of the situation did not escape her. Sophie had travelled the world looking for an interesting life, and now two and a half days at Ellersley had trumped the lot.

A sibling reunion, shonky lawyer, controversial will, secret coffin-building business and the sexiest receptionist in the Southern Hemisphere – now that was a line-up.

Sophie kicked off her sheet and swung her legs over the side of the bed. She sat there naked, surveying the clothes scattered over the floor. Yellow singlet top and denim skirt. Perfect. She rummaged around in her suitcase for clean undies but couldn't find any. Not a problem, she'd go commando. She grabbed her toiletries bag, tiptoed to the door, opened it gently and peeked out. All clear. She scooted down the hall to the bathroom, clutching the bundle of clothes against her breasts.

She turned on the hot water and flicked her hand under the water. Surely someone would be going to Coorong today. Chris was bound to have some business at Barton & Sons. She'd been on the phone to Mr Sloane the afternoon before and she wasn't happy. There was no way she'd leave the will as it was. If Chris was going to the lawyer's office, she'd want moral support.

Sophie hopped into the bath and stood with her back to the spray. The others would be no use to Chris. Dave had been drinking in front of the cricket last night. There was a full case of four-ex when he started, and he'd been going strong when Sophie went to bed. He wouldn't be up for hours. And business meetings were not Jenny's thing.

Their dad hated making an unnecessary trip to town, so he wouldn't be interested either. Sophie turned off the taps and reached down for the towel. He would have been up for hours already. He'd be way out in the paddocks somewhere, fencing, or checking stock. Maybe filling the troughs – it was going to be an absolute scorcher.

He could be doing any one of those things, Sophie thought, as she stepped out of the bath, any one of them, except he was dead.

She wrapped the towel tightly around her and sat on the edge of the tub, looking at the crumpled pile of clothes on the tiles. Is this how it worked? That she'd wake up and start the day, just like a normal person. Choose her clothes off the floor, head down to the bathroom and sit on the loo. Wipe her bum, flush, and step into the shower. And at any point, one thought might lead to another and then bam! He's dead.

It was a stupid idea. He hadn't been so present in years. When she opened the bathroom door, she knew straight away he'd used it that morning. His shaving gear lined up neatly on the shelf; the faint whiff of Sunlight soap; a scrunched-up star in the towel where he'd wiped his face dry.

He was about to yell through the laundry door; he wouldn't want to take his work boots off. He'd be standing on the concrete step, shirt neatly tucked into his work trousers, one hand resting on the doorframe, leaning his head into the house.

'Soph! Come on, girl, get up, I need a hand with the weaners.'

Or maybe he was about to come in for the morning cuppa. It would be nice to get up and put the kettle on, to get his mug out and hers too. She could tell him about all the palaver with the will, the interview with Mr Barton. He'd enjoy that. It would make him laugh, watching her play it out.

But he was dead. The coffin-building was his plan, and he would be the one lying in it. It was mad. It was impossible.

When her mum died, he sat on the side of the bed and picked Sophie up. She leaned against his chest, and she could feel his heartbeat through the pocket of his shirt, that's how strong it was.

Sophie shifted. Her bum was getting numb. She stood up, roughly dried herself and chucked on her skirt and top. A quick tousle of her wet hair, a dash of mascara and light rouge and she was ready to face the world. The outside world, anyway. Light rouge was all it took to front up to that.

29

'Honestly, Sophie, what is that get-up?'

Christine looked at Sophie in disbelief. A cut-off denim skirt and a singlet top; what was she thinking? The strappy sandals didn't help.

'For a meeting with a solicitor, this is what you choose? Do you even own a suit?'

'Nope.' Sophie didn't appear to be the slightest bit concerned.

'Did you bring something to wear to the funeral? Or is this,' Christine gestured at Sophie's outfit, 'what we've got to look forward to?'

Sophie was spreading peanut butter on her toast and was so absorbed by the task she didn't seem to hear Christine's question. She certainly didn't answer it.

It was odd for Sophie to be out of bed and making breakfast at this hour. It was also odd that she wanted to join Christine for the visit to Barton & Sons. Normally Christine would have said no, but she was feeling apprehensive about the meeting.

They reached Barton & Sons at nine sharp. Christine flipped down the visor to refresh her lipstick, tucked her handbag under her arm and led the way across the street. Sophie was dithering in the car but eventually managed to get out, dashing across the road to catch up. She reached the door just before it closed and tumbled in, puffing and laughing, a strap falling from her shoulder.

Christine ignored her. She took her sunglasses off and addressed the young man behind the desk.

'Christine Minehan for Mr Barton.'

He picked up the phone and said, 'She's here.'

Christine pushed her hair into place and shifted her posture. By the time Vince Barton opened his door she was quite composed. She turned to Sophie, who was flicking through some motor sports magazine, and coughed. Sophie didn't respond, so Christine hissed at her, but it had no effect. Sophie was an appalling support person. Christine decided to leave her in the foyer.

'Mr Barton,' Christine spoke as soon as she was in the office. She marched to a client chair and sat down. She barely waited for Vince Barton to reach his seat before she continued.

'You have been contacted by Mindle, Seifort & Sloane.'

'Yes, yes, we had a conversation.' Vince Barton was shuffling papers on his desk. He did not seem comfortable. He was nervous about their interview, which was exactly as it should be.

'I spoke with Mr Sloane yesterday afternoon, and he said you were most unhelpful.' Christine's composure improved as she watched the solicitor's uneasy fidgeting.

'I'm sorry it appears that way, Mrs Minehan, but you will understand that –'

'Oh, I understand perfectly. You want to make the Edwards the laughing stock of this town. And if we don't participate in this farce, you are proposing to deny us our rightful inheritance.'

'Again, Mrs Minehan, I am sorry you feel that way, but –'

'It is not a question of how I *feel*, Mr Barton,' Christine cut him off again. 'It is a question of fact. Mr Sloane explained that unless you co-operate, there is very little we can do about it now. Contesting the will, as I'm sure you are aware, is a costly and drawn-out process, and it will not solve our immediate problem. However, if we are unable to come to a suitable arrangement, I will pursue that option without hesitation.'

Vince Barton's gaze had fallen to the desk. This time he did not try to interject, which was just as well because Christine hadn't finished.

'Right now, I don't have time to contest the will. I certainly don't have time to build a coffin. I have more important things to do.'

Mr Barton gave no answer.

'Such as arranging my father's funeral,' Christine said pointedly. Vince Barton nodded. It was a non-committal kind of nod, but it was acknowledgement enough for Christine to continue.

'It seems to me, Mr Barton, the question is a simple one. What do you need to drop this ridiculous condition?' Christine paused, steadying herself. 'What, or should I say how much, do you need to sort this business out?'

He said nothing to this, but he slowly lifted his head and looked directly at Christine. As though he was assessing her. Christine flushed. He smiled slightly. His eyes glinted.

'Mrs Minehan,' he began, swelling with self-righteousness, 'I am bound by rules and regulations that do not permit me to enter into financial negotiations of this nature. Particularly in relation to an estate for which I am the executor.'

He pulled the lid off his fountain pen, opened a notepad, wrote the date, and drew a line under it.

'I am afraid I am unable to alter Mr Edwards' will, no matter what the incentive. Now, if that is all, thank you for your time. I won't detain you any longer.'

He rose from his chair.

Christine stood up shakily, one hand on the desk.

Dismissed! Dismissed by such an insignificant creature. It was mortifying. But Christine knew this was the consequence of a far greater betrayal. A betrayal made months, perhaps years, before.

Christine gripped her purse and walked to the door. She tried to hold her head up, but it was hard. When she reached the foyer, she abandoned the effort and rushed, head down, towards the sunlight.

'Chris? Chris!' Sophie called after her. Christine had forgotten she was there.

'See you tonight?' Sophie was talking to the receptionist. The door was caught on a bump in the lino and her voice floated out, clear as a bell.

There was a pause, then Sophie laughed. 'Drugs? In Coorong? Sure.' More laughter. 'I'd better go.' Then she shouted out, 'Chris! Wait – I'm coming with you!'

Christine beeped the car unlocked and kept moving.

'Wait!' Sophie called, skipping across the road. 'Chris! I'm here. I'm with you. I'm totally with you.'

But she wasn't. None of them were. This humiliation was Christine's alone.

30

Jenny had woken at five and was outside working by five thirty. It didn't take long to put on a dress and work boots. A cup of tea and a piece of Vegemite toast took only a few minutes more, and she was out the door. Pre-dawn. Only just, but it changed everything to start the day before the sun came up.

She took the Hilux for a drive around the stock first, checking water troughs and the cattle. She'd gone out on Monday morning, and again yesterday afternoon. Maybe she didn't need to do it every day, but she'd prefer to know everything was running smoothly. The cattle looked beautiful. Sleek and fat; knee deep in green grass. There was no need for hand feeding or moving stock. The water troughs were one third full. He must have filled them in his last days. For now, Jenny knew they were coasting on the hard work of their father. The others didn't see it yet. As far as Jenny could tell they hadn't considered the animals. They hadn't noticed his dog was gone. Beautiful Nell.

He'd put her down. Jenny had found her in the dead animal pit, stretched out on a pile of carcasses, drying in the sun. It was sad, but also something of a relief. Jenny could never have done it.

By the time she got back from checking the stock, sunlight was spilling into the machinery shed. Jenny did a quick appraisal. Vehicles took up most of the floor space. The tractor, the old Holden ute, two motorbikes – the first job would be to move them all out of the shed. They would survive in the open for a week. They might enjoy the change.

It was a new tractor and Jenny wasn't sure how to drive it, but it was a diesel engine so she thought it would be much the same as the Hilux. She climbed up onto the seat and rattled the gearstick to check it was in neutral. She turned the ignition key and pumped the accelerator. Nothing. Same again – nothing. No doubt there was a button somewhere, or some sort of trick, but Jenny didn't feel confident about experimenting. She spied a lever that looked like a handbrake and considered releasing it. There was a slope away from the shed – maybe she wouldn't need to start the engine at all. Jenny let off the handbrake and the tractor rolled slowly into the middle of the paddock where she pulled the brake on again. That'd do. Now for the Holden and the bikes.

With the vehicles gone Jenny had a clear view of the workspace. It was big. There was a long bench at the back and a shorter one on the left wall. A few shelves, some empty drench bottles, a stack of feedbags and that was it. They were lucky that their father wasn't a hoarder. She'd heard of people who set a match to a full shed, just so they didn't have to sort through it.

Organising the work area was the next priority. If she could get it done before the others showed up it would simplify things a lot. Jenny set the sawhorses apart in the middle of the shed and then sorted through the tools, placing them in a logical sequence around the shed. Then she went over to check the power point in the far corner.

'Hey, sis.'

Jenny turned to face Dave.

'There's power,' she said, holding up an extension cord with wonder. 'Did you know he'd powered the shed?' She stood up and dusted off. 'It's going to save us so much trouble.'

'Right,' Dave said, but he didn't sound very enthusiastic. He propped himself on a sawhorse. 'What's up?' he asked listlessly.

Jenny looked around. 'Oh well, I thought I might make a start.'

'On what?' Dave asked.

Jenny could see that Dave was under the weather, but all the same she was a bit surprised by the question. Surely he knew what she would be working on.

'Holy shit.' Dave finally engaged in the conversation. 'You're doing it. You're building his coffin.'

'Yes, well, there's a bit of a problem,' she said.

Dave was moseying around the shed now, examining the set-up. He looked over towards Jenny and then his gaze shifted to the paddock behind her.

'You don't know how to park a tractor?' he asked.

'Actually, I couldn't start it. I just let it roll.'

'Atta girl.'

By the time he returned to the centre of the shed he had the air of a manager who had just finished a site inspection.

'Where's your timber?' he asked.

'That's the problem,' Jenny said. 'I don't know what to use. The will says rough-cut. I've looked in the old shed. There's not much there, and it's commercial grade. Do you think we're supposed to chop down a tree?'

Dave walked out of the shed and looked around, as though hoping to find a pile of wood stacked in a handy spot. Something caught his eye, and he shook his head slowly.

'You know what he wants, don't you?'

Jenny walked over to see what he was looking at. There was nothing there. Only the hayshed, fifty metres away, which had been there forever.

'No.'

'He wants us to use the family harvest.'

'The hay?' Jenny wasn't quite sure how to respond. She had heard of houses made from straw bales, but never a coffin. They had to be realistic. 'I think we have to make a timber coffin.'

'Not the lucerne, you goose,' he said. 'The mill.'
And then, slow but steady, it dawned on Jenny.
Of course. She smiled at Dave. Of course, that was the answer. They had to go to the mill.

31

Tom Edwards wasn't going to have it said that he didn't make an effort with his son. He tried, bloody hard in fact, to get Dave interested in the property.

The mill was a great example. Living history, that's what it was. A vertical slab hut built by his great-great-great-grandfather; stacks of hardwood milled by every generation since. What more could a boy want?

Helena loved to go there for a picnic, before things got hard. Bundle the kids in the car and take them up by the main road. Tom would join them every now and then. Jenny and Dave climbed all over that timber when they were toddlers. They yelled at each other from the top of the pile – who was the tallest, who was the king. They lost interest though. Like they did with everything else.

He took Dave to muster a mob of cattle when he was about thirteen. He'd been mooning around the house for months, obsessed with his acne and broken voice, and his puppy-dog devotion to his mother. He needed a shake-up.

They were bringing the cattle down the back boundary, and they came across the mill. Dave didn't notice, so Tom had to point it out. He did it as though he were surprised to see the mill himself. He was ready to join Dave in looking over the hut and the timber stacks seasoning behind it. He would have let the cattle spread out a bit while they explored. Hell, he would have lost a couple in the scrub to share that with his son.

But Dave couldn't have cared less. Barely laid eyes on it before he turned his face to the ground again, kicking a stone out of his way. Dry dirt and boredom. It was all he saw. And maybe that's all there was. Maybe. But this was the work of his ancestors, and he wouldn't even look up.

Tom Edwards wasn't proud of that day's work with his son, but he wasn't a heartless bastard either. He was pushed. Any man worth his salt would have done the same.

32

Dave never went back to the mill. He wouldn't have gone with his father then if he'd been given a choice, but thirteen's a hard age to hold your own against both your parents.

He wasn't sure who was harder to forgive – his father for the hiding, or his mother for telling him to go. She was laid up on the lounge, pregnant and swollen, and Dave would have done anything to make her happy.

He never told her what happened. How his father hauled him over to that stack of timber, grabbed him by the hair and jerked his head back hard.

Open your eyes, you little prick. Look at it! It's your fucking heritage. Do you know what you are without this? Nothing. Another fucking useless, ordinary bloke. Is that what you want? Is it? Answer me!

Is. That. What. You. Want?

His father cut the words off, shoving Dave's head forward with each one.

When Dave didn't answer, he lost it. Clenched jaw let loose, spit flying and grunting breath. He spun Dave around and held up his fists like a prize fighter. He flicked one at Dave's face, barely touching. Like he was teasing, or maybe testing his range. Then he hit him hard. Bone crunching on bone, over and over, and then there was one massive blow in Dave's gut. It knocked him back onto the timber, and he couldn't get up. He lay there, coughing and crying and spitting blood, and his father looked on in disgust. He didn't wait for Dave to recover. He gave a quick whistle for the dogs, sent them round the mob and took the cattle home.

Dave hadn't told anyone then, and he didn't plan to tell anyone about it now, but his palms were cold and damp on the steering wheel.

Anyone else and he would have refused to go, but when Jenny stood there in her baggy dress, her face round and hopeful, he couldn't say no.

She was right about the track. It was rough going. She would have found herself in trouble, driving up on her own. It wasn't like his old man to neglect the maintenance of a road. Maybe there was nothing at the end of the track anymore. Dave briefly lit up at this thought. Maybe his father had sold off the mill, or the timber. Or both.

The ute bounced over the last few hundred metres of track and they came out of the bush into a clearing. It was another world. Soft green grass – like it had been manicured. Tall eucalypts on all sides, dappled light. It could have been a fairyland, that's how good it looked. It didn't help Dave though.

He killed the ignition and Jenny stepped down from the ute. She slipped her shoes off and walked carefully across the grass. She reached the hut door, scraped it open and stuck her head inside.

'Oh my!' The words wafted out. 'Dave. Dave! Oh, my stars.'

Dave sat behind the wheel, hands gripping hard. He wasn't feeling so flash. Nauseous. Maybe he shouldn't have brought the slab of four-ex home on Monday night. Maybe he shouldn't have drunk it last night.

'Dave, you've got to see this.' Jenny was further into the hut now, her voice muffled by the slab walls.

'I'll wait here,' Dave yelled back.

Jenny appeared at the door. 'Aren't you curious?'

'I said I'll wait.' Dave kept his hands on the wheel and stared straight ahead.

Jenny watched him for a few seconds.

'All right,' she said. 'Come round the back and help me choose though.'

Dave closed his eyes. Specks of light flickered behind his eyelids, and they didn't disappear when he opened them again. He turned the ignition, slowly and deliberately let out the handbrake and drove around. He creaked the driver's door open and stepped onto the dirt. He leaned against the door, waiting for the lights to stop dancing.

'You'll be right, mate.' He spoke softly to himself. 'You'll be right.'

He worked his way around the front of the ute, keeping a steady grip on the bull-bar, and then let go to take a step towards the timber. Help her choose, Jenny said. Help her choose.

He leaned forward, hands on knees, light-headed. He was waiting for the pull on his scalp, his neck to crack back, when Jenny emerged from the hut.

'Are you all right?' Jenny had a soft voice, and Dave only just registered it.

'Dave?' Louder, this time.

Slowly, very slowly, Dave lifted his head.

He opened his eyes to find his sister in that shed. Standing stock still before him, waiting.

Dave bent over double and started vomiting. Bilious liquid splattered the dirt and Jenny's bare feet. She didn't move an inch. She stood there as Dave heaved, coughing up mucus and specks of blood.

When the retching ended, he found that he was weeping, that he had been sobbing all along. He lifted his head and stumbled towards the nearest pile of timber. He sat down and put his head between his knees, tears and snot clinging together, trailing to the ground.

And Jenny sat beside him in her baggy dress, waiting.

She waited until his dad had turned away and whistled to the dogs. Waited until the sound of dry bark crackling under cattle hooves had faded away. Waited until the coughing settled and the tears had slowed. Waited until Dave knew he was still breathing, still there.

And then she said, 'You're right, Dave. You're all right.'

She put a hand on his shoulder and pushed herself up. She walked over to the piles of timber and returned to her search. Dave watched as she counted boards, examined cut ends, and wiped dust away to look at the grain. By the time he stood up, she had chosen her timber. They stacked the boards on the ute and Dave tied it down. Then they drove home.

33

Wow. Sophie had no idea what went down in Vince Barton's office, but it sure hadn't agreed with Chris. On the drive home she'd been completely silent, then the moment they got in the house she started making an insane amount of noise – slamming doors and opening cupboards and throwing stuff on the floor.

She practically upended the sideboard. Yanked out the drawers of placemats and coasters and everyday napkins, then got down on her knees to reach into the main cabinet, pulling out anything she could lay her hands on. Wooden boxes of silverware. Cake servers. Weird soup ladles and curved knives. It all looked super-posh, but Chris barely glanced at it. Except for the table linen, and she didn't really look at that either. Just swept up a pile of white and stormed out, leaving a trail of napkins behind her.

An old cigar box had sprung open when it hit the carpet. Sophie crouched down to check it out. It was full of tiny teaspoons with pictures on the handles. Huh! They were so cute. Sophie picked up the box and carried it to the kitchen. She opened the cupboard under the sink and peered into the dark. Silvo. It had probably been there since the forties, but so what? She wasn't planning to drink it.

Sophie was starting to get hungry, but she didn't feel like eating on her own. She'd wait for the others to get back. She could polish spoons in the meantime.

Coronation. 1953. Queen Lizzie looked young and fresh, the crown sitting perfectly on her curls. Sophie tipped some Silvo onto a rag, inhaled deeply and gave the spoon a rub. Her Majesty was so shiny! Encouraged, Sophie chose the next in line – CWA, 1965.

She settled into a rhythm of selecting, polishing and lining up the gleaming teaspoons, and only occasionally sniffed the Silvo.

It didn't have much effect. But cleaning the spoons did. It was a very soothing activity. In a time when cannabis wasn't freely available, polishing teaspoons would have really helped a woman get through the day.

Maybe it wasn't such a bad life – keeping house. Okay, so she hated vacuuming with a passion, but when she had children, she could delegate the vacuuming to them. Or possibly employ a maid.

It was a new line of thought for Sophie. Homemaking. Procreating. Polishing spoons turned a girl's mind to settling down. And why not? Farmers needed wives. There were nursery rhymes about it. TV shows too.

A man like Ben Taylor would definitely want a wife. A bit of loving; some wild sex. Okay, so wild sex wasn't in the nursery rhymes as far as she could recall, and it wasn't *shown* on the TV, but it must have been happening off screen. How else did the farmers get children?

Sophie pushed her chair back and stood up. Now she was really hungry. Where were they all? She walked out to the porch and scraped the screen door open.

Jenny's ute was still missing.

Chris was at the Hills hoist, pegging linen like it was a combat sport. Sophie opted not to join her. She took a wander around the house instead.

A tyre swing hung from the biggest branch of the elm tree, but the rope was old and fraying. Sophie gave it a shove and watched it spin in clumsy arcs. The ground flipped in and out of view as it turned. She stopped the tyre and traced a flatweed heel-toe to the edge of the verandah, then tiptoed over the pavers, avoiding the cracks, to the tap on the corner.

She bent over and turned the tap on, flicking her fingers under the water until it was cool and then put both hands under, slapping wet patches on her legs, throwing handfuls over her face, her hair.

She let it drip under her t-shirt, shivering a bit with the trickling, and continued her round.

On the eastern end of the house, where the pavers ended, the grass was hard and prickly. Desiccated bindies waited, barbs up, ready to spike. Sophie flicked one from between her toes, and when she straightened up, she noticed the bathroom window was still propped open. She reached a hand up to tap it shut and then picked her way around to the laundry where a patch of green was still surviving, watered by the washing machine run-off.

Sophie paused to feel the softness of living lawn beneath her feet. She would have a lawn when she got married. She would sit on it in a wrap-around skirt and watch the children frolic.

Oh man, where *were* those guys? She had done everything she could think of to pass the time. She was going to die of hunger if she didn't eat soon.

Sophie decided she would sit on the lawn and count backwards from one hundred. If they hadn't arrived by the time she hit zero she would eat lunch on her own.

34

Christine gave the Hills hoist a shove and it whined around a quarter turn. She hauled a tablecloth over the outer line, pegged it in place, and gave the metal frame a push. When it stopped whining, Christine noticed another noise. The ute. It circled round to the shed and cut out. She heard doors slam, then the murmur of voices.

Christine bent down to pull a hand-embroidered serviette from the basket. She flicked the wrinkles out of the fabric and pegged it on the line.

Apparently, Jennifer and David had been out for a little jaunt.

Why not? Christine thought, and jabbed the next serviette up.

Why not just go out and enjoy yourselves? It's not as though there's anything to do around here. Not as though our father died five days ago and left us at the mercy of a ridiculous little man.

It's not like I have spent the entire day trying to find a solution to our predicament, with no help from anyone.

No, today was the perfect day to head out for – what?

What on earth had they been doing? Having a cheerful picnic? A team-building exercise for two? Christine would have joined them herself if she were not having such a wonderful time being accused of bribery by Mr Vince Barton.

A hot flush of humiliation rose up her neck. She hadn't planned to bribe him. She had no desire to 'enter into dealings' with a man like that.

She just wanted to sort it out. Efficiently. Reasonably. With enough time to prepare a decent, normal burial for their father. How was it possible to twist that desire into such a dirty, tangled thing? This was the reason she left in the first place. No one was normal in Coorong. And no one was normal at Ellersley either.

She wouldn't say Stephen Minehan was the most attractive man she'd met, even then, but he was smart – smart enough to become a specialist. And he was from Sydney. He was always going to go back. Returning with a pretty, young nurse on his arm, primed and ready to support him in his career, was the icing on the cake.

He chose well, Christine had to give him that. She was so determined to make it work. She watched the other wives and worked out quickly what was expected of her. In a short time, Christine had learned to be normal in any company. At home, at functions, at the reception desk, until the children came along.

Mother's groups, P&C boards, birthday parties – nobody did it better than Christine Minehan. Other mothers said it, and Christine knew it.

So how had she become the odd one out here? How had objecting to the insanity of this situation all of a sudden become a crime?

She heard Sophie run past and shout, and Jennifer spoke softly in reply. The screen door squawked, and there was a moment's quiet, then Sophie started talking again. She and Jennifer approached the house, but neither of them stopped to help. Christine was nearly done, but they didn't know that. They could have offered, at least.

Christine shook the last serviette out with a snap and pinned it to the wire. She left the empty basket in the dirt and walked between the layers of cotton to the centre of the Hills hoist. She stood there, waiting for them to go inside.

The screen door screeched open and closed again. Christine blinked and leaned her back against the metal pole. A vertical line of heat seared through her blouse, scorching the skin between her shoulder blades. She slid down to the ground and sat on the concrete. Clean linen swayed gently in her face, giving a hint of cool, a glimpse of calm. She inhaled the washed air and closed her eyes, resting her head on the pole.

Perhaps she could stay here for a while. Let the world go through its wash cycle without her. She could watch from outside the machine and see how her siblings coped in there. Let Vince Barton join them, why not? They could all tangle together, and when they were properly wrung out she would remove them from the machine, separate them and hang them on the line to dry.

35

Contemporaneous notes are the secret to a successful legal career. Vince could not recall which of his lecturers made this comment, but it certainly made an impact at the time.

From the beginning he was diligent about taking notes. It gave him something to do when legal cases were few and far between. He took pride in his handwriting, a fine cursive script with decisive strokes. No unnecessary flourishes; no wavering, wandering lines.

An interview was not complete until it was recorded on paper. Indeed, his clearest thinking often occurred while writing notes after an interview. Such was the case when he began to document the morning's conversation with Christine Minehan. As he wrote, phrases jumped out from the paper as though they were tap dancing on a lit stage.

'What, or should I say, how much . . .' Yes. Those were her very words. 'Or should I say, *how much* . . .' He was impressed by his own answer as he transcribed it further down the page. 'Bound by rules and regulations which do not permit . . .' Vince did permit himself a slight smile at the recollection of his speech. It was a pleasure to watch a woman of Christine Minehan's stature squirm. She twitched in her seat most uncomfortably while Vince explained, calmly and professionally, where she had gone wrong. He was not unkind, but he was firm, and Christine was shaking as she stood to leave.

He had not expected this turn of events, he would admit, and yet it was so predictable. From the moment Vince set foot in Coorong Tom Edwards had treated him with contempt.

Oh, Vince could weep for that 22-year-old boy! Arriving at his welcome dinner in a purple suit, hair meticulously styled. Vince had thought carefully about how he should dress. He had already given up his name; he understood changes would have to be made. But it was an evening party! Surely he was allowed to show some flair.

If Tom Edwards remembered what happened that night, which was doubtful, Vince suspected he would have said it was just a joke. Perhaps it was. It certainly kept the people of Coorong laughing for a long time.

Under normal circumstances Christine Minehan would not even notice a person like Vince. Now that she had to pay attention, what she saw was an irritant. A rank outsider who should be grateful to receive her gaze. Indebted to her for her scattered largesse. Only the largesse was not hers to scatter. Not yet, at any rate. And time was getting tighter for the Edwards siblings. Wednesday morning already, and no sign of a coffin. No plan. Not even the whisper of an idea as far as Vince could see.

He waved the ink dry, flapping the paper gently. It might come to nothing, this interview, or it might come to something. In either case Vince had it documented. Dated. Ready to present at any time it was required.

36

It was a silent drive home, mostly, but it was a gentle silence. Once Dave had stopped vomiting and had a sit, he was ready to help her carry the planks to the ute and tie them down.

River red gum. That's what Jenny chose. There was some beautiful timber: yellow box, stringy bark, ghost gum. Sometime, when this was all over, she would go back to the mill and take the time to acquaint herself with it. But for the coffin they would use the river red. He would have wanted it. It was a dignified timber, fit for a king.

Also, practically speaking, the selection of widths in the red was the most useful. Plenty of four- and six-inch boards, even one eight-inch board. Jenny could hardly believe her luck. The boards were cut to a depth of two inches, so they'd get two, maybe even three, planks from each of them. How they would do this was another question altogether.

Dave had reversed up to the shed, and they were starting to untie the load when Sophie came running across the paddock.

'Hey, guys!' she called out. She was waving like a desperate hitchhiker. 'Wow. That's a ton of wood.' Sophie was only a couple of metres away by now, but she was still yelling. 'Where'd you get it?'

When she got closer to Dave she reeled back.

'Shite, Dave, you stink!'

Dave stopped untying, shook his head and walked off.

'Gross. Did he have a chuck in the car?' Sophie didn't wait for Jenny to give an answer. 'Did you have lunch yet?' she asked.

'Not yet.'

'You want some? I'll make it.'

Jenny followed Sophie down to the house. Now she had stopped working, she realised she was hungry.

'Do you want to hear about our morning?' Sophie shoved a pile of fancy teaspoons and a can of Silvo to the end of the table and opened the fridge, pulling out random items and throwing them onto the table.

'I thought I'd better keep Chris company on her Mr Barton mission.' Sophie slapped bread on two plates. 'Sandwich?' she asked Jenny, who barely nodded before she ploughed on.

'Anyway, Chris was in a foul mood. I mean, absolutely *foul*. She marched straight into Mr Barton's office and left me in the foyer like a shag on some sort of foyer-rock.'

So far, Jenny thought, the story had a number of holes. The idea of Sophie choosing to keep Chris company was the first and truly gaping one: as far as Jenny could recall this had never happened. Not in their family's whole history. And if Sophie had wanted to get into Mr Barton's office, which again was difficult to imagine, a closed door wouldn't have kept her out. Sophie knew how to get to the action when it suited her. Perhaps the action was somewhere else.

'And it turns out his receptionist, you know, that guy in the sling?'

'Yes.' Jenny smiled. 'I do.'

Sophie didn't need to say anything more, but Jenny would happily listen if she did. Even watching her move was a delight. Such a slender form, standing on her toes to reach the top cupboard.

'Anyway, he knew Dad. He even bought cattle from him. Isn't it amazing?'

'Mmm.' Jenny took over construction of her sandwich. Sophie was no longer showing commitment to the task, and Jenny had no interest in eating a piece of mangled bread and butter.

'He said he'd pick me up on Saturday morning and take me to the sales. Six am. Can you imagine me getting up that early? I fibbed though, Jen. I told him I loved the early morning. Which I guess I might if I was ever up for it.'

Sophie paused, butter knife in hand.

'The truth is I'm more of an evening girl. I won't be looking my best at six am. He needs to see me in the twilight to get a proper idea of my sex appeal. Plus, why wait until Saturday? What am I going to do for the next three nights?'

'You could help with the coffin,' Jenny suggested.

Sophie laughed. 'Good one. Luckily, I remembered tonight is movie night at the town hall – I had to ask him quickly before I lost my nerve. Wow, Jen, it was awkward. I mean, *totally* awkward.' Sophie plastered peanut butter on her bread.

'He said yes, but I'm not sure if he *meant* to say yes.' Sophie took a bite. 'It was more like he blurted out the first word that came into his head.' She took another bite. 'I don't even know what the movie is. He said it was something about drugs. Strange for Coorong, hey?'

'Maybe.' The CWA didn't have the hold on Coorong it once did. Jenny had heard there were movies with swearing and violence and sex and all kinds of things at the town hall now.

Jenny finished her sandwich and took her empty plate to the sink.

'What are you doing now?' Sophie shoved in the last mouthful of bread and stood up too. 'I could help you if you like. I mean, obviously I have to get ready for my date a bit later, but I could hang with you this afternoon.' Sophie said it like she was offering Jenny a personal favour.

'I'm working on the coffin,' Jenny said.

'Great,' Sophie said. 'I'll help this afternoon and then you guys can finish it tonight. If there's anything left to do, I can help tomorrow.'

'Thanks.' There was no way Jenny could describe the dimensions of the job to Sophie. A full-length coffin from rough-cut timber in less than ten hours? Who was she kidding?

Right now, it didn't matter. The important thing was having Sophie on board. '*All four must participate in building the coffin, and each of my children must physically work on the construction of the coffin.*'

That's what the will said. Everyone had to be involved. Dave had already helped with lifting the timber. He wasn't fully committed to the project, Jenny could see that, but he'd come around.

Christine was the one. It wasn't possible to talk Chris into doing something she didn't want to. She thrived on resistance. Perhaps she even needed it to survive.

37

The concrete was rough, jabbing into her buttocks, and the pole was burning Christine's back, but she refused to go into the house until the others came out. Jennifer and Sophie took long enough, but at least they did appear. They took no notice of the white washing or Christine, though they must have known she was there. Instead, they walked towards the shed, chatting and laughing.

She waited a while longer for David to emerge. Long enough to make the pockmarks permanent, but he didn't come out. Perhaps he wasn't feeling well.

Christine hoisted herself up. Neither should he be. Two nights of drinking in a row. He must be aware of the risks of alcohol consumption by now.

Christine brushed off her skirt, then stood still and listened for a moment. There was no sound coming from the house. Right. She decided to take a chance on David. He was probably lying in a stupor somewhere, unable to notice another person's presence. She pushed her hair back, straightened up, and slipped between the layers of linen to re-enter the appalling day.

A peal of laughter burst out from the shed, and the sound was swallowed by the mid-afternoon heat. Christine walked across the dry yard, picking bits of grass off her skirt as she went.

The kitchen was dark and cool. She wasn't hungry, but all the ingredients were on the table, so Christine made herself a sandwich anyway. Getting out of routine wasn't going to help matters.

She took a bite of the sandwich. What next? Out of habit she reached into her handbag for her mobile. In the normal world it would remind her of what to do. A message from one of the kids, an email, an alert in her calendar would pop up. The absence of mobile reception was very disorienting. Occasionally there was some blip in the atmosphere and an SMS made it through. *Hi Mum, miss you xoxoxoxoxo* from Claudia yesterday, and *Cricket stumps?* from Nicholas at 3 am. She sincerely hoped it was a delayed transmission. Nicholas sending texts at that hour was unthinkable.

Christine tapped the screen and saw two missed calls. Missed by the inadequate coverage and not by her, she would like to put on record. There was one from Robert Sloane at 11.30 am, and one from Stephen at who knows what hour. She perked up briefly. A call from Robert might indicate further negotiation with Vince Barton.

Christine finished her lunch, put the rest of the food back in the fridge and went out to the porch. She dialled Mindle, Seifort & Sloane and was once again put through to the junior lawyer who transferred her to Robert Sloane quick smart.

Robert's news was minimal. His advice was unclear and contradictory. He seemed unable to make a decision regarding contesting the will, and he was, if anything, suggesting they build the coffin. Christine had this instruction already; she didn't need Robert to back it up. She certainly didn't need to pay him for the privilege of hearing it twice.

Christine waited for him to finish speaking. So many words, so little action. No wonder she had taken matters into her own hands. She said as much to Robert, mentioning the interview with Vince Barton that morning. This had not been Christine's plan, necessarily, but it seemed reasonable to expect something from M, S & S after paying such exorbitant fees. Even if it were only moral support. It would be reassuring to have a sane professional backing her up.

Unfortunately, Robert was unwilling to provide such reassurance. He went quiet as she recounted the event. The scratch of his pen was the only noise coming down the phoneline. When Christine finished, he asked some questions. Was there anyone else present during the conversation? Had she discussed it with anyone else? And was she sure she had used the words *'how much will it take?'*

'No, no and yes,' Christine snapped back. She felt like shouting at the man. He had missed the point entirely. If anything, he appeared to be taking Vince Barton's side.

'It's not a matter of taking sides, Mrs Minehan,' Robert said carefully, and as he spoke Christine realised what he was doing. He wasn't taking sides, that was true. He was starting the legal retreat. Backing away, far away from anyone's side.

She had seen her husband do it more than once. One minute he was 'Stephen' and the patient was a close friend. The next a guidewire had perforated a blood vessel and he was 'Dr Minehan' once again, standing at the foot of the bed, as far away as he could from the patient and the procedure that did not go according to plan.

'Not a matter of taking sides, Mrs Minehan, not at all,' Robert continued. 'However, I must inform you of the risk of your suggestion being misinterpreted in an unfavourable light.'

Christine shook her head in disbelief.

'It may be prudent for you to jot down a few notes about the interview while it's still fresh in your mind. Perhaps outlining what you really meant, how Mr Barton misunderstood your purpose. Because I'm sure, Mrs Minehan, I am absolutely sure you would not offer money to a lawyer to encourage him to alter a legal document. Would you?'

'Oh, don't be such a dickhead! I was offering him money to do exactly that. But what else could I do? Can't you see what a farce this is? It's like some sort of musical comedy. And what part are you playing? The villain? The buffoon? A chorus boy?'

What a pleasure it would have been to say it out loud. She didn't, though. Instead, she held her tongue. She said, 'Certainly,

Mr Sloane,' and 'thank you, I'll do that,' and 'no, of course not'. Then she put the receiver down.

'Shit.' Christine stared at the phone. 'Shit!'

Surely this wasn't real. Surely this could not be happening? Somewhere there had to be a sane voice, a person who would use their common sense to confirm what she knew to be true.

Stephen. He wasn't a particularly good listener, but at least he was normal. Normal to a fault, according to her father.

She would ring Stephen and see what he had to say.

38

'Come on, Jen. I'm helping, aren't I?' Sophie was perched on the ute cab, heels tucked into the rails, watching Jenny untie the knot. Jenny raised her eyebrows.

'Okay, okay. I'll come down.' Sophie jumped off the ute in time to catch the rope that Jenny flung over.

'You must know *something* about him.' Sophie unlooped the rope on her side and threw it back. She wasn't giving up yet.

'Age? Girlfriend? Wife? Kids? Come *on*. Anything.'

Jenny was the only one who would have information. The others had been away from Coorong for too long. Sophie looked through the gap between the timber and the ute tray to check out Jenny's response. She seemed distracted, studying the load. A vertical crease had appeared in the middle of her forehead. Sophie looked at the load too. It was a stack of big, rectangular logs, lying on an angle. Hard to say whether it was good or bad. Maybe she'd have to engage with Jenny about the coffin stuff and then bring her around to the topic of Ben Taylor.

'Aren't they a bit chunky for a coffin?'

'Yes,' Jenny said, 'they are.' She slipped a log down and indicated to Sophie to take one end. They carried it into the shed, lying it alongside the sawhorses.

'How do you make them thinner?' Sophie put on her best 'I'm interested in what you are saying' face. It was totally wasted. Jenny wasn't even looking at her.

'I don't know yet.'

'You'll think of something, I know it. Anyway, how old do you think Ben is?'

Unloading the timber was hard work, but Sophie was willing to hang in there. Provided Jenny started talking. Which, like a mind reader, she did. Only she wasn't saying anything about Ben Taylor.

'Six for a cat, eight for a kelpie, ten for a Labrador. So, what for a man? Fifteen?' She was sort of singing it. Like times tables.

'Fifteen what for a man?' Sophie got curious.

'Fifteen millimetres.' Jen was looking at the logs on the ground.

'Fifteen millimetres what?'

'Thick. The planks.' Jenny was seriously distracted.

'The planks? Fifteen millimetres for a ... oh, man, how did I not think of that?' Sophie slapped her forehead. 'Cats. And dogs. Of *course*. I was thinking murdered infants. Pet coffins are way less interesting, but I'm guessing they're legal, so that's a positive.'

Jenny squatted down and peered at the end of a log.

'Quarter sawn,' she said softly. 'Properly quarter sawn. Lovely.' She smiled, and the crease fell away from her forehead.

'Jen!' Sophie said it like a firecracker going off. She hadn't meant to, it burst out on its own. Jenny looked up at her.

'How old is he?'

Jenny waited, like Sophie wasn't giving her all the information.

'Have you heard *anything* I've been saying? Ben!'

'I don't know, Soph, twenties, maybe? Thirties?'

'Oh, come *on*, you're not even trying to help me!'

Jenny was running a hand over the splintery surface of the top board, muttering, 'No commercial mills, no comm–'

'Jen! Wife? Partner?'

Jenny paused for a moment.

'Matthew,' she said.

'He's *gay*? Wow. I did *not* pick that. Are you sure?'

Jen nodded slowly. 'Matthew will know,' she said. 'I have to ring Matthew.'

Sophie realised Jenny was still talking about wood. She gave a sigh of relief.

'Oh, *your* Matthew. Okay. Happy with that. No problem at all.'

'What?' Jenny looked blankly at Sophie. The forehead crease was back.

'To clarify,' Sophie said, while she half had Jen's attention, 'Ben is definitely not gay?'

'Not as far as I know,' Jenny said. She stood up slowly, steadying herself with a sawhorse. Her dress was stuck to her hips and her face was trickling sweat.

'Are you okay?' Sophie briefly forgot the main topic of the day.

'Me? Yes. I'll get a hat.'

'Good idea!' Sophie called out as Jenny walked away. Maybe she needed a rest. She looked really hot. Jenny had been a hopeless informant, anyway. It was almost as though she didn't care about Ben Taylor's stats. It meant Sophie had nothing to go on, except a reasonable chance Ben was straight.

Also, he'd said yes to the movie. *And* he'd blushed as he said it. That was useful information. Sophie hoped it was, anyway.

39

Tom would concede it wasn't only Dave. The girls were just as bad. Couldn't be bothered with any of it. No interest in their family, their heritage, or Ellersley. They sure as hell had no interest in running the property. Hightailed it out of there at the first hint of hard work. Bolted. Never looked back. In fact, even setting Ellersley aside, Tom wasn't convinced his offspring knew how to work at all. There was bloody little evidence of it.

Dave's business was a form of glorified gambling, as far as Tom could tell. And the three girls had been unemployed, one way or another, since leaving home. Which meant, assuming Jock had no children – which was a big assumption, Tom would admit – a whole generation of Edwards had escaped the fact that life was hard work and hard work was not optional.

If you don't plant seed, there's no crop. If there's no crop, there's no feed. If you don't have feed, the cattle die. And if you don't work, there is no seed, no crop, no feed and no cattle. And without stock, there is no income. No food on the table. No roof over your head. Every single day, until they left home, his kids had been exposed to this reality. How the hell did they miss what was going on?

Tom Edwards would never dishonour his wife's name. Not when she was alive, and certainly not since she had died. But he did wonder sometimes if it was genetic. If there was some sort of diplomat's daughter gene that his children had inherited: an innate belief that life was about dances and pretty dresses and someone else doing the work.

Helena never held it against him that she didn't have those things at Ellersley. She didn't complain when the money got tight, and she didn't sulk either. She took economic measures. One time she made a set of curtains from old sheets. They were a bloody disaster. But she tried, and Tom respected her for it. Cooking, cleaning, kids: she had a crack at everything, at one time or another. But it took its toll.

40

Christine dialled Stephen's number. Her husband had enjoyed twenty years of wifely support from Christine – it was time for him to return the favour.

Stephen's mobile went through to message bank, so Christine phoned the surgery. Nicola was irritating as always.

'Honestly, Nicola, you don't get social status from being a medical receptionist,' Christine wanted to tell her, but today there were more pressing matters to deal with.

By the time her call was transferred Christine was ready to let the whole mess tumble out. She thought she might cry, which would have shocked them both. But, due to years of habit, Christine asked her husband how he was going first. Mistake number one. Mistake number two was leaving a long enough pause for him to answer.

His answer was odd. It was difficult to tell initially if he was in a positive or negative state. He didn't seem to know himself. Then he started saying phrases like 'I'm realising how unhappy I've been' and 'I need to find myself again' and 'I've found something new' and several other lines she was familiar with from years of watching *The Young and the Restless* while breastfeeding his children.

'And you, Christine, will understand more than anyone that I have devoted my life to looking after others. It's time to look after myself.' He was gaining strength now, really getting into the flow of it. Was he reading from a script?

The most impressive feature of his speech was that he was taking himself seriously. Apparently, Stephen believed he was saying something important. Something real.

Devoted his life to helping others – who the hell was he kidding? She'd never met a man more pandered to. Patients, nurses, theatre technicians, receptionists . . .

Of course.

The receptionist.

That's who he was kidding. Nicola.

Which explained the snippy voice. Working as a receptionist didn't give a woman social status, but sleeping with a cardiologist did. Christine understood that. She understood it when she was nineteen years old and decided marrying Stephen was her ticket out. She understood it as her orgasm faded into the dim, distant past and his came quicker and quicker. At least two nights every week for two decades she had understood what she was paying for, and she knew it was the way the world worked.

And this, too, was the way the world worked.

Twenty years younger. Breast implants. Adoring eyes in false lashes. A sunshine smile and an ever-ready laugh, even for a man with no sense of humour. And all that youthful energy! Nicola would have decades of pandering in her.

And what was there to hold him back?

His children weren't children anymore. Adolescents were so painful. So awkward. It took some effort to love them now.

Perhaps his twenty-year marriage had become painful too. All the pressure of being waited on hand and foot. Christine couldn't imagine how hard it had been. No wonder he 'needed space' and wanted to 'find freedom'. Did he really say those words out loud?

She imagined him gazing with steely eyes into the distance; Nicola standing three feet behind him in soft focus, a vicious smirk in place of her usual pout.

It would be a Friday episode. The shocking moments were always kept to the last day of the week. And Christine, a 32-year-old mother breastfeeding in front of a widescreen TV, would weep.

Devastated by sleep deprivation and loss; her ideal life reduced to a shooting pain in her left breast, an unbearably sharp stab every time her baby sucked.

Christine wept rivers of tears and let them fall onto her daughter's face, startling her dark eyes open briefly. Christine would weep and believe she was mourning the poor wife's betrayal, and the harsh daytime drama world that let such a thing happen.

Not now though. Now that it was happening in real life, now everything really was lost, she just felt tired. She held the heavy handpiece away from her ear while Stephen babbled on and asked herself, 'Is there any reason I need to listen to this?' And at that moment she couldn't think of a single one.

Christine laid the handpiece gently in its cradle and a *ting* cut her husband off.

'Fuck you, Stephen Minehan,' she said.

Then she got up and walked into the house. Walked down to her bedroom and closed the door behind her. She untied the curtain loops and let them down, shrouding the room in darkness. And then she undid everything else. Unbuttoned the $399 Bentley silk blouse and let it fall to the faded rose carpet. Unclipped the $179 Belle Epoque underwire bra and dropped it on the crumpled blouse. Unzipped her $563 Moschino skirt and held her legs together, the silk lining catching on her hips and billowing up over the waistband as the pinstripes slipped to the floor.

She removed pantyhose and invisible underwear in one tight elastic roll, pushing it down her legs and over her ankles, pulling cracked heels and polished toenails out of their casing and exposing them to the air. And she left the whole straggling mess there, gaping with astonishment at the sight of a middle-aged woman wearing only a touch of mascara and hair mousse, walking towards her perfectly made single bed.

Christine untucked the cover, turned it back and slipped between the crisp linen sheets. And there she lay. Flat on her back, with her arms placed carefully by her sides and her legs in a straight line.

She lay there with her eyes wide open, staring at a water stain on the ceiling, a yellow discolouration that had grown slowly over decades, a fine brown outline pushing into the white paint around it. She blinked occasionally, unintentionally. And she lay there. Just lay there. There was nowhere else to go.

41

Sometimes it was the smallest noise that woke him. He could have a party roaring around him for hours and lie comatose the whole way through it; then the tinkle of his mate pissing in the sink would wake him up with a start.

Dave had a vague awareness of Sophie's yelling as he nodded off. The clatter of planks being unloaded was like a gentle rustle, hushing him further into a deep and dreamless sleep. Then a small *click* outside his bedroom door brought him back to consciousness.

He woke up curious, which was a nice change. Not feeling too rusty, either. He got up and poked his head out the door, scanning the hallway. No action, but Chris's door just across the hall was shut tight. That'd be the click. It was a bit odd. It wasn't Chris's style to take a midday nap, but maybe she had a hangover too.

Dave reached up to scratch the back of his head and got a whiff of his armpit. Whoa. Shower time.

He ducked into the bedroom to get his towel and heard the screen door screech out the front. Then, strangely, another *click*.

He tiptoed over and looked down the hallway. The door to the porch was closed. Dave didn't even know there *was* a door to the porch, that's how rarely it was used. It was shut now, though. The shower could wait; he wanted to check this out first.

Running his hand along the wallpaper, he felt his way down the darkened corridor. Nice and quiet. He didn't want to disturb the door-closer. He wanted to know what she was up to.

'JENNNNY!' Sophie's voice blasted out from the shed. 'JE-ENNY, WHAT DO YOU WANT ME TO DO NEXT?'

Bloody hell, Soph, work it out for yourself. Don't disturb Jenny, she's up to something interesting.

The screen door stretched out another whine and Dave listened to Jenny's work boots clumping out. Bugger. He slid down the wall and sat on the carpet. A wave of nausea hit him from behind, and a vomit burp spilled into his mouth. Maybe it wasn't the miracle recovery after all. He sat upright and leaned his head against the wall.

The screen door slapped again. Aha. Jenny back. That was quick for Jen – it must be something important.

The dial on the telephone whirred two, three ... eight times. A local number. Then, just audible, Jenny's voice. Dave bum-shuffled across to put his ear against the door, hoping to get a clear sound. If it were Sophie or Chris, he wouldn't have had to bother. He would have understood every word from a paddock away. But Jen, curse her, had perfected the art of speaking softly. He could barely make out a sentence. Then she hung up. She might as well have phoned the weather. It was a disappointing outcome for Dave.

He heard Sophie's voice outside the window and Jenny answered. Something about sunscreen and a hat. Yeah, right. Dave snorted and propped himself into a squatting position. He was waiting for the head-spin to settle when the door burst open and Sophie ploughed into him.

'Whoa! Dave! What are you doing? You scared the hell out of me.'

'Yeah, rightio, settle down.' Dave stood up, back against the wall to stay steady.

'You smell shocking. How about a shower?' Sophie waved her arms around like she was signalling aircraft.

'Settle, mate. I know how to have a wash.' He wasn't fussed about Sophie, but he didn't want to upset Jen. He could see her wringing her hands in the porch behind them. It looked like she was getting herself into a state.

He looked over Sophie's head and gave Jen a reassuring wink, as if to say, 'your secret's safe with me'. He hadn't heard anything, but Jenny didn't know that. Anyway, with Soph around there wasn't much else he could do, so Dave decided to make a quick exit. They could talk about whatever women talked about once he was gone.

The shower was calling. Add clean clothes and a bite of lunch; he'd be a new man.

42

'Shit, shit, shit, shit, shit.'

Jenny waited until they had both gone before she sat down. Sweat was prickling up through every pore, a slick layer gathering on her skin. She watched droplets slide off the tip of her nose one by one, freefalling to the floor.

It was too close. Sophie outside the window, Matthew on the telephone and Dave behind the door, listening. Why would he do that? Why would Dave, of all people, sneak up and eavesdrop on her private conversation?

'This is why,' Jenny whispered to herself. 'This is why they can't meet him.' She pressed her palms against her forehead and started a low, monotonal hum.

Matthew had said he'd come to Ellersley. He said they'd need the bandsaw and he'd bring it out. It happened so fast she didn't have time to think, and he hung up before she could say no. And then Sophie was there, and Dave, and now she had the pressure in her chest and pounding in her ears, and she knew she was trapped.

If Matthew came, she couldn't keep things separate anymore. And if she couldn't keep them separate, how could she keep herself together?

'Is Uncle Jock coming to the funeral?'

Jenny heard a far-off voice and turned.

'Wow, Jen, you weren't wrong about needing a hat. You are fire-engine red. I mean, sirens blaring and everything.'

Sophie was in the doorway, a glass of water in her hand.

'Seriously, I think you've overheated or something.' Sophie stepped down into the porch, crunching on an ice cube. Jenny was surfacing slowly; she heard the words, but she didn't understand what Sophie was saying.

'What?' Jenny asked.

'Fire engine. That's how red you are.'

There was something else. Something about the funeral.

'Before that.'

'Oh, right. Uncle Jock. Does he know Dad died?'

'Who?'

'Uncle Jock! Come on, Jen. Jock. The one who ran away and left his family in the lurch. Ringing any bells?'

'I don't know,' Jenny said.

'You don't know who he is, or you don't know if he's coming?'

Jenny shrugged. She didn't have an answer to either question.

Sophie nodded to herself. 'Chris'll know.' She wandered back down the hallway, ice cubes clinking like a wind chime in her wake.

It was a cooling sort of sound. Calming enough to encourage Jenny to her feet and into the kitchen. She turned on the cold tap and let the water run over her wrists, then poured a glass and wandered back to the porch.

She had to get out. Somewhere quiet where she could take her boots off. The laundry steps.

Jenny sat on the second step and hitched her dress up above her knees. The afternoon was quiet, disturbed only by a voice drifting from the bathroom window.

Matthew said a bandsaw would be just the thing. Jenny had never used it before so he would have to show her how. He'd offered to bring it out straight away and set it up for her. It would be no trouble at all, he said. In fact, it would be a pleasure.

Jenny started to feel hot again. She flapped her dress and noticed she still had her boots on. She wrenched them off, peeled off her socks and put both feet in the patch of green grass. Better.

The laundry door opened behind her, and Sophie poked her head out.

'Can I join you?'

Sophie was everywhere today – in the shed, outside the porch, in the porch, on the laundry steps. There was no getting away from her. This time she was uncharacteristically cautious, even subdued.

'If you like,' Jenny said.

Sophie sat down beside her. 'What's going on?' she asked.

'What do you mean?'

'What's up with you guys? You said you needed a hat, but when I came down you were on the phone – I saw you hang up – and now you're all upset. And Dave was sitting in the dark, covered in vomit and now Chris is lying in bed in the middle of the afternoon. It's not normal.'

Jenny looked up. 'Chris is in bed?'

'Flat on her back. She didn't even budge when I whispered her name. And it was a loud whisper.'

'Is she awake?'

'I think so.'

'How long has she been there for?'

'How would I know? I've been helping you all afternoon.'

'Is she breathing?'

'I think so. I hope so. Wait, do you – shite!'

Sophie leapt up, gave a yell and ran back into the house.

'Chris! Chris! I'm coming in!'

It had been a semi-serious question, but Jenny had mostly asked it to get Sophie off her back. The fog was lifting, and she had to think. She had to work out what to do about Matthew. It was too late to call and put him off. He said he'd head straight out. He'd have the Ford loaded up by now – he was probably already on the road. Matthew was a slow driver, but even with that in her favour there wasn't much time. She'd have to move fast to prevent the impending crash.

43

Vince walked at a respectable pace up Main Street, nodding at the occasional passer-by, but internally he was skipping like a sailor in a Broadway show. Forty years of legal practice and not a thing to distinguish one day from another. And here he was embroiled in a plot that would make a gripping tele series. Coffins; will conditions; a tête-à-tête with Robert Sloane. Admittedly the chat with Robert would not have the audience on the edge of their seats, but the next event might. A bribe. By Christine Minehan, of all people. How marvellous.

Once he had filed the interview notes, Vince had turned his mind to lunch and then his feet towards the pub. It would be a nice little celebration. Nothing ostentatious. Nothing to attract attention. But festive, all the same.

A bribe, no coffin progress and it was Wednesday already! He couldn't be sure about the coffin, but Christine's visit certainly suggested work had not commenced.

Vince paused outside the pub to catch his breath and peruse the menu board. Wednesday – steak day. Wonderful. The Royal Hotel was not a five-star venue, but Shirley did know how to cook a steak. Vince went into the bar and ordered a scotch fillet – three hundred grams, rare – and took a carafe of water upstairs. A glass of red would have been preferable, but it would also have been frowned upon. Not before twelve, was the rule in Coorong.

An elm cast a dappled shade over one end of the verandah, and Vince chose a table to his liking. He sat down and poured a glass of water.

The bribe was an interesting development. As far as Vince could recall, offering a bribe was a criminal offence. Christine Minehan was unlikely to enjoy being the accused in a criminal case.

Vince had no desire to pursue this in the courts. In his experience courts were to be avoided at all costs. But Christine didn't know that. The more important thing about the attempted bribe at this stage was the question of social standing. A conviction was not required to taint a person's reputation. But if her illegal offer were made public, life could become quite uncomfortable for Mrs Minehan. Her attempt to wield power over him had the potential to bring about her downfall. At the very least, it could prove to be a disruption to the family building project.

Vince took a large sip, and before he had swallowed, he felt a hard slap on his back. He choked, spurting water over the table.

'Afternoon, Vince. What are you doing here?' Vince looked up to see Charles Briggs. Charles was eyeing off Vince's cutlery and he put on his disapproving doctor voice. 'I hope you're not having a steak.'

'Oh, hello, Charles. Ha ha. As a matter of fact, I am. You know, just a one-off.'

'Sure it is, Vince; you Italians love your food, eh?'

It was the one downside of Tom Edwards' will: the decision to appoint Charles Briggs as co-executor. Vince had strongly advised against it, but Tom wouldn't budge. Vince argued that Charles could not possibly remain impartial, which was true, but Tom said something about balancing the scales and, regardless, it was how he wanted it.

'Suppose we'll be certifying job done in a couple of days,' Charles said.

'Yes, I suppose so. Ha ha.'

Charles looked like he was settling in for a chat, but thankfully Vince's meal arrived, in all its cholesterol-elevating glory.

'I'll leave you to your poison, Vince. Make sure you go for a brisk walk.' He whacked Vince on the back again and headed down the stairs. He wasn't moving that fast, himself, Vince noted. Perhaps Dr Briggs would also benefit from some regular exercise.

Vince picked up his knife and fork and gently cut through the middle of the steak. Only just seared on the outside and oozing juices. Perfect. He set to with gusto.

Maybe Charles would certify any coffin put before him, but Vince was an executor too. And there was no getting past the coffin criteria. They were highly specific. Not to Vince's taste, he'd hasten to add. Who would choose to be buried in an unadorned coffin? But that was of no significance. It was Tom Edwards' condition of inheritance.

Vince dabbed at the corners of his mouth with a napkin and placed his cutlery neatly on the plate. Charles was not going to dampen his mood today. Not with a fabulous lunch under his belt and an unscheduled afternoon ahead.

It was the perfect time to do some research. He could familiarise himself with a subject he hadn't looked at in recent years. Bribery.

44

'Chris! I'm not joking. I'm coming in now!'

Sophie barged through the door and ran to the bed.

'Chris? Are you awake?' It felt ridiculous to ask, given her sister's eyes were wide open, but how else did you work out if someone was alive?

A pulse. That was it. Sophie quickly knelt by the bed and put two fingers on Chris's neck. The skin was warm. It was hard to say if there was a pulse though. Maybe she wasn't feeling in the right place. The body still didn't move.

'Chris? Can you hear me?'

Breathing. ABC. That's right. B for breathing. So how did you know? Stop, look and listen? No, that was crossing the road. Slip, slop, slap? *Oh, stop it, Sophie, get a grip.* Look at her chest. Is it moving?

Sophie couldn't see even a hint of movement. The covers lay flat on Chris's chest, and she continued to stare glassy eyed at the ceiling.

This is it. Sophie took a deep breath. She pinched her sister's nose, pulled her mouth open and leaned over to give her a life-saving breath.

'AAAAAAAAAAAAAAAAAHHHHHHHHHHH!'

It was the longest, loudest yell Sophie had ever heard in real life, and it knocked her back on her feet. She lost her grip on Chris's nose, who immediately clamped her mouth shut and resumed her stone-like position.

Okay. So she was breathing. She'd have to be if she could let loose like that.

'Chris?' Sophie got up from the floor and sat on the side of the bed. 'What are you doing?'

Chris stayed silent.

'What's going on?' Sophie was aiming for an empathetic tone. 'Has something happened?'

She considered patting Chris's leg but decided against it.

'I mean, apart from Dad dying. And the coffin and all that stuff.' Sophie had never had to encourage Chris to talk. The past twenty years had been all about shutting her up; Sophie wasn't sure where to start.

'Did you find something in the sideboard?'

Nothing.

'Chris, please say something.' Now she was begging Chris to talk. She hoped someone was taping this.

'What do you want me to do?'

Sophie scanned the room, hoping for a clue. What would she want if she were catatonic?

'I know! I'll ring Stephen. He'll know what to do, right?'

'No.' It was a breath out. Sophie wasn't sure if Chris had meant to speak.

'What?'

'No.' She barely opened her lips, but there was no mistaking the word.

'Are you sure?' Sophie stood up and shifted her denim skirt on her hips.

Christine said nothing. She rolled onto her side and faced the wall, her back set against the room.

Sophie went over to the pile of wrinkled clothing. They were designer clothes; super posh. They didn't belong on the floor. She picked up each item, placed it carefully on a hanger and hung it in the wardrobe. She put the shoes in a row under the wardrobe. She tucked the underwear into an empty suitcase. And then she left, pulling the door closed behind her.

45

It wasn't Matthew. It was what they would make of him. Dave would size him up and put him down. Chris would ask about his family connections – he had none – and comment for days afterwards that he was quite nice looking for his age, but surely someone could have taught him how to use a knife and fork. Sophie would make fun of whatever struck her at the time – his bald patch, his paunch, his stutter. They would turn him into a second-class citizen – no, third-class. She would never be able to see him untarnished again.

Jenny set off for the machinery shed at a brisk walking pace. Matthew wanted to come. It was the only explanation for him offering so quickly. She walked faster, dodging dry thistles. He wanted to be with her, and she didn't want him.

She reached the shade of the shed and paused. She could get through this on her own. But she'd be laid bare, thrown open, if Matthew came.

Jenny peered into the shed and tried to focus. He would want to show her how the machine worked, so she'd need wood. She hauled a plank onto the sawhorses, plugged in the circular saw and whizzed a block off the end. Then she took her block of wood and got into the ute.

If she caught him on the road, even if it was only a couple of kilometres away, they'd be safe. He could show her how to operate the bandsaw, step by step, as slow and ponderous as he liked, and there'd be nobody but the birds to laugh at him. Then he could go home, and Jenny could drive back to Ellersley.

Matthew's Ford kicked up such a cloud of dust she couldn't have missed him. He smiled when he saw her frantic waving, slowed to a stop and wound his window down. He rested his chin on his elbow while Jenny babbled about 'family only' and Chris being too fragile. He listened properly, nodding slowly, but he knew she was making excuses. He pulled his head back into the cabin, drove ahead a few metres and pulled off the road in a shady spot. He stepped down from the truck and let the door swing shut behind him.

He stood quietly with his hands hanging loosely by his side, looking into the mid-distance as he waited for Jenny to come over. She brought her chunk of wood, prickly in her sweaty hands. He didn't really need it – he couldn't make a cut without electricity – but he was kind enough to use it in his demonstration anyway.

He started with a general overview and showed her all the components of the bandsaw: the table, the frame, the engine and the saw assembly. He showed her the two wheels that held the blade, and how to line the blade up properly. He showed her the blade guides, and the fence that would hold the timber in line as it moved through the saw. He showed her how to adjust the fence to the desired width, and how to position the board and push it through the saw. He gave her a feather board, one he made years ago, a prop to hold the plank steady against the fence and stop it from swaying out. He had brought spare blades – he said they'd need a few to get through that much hardwood.

He went through it all carefully, giving instructions in clear and simple language. He took more time and care than any other human would. He made sure she knew what she was doing. And he didn't stutter once. He asked Jenny to bring her ute alongside his, so they could slide the bandsaw across. They did it together, and although it was heavy, they made it across the gap just fine. Then Matthew tied the bandsaw securely to the rails, hard up against the cabin, with an old piece of foam wedged in to prevent the metal scraping.

He didn't make eye contact with Jenny at all. Not during the demonstration, not when they moved the saw across, not when he was tying it to the railing – not until he was completely finished. Then he looked straight at her and said, 'That's it then.' His face was as blank as a sheet of paper. 'We're done.'

Then he walked over to the Ford, got in, and drove home.

It went exactly as Jenny had planned. Matthew brought the bandsaw. Taught her how to use it under a tree by the roadside. No one laughed. He went home.

But she hadn't thought of what he would say. Hadn't imagined the words 'we're done'. It hadn't occurred to her that when he drove away, she would be left behind.

46

Dave scrubbed away, humming. Whistled even, once or twice. The miracle recovery had come through. He felt terrific. He got out of the shower, towelled off and took a look at himself in the vanity mirror. Not bad, considering. Give up the grog, a couple of weeks training and he'd be as good as twenty-one. Thirty-one anyway. He put on a pair of stubbies and a Bonds singlet and headed down to the kitchen. He was starving.

The fridge was stocked – everything you could want to make a nice sanger. Dave hauled out bread, margarine, cheese, tomato, lettuce, beetroot. A greasy hamburger would have trumped it, but Dave was too hungry to go into town now. He made a couple of sandwiches and a cup of tea and headed out the front.

It was baking. The dirt scalded the soles of his feet, so he scooted round to the shady side of the house. The laundry step was warm, which was a bit odd. Cool grass and a warm step, but there you go. Retained heat was something else.

The sandwiches were excellent, the tea good and strong. Black with three sugars – the only way to drink it. When he was allowed. He took a mouthful of sandwich and started chewing, his only company a few flies. Little buggers. He waved them off his plate. He'd head over to the shed after he'd finished and see what was happening.

Dave drained the last of his tea, stood up and nudged the laundry door open with his elbow. He put his plate and mug on the washing machine, grabbed his boots and an old cricket hat, and wandered up to the shed.

The sun had shifted to the west. The tin roof gleamed, and the shed was too dim to see inside.

'Jen? You here?' Dave called from a couple of metres away. 'Soph?'

Maybe they'd done a runner. He checked the position of the sun. About five o'clock was his guess. And what day of the week? Wednesday? He counted on his fingers. Yep. It was Wednesday. Bloody hell, that went fast. Weren't they supposed to have it done by COB Friday? Or was it by sunset? Maybe they were allowed to keep building on the weekend. Dave hadn't troubled himself with the details at the time. Jen would know, though. She paid attention.

Dave stepped into the shed and waited for his eyes to adjust. The girls had unloaded the timber. One plank was lying across the sawhorses, the end freshly cut. He wandered around and had a look at the set-up. Apart from the circular saw dropped in the dirt it was very tidy.

A stack of hand tools were lined up on the workbench, and they were top quality. Router, heavy-duty drill, orbital sander, power plane. Four old-fashioned hand planes, too – varying sizes. A wooden toolbox was propped open to the right, removable shelves lifted out for easy access to the equipment. Set square, spirit level, chisels, drill bits – all oiled and sharpened. Where the hell did the professional kit come from? Dave picked up the power plane and inspected the blade underneath. Straight off the whetstone. Bloody hell it was sharp.

It had to be her man, Matthew. Jenny never spoke about him. She'd never said what he did for a living. They wouldn't have known he existed if Chris hadn't sniffed him out.

Maybe he was some sort of master craftsman? Unlikely. Chris had a long-range radar for status. If he was a master craftsman, they would know. No, he'd be a middle-aged man with a hobby – model aeroplanes or something.

Dave wandered around to the end of the sawhorse and took a look at the timber pile. The boards were all milled to two inches. Four by two, six by two, eight by two. They were going to have to trim it down all right. Unless they hired professional weightlifters as pallbearers.

The rattle of Jenny's ute approaching distracted him, and Dave straightened up. The ute came into view at the bottom of the paddock, and, revving high, burned up to the shed. It had a load – a big, chunky piece of machinery standing against the backboard. About twenty metres out, without cutting the revs, Jenny pulled the wheel down hard and did a full one-eighty. The machine rocked precariously on the back and a dust cloud billowed from the spinning tyres. Then Jenny wrenched on the handbrake and the ute skidded in the dirt.

'Jen?' Dave approached the ute cautiously. The driver's door flew open, and Jenny's boots hit the ground. The cloud of dust settled, and she emerged, hot and flustered and apparently unaware of Dave's presence.

'Jen, hey. You right?'

Jenny turned her head slowly towards Dave, but she wasn't seeing him. She didn't blink, or move her face, she just stared.

'Jen? It's me, Dave.' It was a bloody stupid thing to say, but he couldn't think of anything else. Jenny turned to the ute, slammed the door shut and marched towards the house.

'Jen? Jen!' Dave was yelling now, but she didn't answer. Face to the dirt, she trudged on. There'd be no stopping her now.

Dave shifted his attention to the ute, and the machine that, miraculously, was still upright. He jumped on the tray and took a closer look. The bottom half was a stand. Solid though, it looked like steel. The top was an enclosed vertical case, with a smooth steel table, and the table had a blade going straight through the middle of it. He shook his head and whistled softly. It was a fucking bandsaw.

47

Sophie and Jenny crossed paths at the hedge.

'Hiya, Jen,' Sophie said. 'What do you think?'

She twirled around to show off her bright red evening dress – short, with a bit of a sway in the skirt. Sexy, but still rural. Sophie was chuffed that she had brought it with her. It confirmed her view that packing for any eventuality was the only way to go.

Jen stomped past as though Sophie didn't exist. She didn't even look at the dress.

'Chris is alive,' Sophie yelled after her. Surely, she'd be interested in that. But Jenny didn't turn around – she didn't even change her pace. What was wrong with everyone today?

Sophie needed one of her siblings to be functioning normally. Enough to drive into Coorong, anyway. If Jenny wasn't speaking, she probably wouldn't want to go for a drive. And crazy-haired Chris was out. Dave was her last hope.

When Sophie reached the shed, he was reversing Jenny's ute into it. He killed the engine, jumped down and walked around the ute, checking out a machine on the back. He lifted a ridiculously fat chain and peered up at the roof. Sophie had no idea what he was doing, and she didn't care either. She needed Dave to switch focus.

'Hiya,' she called out as she approached.

Dave turned and let loose a slow whistle.

'Mate, you look incredible.' He smiled and shook his head, like he could hardly believe it was her. Sophie shrugged her shoulders and grinned back.

'Hey, while you're here,' he said, 'give me a hand?'

Turd. He was only buttering her up.

'What with?' Sophie was suspicious.

'Holding a ladder.'

'That's it?' Sophie had been roped into this sort of thing before. One job led to another, and another, and then fifty years had passed and there was still 'just one more' thing to do. She didn't have that much time to spare.

'That's it.' Dave put on his most trustworthy expression.

'Fine. I'll help you. But only with that.'

Dave ducked around the side of the shed to get a ladder. He positioned it on the back of the ute and reached down to help Sophie up. He hadn't mentioned she'd be standing on the ute – next to a huge, filthy machine.

'If I get grease on this dress, you are dead.' Sophie gave him a warning look.

'You'll be right.' Dave winked and showed her where to get a grip on the ladder. He picked up a chunky yellow hook and clambered up. There were a bunch of chains swinging around behind him, dangerously close to her dress. She held the ladder firm, though. There was no way he'd give her a lift to town if he broke his leg.

'Thanks,' Dave said as he came back down. 'There's one more thing . . .'

'Nope. No way.' Sophie put her lips tight together.

'Come on, mate, it'll be three minutes. Tops.'

'No, it won't. It'll be ten, or twenty, or way more. Anyway, you owe me a favour now.'

Dave looked wounded, like she'd let him down, but Sophie kept going.

'I need a lift to town.'

'What for?'

Sophie ignored the question. 'It's only a lift in. I'll catch a cab home.'

Dave snorted. 'Good luck finding a cab in Coorong.'

'Or I'll hitchhike or something. Come on though, or I'll be late.'

'Late for what?'

Sophie wouldn't mind Dave knowing, usually, but it was the first date. She didn't want him getting out of the car and giving Ben the once-over.

'The movies. It's movie night at the hall.'

'That's what you're wearing to a movie in Coorong?'

'Oh *come* on, just give me a ride. It starts at six.'

'What's on? I might come.' He was stirring her. The only thing Dave watched in summer was cricket.

'You won't like it; it's not your thing.' Sophie pushed Dave towards his Commodore and broke off for the porch. 'Just grabbing my shoes,' she said. 'Get in the car!'

She flew back, chucked her heels on the floor, and tugged at the seatbelt.

'It's some chick flick. The receptionist at Barton's asked me to go. We went to school together.'

It wasn't totally true, but it wasn't totally a lie either. Dave was so gutted about the will he would barely have noticed Ben. She hoped. If she kept talking, she'd easily distract him. She talked about school, summer holidays, the crazy chlorine levels in the Coorong swimming pool – pretty much anything that came to mind – and when they got to town she jumped out of the car and tried to wave Dave off.

She glanced at the small clutch of people hovering at the door and couldn't identify Ben. She turned to wave at Dave again, but he didn't seem to be in any rush to leave. Then she saw Ben. He was approaching on the footpath, about fifty metres away. He'd spruced up. Moleskins, chambray shirt, leather belt. The full country boy uniform. And it suited him.

Dave was lodged in his parking spot and Ben was getting closer, and Sophie was getting agitated. She felt a trickling in her armpits and remembered that the red dress totally showed sweat.

Shite. She was trying to decide whether to greet Ben or shove Dave off and then Ben was in front of her, and she *had* to do something. She turned her back on the Commodore and stepped up to the footpath to meet Ben.

'Hiya.'

She was so nervous she didn't know whether to kiss his cheek or shake his hand. Her palms had started sweating, so she went in for the kiss. Ben went for the handshake and somehow Sophie's arm got tangled in the sling. By the time she extracted it they were both blushing. Sophie started babbling and Ben said nothing at all, and it was hideously awkward. But when she got the courage to look at his face, she saw he was smiling. And her heart thumped. Literally.

'Okay,' Sophie said and looped her arm through his. 'Let's do some drugs.'

A woman in slacks and an ironed pink shirt turned sharply. Her perm must have been glued on; it didn't shift a millimetre. Sophie beamed and gave her a wave.

'She's from Sydney,' Ben said apologetically. 'They're used to drugs up there.'

'I dare say they are.' The woman wasn't giving an inch.

That would have been enough chit-chat for Sophie, but Ben held up his end of the conversation politely. He introduced them properly.

'Dawn Turner, meet Sophie Edwards,' he said. Sophie was still grinning, but then she noticed Dawn's expression. Her frown had fallen away, and her eyes were searching, seeing Sophie for real.

'I should have known,' she said. 'You're so like him.' She stepped closer and reached out. 'I am so sorry,' she said, 'it's a terrible loss.'

Then she touched Sophie's cheek. Like they were family.

Ben squeezed Sophie's arm against his chest, and Sophie stood between them, lost.

'Will we go in?' Ben directed the question at them both, and Dawn turned around to follow the queue.

'Sorry,' Ben leaned down and whispered. 'I didn't think.'

'That's okay,' Sophie said, but it wasn't.

The people in the line were moving happily, jostling one another. There was laughter and chatter, and everyone knew each other.

Sophie clung to Ben's arm, willing herself to stay upright, and stared straight ahead.

She had forgotten her father again.

48

Helena. Helena Smit. Who knew a woman like that existed?

After Jock buggered off and his old man died, Tom became a favourite with the mothers in the region. He didn't see it to begin with. He had enough on his plate with running Ellersley and looking after his mother. That's what he thought he was doing. She was in charge though. Had her eye on him the whole time. She told him to slow down, but he didn't hear it. Didn't want to. But eighteen-hour days take their toll. He couldn't keep it up forever.

After a few years, once he could see his way around the property, Tom pared it back. Then he noticed the girls. And they noticed him. A young bloke with ten thousand acres and all his limbs intact was a bloody good catch. For the girl as well as her mother. Even if he'd been a dog to look at, they'd have lined up. He wasn't, though. Tom scrubbed up all right, and he knew it.

He had a lot of fun, at the time. He was honest, though. He never stuffed them around. And he wasn't rough either. Everyone enjoyed themselves.

There were some nice girls, but Tom never settled on one. Looking back, Kate Belford would have been a good pick. She was bold. Plenty of spark. He could have chosen Kate. Would have, probably, if Vic hadn't invited him to that ball. A diplomat's party, no less. How the hell Vic got tickets Tom couldn't say, but he didn't turn the invitation down.

He packed an overnight bag and drove up to Canberra. Vic lent him a suit. It wasn't until they were on their way to the party that Vic mentioned the German embassy. That's where it was. Tom was cranky about that. Twenty years since the war ended and everyone, including his best mate, was pretending it never happened.

There were blokes scattered around the walls and girls in party dresses. A proper parquetry floor, and chandeliers dripping from the ceiling. Bloody hell. Chandeliers in a German embassy – was this what his father fought for? Tom was winding himself up, spoiling for a fight. But Vic caught him at it. Vic was there for a big night out, not an early eviction. He distracted Tom with the best distraction there is. A girl.

'Hey, mate.' Vic was looking at Tom but cocking his head to the side. 'Ten o'clock, check it out.'

Tom did. And his chest fell clear through the floor and hit the ground below. There was no scraping it up. She wasn't a German, thank God, but she wasn't far off. Helena Smit. The daughter of a Dutch diplomat. She entered the room on her father's arm, and she could have been a bride, he guided her with such care.

Tom dropped to his knees as she approached. Hit them hard on the parquetry floor and the room hushed. Or so he thought, but the band must have kept on playing. Tom clutched a hand to his chest, as if to steady his heart. And he waited for her to look him in the eye, to make sure she knew it was for her. It was a joke, of course it was. A joke to make men laugh and women blush. But he meant it too.

He wouldn't let up until she took his hand. It took some work, but she was worth it. She was unbelievable. And Tom won her over. In the photos he's bursting with pride. Grinning from one side of his face to the other. Talk about the cat and the cream.

Magic, it was.

Pure bloody magic.

49

Jenny had her head down, eyes on the cracked dirt.

'No. I'm not right.'

She muttered as she marched to the house.

'I am not right.'

The heat was ferocious, but Jenny didn't care.

'I don't care about Chris. I don't care about your dress.'

She wrenched the screen door with enough force to rip the top hinge off. She left it hanging crooked and continued down the hall to the linen cupboard. She had no plan. No reason to pull a chair over. But when she stood on her tiptoes and reached into the very back of the top shelf, she understood what she was looking for.

A box of toys was at the front. Blocks and train tracks and Matchbox cars. Further back, hidden in the dark, was a dusty shoebox. Jenny pulled it out and placed it on the top of the toys. She got down from the chair, closed the cupboard and carried the boxes down the hall. She took them into the lounge room, stepping over piles of crockery to find an area of carpet big enough to spread out and work. Then she fetched the kitchen scissors.

The lid of the shoebox barely fit the collapsing walls, but they were still there, in a tidy pile, resting on top of each other. Mum and Dad at the bottom, and three smiling children in a pyramid on top. A girl, a boy and a baby. They had open eyes and red lips and perfect white teeth. The mother had pointed breasts, the father wore braces and there was a change of clothes for everyone. They were, in every way, perfect.

It was the best present she ever got. It was five months after Christine was born and Jenny didn't know who belonged in her family anymore. The plastic people made it clear. Jenny was the girl, Dave was the boy, and Christine was the little plastic blob.

Jenny had played with the figures, on and off, for years. She was always the eldest child, and one day she would be promoted and become the mum. She would have pointed breasts and a tiny waist and a husband wearing braces too.

One by one, Jenny extracted the dolls from the shoebox and stood them in a line. Then she picked up the father and laid him on her lap. Holding his shoulders firmly she put the scissors to his hollow, pink waist. She cut as hard as she could, hacking and bending where the plastic was strong, until she had severed him in half. Then she chucked both pieces into the crumpled shoebox.

'One down,' she said, 'four to go.'

50

Alive. Dead. Alive. Dead.
Arrive. Bed. Arrive. Bed.

Sophie says, 'She's alive!'
Sophie says, 'I checked.'
Sophie says, 'I'm coming in.'
Sophie says I'm not dead.

Alive. Dead. Alive. Dead.
Survive. Wed. Survive. Wed.

Stephen says, 'It's something new.'
Stephen says, 'It's something else.'
Stephen says, 'It's time to find.'
Stephen says:
Myself.

                    And you
                    Will under
                    Stand better
                    Than
                    Anyone
                    That I have
                    Devoted
                    My life
                    To
                    Helping others.

51

Vince had been some hours at the books – or laptop as the case may be – and he had thoroughly enjoyed himself. Bribery and corruption law was fascinating.

Take, for example, the hypothetical case of a public official who is offered a bribe. The public official would have to accept the bribe prior to any conviction of wrongdoing. And rightly so, was Vince's feeling on the matter. The *briber*, however, could be convicted purely on the basis of offering inducement. That is, the bribe would only need to be offered – not, in fact, given – and the person could be liable to up to seven years' imprisonment.

Seven years' imprisonment was quite a sentence. Shocking, some might say. Vince suspected Christine Minehan would think so.

He had been working at one end of his dining room table. The grandfather clock at the other end chimed the half-hour and Vince folded his laptop shut. Five thirty. The end of a working day.

He pushed back his chair and turned to face the floor-to-ceiling wine rack. He selected a shiraz and put it on the sideboard while he rummaged around for a glass. Holding the stem, he poured a generous measure, watching the colour deepen as the glass filled. He took a sip, swilled it around in his mouth and swallowed. Rather a nice drop.

Vince picked up the bottle and made his way to the lounge room. He divested himself of jacket and tie and plumped up the cushion on his recliner. He raised a glass in one hand and the TV remote in the other.

'Salute!'

Vince drank deeply. It had been a wonderful day.

52

Alive. Dead. Alive. Dead.
Denied. Said. Denied. Said.

Sloaney says, 'I won't take sides.'
Sloaney says, 'Who was there?'
Sloaney says, 'Jot down notes.'
Sloaney says, 'Because I'm sure,

        Mrs Minehan, I am absolutely sure you
                    would not
              offer money
         to a lawyer
      to encourage
   him to alter
             a Legal Document.

Would you?'

53

When the pieces of family were piled into the shoebox, Jenny decided to build them a tomb. She dragged over the main toybox and started unpacking. A few pieces of railway track came out first, then Evel Knievel on his white stunt bike. A Rubik's Cube with half the stickers missing, an open tin with beads spilling out and a few farmyard animals. There was even a Ken and Barbie couple. They were already missing limbs, though, so she didn't need to cut them up.

The wooden blocks were at the bottom. There were blue squares and green pillars and orange rectangles with arches underneath. Jenny reached in and touched them, the smooth blocks and the lines in between. There was an occasional chipped corner or splintered edge, but she could work around those. Like an earthmover at a construction site, she pushed the jumbled pile of toys aside. On the edge of the cleared area, she unpacked the blocks.

The box full of severed people went in the middle of the clearing. A green pillar at each corner set the dimensions of the tomb, then Jenny started building the walls.

The counsellor at Coorong High School didn't believe in traditional roles. She was progressive. That's what she said. One day she invited Jenny into her office for a chat. A teacher had noticed Jenny had gained weight and gone quiet, so the counsellor was just 'checking in'.

There were no windows in the counsellor's room, but there were posters on the walls. Posters about Careers and Further Education and Next Steps. That day the counsellor wanted to talk about A Woman's Choice. She explained that Jenny didn't have to have a baby. She had her whole life ahead of her. She could go on to do Further Education and have a Career.

Jenny knew she was pregnant, of course she knew. But she didn't know what to do about it. So she did what the counsellor told her. She woke up one morning and put on her uniform. She got on the bus at the Ellersley grid and off again at the school gates, and the counsellor was there in her car, ready to take Jenny to town. Except it wasn't really town. It was a crackly gravel car park behind the hospital, with a door that said CLINIC.

They gave her a form to sign, then they put her in a cubicle. There was no window, just a plastic chair and a hook on the wall to hang up her school uniform. She put on a stiff, white, cotton gown and walked barefoot to a surgical trolley.

Then she woke up. She was lying on her back, and she had stomach cramps and a warm trickle of blood between her thighs.

They explained the procedure, and she signed the form. It was a sort of consent. But nobody talked about the other choice.

No one told Jenny she could have a baby. Nobody asked if she wanted a beautiful, soft, crumply baby to fall asleep on her chest. No one asked if she had always and only ever wanted to be a mum.

It wasn't their fault. They did their best.

They just got it wrong.

54

Dave stepped out of the air-conditioned Commodore into a wall of heat. It was six thirty, for fuck's sake. Did it ever let up? He put his head down and pushed his way across the front yard. When he reached the porch, he kicked off his boots and gave a yell. 'Jen! Chris? Anyone home?'

Nothing. He walked through to the kitchen and opened the fridge. Cold air tumbled around his ankles, and he took his time locating the beer so he could enjoy the chill. He wasn't going to have a big night, but there was nothing more refreshing than a cold lager on a hot day. He scanned the fridge for something to eat, but there were only ingredients he'd have to prepare. No snacks. It didn't matter. A bevvie was the main priority.

'Hey, girls!' he yelled again. 'Want a drink?'

He cracked open a stubby and wandered out to the hall, ducking his head into each room as he passed, checking for any sign of life.

The lounge room was closed-curtains dark. There was a whole heap of plates and whatever else piled up on the floor, and the telly was off. Nothing to see there.

Jen's door was open and her bedroom was empty. Chris's door was closed. Still? Maybe she wasn't in there. Dave took a swig and tapped on the door. Silence. He turned the handle and pushed it open a fraction.

It was dark, but his eyes adjusted enough to make out a Chris-sized shape in the bed. She didn't move when the door creaked. The covers were pulled up to her chin so he couldn't see her face, but she had to be asleep. He decided not to wake her. He'd have a look at the cricket instead.

Dave returned to the lounge room and made a beeline for the TV. It was like a bloody obstacle course, getting around the plates and toys on the floor. He was doing all right until he ploughed into a block tower, and then tripped over something solid.

'What the fuck?' He rolled over and saw it was Jenny. She was sitting on the floor with her legs splayed out, staring at the tumbled down building blocks.

'Jen?'

Jenny didn't answer him, but she was saying something. Was she talking to herself? Or the blocks? Dave wasn't sure, but it was bloody strange.

'Jen? What's up?'

He shouldn't have asked. Never ask a question if you don't know the answer. Management 101. Dave sure as hell didn't know the answer this time.

'I wasn't always this fat,' Jenny said, rubbing at her shin.

Dave backed off in alarm. 'No one's calling you fat, Jen.'

Jenny was retrieving the scattered blocks and sorting the colours. She started a new project – a single blue tower. 'I was tall and slender. Do you remember?' She was talking to the tower, as much as Dave.

'Do you remember him?'

Dave had lost the thread. 'Not sure I'm following, mate.'

'James. He was on your team.'

Dave had been on plenty of teams, over the years. There was a James or Jimmy or some other version on most of them.

'He was at your party. The one out the front, with the fairy lights. There were sparklers and steak sandwiches. And beer. Even though you were sixteen.'

The tower was getting taller, and Dave was nodding. He did remember that party. It was a cracking night. They'd just won the semis, so they were all on a high. Everyone came. Everyone. It was massive.

'He winked and tipped his head. I was wearing my cream dress. I loved that dress. When I wore it, I floated.'

The tower reached its peak – there were no blue blocks left – and Jenny commenced deconstruction work. She removed the blocks two at a time and put the pairs in a semicircle. It looked like an arena, or seats at a school play.

'You saw us leave. Do you remember that? You watched us go.'

He didn't remember. But he was sixteen and pissed, he could have done anything.

'You held up a can and smiled. I thought you knew him, and he was all right.'

Jenny looked straight at him.

'I didn't know,' she said.

'I didn't know a kiss could turn rough.

'I didn't know my dress would get ripped and stained with blood.

'I didn't know about pain like that, I didn't know.

'He pounded so hard, it cracked me in half.'

55

Alive. Dead. Alive. Dead.
What was that noise? What's that he said?
Who is talking, disturbing the peace? And where is my sleep?
Where did my numbness go?

Christine's bladder had begun to hurt, threatening an accident. Which would be fine for a short time, but how long could a woman lie in her own urine? And what if she needed to pass a bowel motion? That was not a thing to do in bed.

Hunger was prodding Christine, too. These things were prompting her to move, which she was determined not to do. But her body won out. The arm she had been lying on was numb, and she rolled off it without thinking. Pins and needles started pricking, and her fingers flexed and stretched without her permission. *Blast!* She closed her eyes tightly.

Wet the bed, let your arm die and don't think, don't let yourself think.

Christine's hand continued to curl.

Stop it. Stop moving!

What she needed was a bedpan. She could pee in a potty without truly waking up. Christine let one eye open to scan the room. On top of the wardrobe, in the back corner, she spied a dusty bowl. She couldn't believe her luck. She sat up and let the other eye open. Yes, it was! Cracked white enamel, royal blue rim and a handle on the side. It was a real, old-fashioned chamber pot.

She pushed the covers back, tiptoed to the wardrobe and reached up. She could barely get her fingers over the edge. *Damn.* Keeping her eyelids drooped as much as possible, Christine pulled the chair across.

She stretched her arms out like she was blindfolded, feeling around for the pot. It didn't take long to find it, even though she was concentrating on being blind and semi-comatose. Her bladder was pressing with increasing urgency.

Christine hopped down, tiptoed to the bed, put the enamel pot on the carpet and squatted down, waiting for the sweet release. It really did tinkle in a pan. It also splashed onto her legs – a gentle, warm sprinkling. Christine was surprised by how long it took. She hadn't done a pee that long in years.

She groped in the air for paper, without success. She opened her eyes again. There was no paper. Because she was squatting in a bedroom. Drip-drying was her only option. She jigged up and down a couple of times.

Fine. Bedpan under and body in bed before someone came in. It was bad enough that she had woken up; it would be unbearable to be caught. She lay down, pulled the covers up and closed her eyes firmly. She was about to switch her mind off when a thought slipped in. *What about the chair?*

Damn again. Better put it back, otherwise they'd notice.

Christine got up quickly this time, put the chair in place and skipped back into bed. *Close your eyes. Don't think. Don't wake. Nothing has changed. You still want to lie here and never get up.*

It sounded a lot like suicide. Christine felt bound to question this idea. Was suicide really her plan?

Stop thinking. It's not like that. It's just a very long sleep until everything is sorted out and I can wake up in another life.

But that could only be achieved by taking drugs. Bex powders like Great-aunt Charlotte. And wasn't she impressive? Drowsing around in her dressing gown and hair rollers, smoking with her smelly, stained fingers and coughing up yellow phlegm when she laughed.

Stop it! Keep your eyes closed and let it pass.

But her efforts to remain unconscious had woken her up. Her eyes popped open, and she scratched her leg. She blinked twice and looked at the ceiling stain. Somebody needed to deal with that.

56

It was magic, all right. Two weeks up the coast for the honeymoon and then home to Ellersley, laughing and kissing the whole way.

There were some teething problems settling in, but that was to be expected. They all did their best. Helena, his mother, and him too. Especially his mother, though. She worked hard to welcome Helena. Gave up the big room – said it was Tom and Helena's place now – and moved into Jock's old bedroom across the hall. She handed over the reins in the kitchen and never once made fun of Helena whose cooking was, at best, bloody terrible.

They rubbed along for a few months, then one day, out of the blue, Helena said she couldn't take it. She didn't want Tom's mother living with them anymore. Either she went or they moved out. As long as his mother lived in the house, she would be the one in charge and Helena would be a guest. Helena cried and Tom gave her a cuddle, and when she'd calmed down, he tried to reason with her. But there was nothing doing.

It took him a few days to work up the courage. He told Helena to go into town and he sat down with his mum on the verandah. She already knew. Started talking before he'd opened his mouth. Told him she'd decided to move into town with Aunty Charlotte. Wanted to be closer to the shops and the cinema. As far as Tom knew she'd never been to the cinema in her life, but he didn't argue. God, he was relieved.

The day she left, though, that was bad. Packing her into the truck with a few sticks of furniture and driving her to Aunty Charlotte's – it was a terrible business. They both knew she wanted to stay. She'd been running Ellersley for over forty years. He and his dad did their share of the work, but she was the brains. Ellersley needed her, and Tom was kicking her out. It was the worst thing he'd ever done, but he couldn't think of anything better.

A few years later she tripped on a concrete path and cracked her hip. And that was it. Three weeks in hospital and a blood clot in her lung and she was dead.

Jock didn't come for the funeral. If he had, Tom wasn't sure what he would have said. More than he should have, and nowhere near enough, was his guess now.

But back then, when the funeral was over and the mourners gone, Tom wasn't thinking about Jock. What he was thinking, and he thought it still, was that at Ellersley there was no concrete. And if she'd fallen, which she might never have done, dirt would have been kinder on an old woman's hip.

57

'Hey, guys. What's happening?'

When Christine spoke, Dave jumped and put his hands up like she'd fired a gun. When he saw her in the doorway he gasped, and quickly turned his head to the side, saying, 'Fucking hell. What the fuck?' His hands stayed up.

Jenny was sitting on the floor, in a sea of blocks. She looked at Christine.

'You're not wearing any clothes,' she said.

Christine assessed her front and found that Jenny was telling the truth. It made sense. She had taken her clothes off before going to bed.

'I've decided to become a nudist.' Christine entered the room and stepped over some plates to get to the couch. Dave was backing towards the TV slowly, his eyes fixed on the carpet.

'Rightio,' he said. He sounded panicky. He was reaching out for the wall behind him. When he found it, he started inching towards the door.

'No, I mean sure, that's great . . .' Dave made it to the doorframe but accidentally hit the light switch.

'Whoa! Fuck!' He quickly averted his eyes, jabbing at the switch like it was an emergency button in a stuck lift. He flicked it off and fled from the room, leaving Christine and Jenny in the semi-dark.

Christine squatted to inspect the blocks, but she was struggling to work out what the construction was meant to be.

'A nudist?' Jenny asked.

'Why not?' Christine found a scrap of cardboard to sit on and shuffled back to lean against the couch. She might be a nudist, but the carpet was disgusting. There were limits.

'How will you keep safe?'

'Safe?' Christine reached for an orange arch and balanced it on her knees.

'Yes. Safe from people. And their deciding eyes.'

Christine paused. The judgement of others was worth considering. 'What do other nudists do?'

'I don't know. I've never met one.'

Christine leaned back against the couch and closed her eyes, letting the orange block fall. What did nudists do? Day to day. Did they go to work? Or stay at home with their friends and take groovy drugs? She put the question to Jenny.

'Do nudists do drugs?'

Jenny thought about it. 'Some do, I guess.'

'Do we have any drugs here?' Christine sat up.

'I have blood pressure tablets.'

'Not quite what I had in mind,' Christine said, disappointed.

'Would Valium count?' Jenny asked.

'Yes, I'd say so.' Christine had never taken Valium, but she knew doctors hated to prescribe it. This was a sure sign it was fun to take.

'Sophie has some Valium.'

'Really?' Christine perked up. 'How do you know?'

'She left her toiletries bag in the bathroom this morning. I picked it up to take it to her room and everything flew out. The zip wasn't closed.'

'She is so careless.' Christine settled back against the couch. 'Let's try some.'

Christine didn't expect Jenny to agree, but now she was a nudist she felt duty-bound to make the suggestion.

'All right.' Jenny pushed herself up from the floor. Her dress was stuck to her back and rucked up on her bottom, baring her wobbly thighs. Christine could see why Jenny didn't want to become a nudist. She was too fat. She would definitely be judged.

58

Ben dropped Sophie at the grid. She stood by the track in her high heels and waved him off. Once he was a little way down the road, she blew him a kiss and laughed.

The heels had to come off. Immediately. There were balloon-sized blisters down there and Sophie didn't want to give them any more chance to grow. Also, she wanted to inspect them before they popped. It was a total bummer to miss blisters in their most dramatic state.

Walking across the grid was fine, but the track was littered with sharp stones.

'Ow. Ouch!' Sophie tried hopping from foot to foot, but she couldn't see well enough to avoid the vicious, pointy ones, and her feet were soft. She'd been in the city too long. She slowed down to a careful tiptoe and chanted softly as she went.

'One, two, three-four-five. Once I caught a fish alive.' She laughed again. Where did that come from? Some childhood place she hadn't turned her mind to for a long, long time.

'Six, seven, eight-nine-ten. Then I let him go again.'

She tried a twirl, but she had to haul up halfway. 'Ow. Ow! Okay, okay. I won't let him go.'

Sophie was talking to the stones, to herself, to the universe. To whoever was listening. Her smile wouldn't let up. Her cheeks hurt, but that just made her smile more. And laugh. And she would have danced, too, if it weren't for the rocky track.

She tipped her head back to look at the stars. She hadn't realised, until now, how much she had missed the stars. The black sky, and thousands of points of light. They weren't visible in the city. In any city. Only at Ellersley.

Sophie rounded the hedge to see the porch light on, and someone sitting on the step. She would try to keep a straight face and say goodnight. Unless it was Jen. With Jen she could smile all she liked.

59

It was only nine thirty, but Sophie was tiptoeing as though it were the early hours of the morning, and their parents were waiting up. It made Jenny smile. This was partly because of Sophie, and partly because of the Valium. Taking a Valium tablet was a wonderful way to settle anxiety. To soften despair. Taking a few in one handful, however, was more likely to result in unconsciousness.

Jenny didn't have the heart to ask Dave for help with getting Christine to bed. He was still shaken by their sister's appearance as a nudist; a second encounter might have brought him undone. Hopefully Chris wouldn't be upset about the carpet burn on her back. She was too heavy to carry – dragging her by the feet was hard enough.

Dave had mooned about outside for a bit with his beer, but he'd come in when he got hungry. They'd shared a dinner of sandwiches – neither one of them felt much like cooking. It had been quiet at the table, but not mean-quiet. Just two adults chewing food because, no matter how painful the day has been, a person has to eat.

Valium sure did ease the pain, though. Jenny already knew this because Matthew had been prescribed some to help him give up alcohol. He had a few left over in his bathroom cupboard, and one morning when she had a panic attack, he gave her one. It was wonderful. It calmed her right down. She asked her doctor for a prescription, but he had been cagey about it. It was like she was asking for heroin. Which she wasn't, she was only asking for some relief.

Anyway, it helped get her off the lounge room floor. It knocked Chris right out, but that wouldn't hurt. Maybe she'd wake up seeing the value of wearing clothes. And here was Sophie, barefoot and humming happily.

'Hiya, Jen.' She stood with a strappy sandal in each hand and shrugged her shoulders, shivering like she was cold.

'Hey.' Jenny leaned back on the step, looking up at the sky.

'What's everyone up to?'

'Dave's watching telly, I think. Chris is in bed.'

'Still?'

'She got up for a bit, but then she went back.'

'Fab,' Sophie said, 'I might crash too.'

She leaned down and gave Jenny a kiss on the cheek – a perfume-scented, butterfly kiss – and lightly squeezed her shoulder as she passed. 'Goodnight,' she said and stepped up behind Jenny to slip into the house.

It could have ended like this, the night of Dave's party. With Jenny tiptoeing home in her cream dress, her hair a bit messy, a shoulder strap falling off. She would have taken her heels off to stop the rubbing, and kissed her mother's cheek as she passed her on the steps.

60

Vince snorted himself awake and wiped at the drool trickling from the corner of his mouth. His tongue was thick and dry, and his teeth were furry with stale wine.

He lifted his head slightly. There were two empty bottles on the table beside him, though he only remembered opening one. He felt around on the side of the recliner and pulled the lever, his legs collapsing at the knees as the footrest tucked in. He shuffled his bottom forward until his feet reached the floor and rested his head in his hands.

It was coming back to him. The interview with Christine, the bribe, the afternoon's research. By the evening he was on something of a high – hence the two bottles of red. This morning he felt less optimistic. Vince had been reasonably successful in pushing Dr Briggs' booming voice aside yesterday, but now it was filling his head.

'*Suppose we'll be certifying job done in a couple of days,*' he said.

Perhaps the coffin-building had not commenced by 9 am yesterday. So what? There had been a full – what time was it? Vince turned to the clock behind him: 8.39 am. *Merda!* He had to get moving.

Vince pushed himself up and stood for a moment, waiting for the spinning to settle. His temples throbbed, and there was a stabbing pain behind his right eye. He walked down to the bedroom, a steadying hand on the wall, and sat on the bed to extract himself from yesterday's clothes. The reality of the situation was gradually dawning on him. If he allowed this matter to run its own course, it was a near guarantee that he would not inherit the property.

He went to the bathroom, reached into the shower and turned the hot water on. He waited a minute before stepping in. What was he thinking? Or more to the point, when did he stop thinking? Vince lathered soap all over his body, watching the bubbles slip down the drain.

A measly attempted bribe – where would that get him? Nowhere, if he didn't show some initiative and make use of the event.

The water pipes shuddered as he turned off the taps. He reached for a towel and stepped onto the fluffy mat.

So how did he do that? Press charges? That would antagonise the Edwards, without question, but would it impede their progress? Unlikely. It may even bring them together, spur them on. No, today he needed to stop them in their tracks.

He inspected his face in the cabinet mirror. He hadn't shaved yesterday afternoon, and it showed. Twice a day was a bare minimum for Bartolo men.

He surveyed the row of suits hanging in his wardrobe. His eyes lit on a fresco in charcoal. Subdued. Professional. He chose a white shirt with mushroom pink trim and a light pink tie.

He needed information. About each of the siblings: their blind spots, their weak points, their criminal histories – it was surprising how many people had one. And he needed information about the project too. They were certain to be failing to comply with the instructions in one way or another, but how would he know if he didn't inspect their work?

Vince did up his belt and made a final adjustment to his tie. He slipped his feet into leather moccasins, picked up his briefcase and walked out the door. The brightness of the sunlight was excruciating, but he was determined to carry on. He would go to Ellersley. As the executor of the will, ensuring compliance with legal instruction must be his first concern.

It was not the time to leave matters to chance.

61

The house was quiet. The bedroom doors were closed, the bathroom empty, the kitchen table clear and no mugs on the sink. All the signs suggested Dave was the first one up. At least they would suggest that if he was in a normal household.

Dave flicked the kettle on and put a slice of bread in the toaster.

He'd stayed up to the end of the innings, but it didn't help. It didn't wipe out the image of Jen's face, hollow and empty. And it didn't erase the image of Chris butt-naked either. Bloody hell, he could have done without that.

The toast popped up and he scraped some butter and Vegemite on it. It was burnt around the edges, but he was still eating it. It was the last piece of bread.

Sharon had called. Three overs into the second session. Australia six for 275, the skipper three runs off a century. He'd had no mobile reception for three days and all of a sudden it decided to come to life. It hurt, to quit watching at that point, but he did it. Didn't even mention the match to Sharon which, in retrospect, was a wise decision.

Councillor Adams had dropped by. Bloody moron. Offered his condolences for the death in the family, which Sharon thanked him for, but she didn't invite him in.

He said he'd heard there was some trouble with the will, that Dave wasn't inheriting Ellersley after all. He asked Sharon to pass on his concerns. His, and 'a number of his associates'. What a fucking idiot.

Sharon stood her ground. Said she'd pass it on and stared Trevor down until he'd backed away.

Sharon recounted the conversation to Dave, then added her own bit at the end. 'He is a slimy piece of shit, Dave. Coming by when it's just me and the kids. It's not on.'

'Of course not, love.' Dave tried to be soothing, but Sharon wasn't finished. Nowhere near it.

'I don't know what you owe Trevor Adams,' she said. She had that measured tone, the one she used with the kids when it was serious. 'I don't know, and I actually don't care, so long as it gets paid.'

'Of course, Shaz, I'm sorting it out.'

'You've crossed a line, Dave. I don't know how long ago you did it, but –'

'I'm sorting it, Shaz. I promise.'

'I hope so. I really do. Whatever pile of crap you're in, you better pull yourself out.'

Dave turned around to see the cricket ball flying over the fence, and a bunch of blokes reaching up to catch it. One hundred and eight. Fuck it. He'd missed the century.

'Are you listening to me?'

'Sure, love, of course.'

'You bring a solution back from Coorong, or we're done.'

'What's that?' Dave turned his back on the cricket and pressed the mobile hard against his ear. He wasn't sure he'd heard her right.

'Real numbers, Dave. Sums that add up. If you can't do it, I'm out of here.'

He couldn't be hearing right. Sharon didn't pack her bags. She stood by him. She always stood by him.

'The kids too.'

Dave was silent.

'Did you get that?' She hated it when he wasn't listening properly. But he was, this time. He was leaning against the back of the couch with his eyes closed and the phone held tight.

He got it.

'Dave?' Gritted teeth now.

He wanted to answer, he really did. But he didn't know what to say. He couldn't sweet-talk Sharon. He couldn't lie.

There was a tiny ping when Sharon ended the call. Dave held his phone out to double check she was gone. She was.

'Fuck. FUCK IT!' Dave bellowed. He drew his arm back and threw the mobile as hard as he could. It smashed against the wall and fell into a pile of cracked glass and broken plastic. Dave put his head in his hands and started crying.

'No, no, no. Please no.' He was rocking back and forth, his palms pressed against his eyes. He had nothing. No idea what to do. And now he needed a fucking new phone.

62

Who the hell doesn't come to their mother's funeral? Tom would prefer not to know the answer to this question, but he does know. Jock.

Jock never showed up for anything.

Not work, that was for sure. From the minute Tom could hold a pair of pliers, Jock took off and left him fixing the fence on his own. Same with mustering, feeding, watering. As soon as Tom had a handle on the job, Jock pissed off. Their father was too soft. He'd had the fight knocked out of him in PNG, was what their mum said. He'd shake his head as he watched Jock go, and say, 'We'll be right, won't we, Tom?'

After five years of boarding school – at King's, no less – Jock graduated with a posh accent and a belief he should be richer. Somehow, he conned his mother, his grandmother and any woman who came within a ten-mile radius, into believing the same thing. Their mother bought him a suit and a Stetson hat. To wear to interviews, she said. But Jock didn't apply for jobs. He weaselled money instead. He coaxed his mates to shout him drinks, his girlfriends to give him lifts and loans, and God knows what else, but Jock never did a day's work. Not one.

It was a shabby way to behave, but at the time, Tom forgave him. Jock was his big brother. And he was bloody great company when he was home. He made them laugh. Lightened the atmosphere, which no one else could do when their father was low.

When Jock deserted for good, though, that was something else. He was needed. Badly needed. It wasn't a sagging fence. Or a day's mustering. Jock knew it, and he left Tom to face it on his own.

Nineteen years old, a dying father, a grieving mother and ten thousand acres to run. What a prick.

The farming was hard, and so was looking after his mum. But they were nothing on the repulsive task of nursing a dying man. His sagging body was so skinny it barely dented the mattress. He was too weak to move. Or wipe his own bum. He expelled pellets in liquid shit, and it was Tom's job to collect the mess in newspaper and carry it away.

Jock pissed off and left Tom to it. Didn't look back.

When their mother broke her hip, Tom visited her in Coorong Hospital every day. She asked after Jock, and Tom made excuses for him. Like everyone did. Tom rang him a few times. Left messages. But Jock didn't answer his phone. He never rang back. It was a bloody terrible thing to watch, his mum dying and hoping her eldest son would call her before she went.

Tom knew his mother had spoken with Jock over the years. Every now and then. But he had no idea how often it was, or what they discussed.

When Tom found out, it surprised him Jock hadn't shown up. Not out of decency. Tom would hardly have expected that. But Jock must have known what he stood to lose. Surely it would have been worth a few days of handholding to shore up his position. But he didn't come.

63

On Thursday morning, Sophie was the first one at the shed. She wasn't totally clear on what work she should be doing, so she wandered around looking at drills and saws with sharp teeth. The massive machine was standing against the side wall. Sophie had no idea how Dave had got it off the ute. All the chains were still hanging from the roof, though, so probably he swung it like Tarzan.

She leaned on a sawhorse for a few minutes, but no one else arrived. She kicked off her shoes, jumped up and walked along the sawhorse, balancing with her arms out. She reached the end and, as she turned, she spied Dave trudging across the paddock.

'Finally!' Sophie yelled. 'I've been waiting for you guys for *ages*.'

Dave didn't say anything. It didn't matter. Sophie could easily keep the conversation going for both of them.

'I've assessed the shed situation, and it seems to me our main problem is how thick the logs are.' Sophie pointed at the pile of logs.

Dave was inspecting the timber.

'Okay, so maybe I didn't work that out on my own. Jen might have said something about fifteen millimetres for a man. But that was days ago, and I remembered it, so that's worth something, right?'

He didn't respond.

'Dave? You hearing me?' Sophie prodded his arm. 'We have to trim the logs.'

Dave nodded, which maybe meant he was listening.

'So how do we do it?'

'Bandsaw,' Dave said, which wasn't much help to Sophie.

'What?'

Dave waved an arm towards the behemoth against the wall.

'That? Are you serious?'

'Yep.'

'Wow. Do you even know how it works? Also, top job getting it off the ute. But do you know how it works?'

'Near enough.'

'Okay.' Sophie wasn't totally convinced – it didn't look like a near-enough kind of machine. Fortunately, they were interrupted by a loud whoop, so she didn't have to quiz grumpy Dave.

'Good morning, family!'

Sophie put a hand up to the sun and squinted at the approaching figure. Chris. Of all people. On the bright side, she was out of bed.

'Good morning, good morning!' Chris was singing the words, like she was Maria in the Alps. She was trying to get across the paddock, but it wasn't going that well. She was wearing undies and an old cotton shirt of their father's. That was it. Bare legs, bare feet. Hair spiking at crazy angles.

She stumbled up to the shed and smiled broadly, throwing her arms wide.

'My family!' she shouted. It was way too loud for close range. Sophie watched with interest.

'What's happened to her?' she asked Dave, but he had turned away and was staring determinedly at the back bench.

'She's decided to become a nudist,' he said.

'Nudists don't wear clothes,' Sophie said. 'Not unless it's an emergency. And they never wear undies.'

Dave looked sideways at Sophie. 'She's wearing undies?'

Sophie nodded.

'Are you sure?'

'One hundred per cent.'

He let his breath out and turned around to face Chris, who was now lying on the ground, cackling wildly.

'She's taken something,' Sophie said. Nothing else could explain her sister's current state.

'Yes!' Chris said and rolled onto her belly. 'Yes, I have!'

'What?' Sophie was getting curious.

'Well you might ask, my sister.' Chris rolled onto her back again. 'Well you might ask. Straight from the bathroom bag into the mouth. That's how you take something in this place. A few at night and one in the morning, one or two, or a few, and pop away! Pop, pop away!'

'Whose bathroom bag?' Sophie crouched beside her. 'What did you take?'

Chris started to giggle again.

Dave put on his serious face. 'Was it yours?'

'Maybe,' Sophie said. 'Probably, I guess.'

'What were her options?'

'Oh, I don't know.'

At this stage Sophie wished Dave's bandsaw competence was the topic of conversation.

'I was coming back to Ellersley, Dave. For Dad's funeral! I had no idea what to bring. Sometimes you've got to pack a bit of everything.'

Dave shook his head disapprovingly. He was acting like she was the irresponsible one, but she wasn't. It was the exact opposite. She'd come prepared for all contingencies. Except Chris stealing her drugs. But really, how could she have predicted that?

64

Vince was about to drive to Ellersley when he had a rather clever thought. Why not pop into the office first and pick up his dictaphone? He could put it in his breast pocket and switch it on before he got out of the car. A recording of this nature would not be permissible evidence in court, but it could prove useful in conversations with the Edwards siblings.

Smart thinking, Vincenzo. Smart thinking. It was encouraging to find that, despite the hangover, his brain remained sharp.

He arrived at the office at 9.16 am. Ben Taylor was sitting behind the reception desk, hair combed and neatly dressed. He was in casual attire, but he looked as uneasy as if he were wearing a hair shirt. He always looked this way, Vince had noticed. This morning, though, there was something else. A heightening of colour, a hint of self-consciousness. It was rather intriguing. Vince decided to stop for a chat.

'Good morning, Ben.' Vince hitched his trousers and perched on the edge of the desk. He was friendly, but not too personal. Vince had learned how to converse with the rural man.

'Morning.' Ben was brief, as always.

'How are you this morning?'

'All right.'

The hue of Ben's face was changing, and by now had turned a deep pink. Something clicked in Vince's mind. He had seen this blush before. Yesterday, in fact. At the end of his meeting with Christine, Vince was closing the door and caught the tail-end of a conversation in the foyer. It was Sophie Edwards, talking to Ben.

'See you tonight,' she had said, and then dashed out. Vince had hovered for a moment, and witnessed his receptionist nodding slightly, his cheeks as flushed as a new rose.

Vince smiled indulgently at Ben. 'Not too tired after a late night?'

Ben stared at the desk, stone silent.

'Young Sophie, now she's a livewire, isn't she?'

A deepening blush, but now his jaw was clenched, lips set tight. Vince backed away. No point in getting Ben offside now. He might be required later, and it would be much better if they were on speaking terms.

'Well, I hope you had a nice time.' Vince stood up. 'I'm popping out for an hour or so. Write down any messages. I'll attend to them on my return.'

Nothing gained, but nothing lost either. Vince retrieved the dictaphone from his office. The weight of it in his breast pocket was most reassuring.

'Goodbye then.' Vince nodded to his receptionist and walked out the door with purpose.

65

'There's a funny little man, trotting through the hedge. Trot-trot-trotting!'

Christine was propped on a chair with Sophie holding her upright. She would have liked to be rolling on the ground but sitting up wasn't going to spoil her fun. Not when a little man was coming to join them.

'Hello there!' she called out. 'Hello, Mr Trotting Pony!'

Sophie shushed her, but Christine was undeterred.

'Would you like some hay?' She started to giggle, rolling to the side. Sophie grabbed her arm and pulled her up again.

'Ow! Oh, good!' Christine hooted, then yelled happily, 'No hay today, but three bags full. One for you, Little Trotter? Two? Three?'

She flung her head back and kicked her legs out. 'Giddy up! Clk-clk. Off we go!'

Both of Sophie's arms were circling her chest and impeding her horse-riding. Christine was momentarily distracted. She pulled away from Sophie, grunting, trying to get loose.

'Good morning, David, Sophie.' The voice was familiar. Christine looked more closely. Was the Trotting Pony someone she knew? Yes! It was Vince!

'Hiya,' Sophie said. Dave said nothing.

'Hiya,' Christine echoed Sophie, then took it one step further. 'Hee-YA!' she yelled. A whip crack would have improved the effect, but Christine didn't have one on hand, so she yelled again instead. 'Hee-YA!'

Everyone else was silent. Dave had his arms crossed; he looked cranky. Sophie had loosened her hold slightly, but not enough for Christine to gain freedom.

Christine kicked a clod of dirt at Vince the Pony Man. He jumped aside and she laughed. He looked funny when he jumped. She inspected the ground for a second missile, but before she'd had the chance to launch it Sophie spoke.

'Time for us to go, Chris.'

'What?' Christine was surprised. It was a silly time to leave. She had only just begun flinging dirt at their guest.

'Come on.' Sophie was offering her hands. Christine considered the hand-holding activity and decided to try it.

'Up you get,' Sophie said, and tugged. Christine stood up.

'Nice work, Chris.' Sophie let her hands go.

Christine agreed. 'Yes, nice work, Chris.' Sophie steered her towards the house and Christine allowed it.

'Clk-clk, clk-clk,' she said as she passed Vince Barton, and lifted her feet high.

She ignored Dave entirely. He had been no fun at all.

66

Dave stood with his arms crossed and said nothing. If Vince Barton wanted to visit, he could do the talking.

'Warm, isn't it?' Vince was dabbing at his face with a hanky.

Dave stared straight ahead.

'Sorry to bother you, that is, I hope I'm not intruding...'

Dave snorted. Bullshit. He knew he was intruding.

'I want – that is, I have to – see the coffin. Execute my appointed duty...' Vince faded out. He was sweating, and it wasn't just the weather. He looked nervous. Very nervous. And so he should. Coming onto Ellersley uninvited. Demanding to see the coffin. 'Appointed duty' – what a load of shit.

'Is Mrs Minehan unwell?' Vince changed tack. Dave waited.

'Perhaps she has taken a substance of some sort?' Vince held his elbow out, nudging the air. He was being fucking bold, spraying accusations about.

'Now then, let's see this coffin of yours.' He said it like he was a businessman, or a real lawyer. Like he was the one in charge.

Vince took a step towards the shed and Dave put a foot out in warning, fixing his eyes on the little man. Vince was sweating profusely, but he didn't stop. He made a move to step over the imaginary line, and Dave unclenched his jaw.

'Don't fuck with me, Vince.'

Vince paused, his foot hanging there.

'I mean it. Do not fuck with me.'

Vince wavered. His foot went down on the wrong side of the line and Dave exploded.

'You fucking little prick, who the FUCK do you think you are?'

Dave grabbed Vince by the knot in his silk tie and lifted him nearly off the ground.

'No one, David, no one –'

'Correct. Fucking no one.'

'That's right.' Vince was nodding as well as he could with Dave's fist wedged under his chin. 'I'm –'

'What? You are fucking what? You're fucking trespassing, that's what. You are fucking perving on my sisters. And you are pushing the last fucking millimetre of luck you have.' Dave shoved Vince in the chest with each charge, throwing in a couple of extra at the end.

Vince was tripping over himself, agreeing frantically.

'Yes, David, yes. I –' He stumbled backwards with his hands held out to ward Dave off.

Dave followed him and leaned in close. He lowered his voice and made the words distinct, so Vince wouldn't miss a single one.

'You want to keep your shiny little balls attached to your runty body you can run. Now.'

Vince was nodding hard. Dave gave him a final shove, and Vince gave a desperate thumbs up, turned around and started walking.

'Run, you little prick!'

Vince picked up the pace to a fast walk.

Dave growled. 'I'm not joking. Run!'

67

It was the scream that got her out of bed. Jenny had been drifting in and out of consciousness, listening to the sounds of the morning. Sophie humming to the bathroom and back, the flick of her thongs down the hallway and out. Dave grunting and stomping around, then leaving every step a heavy thud. After a brief period of quiet, Jenny heard Chris open the door of her room. She tripped, and stumbled into the hallway, giggling. She made her way down the hall, ricocheting off the walls and whooping with every collision, the screen door screeched and there was silence.

When Chris had gone, Jenny realised she was awake. She closed her eyes and rolled over, hoping there was still enough Valium in her system to knock her out. There wasn't. But she didn't get out of bed. Not straight away.

She heard a car come down the track. Not long after, Dave started bellowing. Violently. Jenny didn't have to worry. She was safe in her room.

She watched the wall and listened to the car drive away. Then Dave stopped shouting, and for a moment all was quiet. In the stillness, Jenny heard her own voice.

'Sorry, Matthew, sorry. It's just . . .'

He waited so patiently for her fumbling words.

'Chris, she's a bit fragile . . .'

He watched her face, red and hot, and waited. He knew she was making it up, but he let her finish what she had to say.

'Just for today, it's better . . . just family.' She was so desperate to see him go.

The loop of her conversation with Matthew was set to replay when she heard Sophie's voice in the porch.

'Come on, Chris, you're doing really well.' Sophie? Encouraging Chris?

'It's all right, Chris, it's okay. We're going to make a cup of tea.' Sophie *calming* Chris?

Their voices hushed, so Jenny guessed they had moved into the kitchen. Maybe that's why they didn't hear the scream. Maybe the kettle was on and they mistook the sound.

Jenny heard it though. It was a high-pitched shriek, getting louder and louder and then snap! It stopped. Jenny wasn't sure if it was human or something else. It might have been mechanical, but it was too anguished, too uncontrolled. Either way, it sounded serious. Serious enough to get her out of bed.

Jenny rolled over and levered herself to sitting. She was still wearing her dress from yesterday. It would do. She patted down the wrinkles and pushed her hair off her face and the shame washed over her again. It was coming in waves, like nausea, or home sickness. The loop changed, just a little, and started playing again.

'I'm sorry, Matthew, I really wanted you to come.'

But she didn't, and he knew.

'Thank you, bye, bye!'

Jenny held her head in her hands. She wasn't sure she could do this.

'Bye, bye!' she said, and he was gone.

68

Dave chose the biggest piece. Eight foot long by eight inches wide, and it wasn't big enough. It was nothing to lift.

He switched the bandsaw on and listened to the hum of the motor.

Fucking Vince Barton, the little bantam cock. Strutting across the yard, fucking owning the place. Like he has the right.

He lifted the timber, balancing it on his hip, and slid it onto the table on its narrow edge.

Fucking Trevor Adams. Going round to my place. Bailing up Shaz while I'm away. Like he has the right to do whatever the fuck he wants.

Dave lined the flat surface of the board against the fence and pushed the end into the saw. A shrill, grinding noise started, and he winced.

Fucking investments. Fucking everything falling through.

Dave was steering reasonably well, despite his vibrating arms.

Fuck it all. FUCK it.

He was doing his best to keep the board hard against the fence, but the length was making it awkward. He held it as steady as he could and kept going.

And fuck you, Dad. Seriously. Fuck you.

It's what you wanted, isn't it? To see me fail. Business. Property. The whole fucking lot. How about the wife and kids? Did you want me to lose them too?

The board was halfway through, and Dave was struggling. He wasn't in control of the timber at the other end.

You win, Dad. Congratulations. I'm the loser. Just like you said.

The cut was two thirds done when a piece of sawdust flicked into Dave's eye. He was standing too far behind to switch the saw off, and the timber was too far through to pull it back. He squinted his way forward, concentrating hard, but he couldn't see if the board was against the fence. When it started to swing out the cut went wonky. Fast. He tried to pull it back in line. He put some weight into holding it against the fence, and the board shifted across, but so did the blade. A high-pitched squealing started. Smoke, the smell of burning timber. The side of his face felt hot, and he knew the heat was radiating off the blade, but he couldn't see it with that fleck in his eye, and he couldn't let go of the board either, so he did what he had to do. He held on tight and kept going.

When the blade snapped it flung out at his face. It threw him off balance, and he let go of the half-sawn board, which flipped and tumbled to the ground. Dave stumbled backwards and put a hand to his cheek. It stung with the touch, so he pulled it away again.

Spots of blood tracked across his palm. A single line of lacerations from the teeth of the blade, spaced at perfect five-millimetre intervals across his face. It would have pleased his old man. It was a precision cut.

69

Tom's mum managed the finances of Ellersley until the day she died. There was no reason to change the arrangement, so they never did. She knew what she was on about. Helena hated her mother-in-law looking at her bank statements. Tom said his mother wasn't nosy, but he had to admit she'd be checking the sums.

They opened a separate account for Helena, then they carried on as usual. A finance meeting once a month, just Tom and his mum, and the decisions about buying and selling were made after that. She ran the business, he ran the farm and they both knew their place in the partnership.

It never occurred to him to check the figures. Unless it was shoved right under his nose, he wouldn't have noticed a regular deposit into a Bankwest account. And if he did, he wouldn't have thought of Jock.

But after his mum died, Tom had to take notice of the money. He took her accounts diary and bank statements to the accountant. The accountant had a skinny tie and a nervous cough, and he didn't look Tom in the face. He kept his eyes on the paperwork, and tapped a calculator as he went. He asked Tom a few questions that were easy enough to answer, and then he asked if Tom would continue the regular transfer of funds to John Hinkley Edwards in WA. Even then, it took Tom a couple of seconds to think of Jock.

When he did, the fury rose in him quick as a firestorm. It was fifteen years since their father died. Fifteen years of hard work for Tom. Brutal days. Punishing weeks. Years that seemed to stretch out for decades, and decades gone in the blink of an eye.

And the same years had passed for Jock. Fifteen years of doing piss-all, while Tom slogged it out, earning enough money to run the property and fund his older brother's pay cheque. Every month, he had a meeting with his mum. And two days later, every month, she gave away their hard-won dollars. It turned out they weren't a team. His mother had been in another partnership all along.

When the accountant said how much money had been sent, Tom gripped his hat so hard his fingers turned white. The accountant had to ask him twice about sending the money, but Tom had no doubt about the answer.

'No,' he said.

No bloody fear.

70

Guiding Chris across the paddock was easy. But when Sophie opened the screen door and ushered her into the house, her older sister baulked and stopped short at the doorway.

'Come on, Chris, you're doing really well.' Sophie pushed her gently, but Chris resisted. She was making a whimpering noise.

'It's all right, Chris. It's okay. We're going to make a cup of tea.' Sophie had some experience with getting others through the comedown, so she knew to remain calm and firm. It had to be the ecstasy – the signs were typical. Hopefully Chris had only taken one.

'A nice cup of tea and a piece of toast. Or maybe a biscuit. You'll feel so much better.' Sophie kept up the chit-chat. Chris allowed herself to be nudged forward, but she was steering away from the office desk.

'I know you're feeling rubbish now, but it will totally pass. I might have some medicine that'll make you feel better.'

Chris was holding both hands out towards the desk as she edged past, making a hushing noise, as though pacifying a wild animal. Sophie laughed. Chris had probably never taken ecstasy. Strange things could happen the first time around.

'A few more steps, Chris, that's all.' Sophie took her into the kitchen and sat her down at the table. 'Stay here and I'll be back in a minute.' Sophie made eye contact with her to make sure she'd heard. Chris nodded. Great. Sophie ducked out of the kitchen to find her bathroom bag.

It was on her bedroom floor, open as she had suspected. Chris had definitely taken ecstasy – there was only one tab left in the side pocket. The trouble was it looked like she had taken the Valium too. All of it. Sophie wasn't exactly sure how much she'd brought, but it was a whole lot more than none.

It had to be said – Chris did not know how to take drugs sensibly. It was *essential* to have sedatives on hand for the comedown. Without benzos it was hideous. Tea and toast could only do so much.

Sophie went back to the kitchen empty-handed. Chris was sitting with her hands folded in her lap, weeping.

'Oh, Chris.' Sophie felt a pang of sympathy. 'It's okay, it will pass, it absolutely will. Today will be hell, but tomorrow will be so much better.' She squatted and put an arm around Chris's shoulder.

'I bribed him.'

It was a new direction for their conversation, but Sophie rolled with it.

'Who?'

'The lawyer.'

'Which lawyer?' Sophie decided to keep it real – in case it was – but it seemed unlikely. As far as she knew Chris had never broken a rule in her life. Let alone an actual law.

'Stephen is sleeping with his receptionist.'

'What?'

'Stephen and Nicola are having sex.'

Okay, so that could be real. Sophie would want to sleep with the receptionist too if she was married to Chris.

'Mr Sloane says I have to take notes.'

'About sex?'

'About the bribe.'

'Okay.'

'The bribe, and the lawyer. And how I didn't bribe him.' Chris clamped her mouth shut, as though she'd said too much already.

'Okay,' Sophie said lightly, 'let's have a cuppa, then.' It was all she had to offer, and she was determined to put something therapeutic on the table. She was reaching up for mugs when Chris spoke again.

'He's got blood. Dripping.'

'What?' Sophie had really lost track.

'On his face.'

Chris was looking towards the door. Sophie followed her line of sight to see Dave leaning against the doorframe. His face was swollen and there was blood dripping from his cheek.

'Shite!'

Dave didn't respond.

'What happened?'

He still didn't answer.

And then he collapsed. He buckled over and smashed his bloody cheek on the floorboards.

Sophie dropped her mug. 'Dave! Shite, DAVE!' Sophie jumped over the shattered porcelain and rushed to his aid. He was totally unconscious. And lying face down, which was not right. Sophie was sure about that. But he was so heavy. She wasn't sure she could turn him over by herself.

'Chris! You have to help.'

Chris was watching with interest, but she clearly wasn't hearing Sophie.

'Chris! Come here!'

Chris still wasn't registering, so Sophie upped the volume.

'HELP! Chris. NOW!'

Sophie had been pushing at Dave's shoulder, trying to roll him over, but it wasn't working, so she tried levering his knee instead. By some miracle she heaved him over. Then she picked up his legs, because she'd seen them do it on *ER*. His face was still bleeding, and Sophie wondered if she was making it worse, but then Chris keeled over and fell off her chair and Sophie forgot about the blood. Shite! What was she supposed to do now? Should she stay with Dave or help Chris up? And, she couldn't believe she hadn't thought of this yet, where was Jenny?

'JENNY!'

Sophie was done. Too much responsibility had been laid on her this morning. Dave's mood; Chris's trip; Vince Barton's random visit; *all* her Valium gone and now a bloody face and two unconscious people. She wasn't the right person for this job. She was *not* the one who kept the family on its feet.

'JENNY!' Sophie was yelling so loudly now she was hurting her own ears. She was mid-yell when Jenny appeared.

'FINALLY!' Sophie didn't mean to shout it, but she had gotten into the habit.

Jenny was in a crumpled dress and her hair was wild. She looked like a crazy lady, but Sophie knew Jenny was the best chance they had of coming out of this intact.

'Jen, finally!' Sophie said, at a regular volume now.

Jenny bent down to touch Dave's face and he flinched, his eyes flickering open.

'He's all right, Soph,' she said. 'He must have fainted. He's coming round now. Keep his feet up.'

'Sure, but what about her?' Sophie indicated Chris lying on the floor, now moaning. Jenny walked over and gently patted Chris's shoulder, then untangled her legs from the chair.

71

TO SUMMARISE:

MONDAY

i) Reading of the Last Will and Testament of Thomas Hinkley Edwards.
Jennifer Edwards, David Edwards, Christine Minehan nee Edwards and Sophie Edwards present.

TUESDAY

i) Robert Sloane of Mindle, Seifort & Sloane calls to discuss contestation. Vince Barton of Barton & Sons gives him pertinent advice.

WEDNESDAY

i) Christine Minehan offers Vince Barton of Barton & Sons a bribe. Vince Barton refuses this offer. (Witness account, contemporaneous notes)

THURSDAY

i) David Edwards threatens Vince Barton with physical violence. (Dictaphone recording)

ii) Christine Minehan is witnessed half naked and incoherent, in a state of apparent intoxication.
(Witness account, contemporaneous notes)

iii) Jennifer Edwards is absent from coffin-construction site.
(No legal bearing, observation only)

iv) Regarding coffin construction:
Power tools, sawhorses and planks of timber noted.
No evidence of a coffin, a partially constructed coffin, or any box-like object. Inspection limited by inadequate access to site.

(No legal bearing, observation only)
v) Regarding time constraints:
Deadline for completion of the coffin is close of business on the fourth working day following the will reading. Which time is 5.30 pm this Friday.
(The Last Will and Testament of Thomas Hinkley Edwards, Disposition of Estate, clause 2(g))

By the time he had written this summary Vince was in excellent humour. His hangover had lifted, and he had quite forgotten the state of despair with which he had started the day. He got up to put the kettle on.

It was now 10.40 am. Less than thirty-one hours until the deadline for completion of the coffin. Now that he had been out to Ellersley and observed the situation for himself, he would have to say that everything seemed to be going rather badly. Or well, depending on your point of view.

Although disquieted by David's threat, Vince could see the positive side. David was, surely, the lynchpin of the operation. The construction of a coffin would present no challenge to a man of his expertise. If David was not fit to lead his sisters, the whole project would be in doubt. And, in light of the morning's events, Vince would question whether David was fit for the job. His behaviour had been frankly unstable.

If it came to the crunch, Vince would pursue common assault charges against David Edwards. But it took weeks, sometimes longer, for such charges to be prosecuted. It could be useful down the track, but it wasn't going to stop the work now. David's volatile state was encouraging, but it was no guarantee. Vince could not afford to lose focus.

Surveying his notes, Vince was struck by an omission in his record. He had not mentioned Sophie. Although David was violent and Christine out of control, Sophie had appeared remarkably at ease. She seemed unconcerned about Christine's state. A state, Vince reflected, which was rather bizarre.

Could it be that Christine had imbibed a substance other than alcohol? Vince's mind was whirring. He had heard someone talk about drugs recently. Who was it?

After his interview with Christine, that was it. When Christine left his office, she said something on her way out. Vince rubbed his temples. Drugs and Coorong – was that it? Why would she say that? He pressed at his temples, hard, and after a moment lifted his head up and smiled. He slapped the desk triumphantly. It wasn't Christine. It was Sophie.

'Drugs in Coorong,' is what she'd said. He remembered it clearly now. She was talking to young Ben. Sophie had drugs and Christine had taken them. It was the logical explanation. All that 'clippety cloppety' talk. Of course it was drugs.

It was quite possible there were drugs at Ellersley. If that were the case, it could change the situation rather quickly. Sophie could be removed from the equation altogether if she were arrested. He needed information. Enough to convince Officer Greaves to do a search of the homestead.

Vince picked up the phone and punched in Ben's extension number.

'Ben? Would you care to come into my office for a moment?'

Ben appeared at the door and Vince stood up from his chair.

'Ah, good. I was just about to have a cup of tea. Would you like one?' Vince smiled his most winning smile. Ben hovered at the door warily.

'Come on then! Kettle's boiled.' Vince held up the plastic kettle as evidence. 'How do you have it?'

'Black.'

'Sugar?'

'No.'

Extracting information from Ben Taylor was not going to be easy, but if he spoke up it would be absolutely worth the work.

72

'I took Great-granny's earrings,' Chris said. She was conscious and upright, which was a plus. Sophie was boiling the kettle – again – and Jenny had taken over the job of holding Dave's boots.

'You what?' Sophie stepped away from the kettle.

'I took the sapphire earrings and necklace. Oh, and the pearls. And her engagement ring. For Claudia.'

Chris was coming back to her senses, Sophie realised. Taking the jewellery was absolutely something Chris would do. She wouldn't look on it as stealing, more like claiming her inheritance. The only unusual part here was the free confession.

'Okay. Thanks for sharing, Chris.'

Chris nodded graciously.

Dave started to groan, and Jenny lowered his feet to the floor. She brushed off her dress, but it was filthy. There must have been a wheelbarrow of dirt lodged in Dave's boots.

'What about Stephen?' Chris spoke again. 'Did I tell you he's bonking his receptionist?'

'You did mention that,' Sophie said.

Jenny was kneeling by Dave's head, touching his forehead lightly. 'It's all right, Dave, you're all right.'

Sophie got a bit closer. He had one eyelid open but there was swelling all around the other, and globules of blood on his cheek. Lucky Jen was dealing with it. It was gross.

'Could you pour some water into a bowl, Soph? There should be antiseptic under the sink. And get some clean towels. Face cloths.'

While Sophie was searching the linen cupboard, she remembered Chris's other confession. If the part about Stephen was real, how about the rest? Only one way to find out.

'Hey, Chris, what about the bribes?'

Chris didn't answer straight away, but Dave started like he'd had an electric shock. His one eye popped open and his whole body went rigid.

'Who told you about the bribes?' he said.

'Chris did.'

'Who told Chris?'

'Dunno.' Sophie looked at Dave curiously. He was getting paranoid, but whatever he'd taken hadn't come from her bag.

'Fuck!' Dave sat up. He put his head in his hands and pulled back, looking at his left hand like it had bitten him. He touched his face more gingerly, wincing. 'What the fuck's going on?'

'You've had an accident,' Jenny said, swishing a face cloth in the water.

'Did they come for me?' he asked, grabbing her arm.

'No,' Jenny said. 'No, Dave, they didn't come for you.'

'Who?' Sophie asked.

'It doesn't matter,' Jenny said. She unclamped Dave's fingers, squeezed the excess water from the cloth and applied it to Dave's cheek.

'It might.' Sophie felt like investigating this further. Maybe it wasn't just paranoia.

'Oh, stop it, Sophie.'

Jenny said it as though Sophie was stirring up trouble. Which maybe she was, a bit. Bribes and lawyers had high entertainment potential. But also, it could be important for the coffin. Sophie didn't know how exactly, but they'd never know if she didn't ask, right?

'This is not good,' Dave was muttering, 'this is not good at all.'

'Shhh, Dave, it's all right.' Jenny put a clean hand towel to his cheek and guided his hand to hold it there.

'It's not. Me and Sharon, we're done for.'

'Wow, Dave. Really?'

Jenny shot Sophie a warning look.

'You don't get anywhere if the council's not on board.'

Jenny nodded sympathetically. Like she was constantly having trouble with getting the council on board.

'You can't build a granny flat, let alone a real development.'

'I know, I know,' Jenny said and shushed him. Sophie bit her tongue.

'You've got to grease the wheels, don't you?'

Jenny continued nodding. Sophie fixed her attention on pouring a cup of tea in a responsible manner. Then Chris, who had been silent for a while, spoke.

'Don't worry. I bribed a lawyer and nothing bad has happened.'

'Really?' Dave looked up hopefully.

'Yes,' Chris said. 'I offered Mr Barton money to change the will.'

'And?'

'It didn't work. He just got all huffy and said it wasn't legal.'

'It's not, is it?' Sophie asked. Chris said it like the problem was Mr Barton's crabby mood, not her breaking the law.

'Nope,' Christine said. 'You can go to prison for seven years.'

'Really?' Dave looked less hopeful now.

'Yes. Robert Sloane told me. He said I should take notes, but I was too stressed. I took drugs instead. Sophie's got them,' she said to Dave. 'You should try it.'

'I can't,' he said. 'I promised Sharon. When we first got together. She made me promise I'd never do drugs, no matter what.'

'Does Sharon know about the council?' Sophie asked. They could talk about drugs some other time.

'She does now,' Dave said.

'Shite,' Sophie said, 'that's got to be a problem.'

'Insolvency's worse.'

Sophie wasn't totally sure what insolvency meant, but it was definitely financial, and it was definitely bad. Maybe like bankrupt.

Which, if you had a wife and kids, and you owned stuff as well, was meant to be a disaster.

'Wow. What do you do about that?' Sophie was genuinely sympathetic now. This was not a scandal. It was a life falling apart.

'You build a coffin,' Jenny said.

They all stared at her.

'We build a coffin, I mean.'

They stayed silent, waiting.

'You're all wasting time bribing lawyers and taking drugs and having fights and heaven knows what, and the only thing we have to do is build a coffin.'

When she put it like that, it sounded simple. It made Sophie wonder why they hadn't started yet. Jenny pushed her chair back from the table and stood up. She gathered the mugs together and took them to the sink.

'Eleven thirty.' Jenny checked the clock above the mantlepiece. 'It's time we made a start.'

73

Jenny led the family procession across the paddock. She looked over her shoulder to make sure her siblings were keeping up.

Dave was trudging along, holding the wet rag against his swollen cheek, drooping like lavender in the midday heat.

Christine was next. She was picking her feet up high and watching closely as they came back to earth, testing the ground to see if it held firm. She wasn't quite back to normal, but she had a freshly washed face and neatly brushed hair, thanks to Sophie. And she was wearing clothes, which was a relief to everyone.

Sophie followed a few steps behind Christine, watching her progress. Sophie seemed to have taken charge of Chris's wellbeing; Jenny wondered how long she could keep it up.

The hot sun pricked Jenny's scalp, and she could feel the skin burning on the back of her neck. When she crossed the line of shade and stepped into the machinery shed the heat only intensified.

Jenny went straight to the scene of the accident. The others followed. They stood in a semicircle around the bandsaw and the fallen timber – their only eight-inch board.

Christine went to the board, squatting like a curious child to look at the cut. It was straight as a die for a couple of feet, then all crooked and diagonal. The edge closest to the bandsaw became thinner and thinner until it ended in a splintered rip away from the main board.

Dave was staring tragically at the scene. Wallowing in his helpless state.

But there was no time to mourn. Jenny stepped over the board and opened the box on the bandsaw that housed the new blades.

Matthew had told her how to change it. All she had to do was recall his instructions and keep her mind on the words. Just the words.

'It's easy if you work with the blade and not against it.' His voice was steady, reassuring.

'It will want to spring out from the coiled loop, and that's okay, you just take the top loop in one hand and the bottom in the other and stand back to let it go.' Jenny did, and it worked. She kept listening and Matthew instructed her, step by step, how to change the blade.

She managed just fine. Put the new blade in, lined it up between the guides and adjusted the tension. And then she stood back so she could get a wider view. She looked at the saw and the half-sawn board lying on the ground beside it, at the tools lined up on the bench at the back wall and her three siblings watching her, waiting on her instruction.

And Matthew said, *'This is it, Jen.'*

It was not so different from what he'd said when he left her by the roadside. But 'this is it' was a world apart from 'that's it'.

'This is it' was an invitation. Not a final farewell.

74

It was unexpected, but apparently it was true. Jenny was the boss of the Edwards family after all.

Christine was resurfacing bit by bit. The pieces of reality filtering through, however, did not feel real at all. Jenny taking the lead, for example. And no one challenging her.

This was not the way their family worked.

Dave was standing around looking helpless with that silly scrap of towel clutched against his cheek. Sophie was watching Jenny with an interested expression on her face; she appeared to be actually listening.

And Jenny was issuing orders. Directing Dave one way and Sophie another. Steering Christine by the elbow to a pile of big logs. Apparently, they were going to feed the logs into the bandsaw.

Jenny gave them earmuffs and safety glasses and insisted they pay attention while she explained how the saw worked.

Christine tried to concentrate, but she found words slipping out of her mind as fast as they came in. She kept her eyes on the bright red button that said STOP and imagined pressing it if something went wrong. That would resolve most problems, surely. Thankfully Sophie was the one near the blade. Christine's job was to hold the piece of wood steady. That was it.

Imagine. Christine Minehan doing manual work. Under someone else's instruction. All those years of striving to get ahead and look what she'd become: a labourer lifting logs in a hot tin shed.

75

'**B**rilliant!' Sophie's eyes shone with anticipation and Jenny had a moment of panic. Perhaps it was unwise putting Sophie and Chris in charge of the bandsaw. But what other option did she have? Dave couldn't do it. It was going to take hours, and she had to get on with more complex tasks.

'You right?' Sophie raised her eyebrows at Chris, and Chris nodded. Sophie put her earmuffs on and yelled, 'Ready, set, go!' She flicked the switch and the bandsaw hummed.

Sophie fed the board in carefully, which was somewhat reassuring. A spray of sawdust flew out as the saw cut into the hardwood, and the humming noise changed to a high-pitched squeal. Dave jumped and turned around. A positive sign, Jenny thought. He'd been mooning about, refusing to get involved; at least he was paying attention.

Jenny grabbed a pair of earmuffs for Dave and went over. He had to let go of his face cloth to put them on; another positive. Jenny led him to the back bench and got a pencil and a pad of graph paper from the toolbox underneath.

The first page was a sketch of a human coffin. The second was a list of cuts, and the third was a diagram of the construction. Dimensions, angles, joins – Jenny had done the maths a couple of days earlier and drawn it to scale.

She showed Dave the sketch and went through the steps of putting a coffin together. On a fresh sheet of paper, she outlined the timber preparation. Thicknessing to 15mm planks – three from each board, then planing and sanding every plank. All before the construction could begin. Dave picked up the diagram of the coffin and inspected it. He performed a similar appraisal of the list of jobs for timber preparation. He was buying in.

'I'll need help to manage –' Jenny cocked her head over to their sisters at the bandsaw. She needed Dave on board, and he needed status. Also, she probably did need help to manage the girls.

'They'll be right,' Dave shouted. 'Born carpenters.'

Jenny paused to watch them. They were nearing the end of the cut and Sophie was struggling to keep the board on the table. Chris had lost concentration entirely – she was resting one hand on top of the board, looking absent-mindedly around the shed.

Jenny's hands flew to her face and she shut her eyes. Then there was a tap on her shoulder – Dave. She looked up.

'I'm on it,' he yelled. He crossed the shed in no time and caught the timber before it dropped. Jenny smiled.

What was happening to her? The lone builder, smiling because she had a partner on the job.

76

After Tom cut Jock's payments off he heard more from his big brother in two months than he had in ten years. It's amazing how close family ties can be when there's money involved. Tom spoke to him a few times, but then he got Helena to answer and tell Jock he was out. Tom wasn't going to give him the money, and he didn't want to hear his brother beg.

Then Jock came for a visit. All charming and happy; carrying big plastic toys for the kids. Left quick smart when he knew he wasn't going to get any money though.

Tom looked at his kids with new eyes after that. He decided they weren't going to turn out like Jock. Not on his watch.

Helena said he was too hard on them. He said they had to learn. After a while he got sick of the conversation. He was better off keeping his trap shut.

He had Jenny and Dave out on the property with him all the time. They were still young – Jenny was about five or six. It took time and patience, and they got in his way, but he taught them some skills. Taught them how to work. There was no allowance, no easy jobs for cash. No money unless they earned it and then they got the minimum wage. Same as anyone else.

He would have taken Chris out too, but Helena said no, she was only a toddler. Tom gave in on that one.

Everyone niggled along for the next few years. They got the work done. They had some laughs. But then it all went south.

The wool prices took a dive, and he was working overtime, diversifying, to keep the business out of debt. Then the dry set in – it wasn't called a drought. Not yet. And Helena got crook.

He was working so hard he barely noticed what was happening. Helena was falling into herself, somehow. Wouldn't eat. Wouldn't talk. Then one morning she didn't get up. Couldn't, maybe. Tom called Charles Briggs – he came out the same day. He said Helena had depression. Tom said, 'Don't we all?' and Charles said, 'No, we don't, Tom. The rest of us can get out of bed.'

He took Charles' advice and packed Helena off to her parents. She stayed a month, and it did her good, but it didn't last. That was it, for years. A month away and then back for a few, in and out. She was never fully with them, even when she was there. When she got pregnant, her depression got worse. It was a terrible time.

There was no rain on the horizon. No grass in the paddocks. The dirt had turned that drab, lifeless grey that says there's nothing left in the ground. Tom no longer had the time or inclination to teach his kids not to be idle. He was getting out of bed and getting the day's work done and that was as much as he had in him.

Then Sophie was born. Into that never-ending dry spell, into the heat and weariness, into a family just scraping by. She had a dimple before she smiled, and from day one Tom could see she was laughing at them.

Tom didn't spoil her. He took her out on the property, the same as the others. She went to the local school. No money when she was a kid. No handouts. But he couldn't deny it, she had an easier time. Life had changed by then. He had other things on his mind.

77

The spoken word, provided it was relevant to the case, was usually considered admissible evidence. Bright red cheeks, on the other hand, were not. Ben Taylor's cheeks did not lie, Vince was certain of that, but his lips were pressed together like a ziplock bag. He sat rigidly in the client chair, mug clenched between his hands, and eyed Vince distrustfully. It was unsettling.

Vince decided to end the interview before they'd finished their tea. He had Sophie Edwards' disclosure of drugs in Coorong and Ben Taylor's embarrassment. It was far from conclusive, but it was a start. Confirmation of drug use by Ben would have been ideal, but he was refusing to speak, and Vince was running out of time.

Obtaining a search warrant at such short notice would be a stretch. But people – including police officers – were nosy, and if Vince had enough evidence to make him curious, it was possible Michael Greaves would visit Ellersley.

Vince booted Ben out and flicked through the Edwards file.

Sophie lived in Newtown. It was a nice suburb. Much nicer now than it was in Vince's university days; but it still had rough pockets. Sophie could easily be occupying one of them. It wouldn't be hard to obtain illegal substances in Newtown. And it shouldn't be too hard to track down a record of arrest for possession, if one existed.

Vince dialled the Newtown Police Station. The young constable was polite but told him disclosing this information would be a breach of privacy, and he would need to apply for a subpoena. Vince hung up, irritated. The youth of today were so law-abiding.

He moved on to the next possibility – Newtown Court. Here he had a stroke of luck. The clerk, Tessa, was an acquaintance from Vince's younger years. He would go so far as to call her 'an old flame'. They'd parted on reasonable terms, and Tessa said she'd do a search of the court lists for him.

Vince now had three potential sources of information. He knew he had to speak with Michael before he closed the station for his afternoon nap. Otherwise, there was no chance he would search Ellersley before the end of the day.

His call went through to the answering machine, so he decided to walk to the station. It was only about eight hundred metres, but it was a steep incline. Charles Briggs would be impressed. After a hundred metres or so Vince shed his jacket. After another hundred, he loosened his tie and removed his hat. Despite these measures the sweat poured from him as he puffed up the hill.

The screen door was unlocked, a positive sign. Vince replaced his jacket, smoothed his hair, and stepped into the cool office. He tapped the bell on the counter and after a few minutes Michael Greaves appeared.

'Vince?'

'Michael, yes, good morning.'

'If you say so.'

His tone was not welcoming. Vince decided to cut straight to business.

'I need a few minutes of your time.'

'Not too many, I hope.' Michael Greaves was decades younger than Vince and had only been in Coorong for six years, yet he was the one with authority. There was no justice.

Vince ploughed on. 'I'm sorry to say it, but I have concerns about possible drug use at Ellersley.'

Michael Greaves raised his eyebrows and picked up a pen.

'Go on, then.'

Vince gave an account of the episode at Ellersley, Sophie's conversation with Ben, and the awaited information from the Newtown Court.

'Not much to go on, Vince.'

'No, Michael, there isn't. I quite agree. But if the premises aren't inspected today, I fear the drugs will be moved off site.' That sounded rather serious, Vince thought. Not something a responsible policeman would allow without investigation.

Michael Greaves put his pen down. He hadn't written a word. But he had listened.

'All right,' he said. 'I'll head out there and say g'day –'

Vince nodded seriously.

'– if I get the chance.'

It wasn't promising, but Vince could see it was the best he would get.

'Much appreciated, Michael. It's reassuring to know our community is in safe hands.' Vince backed out, saluting as he went.

If Sophie was detained on a charge of possession that would be ideal. But Vince knew there was only an outside chance. He mustn't lose focus. He needed an immediate, definitive disruption.

The walk back to Barton & Sons was much more pleasant: downhill, in the shade of the pepper trees. When he got back to the office, he would review the entire Edwards file. Who knew what he would find?

78

Sophie was focusing on holding the timber firm against the bandsaw fence. She had the hang of it now and was determined to keep it steady until the board was completely through. Dave's face looked shocking – worse as the afternoon wore on – and Sophie couldn't afford to get disfigured right now. It would totally jeopardise her chances with Ben.

They had done a four-inch board first, to learn how the bandsaw worked, and then Jenny had helped them lift the damaged eight-inch board onto the table, with the flat surface against the fence. She wanted it done early because it was for the lid. Jenny joined them, positioning herself at the end where the cut board came out, to steady it until it was all the way through. The second cut was trickier, especially when they got to the damaged part, but they got two proper planks out of it and Sophie could see Jenny was pleased.

At the end of the second cut Christine hit the STOP button. Sophie was massaging her arms and Jenny mimed a bowl and spoon.

'Lunch?' Sophie had the earmuffs off before Jenny had finished her one-word question. She didn't have to be asked twice. They had been working for hours. At least two, anyway.

She followed Jenny out to the shady spot on the south side of the shed and sat on a drench container. Dave had pulled his over to the shed and was leaning against the wall with his cap tipped forward, all grumpy, like he'd been the only one working hard.

Lunch was ham and tomato sandwiches. And green cordial, ice-cold, to wash it down. Brilliant. Sophie was starving.

Once Jenny had unpacked the sandwiches, she reached into the esky and pulled out cold, wet tea towels to sling around their necks. It made Sophie shiver, but in a delicious way.

They ate quietly for a bit, then Sophie broke the silence.

'So, guys,' she said. 'What are you going to do with the loot?'

No one was rushing to answer, but after a moment Chris piped up.

'I suppose I'll have to give it back,' she said. She was sitting up politely, eating small mouthfuls with her mouth shut. It looked like she was almost back to her normal self.

'Now that you know I took it, I mean. It seems like the right thing to do.' She took another delicate bite. 'Not that I would call Great-granny's jewellery "loot".'

Chris looked around at the others. 'That is what we're talking about, isn't it?'

'No,' Sophie said. 'I'm talking about the whole lot. Farm, shares, money – remember?'

'Oh that.' Chris said it like the property was of no value compared with the pearls.

'I suppose when Nicholas grows up, he might want to muster some cows. Who knows?' She looked out towards the river flats dreamily, as though imagining a scene where cattle grazed the pastures, and her son rode by in immaculate moleskins and an Akubra hat.

'You really have no idea, do you?' Dave was staring at Chris in disbelief.

'What?'

'How can you have no idea of what it all costs? Mortgage? School fees? Food on the table? Ringing any bells for you?'

'Stephen will be taking care of that from now on,' Chris said matter-of-factly. She was definitely returning to normal. 'Playing lovebirds with Nicola the receptionist comes at a price.'

Sophie almost choked on her sandwich.

'And I think,' Chris was on a roll now, 'in fact, I'm almost certain, that in the case of an interventional cardiologist whose wife has supported him for over twenty years, the price is rather high.'

She dabbed at her mouth with the corner of her wet tea towel.

'High enough to pay for a mortgage and food, certainly. And if Suzanne Mortimer's experience is anything to go by, it should pay for a family trip to Europe every year or so as well.' She smiled serenely at Dave.

'The poor bastard.' Dave shook his head. 'He's not getting off lightly, is he?'

'No,' she said. 'He is not.'

There was a lull in the conversation while everyone concentrated on their sandwiches. Jenny hadn't said a thing, and Sophie didn't want her to. She hadn't wanted a serious answer from any of them. She had just wanted to break the silence. Once she'd said it out loud, she was slapped back by the list she had cited. Farm, shares, money. As though that's what it came down to. Now that their father had died, land plus money plus shares, divided by four, equalled all that was left.

79

Dave was the first to finish lunch. The throbbing in his face had settled down, and he was keen to keep moving. If they were going to build this thing, they didn't have a lot of time.

He lifted an eight-inch plank onto the sawhorses, turned on his plane and made a start. He was working at roughly one and a half times Jenny's speed. He had two planks done in the time Jenny had completed one, but she'd got the lunch ready, so he gave her half a plank extra. All the same, left to herself Jenny would take forever to get the job done.

Managing a construction company was all about timelines. Co-ordinating contractors, communicating with clients, keeping the whole project ticking over – it took a big-picture man to stay on top of that.

Dave noticed the shavings were coming off a bit thick and he checked the board behind him. It looked all right.

The girls were surprisingly handy but completing the project by close of business Friday was not on their radar. Dave would question whether any of his sisters knew what close of business meant, let alone what time it was.

Five thirty if you were in the private sector, five o'clock if you worked for the government. That's how it was in Wagga, anyway. He assumed it was much the same everywhere else. They might need to confirm it with Vince.

Sophie started the bandsaw and it revved into action, whining as the girls fed the timber in. Jenny had wrestled the other eight-inch plank onto her sawhorses and was adjusting the blade on her plane. She wasn't fast, but Dave had to give it to her, she was strong. And she knew what she was doing.

Dave's plane slipped, digging a minor divot into the board, and he refocused. Two thirds of the way. He checked his watch. Twelve minutes so far. Which meant thirty-six minutes total for both sides of the board. Bloody hell.

The girls didn't know much about keeping time, and they didn't seem to know about money either. They hadn't even thought about what they would do with the inheritance.

In fairness, Jenny and Sophie hadn't said, but he could tell by looking at them they hadn't allocated the funds yet. And Christine was sitting on a gold mine with or without Ellersley. It was a sexist world, that was for sure, and women had it easier than the men. Here were three women who survived day to day without knowing what it took to get food on the table.

He didn't know a single bloke he could say that about. Men knew money had to come from somewhere. And small businessmen knew that better than anyone.

Dave skated to the end of the board and flicked the switch. He shook the shavings off his boots and bent over to look down the long line of the surface. Good enough for the inside of the coffin. He'd be a bit more careful with the other side. He walked back to the start of the board and flipped it over.

It had been a long time since he'd been on the tools. Years. He'd forgotten how satisfying it was. It was why he'd got into construction in the first place.

Getting into the operations side of it never even crossed his mind. Until Sharon said he should try it. She thought he had good business instincts, and she was right. He was good at the human part – managing contractors and clients – and he was good at the economic part of it too. He knew how to pick the market, which way to jump.

Dave kicked the extension cord out behind him and switched the power on.

He was good at all of it. Bloody good. But at the end of the day, anyone can come unstuck. A couple of minor debts, some bad luck, and the whole thing could spiral very fast. It was easy for Sharon to demand numbers, but she had no idea what he was up against.

By chance, Dave had visited his accountant a couple of weeks before his father died. It had nothing to do with the inheritance. He didn't even know his old man was sick. Anyway, Jim broke down the figures. Dave's total debt was six point three million. Four and a half mil for the bank. One and a half mil to suppliers and contractors. Three hundred k to pay off the second mortgage on the house. And the final nail – like he needed one – was the extra three point five mil he'd need to get Eastside Estate to point of sale.

Dave didn't trouble Jim with information about Trevor Adams and the council. That was only a couple of hundred k.

At the end of the appointment Jim said, 'You're fucked, mate,' and opened the door for Dave to go. He sent his invoice, which Dave hadn't paid yet, but he would. When Dave rang him to clarify a few things he was very brief on the phone. The first time. The second time he didn't answer. Didn't return the call. Not a pro bono man, Jim Blackett. He knew how to stay out of debt.

80

It was impossible to imagine the work involved in building a coffin, even a pet-sized one. Jenny knew this because people – especially men – were always guessing, and they were always wrong.

She looked at the eight-inch plank on her sawhorses, and checked the blade on her power plane. Dave had already started planing the other one, and Jenny hoped he was doing a reasonable job. It looked a bit rough from where she stood. Since he had butchered the resaw earlier that day they only had two planks. They would have to be careful with them if they wanted a lid worth looking at. She switched the power on and braced as the plane hit the timber surface.

In Jenny's experience, fathers were the worst. She occasionally went to a burial at the pet cemetery. It was such a peaceful place. So well cared for. And there was a real satisfaction in seeing the coffin fulfil its purpose. She always stood back from the mourners, out of respect, and for a quick getaway. But sometimes the father would find out who she was and sidle up for a conversation.

'That'd take you, what, a couple of hours?' They'd say it in a hoarse whisper, as though that meant the others wouldn't hear.

Jenny would watch the perfect fiddleback lid lowering into the ground and say nothing, usually.

Sometimes they pressed harder. 'No, but really, how long does it take?'

She might murmur something non-committal, but usually she blushed and backed away further, so she could leave as soon as the dirt hit the lid.

Jenny hit the off switch of her plane. It was cutting too deep. She adjusted the blade and tried again. Dave looked over and raised his eyebrows. 'Okay?' Jenny nodded and put her head down, ready to start the next lap.

What they wanted to know, these fathers, was if they got good value for their money.

She occasionally had an urge to give them an honest answer, to explain every step of the job from purchasing the timber to the final coat of finish, and then estimate the hours, which amounted to days, and ask the question the other way around. 'This is what it took to build this coffin, the vessel that carries your child's grief. Tell me, how much did you pay?'

But she could see it would not be a kind thing to do. And not many people had the attention span required for that conversation.

Jenny thought that if one day a person who was genuinely interested asked, she would say this:

'Every join, every angle, is an undertaking on its own.

'Every surface, rib and rail is an independently created object.

'From the headboard to the toe board each piece of timber is carefully chosen, drawn up, cut, joined, sanded and finished. Each task takes time and attention, much more than anyone would expect. And more again, to get it perfect. That's what it takes, to build a coffin for a pet.'

Now they were here, the four of them, building a coffin for a human. The construction alone was a huge job. The added work of dressing the rough-cut timber might make it impossible. It had taken Sophie and Christine two and a half hours to resaw two boards into planks. There were five more to go. If all went well and they worked hard, it might get done by nightfall.

The planing was not much faster than the resawing, and the sanding would be the slowest of the lot. Jenny didn't want to think badly of their father, but it did seem a bit harsh to make them do all this extra work. The poetry of using timber from the mill was nice, but there was also the reality of the situation to consider.

And the reality was that it was 3 pm on Thursday afternoon, the resawing was part way, the planing just started and nothing else had been done.

Jenny finished the lap and went back to the beginning of the board. Everyone was chipper now; Dave was whistling. They could have been building on Sesame Street.

She didn't want to bring them down, but it wouldn't be long before the enormity of the task dawned on them. She would have to stay a step ahead. Have the next job ready as soon as they had finished the one they were on. Small, achievable tasks, so they felt they were progressing. They had no time for discouragement and despair.

81

Something terrible. That's what he would find. A disastrous revelation. Information that entirely changed the coffin landscape.

Vince had reviewed the Edwards' file and found precious little to investigate. He only made the phone call to St Vincent de Paul to be thorough.

He listened to the dial tone and speculated on what he might be told. Perhaps Jenny was incapable of using the cash register. Or not so proficient at hanging clothes on the racks.

But when Susan, Jenny's co-worker at St Vincent de Paul, picked up the phone, she was able to inform Vince that Jenny was far from incapable.

'Jenny is hands-down the most talented merchandiser this store has seen. You have no idea, Mr Barton, what a difference that makes in a second-hand store.'

'Is that right?' Vince closed his eyes and applied pressure between them. Susan talked on and on, and on. He wasn't sure he had it in him to hear the conversation out.

'– and then there's her business.' Susan left a dramatic pause.

'Yes?' Vince feigned interest.

'Her coffin business.'

Vince jerked upright.

'What?' *Could it be a joke?*

'Oh darn! Gaylene said we weren't supposed to tell anyone. I'm going to be in real trouble if Jenny finds out.'

'Don't be concerned about that,' Vince rushed to reassure her. 'I won't tell a soul.'

'Thanks, Mr Barton. I do try to keep it to myself, because I know Jenny is a bit thingy about her privacy, but a friend of mine buried a chihuahua a couple of months ago, and you should have seen its little coffin! Cutest thing ever.'

It sounded dreadful, but Vince had to get more information. 'Did you say it was a business, Susan?'

'Yes! It turns out Jenny's been making coffins for years. She doesn't tell anyone about it, sells them through the vet. But sometimes word gets out, doesn't it?'

Yes, it does, Susan.

'Gaylene reckons Jenny could build a coffin in her sleep, she's that good at it now.'

Vince's mind was racing. All this time he had been madly trying to disable her siblings, and there was Jenny, a highly experienced coffin maker, working uninterrupted on the project.

'Oh my, is that the time?' Susan said. 'I'm knocking off at four. I'd better go and tidy up.'

Vince wasn't ready for her to hang up. He needed something to go on with. He could not allow the Edwards to work unimpeded for the night. It was unthinkable what they might achieve – what they had already achieved! – with a professional coffin builder on the team.

'Oh, Susan?' He tried to be casual. 'I have a few questions I need to check with your supervisor. Confidential matters. Perhaps you could give me her number?'

'Sorry, Mr Barton, it's against the rules. You might be a stalker, you know?'

Vince swallowed his frustration. 'Of course, Susan. You must abide by the rules. I'll give you my details instead – my home phone might be best – perhaps you could mention it is urgent?'

'No worries. Gaylene's coming in this arvo to empty the bins. I'll get her to give you a call.'

'Thank you, Susan, thank you. Don't forget, it's very important.' Vince wasn't clear on what he needed to know, or how he was going to extract the information, but he needed something.

Bringing Jenny down was going to be difficult. Unlike Christine, she had no reputation to keep. She had no money, no children, no property and no job.

If Vince had started with the same advantage as Jennifer Edwards, how far he might have come. But he didn't.

He started as a foreigner at a dinner party. A night of one excruciating mistake after another, of hair oil and Italian arms flailing and too-loud laughter; but how could he have known?

Tom and Helena Edwards were there, and Tom kept the company entertained, mocking Vince in ways he could not possibly understand. But the moment of leaving was the worst. The guests were gathered in the hallway – a bundle of people reaching for coats and scarves – and Vince, by chance, was closest to the door. He opened it, and as he stepped into the night Tom Edwards' voice followed him.

'Ladies first,' he called, and everyone laughed. Vince kept walking and concentrated on keeping his head up. He pulled at his gold insignia ring, twisting it back and forth until it came off his little finger, and wondered why Tom Edwards, a man who had everything, had to cut the legs from under a boy so far from home.

Vince shoved all the papers from his desk into his briefcase.

He had believed Tom Edwards came to Barton & Sons because, finally, he respected Vince's work. But Tom must have known about Jenny's coffin business. He must have known Vince didn't stand a chance. He and Charles Briggs had no doubt been laughing behind Vince's back this whole time, while Vince scurried about, getting documents signed.

He snapped his briefcase shut, picked it up and walked past his receptionist without so much as a mumbled goodbye. He needed a whisky. Badly.

82

Sophie was standing at the front of the shed when the police arrived. Hats, stripey things on their shoulders, guns. The whole kit. They were strolling across the paddock, casual and unconcerned, but Sophie knew they were roasting out there.

She took a quick look at the others. They were concentrating on their work. Dave was changing the bandsaw blade, and Chris and Jenny were hard at it with the power planes. She and Chris had done three solid hours on the bandsaw and Sophie was ready for a break. Also, Sophie was excellent at managing tricky situations. She didn't know why the police were at Ellersley, but she would be doing everyone a favour if she took them down to the house and sorted it out.

She ducked out of the shed and the blistering sun hit her hard.

'Hello, officers,' she said happily, as though she had been hoping they'd drop by. She held out a hand to the first officer. 'I'm Sophie Edwards. What can I do for you?'

The officers looked at each other, and the taller one spoke.

'It might be best if we go down to the house and have a talk.'

'Absolutely. It's so hot out here!' she said. 'I'll let the others know.'

Dave was spinning the bandsaw blade, checking it from all angles.

'Dave!' she shouted. He looked up, irritated.

'We've got visitors.'

He pulled one earmuff away from his ear.

'What?'

'I'm going down to the house for a bit. We've got visitors.'

'Who?'

'Police.'

Dave looked uneasy, so Sophie went into reassuring mode. She was getting good at it by now.

'They're just doing a doorknock or something.'

'Maybe I'd better come down.' Dave switched from uneasy to alpha male.

'No, don't. I'll come and get you if I need to.'

Dave was considering it.

'Chris and Jen need you here.' Sophie looked at her sisters, who seemed to be doing fine without supervision, but Dave nodded, like he knew they were relying on him.

'I'll come up if there's a problem. Okay?' Sophie gave him a thumbs up.

'Okay.'

She spun around and ran down to the house. Now she had to find out why the officers had come.

83

When Tom first brought Helena home, he did the sentimental thing and carried her over the threshold. They both laughed. He dropped her legs and she turned and kissed him. He felt like he'd crossed a finish line.

Life wasn't perfect by any stretch. He had to evict his mum. He had to eat Helena's cooking. One year in, the best dog he'd ever owned ran in front of a truck. The next day, the bitch who delivered him ate a fox bait. Two dogs in two days, a week before marking the calves. Bloody hell. Marking without a dog. It didn't bear thinking about. He paid Les Taylor to come across with his dogs and lend a hand. He was useless. It was a terrible, messy job. Cows bellowing and calves crying out and blood and shit all over the place.

But that was just the day-to-day running of a farm. Tom wasn't complaining. He was willing to take the rough with the smooth. And he did. For nine years. That's how long they loved each other.

He loved everything about his wife. Loved how she moved, before she fell pregnant. Quick, and light on her feet. She barely touched the ground before she'd taken the next step. When she got pregnant, he loved her more. The skin smooth over her swollen belly, the way she leaned on the back of a chair, rocking her hips from side to side. He couldn't get over it, that Helena was his. That she was carrying his child in her belly. Tom wanted to touch her all the time, and she didn't mind.

Three pregnancies, three healthy babies, Ellersley making a profit, year after year. It wasn't a free ride. Tom was working bloody hard. He thought he was taking the rough with the smooth. He actually believed that.

But that's not how rough times work. There's no perspective. No gratitude for the happy days. There is only the three feet ahead of you on a stony track that gets harder with every step.

They didn't have sex for years. Seven, maybe more. It didn't bear thinking about. What kind of a marriage is it when a man can't touch his wife? When Helena got pregnant with Sophie, Tom was astounded. And quietly proud. They'd had sex once in God knows how long, and he got her pregnant. How many men could say that?

Helena perked up a bit after Sophie was born. But nothing like she was at the start. She was a bare outline of the woman he'd married. Sometimes fainter, sometimes darker, but never properly coloured in.

It was Sophie's first day of school, when Helena had the ultrasound. By Friday they had the results. Breast cancer.

Charles Briggs arranged a mammogram and CT scan and bone scan and whatever other scans he could think of. It was in her bones and her liver. All through her. There was no point treating it, he said. It had gone too far.

Tom wasn't sure, looking back, if Charlie made the right call. Other women who had treatment seemed to get better. But he was the doctor, not Tom. They had to trust him. That's how it worked.

In any case, when Helena found out she had cancer and she was going to die, her depression went away. Just like that. Slipped out the back door and never came back.

She smiled when she saw him. And laughed.

Out of nowhere, she laughed.

The kids had left home by then, apart from Sophie, and she was early to bed. Then it was just him and Helena. A second chance. A honeymoon in a good season.

It was a beautiful season, too. One of their best. Rain came, gentle then steady, right on time for germination, and intermittently after that. Tom enjoyed being out in the paddocks, and when he came home to his beautiful wife his heart was full. Her face was thin, with sunken temples and dark, hollow eyes. But she smiled when she saw him. She reached for his hand.

For three months, he was allowed to hold her at night. She curled up, and he held her, in the cave of his chest. She let him touch her breasts, now hard and lumpy, and he wrapped his arms around her, almost twice, by the end. He held her so tenderly and tried to breathe in her time. Willing her to fall asleep, but not forever. Only for the night.

84

Things certainly moved rapidly in the coffin-building world.

Christine had been taken off the bandsaw and wasn't sure if it was a promotion or a demotion. It seemed a shame, but Jenny made it quite clear that she had to move on.

Sophie had gone off somewhere, and Dave and Jenny had a chat and Christine was transferred to the sawhorse area where she was asked to operate a power plane. Apparently Dave was in charge of the bandsaw now, and he didn't need her help.

Christine was allowed to take her own safety equipment to the next job, which was a positive. She felt confident in her use of goggles, earmuffs and gloves. The other aspects of her role, however, were likely to be something of a challenge. Planing was completely different to holding logs steady for the bandsaw. Here, the wood stayed in one place, and Christine moved along it. Furthermore, she was expected to hold a vibrating machine steady as she walked. Jenny gave her a demonstration. There was a sharp blade on the underside of the plane. This was to shave the rough wood and make the surface smooth. It was up to her to make sure it didn't cut too deep or fly off.

The first thing Christine did was to practise holding the plane while she walked along. She wasn't ready to turn it on yet. As she walked, the bandsaw revved into action behind her. Then Jenny started her power plane. Christine realised they were serious about letting her do this job on her own. There was only one thing for it. She turned her new machine on and held it horizontally above the board.

'Ready, set, go!' Christine yelled into the roar of construction noise and set her plane down on the plank. It ploughed into the wood and she wrenched it back. The plane seemed to have its own agenda, but Christine was having none of it. She had managed medical practices, school boards and every parent group known to womankind in her previous life. She believed she could bring one power tool into line.

85

A four-inch board was a whole lot easier to manoeuvre than an eight, Dave had to say. He resawed the first in less than an hour; no problems keeping it hard up against the fence. He would have started the next straight away, but he'd had an idea about the money situation. Feeding the boards into the bandsaw had loosened up his brain. Maybe it was the vibration. Or the white noise. He wouldn't call it an inspiration, but it was the most useful thought he'd had in a bloody long time and he needed advice from Jim. Maybe Vince Barton too.

It was just after four. If he wanted to catch an accountant and a lawyer that afternoon, he had to get down to the house and start phoning now. Which reminded him of Sophie and the police. She'd been gone way too long. Too long for a doorknock appeal, that was for sure. It was time he checked that situation out.

He switched off the bandsaw and went to tell Jenny. She was going a bit faster now, which was good to see. And Christine was planing like a madwoman: hair flying out and arms stretched forward. She was rocketing.

'Going to the house,' he shouted, pointing vaguely in that direction.

'Okay.' Jenny nodded. She didn't look thrilled, but he'd be back soon enough.

Sophie was in the kitchen entertaining the boys in blue when Dave got there. They were having a cup of tea and a merry laugh.

'Oh, Dave, there you are!' Sophie said, like they'd been waiting for him to show up. 'We've just been having a cuppa.'

'So I see,' Dave said. No need to be too friendly.

'Someone told the police we had drugs! Can you believe it?'

Of course he could believe it, but he wasn't about to say so. He looked to the cops.

'Find 'em?'

'As a matter of fact, no,' one of them answered, and they both smirked.

'The officers have been so helpful,' Sophie said. She looked like she was going to launch into a speech of commendation, but she was interrupted by the phone. She jumped up immediately.

'Oh, I'd better get that! So sorry to leave you to it – maybe Dave can let you out? Thank you both *so* much. We're so lucky to have such fabulous local police!'

The officers took their mugs to the sink and did the leaving rituals – clearing throats, patting down pockets, putting their hats on. They obviously saw no need to hang around if Sophie wasn't there. Dave didn't have to see them out. They knew the way. He followed them to the porch anyway because he had to get Sophie off the phone. Pronto.

'Who?' Sophie waved as the officers walked past. 'Gayleen? How do you spell that?'

86

It didn't fix everything, a whisky on ice, but it made most things a whole lot better. Vince was sitting in the dining room, cool cloth on his forehead and glass in hand, recovering by degrees when the phone rang.

'Mr Barton? It's Gaylene from Vinnies.'

'Gaylene, thank you for returning my call.' Vince sat up straight, flung the face cloth aside and looked around for a pen.

'That's all right. We're all so worried about Jenny.'

'Yes, bereavement of a loved one is very sad.' Vince rifled through the sideboard drawers.

'And then there's Matthew,' Gaylene said. 'He must be such a worry to her.'

'Matthew?' Vince found a pencil stub and started scratching on a scrap of paper.

'Most people don't know this, but Matthew's a recovering alcoholic.'

'That's terrible,' Vince said encouragingly.

'Jenny told us – or at least we worked it out – because here at Vinnies we know all about alcoholics.'

'Yes, yes. Professional knowledge, as it were.'

'That's exactly right. But he hasn't been drinking for years and he's a lovely bloke, so we don't judge.'

'No, no, of course not.'

'We have a number of clients with alcohol problems. Mostly men. I don't know why. Not so good at managing life, I suppose.' Gaylene was straying into the philosophical and Vince reined her back.

'A terrible business, terrible. Now, Gaylene, we don't have an emergency contact listed for Jennifer – perhaps Matthew would be an appropriate person for this?' Vince smiled, pleased at this clever way of finding out who Matthew was.

'I should say so, Mr Barton. They've been together for years. Although now . . .'

'Now?' Vince's ears pricked up.

'I wouldn't normally talk about another person's private business, but I heard he and Jenny have broken up.'

'Really?'

'Just a rumour,' Gaylene said quickly.

'Of course,' Vince soothed her, 'of course.'

'The trouble is the alcohol,' Gaylene followed up. 'It's all too easy to start drinking again. And once a man gets drinking, things can get out of control.'

Vince took a sip of whisky. 'They certainly can.'

'I've seen it all. Disorderly behaviour, violence, urinating in public places.'

'Shocking,' Vince said.

'Matthew could be lying unconscious in a gutter at this minute.'

Gaylene had a vivid imagination. Vince encouraged her to the best of his ability.

'That's highly concerning, Gaylene.'

'With Jenny away, and no one to check on him . . .' Gaylene was setting the scene nicely.

'If alcohol is part of the picture . . .' Vince encouraged.

'I didn't think of it until now,' Gaylene said, 'but Matthew could be in serious trouble.'

'With a relationship break-up . . .' Vince prompted.

'We don't know about that,' Gaylene corrected him. 'It's just a rumour. Maybe it was only a tiff.'

'Of course,' Vince retracted, 'of course. But the stress . . .'

'Yes. And his history,' Gaylene agreed. 'He could be a risk to himself.'

'And others?' Vince spoke hesitantly. It was such a fine line between encouragement and offence.

'Maybe,' Gaylene conceded. 'From what I hear, when Matthew was drinking, he could get rowdy.'

'It's not that he would be rampaging the streets.' Vince maintained a cautious tone.

'Of course not,' Gaylene said.

'But if he's been drinking . . .' he said.

'. . . anything could happen.'

'Exactly.'

There was a brief pause, then Gaylene spoke with renewed purpose.

'We need to check on him,' she said decisively. 'We may not have his details, but there's the police. And Jenny, of course! She'd want to know. Even if they've had a bit of a squabble.'

Vince murmured in agreement, willing her on.

'She'll be at the farm, working her little heart out on that coffin, with no one to tell her if Matthew's on a bender. I'd better call her.'

Vince kept his voice calm and steady. 'If Matthew is, as you say, on a bender, a call like that could literally mean the difference between life and death.'

'Right. I'm calling her now. And if I can't get through, I'm calling the police.'

'Do you have the number at Ellersley?'

'I'm not sure.'

Vince handed it over happily. Then he replaced the receiver and smiled. *Thank you, Gaylene. Thank you.*

87

After Dave took over the bandsaw and Christine adjusted to the power plane, Jenny had a moment of real optimism about the job. There was action everywhere in the shed, and jobs were getting done. Even Sophie's absence did not overly concern her. Jenny knew she'd be back. Sophie got bored when she was on her own.

But then Dave decided to take a break too. After resawing a single four-inch board he switched off the bandsaw and said he was going to the house. He didn't say why. Maybe he was in the mood for a snack. In any case, he didn't hurry back.

Jenny had worked out tasks for everyone – small and achievable – but it was difficult to allocate these tasks to workers who weren't in the shed.

Christine was working hard. Very hard. But her method was wild, and her efficiency was impaired by her style. She had managed to complete one six-inch plank. It was a little wonky, but they could use it for the floor.

Jenny's current concern, however, was the lid. She wanted it glued and clamped before they downed tools for the day, and she was not willing to leave this part of the coffin construction in the hands of amateurs. Only an experienced practitioner could do proper tongue and groove joins, and Jenny would not consider anything less. Not for the lid.

Sanding the long boards in preparation for joining was the task she should be doing. But Christine needed supervision and Jenny needed to see progress. Until Sophie and Dave returned, she would have to stay where she was. Supervising the apprentice and planing timber for the sides. And hoping the others wouldn't be gone for too long.

88

'Sorry, Gaylene, I just have to check something.' Sophie put her hand over the receiver.

'Dave!' She beckoned him over. 'Do you know someone called Gaylene?'

'Nope.'

He was in a huff because she had been drinking tea with the cops, but he should have thanked her. Chris had taken the lion's share of the available substances already, but it might have been a problem reputation-wise if anything had been found. Thanks to Sophie the officers left happy and absolutely on the Edwards' side.

'Sorry, Gaylene, who did you want?' It took Gaylene forever to answer and Sophie lost the thread. If it was a thread. It might have been just a bunch of words chucked together.

'Sorry, you *want* Matthew, or you're worried about Matthew?'

'We're worried about him, love. He's out drinking.'

'Really?' Sophie knew it was wrong, but she was intrigued. Maybe it would be another family scandal.

'We think so. And you know how they are. They get dangerous.'

'Who does?' Sophie asked.

'Alcoholics.'

'Is Matthew an alcoholic?' Every minute Sophie was learning something new.

'I won't speak out of turn, love, I just want to pass a message on to Jenny. She'd better go over to his place and check he's all right.'

'What if he isn't at his place?'

'Oh, my goodness. Don't say that! Let Jenny know that Gaylene called. I don't want to worry her, but I don't want Matthew dead in a gutter either.'

'Neither do I,' said Sophie. She certainly did not want that. But she didn't want to be the one telling Jenny that Matthew was on a drunken spree either. Jenny hadn't been all that merry since she'd picked up the bandsaw from Matthew, and Sophie suspected this news would bring her down even more.

'You done, mate?' Dave was standing in the doorway. Gaylene was saying a four-thousand-word goodbye and Sophie said, 'See ya,' and put the receiver down.

'Yeah. Hey, Dave, is Matthew an alcoholic?'

'Doubt it.' Dave stepped down. 'You got your phone?'

Sophie pointed to the landline.

'Your mobile,' Dave said.

'It doesn't work here, only the landline.'

'Thanks, mate, not looking for a technical explanation, I just need a mobile.'

'What for?'

'None of your business. Is this yours?' He picked up a mobile from the desk.

'It's Chris's,' Sophie said. 'I dare you to take it.'

The idea made Sophie laugh, but Dave was getting irritated, and she didn't want to push him too far. She ran to her room and got her mobile.

'Ta.' Dave took the phone, removed the sim and put his in.

'Whoa! Who said you could do that?'

Dave was scrolling through numbers, ignoring her.

'Dave! That's my phone.'

'Don't worry, mate. I'll give it back tomorrow.'

Sophie was ready to battle it out, but Dave had already dialled a number. He put his hand over the receiver.

'Off you go,' he said, 'get up there and do some work.'

Like she hadn't been working all afternoon. She'd like to see him bring the cops round within the hour. Anyway, Sophie wasn't going to the shed without him. If someone had to tell Jenny about Matthew, Dave could do it.

89

Obviously, Dave couldn't tell Sharon about the level of debt. Not now, and hopefully not ever, which is why he'd been trying to get rid of it all at once. That's what had tripped him up. A six point three million dollar debt wasn't going to be paid in a hurry. Add on the three point five mil for Eastside and maybe it would never get paid. But that wasn't his problem today. It was a problem for next month, or even better, next year. Dave wasn't an idiot. He knew the debt was real. But he didn't have to pay it all straight away.

What he needed was a figure that would get him through Christmas. Because that's what it was all about, wasn't it? Christmas was the main game. Time with the family, a few pressies, plastic toys in the pool. Having some mates over for a barbie on Boxing Day. If he wanted Christmas, he needed a minimum figure. Enough to cover the mortgage for a couple of months. Enough to pay his suppliers and contractors – give the boys the Christmas they deserved. He'd need a few grand to get Trevor off his back, but he could sort that out when the rest was covered.

Jim answered his mobile on the second ring this time. Super friendly.

'Dave! Mate! How's it going?'

'All right, Jim. All right.'

'Heard your old man's passed. I'm sorry, mate, tough times. What can I do for you?'

He was happy enough to offer his services now. An inheritance in the offing made a big difference.

'A couple of sums, that's all.'

'Ha ha, well that's my game. What've you got?'

Dave had no idea how accountants worked this stuff out so fast, but Jim came up with a number on the spot. It was bloody big, but it wasn't impossible.

Five hundred thousand. That was the bare minimum he needed to take back to Wagga. If he could raise five hundred k he'd have a fighting chance of picking up the threads in the New Year – contractors still on side, family home intact, and a proper Christmas with his wife and kids who, hopefully, would still be around.

Now he had to work out how to get the money. ASAP. Vince Barton wasn't his favourite bloke. Dave wouldn't trust him as far as he could throw him. But he'd be able to tell Dave the quickest way to get some cash.

Maybe he'd have to sell a few shares. It didn't matter, so long as he got the money. Dave checked the digital clock on the desk. Four forty-five.

'Barton & Sons, Ben speaking.'

Dave was momentarily confused. 'Oh yeah, right. Ben.' Poor bloke. Shit job.

'Dave Edwards here, mate. Vince around?'

'Nope. Gone home.'

'When's he back?'

'Dunno. Tomorrow?'

'It's kind of urgent.' Dave was trying not to be pushy, but he needed information fast.

'You can have an appointment. Nine thirty?'

'Nothing today?'

'Nope.'

'Does he have a mobile?'

'Not that he's told me.'

'Fuck it. All right, make it nine thirty.'

It wasn't ideal, but it was better than nothing. It also reminded Dave about the timeframe for finishing the coffin. They still had to get it done before anything else could be sorted out.

The screen door was barely hanging now, and when Dave gave it a prod it grated across the step.

'Dave!' A shout came from the house, and Sophie ran after him. She hadn't gone back to the shed, apparently.

'Wait, I'll come with you.' She slipped her sandals on and followed him out.

'Did your phone calls go well?'

Dave shrugged. It was none of her business.

'Mine didn't. Gaylene said Matthew's an alcoholic.'

'You said.' Dave kept walking. He had enough problems of his own.

'Do you think Jenny knows?'

He shrugged. He had no idea.

'Anyway, Gaylene says he's on a bender and we have to tell her.'

Dave knew where Sophie was heading, and he didn't like it. Jen was functioning well. She seemed to have recovered from her earlier crisis. News about Matthew could take her down, and he didn't want to be the one to tell her. Sophie could give her the news.

'It'd be better coming from you, Dave.' Sophie linked her hand through his elbow, skipping to keep up.

Dave shook his head.

'She takes you seriously,' Sophie continued. 'You'll know what to say.'

He wouldn't. But as Sophie pranced along beside him, he had to ask himself – was she really a better person for the job?

90

Power planing wasn't so bad after all. The first plank took a while, but once Christine got her eye in, she progressed at a steady rate. Jenny looked across occasionally, but she showed no signs of disapproval, so Christine felt confident about her work.

This was just as well, because Dave and Sophie had gone down to the house, leaving her and Jenny to do the work of four people. Then Jenny decided to switch jobs. She started sanding, and Christine became the sole planing person. It was discouraging doing it on her own. She kept at it, though, and by the time Dave and Sophie returned she had completed four planks. Not that they noticed.

Dave walked straight past Christine and tapped Jenny on the shoulder. The sander powered off and Jenny removed her earmuffs. Sophie was hovering near them, obviously listening. Christine removed her earmuffs. She didn't want to miss out.

Dave wasn't saying anything particularly interesting, though. He was telling Jenny that Matthew had a problem and some woman called Gaylene said he was an alcoholic. He said it as though it was news. But Jenny knew Matthew was an alcoholic.

When Christine had come to Ellersley to collect Great-granny's jewellery, she dropped in at Jenny's for a cup of tea. A copy of the Twelve Steps and Twelve Traditions poked her in the buttock when she sat on the couch. Jenny darted to get it and took it out of the room faster than Christine had ever seen her do anything. When Christine asked Jenny if she had a problem, she blushed and said no. Which meant it was Matthew. Jenny was never going to talk about it. Christine drank her tea, caught a taxi to the airport and flew home. She had so much on her plate at the time she barely thought of it again.

Now Dave was saying something about Matthew 'rampaging'. Jenny was squeezing her fingers, one hand in the other. She looked upset. Christine couldn't quite hear what Dave said next. He patted Jenny on the back and walked off quickly, like he couldn't get away fast enough.

91

In retrospect, Sophie wondered if having Dave break the news to Jenny was the best idea. He was doing a brilliant job to begin with, slow and steady, but when he came to the bit about rampaging the streets, he suddenly sped up.

'He's on a bender, Jen, out of control, sounds like he's dangerous, you better call.' All in one sentence. He patted her on the back, hard enough to knock her off balance, and practically sprinted off.

Luckily, Sophie was there. Dave was at the bandsaw by now, and Christine was standing with a power plane in her hand. Sophie was the only one ready to catch Jen's fall. And she did. Caught her in a kind of bear hug, then manoeuvred Jenny to sit on a sawhorse where she held her steady for a minute or so. When Jenny was stable, Sophie picked up the conversation from the disastrous place Dave had left it. Someone had to.

'Jen? Are you okay?'

Nothing.

'Dave's hopeless, but he might be right.'

Still nothing.

'Do you want to call?'

Jenny was shaking her head, very slightly at first, but increasing in speed and strength until Sophie crouched down and held Jenny's face in her hands.

'I'll do it,' Sophie said. She held Jenny's eyes with her gaze. 'I'll phone him.'

Jenny didn't respond, but she'd stopped shaking her head. Sophie decided to count it as a yes.

'Can you write his number down?' Sophie got paper and a pencil and handed them to Jenny.

Jenny wrote the number in big, shaky writing.

'Thanks, Jen, I'm on it. Back in a bit.'

Sophie dashed down to the house. Dave could say what he liked about her slacking off, but this wasn't about getting away from the shed. No way. This was essential. Like dealing with the police, but even more important. If Jenny didn't perk up soon, the coffin project was dead.

92

When they became friends, maybe only the second or third time they met, Matthew told Jenny about his problem with alcohol. He'd been through it many times before. That's what they did at Alcoholics Anonymous. Told their story. He told her what he did when he started drinking.

First stop would be the pub. He'd drink a few schooners of beer and get 'rowdy'. Jenny didn't know exactly what this would entail, but he said when he got too rowdy they'd kick him out. Then he'd get reckless. Go down to the TAB and place bet after bet until all his money was spent. He could empty his bank account in an hour or two, and he did, many times.

Next, he'd go to the bottle-o and buy whisky. On credit. Jenny wanted to know what kind of shop owner would allow that and Matthew told her most would. He didn't blame them.

He'd drive home drunk, sit on the porch, and drink hard. He held the bottle in one hand and a shot glass in the other and didn't put either of them down until there was nothing left for him to pour. He shouted at people passing by and hurled abuse at his neighbours. They forgave him the first time. But after the second and third they went inside every time he was out in the yard.

Once, he got back in the car. He drove into town, veering off the road and onto the footpath, where he ran into a parking meter and stopped. Then he got out of the car and walked, yelling and howling and swinging punches at anyone in his way. He got beaten up by the police that night. They used more force than was necessary, but Matthew said he deserved it.

He'd been five years without a drink when they met, and he'd told the story many times by then. All the same, he was nervous when he told her. So was she. She was gripping her hands together in her lap to stop them shaking. It was terrifying, hearing a person tell the truth like that.

He had not drunk a drop since they met. Fifteen years he'd been dry. But he'd told Jenny how it went, so if Gaylene said he was dangerous and running riot he probably was. And if he was drinking, it was her fault.

93

Charles Briggs had done a good job. Mostly. He looked after the kids when they were crook, and he took care of Helena. He didn't baulk at coming out to Ellersley if it was needed. Tom was satisfied with his treatment about eighty per cent of the time.

Tom still had his doubts about the breast cancer. But Helena had agreed with Charlie. She didn't want to spend her last months on chemo. Fair enough. It was her choice. There was nothing Tom could do about it.

But other times it was Tom's choice. Times when Charlie's advice didn't seem right, but Tom still took it.

Keeping the kids at home was a prime example. It was Charlie's advice, but it was Tom's doing, and the outcome was a bloody disaster.

The kids were at Coorong Primary when Helena dropped her bundle for the first time.

Charlie came out to Ellersley, and after he'd seen Helena, Tom walked him to the car. Charlie said it was the kids that kept her going. He told Tom to keep them home for high school. A doctor gave advice on everything in those days.

No boarding. No King's. No Abbotsleigh. Tom got his hackles up. He told Charlie it was none of his business where the Edwards went to school. Charlie said Tom had to think of Helena. If the kids were gone, she'd have nothing to get up for. That only made Tom crankier. How about getting up for her husband? How about keeping the homestead running? How about getting up to work like he did, every single bloody day, no matter what mood he was in? Charlie waited him out and when he'd calmed down, spoke again. 'It's no use, Tom,' he said. 'If you send them away, she won't survive. It's not worth the risk.'

Tom took Charlie at his word. And he made his choice. The Edwards children, for the first time in five generations, stayed home for high school. Coorong High. God help him.

Helena didn't get better, but Tom would admit she didn't get much worse. The kids, on the other hand, went downhill fast. Trash talk and chewing gum, untucked shirts and rolled-up skirts. His mother would have turned in her grave.

Going to a private school didn't guarantee a worthwhile life – Jock was testimony to that – but it improved the odds. Gave a kid a real education. Proper values. Discipline. Decency. And the chance to meet people of quality; people they'd never come across in Coorong.

If Tom had sent his kids away, they would have done better for themselves. An unemployed alcoholic, a hairdresser, whatever deadbeat Sophie was involved with – they weren't matches to be proud of. Even Stephen Minehan was second rate. He knew how to earn money, but he was a bore. Christine would have seen that if she'd had some comparison.

When Tom agreed to keep the kids home, he told himself there was no other option. But it wasn't true. Maybe it worked out better for Helena. Maybe. But he should have known better. He should have put his kids first.

94

'Dave! Dave!' Sophie was indicating for him to stop the bandsaw.

Dave pressed on. He was halfway through a cut – it wouldn't kill her to wait.

'Stop the bandsaw!' she shouted.

Dave nodded. 'Gotcha,' he mouthed and kept going. When he reached the end of the board, he flicked the switch and took his earmuffs off.

'He's not answering,' Sophie said.

'Are you sure it's the right number?'

'Yes! I even checked it in the telephone book.'

Dave paused to think, but Sophie had another urgent thing to say.

'We have to go and find him.'

'Hold on, mate. Let's think about the options here.'

At any other time, Dave would be happy to hunt down a drunk bloke, but they were working to a deadline. If he left the project for a few hours, it could collapse into a heap and never recover. He couldn't risk it.

'I already have,' Sophie said. 'Finding Matthew is the only option. If we don't find him Jenny will stay in robot land and we won't get the coffin done and everything will go to shit.'

She was right. But Dave couldn't go to Albury. He was needed.

'You know I'm right. Anyway, I'm going. Even if you won't.'

'Where will you go?' He was stalling, thinking about Sophie going on her own.

'His house. I know where it is. I went with Jenny.'

'What if he's not there?'

'Police.'

'What if he is there?'

'I'll tell him to phone Jenny.'

'Raving drunk?'

'Oh, yeah. No, not then. If he's drunk, I'll assess the situation and reconsider.'

Sophie was over-confident, but Dave was starting to believe she had her head screwed on better than she let on. She'd manage it on her own.

'All right. You've talked me round. I'll have to stay here though. You're it, mate.'

'I need to borrow your car,' Sophie said.

Dave took it back. Sophie's head was not screwed on right. She was insane, making a suggestion like that. There was no way he was handing over his car keys. But then he thought about the alternatives. Jen's ute – she'd never get it going. The Volvo – all buttons and beeps – she wouldn't cope with that either.

'When's the last time you drove a car?' Dave asked.

'Nineteen seventy-five.'

'Don't be a smart arse. How long has it been?'

'Two months. I drove Clarissa home after a party.'

Sophie might have been telling the truth, and she might not. Dave couldn't tell, but his options were limited so he decided to take it at face value.

He walked Sophie over to the Commodore, giving her basic instructions on the way. He got in and started the engine, showing Soph how to do it. He gave her a quick rundown of the controls and handbrake and made her adjust the mirrors.

'Got it,' Sophie said.

'You sure?' His heart sank at the sight of Sophie in the driver's seat. He couldn't believe it was happening.

'Yes! Back off. I've gotta go!'

She released the handbrake and revved, way harder than she needed to. The car skidded in the gravel and Sophie whooped.

Dave winced. If Sophie realised how awesome the Commodore was there was a risk she'd keep on driving and never come back.

95

Vince went to the kitchen in search of ice, and when he opened the freezer a packet of fettucine carbonara fell out. *Dinner is served.* He bent over to pick it up and checked the use-by date – still edible, just. It was a far cry from the pasta his mama made, but it was better than nothing. Vince punctured the plastic with a fork and put it in the microwave, then refreshed the ice in his glass.

It had been a very long day. The visit to Ellersley and David's threat felt like a lifetime ago. Then there was the interview with Ben Taylor; research into Sophie's drugs; a visit to Michael Greaves; and finally, the discovery of Jenny's coffin business and recruitment of Gaylene to interrupt her work – he could rightfully enjoy his whisky tonight. He had earned every drop.

The microwave beeped and Vince peered at the plastic tray. Near enough. He peeled off the cellophane cover, picked up his glass and went back to the table.

It did not feel completely wise, leaving his fate in the hands of a woman called Gaylene, but what other option did he have? Michael Greaves and Gaylene were his only allies now, not that they knew it. Vince was relying on them to act according to their word.

Vince kicked his shoes off, loosened his belt and tie, and poured a generous amount of whisky into his glass.

He had no reason to trust either of them, but if he were to put money on it, Gaylene would be his pick. Gossip and scandal were much more likely to motivate a person than executing a job with due diligence.

Gaylene was the more important of the two anyway. Vince hoped against hope that she had called Ellersley and that it had been enough to stop Jenny in her tracks. With a bit of luck, Matthew would even be drinking. But perhaps that was hoping for too much.

Vince took a gulp of whisky and stuck a fork into the gluggy pasta.

He would say this, he had done his best. He had pursued all relevant lines of enquiry and followed them to their very end. He had worked harder on this matter than he had worked on anything in his entire professional career, and surely that was something to be proud of.

Now it was in the lap of the gods.

96

Dave's car was so powerful. Sophie wouldn't tell him, but when she hit the main road, she got up to one hundred and sixty-five k's without trying. Lucky it was automatic. It was decades since she had driven a manual, but it was only a couple of years since she last drove an automatic. She could basically remember all of it, although she was a bit random with the blinkers.

It was brilliant being on a solo mission: driving a hotted-up car into town at night to find a drunken lover and rescue him from potentially bad life decisions. It was a nice change, being on the responsible side of the equation. She leaned forward, smiling, to see the dark sky above the headlights. *Can you see this, Dad? Can you see me?*

Finding Matthew's house was easy. She drove down the main street, turned left and circled around a few blocks until she saw the enormous shed. The porch light was on, which Sophie took as a positive sign. She pulled in at the curb and killed the engine. She suddenly felt nervous. What was she thinking, barging into someone else's life like this?

Sophie gave herself a pep talk. It was for Jenny's sake. She had to do it. Now.

She jumped out of the car and marched up the path. She pressed the doorbell. She didn't hear it ring inside, so she got up the courage and knocked as well. The door opened while she was knocking, and she nearly rapped on a man's chest. Actually, more like his stomach. If this was Matthew, he was *insanely* tall.

'Hello?'

Sophie had thought about driving to town, about knocking on the door and getting no answer, about scanning the streets and going to the police – she'd played out all of these scenarios, and they had only gotten better when she inserted Dave's car into the picture. She had even imagined telling Matthew to call Jenny, but she hadn't considered 'hello' or 'goodbye' or 'my name is Sophie Edwards' or anything like that. Now there was this super-tall man – taller than the doorway – saying hello in a calm voice, and Sophie was lost for a response.

'Hiya. Yeah, hi. Umm, are you Matthew?' It was a disappointing opening line.

'Yes.'

He didn't add any extra words, and he didn't look away. Sophie wasn't sure if she had ever met someone so steady and sure.

'Hi, hello. So my name's Sophie . . .'

'Yes. I know.'

Wow. Sophie believed him, because there was no way to disbelieve this person, but how did he know who she was? Maybe he was psychic.

'Right, okay. So . . .' and then she started babbling like an idiot, how Gaylene said he was an alcoholic and he was out of control and Jenny was super upset and could he call and let her know he was all right?

Matthew rubbed his chin thoughtfully, and the hall light shone on him from behind. It was like some sort of halo. Like he was totally wise as well as psychic.

'If Jen's worried, she can call me.' He was so dignified.

'But I called, and you didn't answer.'

'I was out.'

'Oh, right.' It came out sounding sarcastic, but it wasn't.

'I'm here now,' Matthew said.

'You and me both.' What was wrong with her?

Matthew waited politely.

'Brilliant. I mean, great. So . . . I guess I'll go now.' Matthew gave her a half smile and Sophie backed off the porch. She caught the edge of the step and stumbled down onto the grass.

'See you then!' she called out as she fell, as though they'd had a cracking time. He raised a hand, and Sophie waved back. When she was in the car, she put a hand to her chest. Her heart was beating double time. She started the engine and pulled away from the curb, like she knew what she planned to do next, and realised her stomach was gurgling too.

Sophie counted the hours since they'd had lunch. Five. Wow. She pulled over and looked around Dave's car, hunting for cash. It would be nice to buy everyone dinner. Chippy's. That's what she'd get, if they still existed.

The glove box was full of CDs, the console had only mints and Quick-Eze, but when she flipped the visor down, she found a credit card. Bingo. And there was the pin, written on a scrap of paper in the same place. Double bingo. He wasn't totally smart, her big brother, but he was generous. Sophie looked up Chippy's Chinese. Two blocks away. She'd head straight over. She could eat prawn crisps while they got the food together and then she'd take home the good news *and* dinner. The others were going to be so impressed.

97

'Hey, everyone! JEN! Matthew's not drunk and I bought dinner!' Christine was between boards, so she heard the announcement, loud and clear. Sophie carried plastic bags that reeked of deep fry.

'It's Chippy's!' Sophie was delighted with her work.

As far as Christine could remember the food at Chippy's was not really food at all. It was a collection of preservatives and food dye, Chinese style, with hot chips on the side. She wasn't complaining though. She was so hungry she would have eaten Chippy's ten years past its use-by date.

'Dinner, everyone!' Sophie yelled even louder than the bandsaw. Jenny and Dave powered down, and Sophie held up the plastic bags.

'Good news!' She waited for them to take their earmuffs off. 'Matthew's not drunk!' Sophie hadn't moderated her volume when the machines turned off, and the announcement reverberated off the tin walls.

'Whoa!' Sophie lowered her voice a few decibels. She was pulling containers out of the bags. 'Matthew is definitely not drunk. He's super tall though! You didn't tell us, Jen. He must be, like, ten foot.' Sophie started handing out plastic forks and bunches of serviettes. 'I guess we'll just pass the containers around?'

There were no plates or cups. No water to cut through the salt. Sophie had no idea how to cater for a group. Christine reached for the stir-fry chicken. A fork and container was better than nothing.

'Anyway,' Sophie carried on, like it was of no real consequence, 'he said if you're worried about him, you should give him a call.'

Dave had slipped out of the shed while Sophie was distributing the food, and after a few minutes he came back.

'No major prangs then?' He interrupted Sophie's chatter.

'What? Of course not!'

'Who paid for dinner?'

Sophie paused. 'It's on the company card,' she said lightly.

'That'd be my company?'

Sophie ignored Dave's question and turned to Jenny.

'It's all worked out now. Isn't it great? You must feel so much better.'

Sophie was fairly bursting with energy, and no wonder. Between her time at the house that afternoon and the return trip to Albury she had enjoyed a four-hour break. Christine had planed six planks during this time. Both sides. Dave had resawn logs, Christine couldn't say how many, and Jenny had sanded the two widest planks, with Dave's help.

For some time, Jenny was sanding one side of a plank, over and over. When Dave noticed what was happening, he signalled to Jenny to switch off. He inspected the sander and put in a fresh piece of paper. Jenny started from the beginning of the board again and Dave went back to the bandsaw. After each cut, he made sure to go over to change the paper, or flip the board, or put the next one on the sawhorses for her. He patted Jenny on the shoulder once or twice, much gentler than before. But she didn't acknowledge him. Each time she'd start the motor, put her head down and ploughed on with the job.

They were all tired. Christine was exhausted. She would never refer to a class at the gym as a 'workout' again.

'What have you guys been doing?' Sophie asked, looking around with interest.

'Work,' Dave said and kept on eating.

'How about you, Jen? What have you been up to?'

Jenny was pushing a sweet and sour prawn around her container with a plastic fork. Her eyes were fixed on the prawn, as it swivelled back and forth. She didn't respond to Sophie. Dave cut across the conversation and asked Jenny a question of his own.

'Lid next?'

Jenny looked up and nodded.

'Tongue and groove?'

Jenny nodded again. Christine wasn't sure what Dave was talking about, but it sounded borderline pornographic.

'Chris can help you,' Dave said. 'I'll need Sophie at the bandsaw.' Jenny looked relieved. Christine felt relieved. Holding planks, she could do. Maybe that was all she could do at this stage. Dave may have saved her from a limb-threatening injury, taking her away from the power plane.

98

'You should give him a call.'

Sophie said it like it was the easiest thing in the world. As though it was an everyday occurrence, picking up the telephone. But she and Matthew didn't talk on the phone. They didn't call each other. They each knew the other's schedule, and they met, every day, at one point or another.

When they first started seeing each other, they finished each meeting by making a plan for the next. They set a time and a place, and they were both reliable so they always met. They had no need for a telephone. Not until yesterday when Jenny phoned him. And look how that worked out. She should have driven to Albury instead. Then maybe none of this would have happened. He wouldn't have suggested coming to Ellersley and she wouldn't have stopped him and there would be no rift, no heartache.

Now that Jenny knew Matthew was sober, she could let go of her worries about his safety. But she still felt sick to her stomach at the thought of what she had done. There was no way she was calling him on the telephone. Not for anything.

Besides, she and Chris had to finish gluing the lid, and there was so much work to do before they went to bed. She would put her head down and get on with the build. It was the task in front of her now. It was the only way.

99

It was after midnight when Dave switched off the power plane. He stretched his neck from side to side and winced. Fuck, he was sore. And tired. Absolutely rooted. It had been a long time since he'd done a seventeen-hour day on the tools.

About two minutes later, Chris finished the six-inch she was sanding and powered down. Sophie's orbital sander was revving into the night, but then her sandpaper tore, and she stopped too. Jenny was head down with her earmuffs on, putting the final touches on her perfect clamping job. For the first time in what felt like decades there was silence in the shed.

Chris pulled all her safety kit off and stood up too fast. She staggered and fell against Jenny's workbench. Jenny looked up, irritated, but then she saw Chris keeling over. They all reached out as if to grab her, but she was on her arse in the sawdust before anyone got close enough. At least it was a soft surface.

Chris shook her head and opened her eyes.

'I think I'm done,' she said. She looked it. Dave wasn't sure if she'd be able to stand up on her own, so he held out a hand.

'Here, mate,' he said, and reefed her to her feet. 'I'll take you home.'

Chris put an arm around his shoulder and slumped against him. She waved at the shed in general and called out, 'Bye!' and Dave took her down to the house.

He took her to her bedroom and put her to bed. Like he did with his kids. Pulled the covers back. Took her shoes off. He didn't tuck her in, though. That would have been weird. He got a six-pack from the fridge and walked back to the shed.

It was strange, the quiet, now they'd hauled up. There was no noise at all. No traffic. No planes. No sirens blaring in the night.

He stood still and listened and all he could hear was a single frog chugging away, down at the creek. Then Sophie laughed, and he got moving again.

'Rightio, girls, refreshment time.' Dave put the six-pack on a sawhorse and pulled out a couple of cans. Sophie looked thirsty as all get out, but Jenny just looked tired. He held one up and raised his eyebrows, and to his surprise she accepted it.

'Thanks, Dave.'

'No worries. Any time.' He wasn't sure if he was doing the right or wrong thing as he handed it over – what with Matthew's problem and all – but on balance it was probably right. It was thirsty work, building a coffin.

They cracked their cans open, and even the fizzing sound was refreshing. They held up a cheers then took a swig and Dave could not remember a drink tasting so good.

100

It was early winter, when Helena died. The morning was crisp and clear. Tom went out first thing to take the dogs for a run and the water in their bowls was frozen. A half-inch layer of ice, which he shattered with a stone. He whistled softly to the dogs to come behind, and a figure caught his eye, climbing over the gate.

'Dad. Dad!' She was trying to whisper loudly. Hard thing to do, but Sophie knew she was meant to keep quiet for her mum.

'Can I come?'

Tom looked her over. She was still in her PJs, but she had gumboots on.

'If you like.'

Sophie was five or six by then, and she was happy just to be invited along.

'Where are we going?'

'Taking the dogs, that's all.'

'Hurrah! Hey, Dad, how about the frost? Did you see it on the barbed wire? It's like little swords. Hyah!'

He couldn't stop her once she started talking, but it was a pleasure to let her go. She'd walk for a bit, then run to catch up, then do a few skips.

They went out for a mile or so, along the track. They turned around when they hit the creek. They couldn't have been gone much more than an hour. Helena was asleep when Tom left. Breathing gently, he was sure of it. When they got back, he tapped on the door and she didn't answer. He walked over and touched her cheek, but she didn't move. She was gone.

Sophie slipped into the room behind him and he picked her up. She leaned against him as he sat by Helena, holding her hand.

There was a big funeral. The older three spoke. They did well. Even Jenny got up. Her voice was soft, but the congregation went silent, so they could hear her all right.

The singing surprised him. It was a bigger sound than he expected. The whole community turns out for a young person's burial. Charles Briggs was there, of course. Vince Barton too, now he thought of it. Everyone came. Except for Jock.

Dave went straight back to Wagga, but the girls stayed a few days. When they packed up Tom was relieved to see them go. Just him and Sophie. That's all he wanted. And he got it too. Ten years of just him and Sophie.

He should have sent her to Sydney when she was ready for high school. He'd already seen the result of sending his kids to Coorong High. Helena was gone, so he had no excuse. But he couldn't do it. Life without Sophie didn't bear thinking about.

At sixteen though, Sophie was busting to get out of Coorong. Tom knew he had to let her go. He'd held her back long enough. London was as good as boarding school, surely. And all that money he'd saved in fees – it was the right thing, to give her a head start.

101

Friday dawned hot and dry, like every other day, but even more parched.

Jenny was at the shed by sunrise. She watched the sun crack open the horizon and wondered why the others weren't up. Maybe they didn't care so much about the coffin, or their inheritance. Or maybe they were tired.

Jenny could never lie in when she had a coffin on the go. Once it was finished, she could sleep all she liked, but mid-build was not the time to rest. Besides, they were in the best part. Plans made, most of the timber prepared and a clear path of work ahead.

She turned to survey the worksite. The sunlight slanted across the ground, cutting a diagonal line to the back corner. The whole shed was carpeted with sawdust: benches, tools, sawhorses and the boards lying on them. It was strangely beautiful; the fallen debris, softening all the sharp edges. The knee-high pile of shavings by the bandsaw would have to go, though. It was an accident waiting to happen.

The sun had not yet reached the back bench, where the lid was firmly clamped. Jenny flicked the light switch and went over to scrutinise her work. Four planks fitted together with three tongue and groove joins, and five hours in the clamps already. She ran a hand over the surface and then squatted down to check the line of the timber. No bowing, no bends. And they'd been sparing with the glue, so there was minimal mess. Once she'd done the final sanding it would come up beautifully.

Jenny would have liked to start with this, but she was still the boss of the project, as far as she knew, so first she had to plan the next steps for the others. It wouldn't hurt to leave the clamps on for another hour or two, then hopefully she would be able to come back to the lid and give it the treatment it deserved.

A certain amount of complexity was creeping into the work now. Measuring, cutting, gluing, and not long after that, construction. Her instructions would have to be clear. Perhaps they should be illustrated, too. Jenny reached into the bottom of her toolbox and pulled out a ruler, builder's pencil and a pad of graph paper. She retrieved the scrap of paper with dimensions and angles jotted on it from her dress pocket and began to rule up a coffin diagram.

It was fortunate the others weren't up, as it turned out. A diagram for beginners takes time. And concentration. They would only have been in the way.

As Jenny measured and marked the lines, she kept her focus narrow. It was essential for this kind of work. One thing at a time. It meant she couldn't think of Matthew. He might be hovering around the edges of her drawing, but she had to pretend he wasn't there.

102

When Christine arrived at the shed Jenny was already hard at work. She was operating some sort of mini leaf blower, and the work area looked like a before and after advertisement. Behind Jenny the surfaces were clean, ahead of her were dunes of sawdust, which were changing shape with the prevailing wind.

'Jenny! JENNIFER!' Christine waved her arms until Jenny noticed she was there.

'Oh. Hey, Chris.'

'Can I have a turn?'

Jenny laughed. Christine had planned to do what she was told this morning, but it looked like such an excellent appliance, she didn't want to miss out.

'Sure,' Jenny said.

She set Christine up with earmuffs, gave a few instructions and Christine was on her way. Three speeds. A flexible nozzle. Long and short range. This was a tool Christine needed in her life.

In the meantime, Jenny was moving quickly behind her, organising tools, shifting timber, setting up the sawhorses. By the time Christine had blown the sawdust into one enormous pile in the corner of the shed, Jenny had the workshop ready for the day ahead.

Dave presented at this point; he looked grumpy again. Christine felt like putting the blower on full throttle and blasting him out of there before he brought the mood down, but Jenny had other plans.

'Hey, Dave.'

Jenny said it like she was pleased to see him.

'Hey.'

Dave said it like she was lucky he came. Chris reached for the blower.

'I've drawn a plan,' Jenny said.

She showed them a bit of paper. There was a diagram of the coffin, with measurements clearly marked. A list of the timber they still had to cut. Approximate times to get the tasks done. It was a level of organisation to warm a woman's heart, and Christine was utterly absorbed.

Dave, on the other hand, was being an arrogant jerk. He was behaving as though he knew it all and Jenny was trying his patience.

'Yeah, rightio, Jen. I think I can manage that.'

He was rushing her, which he knew she hated. Jenny became flustered, but she stood up straighter and continued her instructions.

'Got it. Ribs and rails,' Dave said. He picked up a board and went over to the bandsaw, pretending he couldn't hear what Jenny was saying.

'Two-inch. Dave? Two-inch width,' Jenny called after him. He gave a thumbs up which was no communication at all – he might have heard Jenny, or he might not.

'Will I give him a smack over the head?' Christine asked. She was more than ready to do so. She could use the butt end of the blower. Or maybe just the nozzle.

'No. It's only ribs. Any idiot can cut ribs and rails.'

Jenny was surveying the shed, looking for something. Christine knew what it was. 'Sophie?' she asked.

Jenny was blank. 'What?'

'Sophie hasn't arrived yet. Will I get her?' Christine was ready to do this too. Sophie needed a wake-up call. She was clueless, thoughtless and slack. But Jenny's mind was somewhere else.

'What? No. We need to start sanding. Aha!' Jenny found an extension cord and shook the sawdust off. She plugged the orbital sander in and passed it to Christine. Christine sighed. She couldn't help it. The pile of wood was so big, and her arms were suddenly tired.

Jenny heard the sigh. 'Chris?' She reached over and gave Christine's arm a squeeze.

'I'm here. With you.'

Christine nodded. She thought she might cry.

'Chris?' Jenny's hand was still attached to Christine's arm. Perhaps she didn't know how to take it back. Physical contact was not Jenny's usual communication style.

'Sophie will get here soon enough.' Jenny bent down to find the other extension cord. She plugged in her orbital sander, put on earmuffs, and yelled over the motor. 'And Dave's being a dick, but there's nothing we can do about that.'

Christine laughed. It felt like Jenny had plugged a power cord into *her*. She reached for the sander, re-energised. Jenny was still in charge.

Christine had no idea when Sophie would show her face, or whether Dave would screw up the whole project. But it didn't matter. It wasn't her job to know. Jenny had told her to sand boards, and that was exactly what she would do.

103

Sophie pushed the covers off and inspected her legs in the morning light. Stubble. Just as she suspected. She flipped her phone over. Eight fifty-eight. Which made it thirty-six hours since she last saw Ben Taylor, and he still hadn't contacted her. Hadn't called, hadn't dropped by, even though he lived next door. As close as next door gets at Ellersley anyway.

She wandered over to the windowsill and leaned her back against the glass. Where had he been since Wednesday? What was so important that it prevented him from getting in touch? The receptionist duties couldn't be that onerous.

Did she have to wait until the cattle sale tomorrow? Or could she call him today? Maybe she could drop by Barton & Sons and see what he was doing tonight.

Sophie stretched a foot out to grab yesterday's work singlet from the floor. She gave it a sniff. Gross. It was covered in dirt and grease and sawdust, which was no surprise, given the insane amount of work she had done. And not just her, either. They could have gone on some kind of renovation show for building coffins.

Anyway, there couldn't be much more to do. A couple of tongue joins, a few more cuts and maybe some nails to hold it together – how long could it take? Sophie dropped the singlet to the floor and went for a crumpled dress. It was a slippery fabric and harder to grip between her toes, so she caught it by a strap and pulled it across the carpet. She held it up, inspecting for stains. If she was going to drop in on Ben, she had to look fabulous. Sophie imagined herself opening the door in her cute dress, and Ben blushing, and her saying, 'Hiya' . . . and then she stopped.

Anywhere else in the world, that is exactly what she would have done. But Coorong was different. If she did go, by morning tea everyone in town would know she'd visited Barton & Sons. By lunchtime they would know why she had visited, and by afternoon tea they would be tut-tutting over their grocery shopping that Sophie Edwards had come home to bury her father and all she could think about was getting laid. Which wouldn't bother her, normally, but if she was going to spend the rest of her life here, she didn't want to start off on the wrong foot.

She lifted her arm to check her armpit. Stubble again. The bandsaw started and she turned in the direction of the shed. The other guys were all over it. Maybe they didn't need her help. She should get on with more urgent tasks. Like shaving. And hair-washing. She hadn't even *started* to plan an outfit for the cattle sales. That was going to take a whole lot of time and brain power.

The coffin would get built, with or without her help. She'd take them up some morning tea to cheer them along. As soon as she'd shaved her legs and had a shower. And done the tanning lotion. Her nails could wait.

104

Vince woke in better shape than he might have. He showered, dressed, made himself a coffee and walked the six hundred metres to Barton & Sons. He was there just after nine, which was fortunate, as Ben had taken it upon himself to make a nine-thirty appointment for David Edwards. Ben said David had called yesterday afternoon, wanting to talk about something 'semi-urgent'.

Vince was in reasonable shape, but he was feeling nervous. David Edwards was a big man. At their most recent meeting he had referred to Vince's 'shiny balls' and threatened, by implication, to remove them from his 'runty body'. This was both offensive and terrifying. It was also a misrepresentation of anatomical fact. The human scrotum was far from shiny, unless it was under undue strain. At the time, however, Vince made the decision not to challenge David on this point.

By nine twenty-five Vince had worked himself into something of an anxious sweat. His shirt clung to him like wet washing, and his face was prickly hot. He kept his jacket on to hide the sweat, but there was nothing to be done about his face.

Vince shifted items on the desk while he waited. The pen holder; the phone; the post-it notes; the Edwards file. He was considering moving the desk a few centimetres to the left when he heard the front door scrape open, and Ben showed David in.

He seemed bigger, if anything, in the confines of the office. Vince stayed behind the desk, cautiously reaching into the top drawer to switch on his dictaphone. He wasn't sure how to commence proceedings. He certainly didn't want to provoke David in any way. Then, before Vince had said hello, David reached a hand across the desk.

'Vince.' He smiled ruefully and gave a nod. Vince shook hands cautiously.

'Thanks for your time this morning, Vince. I know you're a busy man.' His tone was conciliatory. Polite. It was something of a turnaround and Vince remained wary.

'Heat's bad. Terrible time of year, isn't it?'

Vince agreed. The heat was, indeed, bad.

'Lost my temper yesterday. Sorry, Vince.' David half-smiled and shook his head in regret. Vince waited.

'No hard feelings though?'

Vince's feelings were not hard, per se, but they were not soft either.

He could have spent some time exploring the subject, but emotional honesty was not highly valued in Coorong.

'No, no, David, of course not.'

He gestured to the client chair. When David had taken a seat Vince sat down too, propping his elbows apart on the desk to increase the airflow to his armpits.

'About this will, Vince,' David began, 'I've got a few questions.'

105

Vince looked shocking. Dave was feeling rough, but Vince looked like a man about to have a cardiac arrest. It occurred to Dave that it might simplify matters if Vince died. Or would it complicate things? In any case, he needed Vince to explain the will first.

Dave apologised straight up – even though he wasn't the man trespassing – then they got down to business.

'I've got a few questions,' he said, and Vince nodded seriously.

'Actually, it boils down to one question. How soon can we get the inheritance?'

Vince didn't answer straight away, so Dave jumped in.

'Provided we build the coffin, of course.' He winked at Vince, as though they were in the game together.

'Hmm, are you hoping to finish it?' Vince asked casually. He wasn't a great actor.

'Sure,' Dave said. 'The girls are at it right now. They'll probably have it done by the time I get back.'

Dave had no idea if they'd get it done, but Vince didn't need to know about the coffin. Five thirty was soon enough. Right now, it was Dave who needed information. And, like it or not, Vince was his source. Dave was pretty sure there was a rule that lawyers had to tell the truth. He bloody hoped so.

'Just between you and me, Vince, I need the money.'

'I see,' Vince said, and then started the textbook spiel. 'The distribution of the bank account funds will be expedited relatively promptly –'

David interrupted. 'Steady on with the legal jargon, Vince. Just say it like it is.'

'My apologies. In simple terms, the money in the bank account will be available soon.'

'The deposit? Fifty grand each? It's not enough.' Dave realised he was shouting and lowered his voice. 'I'm talking hundreds of k's here.'

'What do you know about probate?' Vince asked.

Lawyers had a seriously annoying way of communicating. No such thing as a simple answer. Just big words and more questions.

'What?'

'Probate.'

'Nothing. Fuck, nothing.'

'Well, David, probate is the process by which the court can ensure a will is legal and the deceased's wishes will be upheld.'

Dave was listening hard, and he was fairly sure he understood at least eighty per cent of what Vince was saying.

'Right. Sure. Probate. What's your point?'

'Probate takes time.'

'How much?'

'Months.'

'*Months?*' Sharon had been clear on this point. He had to fix it now. Months was not going to cut it.

'It's a process. One must publish a notice, apply, wait for the courts to respond, deal with requisitions if necessary and so on and so forth. Until probate is granted all assets are frozen.'

Dave leaned forward and started cracking his fingers, one by one.

'What about the shares?'

'The shares are also assets.'

'You're fucking joking.' Dave's fist hit the desk and Vince flinched. 'Sorry, Vince, sorry. Not your fault. Just a bit of a shock.' He could not afford to upset Vince now.

'Have you read the will, David?'

'Of course.' Dave wiped his palms on his pants and tried to keep his temper under control. 'The general gist anyway. Everything divided four ways etc.'

Vince was looking at him closely. Before he spoke again, he rolled his chair back. Out of arm's reach, was Dave's guess.

'Did you read about the condition of sale? Or "non-sale" as the case may be.'

'No.' It didn't sound good.

'Perhaps I should explain it to you?'

Dave looked up at the wall clock: 10 am. He had to get back to the coffin, but he had to hear this more.

'It applies to the shares as well, I'm afraid.'

'Do your worst,' Dave said.

He should have said something else.

106

Christine switched off her sander to give her arms a break at 8 am. Then at nine and again at nine thirty. And she'd done it every fifteen minutes since then. They were so tired. It was only Christine and Jenny in the shed now. Dave had absented himself at nine, and Sophie hadn't shown up, though it was past ten o'clock.

Christine rolled her shoulders and stretched her neck. Out of the corner of her eye she spied a girl coming across the paddock in a skimpy dress. Sophie. She was carrying a picnic basket with a checked cloth. Like she lived in a home and country magazine. Probably on the front cover.

'Surprise!' she said when she arrived. She whipped the tablecloth off to show her wares. Jenny didn't respond, so Sophie went over and tapped her on the shoulder and shouted even louder.

'Surprise!' She indicated the basket. 'I brought you some refreshments.'

Jenny looked as tired as Christine felt, and about as impressed with Sophie too.

'Where have you been?'

Jenny's tone was strict, and Christine's ears pricked up.

'It's the final day, and you arrive in some sort of party dress at . . .' She pulled a men's watch from her dress pocket. 'Ten twenty-three am?'

Nobody except Christine ever pulled Sophie into line. And Jenny had never pulled anyone into line, as far as Christine could recall.

'Where's Dave?' Sophie was looking around the shed, hoping for a diversion. But Jenny wasn't having it.

'Dave is not the issue. You need to go home, get your work clothes on and come straight back.'

'I thought we were mostly done,' Sophie said, a dimpled smile at the ready.

'You thought wrong.' Jenny didn't smile, and she didn't take her eyes off Sophie until she had dropped the basket, walked out of the shed and was halfway across the paddock. Christine felt like cheering. As soon as Sophie was through the hedge she did.

'Hooray!' She was clapping and laughing, and Jenny looked bewildered. Christine took the picnic basket and reached in to see what was there.

'Outstanding, Jen. Best thing I've seen since – I don't know when.' Christine was shaking her head, still laughing. 'Honestly. Where did that come from?' She handed Jenny a cup of cold water and clinked cheers.

'Here's to you, Jen, a woman full of surprises.'

'You can talk, nudist lady,' Jenny said, as Christine was taking a gulp. Christine sprayed a mouthful of water at her. Jenny looked into her cup, as though considering, and then chucked the contents at Christine. They both dived for the basket and pulled out water bottles, laughing; spraying and splashing water over each other. Jenny was tipping a bottle over Christine's head and Christine was trying to grab Jenny around the waist when Dave arrived.

'What the hell?' he shouted, even though he was only a metre away. He seemed cranky. Christine stood up and straightened her shirt, patting down the front.

'I leave you girls for an hour and this is what you do?' He certainly was angry. Christine was about to apologise – it had been irresponsible of them – but Jenny spoke first.

'Why did you leave us?' Her voice was soft, but the tone was downright dangerous. Christine was thrilled.

'What?' Dave was irritated.

'Why did you leave us?'

'That's my business, isn't it?' He was still cranky, but less certain now.

'Maybe.' Jenny was standing tall. Soaking wet, with her hair slicked back and her hands on her hips. There was no apology in her anywhere.

'You left us to do this hard, physical work. On our own.'

Christine was standing still, water droplets trickling down the back of her neck, barely breathing.

'What we did, after you left, is *none* of your business.'

Unlike Sophie, Dave knew when he'd lost a battle.

'Fair enough,' he said. And shrugged. Like it was a menstrual problem, not him.

'What's fair enough?' Sophie arrived in her 'work' clothes and jumped into the conversation.

Jenny ignored the question. She waited until they were all paying attention.

'We can finish it in time,' she said. 'You know that, don't you?'

Sophie and Dave nodded enthusiastically.

'But only if we are on it, all four of us, from now until five thirty.'

Sophie and Dave continued to nod.

'No fights, no leaving the shed on personal business, everyone does what they're told.'

Sophie and Dave were still nodding, but less enthusiastically.

'Right,' Jenny said. 'We're on.'

Christine was the only one who hadn't been nodding. She didn't disagree with the plan. Her heart and mind were absolutely on board. It was her arms that were the problem. Christine didn't think they would do what they were told. They were done.

107

Jenny pulled the coffin plan out of her pocket and sized up her labour force.

'Sophie, you're on sanding.'

'Again?' Sophie hung her head tragically.

'Dave, you're on –' Jenny was about to send Dave to the bandsaw, but he was there before she finished the sentence. Which left Chris. Jenny smiled at her.

'How about we build the floor?'

Christine looked visibly relieved. 'Really? No planing? Sanding?'

'Neither.'

Jenny led Christine to the router.

'Tongue and groove joints,' Jenny said. 'I need you to hold the planks steady while I push them through.'

'Sure,' Christine said. 'Holding planks is what I do best.'

Jenny handed over the safety gear and turned the router on. She hadn't lied to them. There was still time to finish the coffin. But it was tight. There was no room for chit-chat.

When the first tongue was cut, Jenny paused to check on the other two. Sophie was sanding with remarkable efficiency and minimal fuss. Dave, on the other hand, was working at a furious pace. He was cutting two-inch battens for the ribs and rails, and from where Jenny stood, the quality of his work looked sub-standard at best. Also, at the rate he was ripping through the boards he was at risk of shredding their entire collection of timber.

'Dave! Slow down.' Jenny signalled from the end of the board rocketing through the bandsaw, but Dave wasn't looking. Once it was through, she hit the STOP button. The bandsaw stopped, so Dave had to as well. He looked up, irritated.

'What?'

'We only need three boards.'

'You'll need more than that. Six, at least.'

'Three.' Jenny held firm. 'We need three.' She pulled the diagram from her pocket and held it out. 'Twelve side ribs, four for the lid and four bottom rails. That's it.'

Dave glanced at the diagram and flicked it back.

'Won't hurt to have a couple more.'

'It will.' Jenny folded the paper carefully and put it in her pocket. 'We don't have enough timber to overshoot.'

Dave looked down at the cut lengths.

'Fine,' he said sulkily. 'One more.' He started the bandsaw and Jenny walked towards the router.

'Jen? Jen!' Sophie was holding up the orbital sander. 'My sandpaper's busted.' The torn paper was flapping loosely, and Jenny walked over to Sophie, trying to be patient. She was showing Sophie how to replace the paper when Chris came over and tapped her on the shoulder.

'Do you want me to do something else?'

Sophie spoke up immediately. 'She can help with the sanding!'

But Christine was more tired than she looked. She wouldn't have enough muscle power to control an orbital sander. Jenny knew that. Sophie didn't. Jenny held her lips tightly together as she locked the sandpaper in place.

'Chris stays with me.'

Sophie groaned, put her earmuffs on and switched on the sander just as Dave turned the bandsaw off.

'Rightio, Jen. I'm done. I've cut *just* enough.'

Jenny held her tongue. She bit it hard, but she didn't bite at Dave's sarcasm so that was probably the best she could hope for. Dave was in a sulk, waiting for his next instructions. He clearly believed he should be somewhere else, doing more important things than building his father's coffin. Sophie was sanding again, but she was resentful too. And Christine was hanging around uncertainly, waiting for Jenny, because she couldn't do the job on her own.

Thirty minutes before, Jenny had been drenching wet and laughing. Now she was caked in dirt and sawdust and unable to get on with her work because of the constant interruptions.

'*It's not that hard!*' she felt like yelling at her siblings.

'*I've shown you the diagram. I've taught you how to use the tools. You know what needs to be done. Just do it!*'

But she could see it wasn't possible. They didn't know what to do. If she left them to it there would be a pile of two-inch battens that reached to the ceiling, orbital sanders with ripped paper, and measuring and cutting done on the wrong boards in the wrong places.

It suddenly occurred to Jenny that parenting must be like this. If she had children, every day would be full of these interruptions. Silly arguments. Comparisons and complaints. If today was anything to go by, parenting would be an appalling job. Perhaps that's why their mother went away so often. Maybe it was too hard. Maybe she wasn't equipped for the role.

Jenny had spent most of her life wishing it had gone another direction, but what had she been hoping for? A part-time job in a role she was not trained to do? And if her wish had been granted, what would she have missed?

Silence.

Solitude. Which was not the same thing.

The sound of waiting. The chime of a church bell.

A child lost, before they were born, or after, and the women and men who bore the loss.

And Matthew.

If her life had gone according to plan she –

'Jen? What next?'

Jenny hauled herself back to the present. She pulled the plan from her pocket for the umpteenth time.

'Measuring.' She showed Dave. 'Sides and ends. Don't cut until I've seen the mark-up.'

The floor. That's what she was doing. Constructing a coffin floor.

108

It took Tom two years to realise what was happening.

Sophie rang every couple of months, and it was the highlight of his day. Of his week, as a matter of fact, and sometimes his month, too. She was random in her timing, and Tom found himself answering the phone more often than he had any other time in his life.

She had so much to tell him. She was travelling all over the place – France, Germany, Italy – and she planned to go to Holland too, to find her cousins. Sometime.

It took a few months to settle down in London. She found a share house and got herself a job at the local pub. She'd work at the pub until she found her feet, she told him. When she worked out what she really wanted to do she'd give it up. Tom knew she would, too. She was a hair's breadth away from something to be proud of, he was sure of it.

Towards the end of her fourth month Sophie mentioned the high rent and low wages. Tom didn't think twice about helping with the bills. Bloody expensive, a place like London. Sophie would have her work cut out for her, just keeping up.

A few months went by before her next call. She'd been seeing some bloke. Went to Iceland with him. Had a fabulous time, but they broke up. She was in London again, and she needed to pay the bond on a new place. She'd be right when she started back at the pub.

Two years. What a bloody idiot. Depositing cash into her account and waiting by the phone, like an anxious boyfriend, for her to call and tell him she'd got it. She never did though. Instead, she'd call a couple of months down the track when she'd decided on a new life plan. Consulting this or managing that or marketing, God help him. Bloody advertising. He didn't need to get upset, though. She never signed up for anything.

By chance, Sophie rang one day after Tom had been to collect the mail. He was standing in the porch, turning over a letter addressed to Jock. It was an old boys' thing from King's – asking for money, no doubt. Tom snorted. He was about to throw it in the bin when the phone rang. That's what it took to make him realise. A letter in his hand, about money and Jock, and Sophie at the end of the line. She didn't have much to tell him. A new bloke she'd broken up with; a holiday in Slovenia; a job at the pub that didn't pay enough. And a life plan that needed a boost to get started. Tom looked at the letter and listened to Sophie, and it hit him. Right in the gut.

'How much do you need?' he said.

'Two hundred. I think that'll be enough. You'd better make it two fifty. Pounds though, Dad. Not Aussie dollars. Over here they're not worth much.'

109

'*Don't cut until I've seen the mark-up.*' Jenny had to be joking. As if he didn't know how to operate a tape measure. To make matters worse she sent Chris over to help him. Maybe Chris was meant to supervise him, or maybe he was meant to babysit her. Dave didn't know, but she was getting in his way. And talking. Fuck. She wouldn't stop.

'Where have you been?' She was messing with the tools, moving them out of his reach. She had decided to tidy up.

'Dave?'

'Town.' Dave was measuring the short side pieces. Jenny's instructions were very specific. Sixty-three-centimetre lengths of a six-inch board. Three for each side. Then he was onto the long. One hundred and forty-three centimetres each. The woman had to have OCD.

'What for?' Chris checked his nail scratch. Like she'd know if it was below par.

'None of your business.'

'An appointment?'

Dave shook his head grimly, but she wasn't put off.

'Who with?'

Dave lined up the tape measure and scratched another nail mark into the timber, deeper this time.

'Mr Barton?'

Dave fixed his eyes on the board.

'He's the only option, really. Isn't he?'

Chris was like a terrier with a rag doll when she started an inquisition. But Dave wasn't in the mood to be torn apart.

'Fuck, mate, lay off!' he exploded, and Chris stepped back.

'I was just asking,' she said, holding her hands up, 'no need to get aggressive.'

Dave clenched his fists and let them loose again. She had no idea. None.

'You want to know?' he asked.

'Yes. Obviously. Why else would I ask?'

'You really want to know?'

Chris nodded cheerfully. 'Yep.' She was out of arm's reach now, not so worried about his 'aggression'.

'Fine,' Dave said.

Chris sat on a board and waited.

'Yes, I had an appointment. Yes, I saw Vince. Yes, about the will.' Dave tapped a ruler on the board to emphasise each 'yes', but when he got to the main point, he lost momentum.

'I need money.'

He left a pause.

'I can't get it.'

Dave chucked the ruler, and it skidded in the dirt.

'That's it. End of story. For fuck's sake, Chris, let it go.'

He picked up a pencil and pulled the tape measure out. Now he'd said it aloud, finishing the coffin seemed more futile than ever. But what else was he going to do? It's not like he had a better option.

'How much?'

'What?' Dave wasn't sure he'd heard right.

'How much money?'

Unbelievable. Fucking unbelievable. Dave was about to shut her off, but something about her matter-of-fact approach made him pause.

'Six point three million,' Dave said. Chris didn't respond immediately, so he continued.

'Five hundred thousand by the end of the week.'

'Well, that's all right,' Chris said. As though they were talking about lunch money for the kids.

'Rightio. Good on you, Chris, glad to know you're cashed up. I'm not.'

'For goodness' sake, it's a financial problem. Get advice.'

'You think I haven't tried? I've spent the morning sucking up to Vince Barton!'

'Did he help?'

'No. He was all about "probate", and "condition of sale", and property and shares all tied up and blah, blah, blah.'

'Talk to an accountant.'

'I did.' He wasn't a complete idiot.

'Why don't you get a loan?'

Dave snorted. 'What do you think the six mil is? With that kind of debt, who the fuck is going to lend me another five hundred k?'

'I might.'

Dave did a double take. Chris looked serious.

'You?'

'Yes. Me. Why not?'

Dave could think of a few reasons. Such as: forty-eight hours ago, she was planning to be a nudist. Twenty-four hours ago, she was totally off her face. And even if she was sober and wearing clothes now, Dave was not at all sure she was in her right mind.

Fuck, though. He didn't want to say the wrong thing. It was only a matter of minutes before this hope disintegrated like the others, but he didn't want to be the one who destroyed it.

Dave flicked the safety lock on the tape measure by accident. It retracted and snapped at his fingers, and he jumped. He pulled it out again, locked it, and bent over to measure the final cut.

He didn't answer Chris's question, but in his mind, over and over, he was praying. 'Please. Please. Please let this be real.'

110

Sand boards, sand sides, sand head, sand toe – how much sanding could a coffin need?

More than a person could possibly imagine, was the answer. Sophie had foolishly imagined that sanding every piece of wood on both sides would be enough, but Jenny set her straight.

'No less than 120 grit for the body of the coffin, and no less than 150 for the lid. You know as well as I do what the will says.'

Obviously Sophie did not know what the sanding instructions in the will were. What normal person would? Besides, she had other things on her mind.

Jenny was inspecting the pile of sanded planks, running her hand over the surface of one, and grimacing as though there were splinters poking into her skin. Which there weren't. Sophie knew this because she had sanded *all* of those boards on *both* sides, and they were definitely smoother than the surface of the bar at a decent pub. They had to be good enough for a coffin.

'Oh, come on, Jen! You can't be serious.'

'Dead serious. It's the law, Sophie.' Jenny's face was absolutely straight, even though her comment was a bit funny. In light of the coffin work obviously.

'It's going to take years!' Sophie felt like stamping her foot, so she did. It was very satisfying. 'I can't do any more.' She considered throwing herself on the wood pile but decided against it.

'You can,' Jenny said, 'and you will.'

There was nothing to be done.

Sophie hung her head and followed Jenny to the toolbox.

She took the sandpaper and sat on a sawhorse to change it. The pile of wood she had to sand was *enormous*. Sophie thought she might keel over with exhaustion before she got through it. She would probably need a hospital admission to recover. Most likely in intensive care.

It was thirty-eight hours since she'd seen Ben Taylor and he still hadn't called. If he had come by, she would have had an excuse to get out of the sanding. But he hadn't. Her arms were very close to being dead.

Fine. If Ben Taylor wasn't going to come by, she would put on her safety goggles and earmuffs and keep on sanding planks until her arms fell off and it would be all his fault. He had better remember the cattle sales or Sophie would clout him around the ears with her shoulders. It would be difficult, but if she had no arms, what else could she do?

111

Vince watched David Edwards leave the office and felt almost sympathetic. Almost.

David was highly distressed about his financial affairs. He did not, however, appear to be concerned about the completion of the coffin.

'The girls are at it right now,' he said. And even worse, 'They'll probably have it done by the time I get back.'

His tone was confident. There was no hesitation. And no apparent anxiety regarding his sisters' wellbeing. Which gave Vince considerable anxiety. It also gave him heartburn. He searched his desk drawer, found two chalky tablets and started chewing.

What could he do? What weapons did he have left?

Not many. Maybe none. He stood up, removed his jacket, and paced the room in his wet shirt.

When all of this was finished – the coffin completed, the funeral conducted, probate finally granted – what would be left for Vince Barton? What was he going to do in this bigoted, back-block town? Return to life as normal?

Vince loosened the knot in his tie and pulled at his collar. He was finding it difficult to breathe.

Forty years, he'd been in this town. Forty years of living with a made-up name, a limping legal practice, and a permanent apology in his mouth.

Why should he keep on with it? Tom Edwards had moved on. By dying, granted, but he'd gone all the same. Why should Vince stick around?

Vince paused to lean on the desk, puffing a little from his exertion. The carpet squares at his feet were worn, and there were various stains of indeterminate nature ground into the grey synthetic pile. He lifted his gaze, but the situation at eye level was not much better. The bookshelf was shrouded in dust. The kettle and one dirty mug sat forlornly on the back cupboard. Vacated spider webs hung limply from the window frame. A stale, sweaty odour permeated the room. Vince sniffed his armpits, but they were not the source. Had it always smelled like this?

Why was he spending his life in this dark and dreary chamber?

Whatever reasons Vince had relied on in the past deserted him now. He could think of nothing in Coorong worth staying for. Nothing. He straightened up slowly.

Niente più scuse, Vincenzo. È tempo!

It was time. Time to leave Coorong.

Time to find a better life.

112

No wonder Dave was in debt. Christine had just offered him five hundred thousand dollars and he'd barely responded. Apart from the doubtful 'You?' he hadn't said a word. Instead, he dropped his head down and recommenced measuring, as though the conversation hadn't happened.

Christine decided to start measuring too. She was hardly going to pursue the matter. She had made the offer; it was up to him to respond. In the meantime, she would do the work Jenny had instructed her to do. She was on the 'headboard', and she was enjoying herself. Forty centimetres was a nice, manageable length and she'd easily get three from a single plank. She was doing the toe boards next. She'd be happy to keep measuring until the end of the day, but she doubted this was on the cards.

After ten minutes of silent work, Dave spoke.

'Chris?'

'Hmm?' Christine continued drawing her pencil line.

'Did you mean it?'

'What?'

'About the five hundred k. Would you lend it to me?'

'I might.'

'It's a lot of money. Would Stephen even have half a mil lying around?'

'No.'

Dave slumped.

He had no stamina. That was his problem. Or part of it, at least. A businessman ought to show more spine. Christine picked up another plank.

'Stephen doesn't. But I do.'

Dave perked up.

'Really?'

'Yes.'

'How?'

'What do you mean, how?' The question irritated Christine. It was almost as though she had spent the last twenty years doing nothing.

'I mean, how did you get it?' He wasn't improving matters.

'I "got it" by working hard and making smart decisions. Just like any investor.'

Dave looked completely baffled.

'And now I own a home at St Ives, a cottage at Whale Beach and a number of investment properties. Oh, and the share portfolio. That's also mine.'

'How?' Dave was grappling with the information, and then the penny dropped. 'Bloody hell. Tax? Liability?'

'Both. Stephen thought it was a smart thing to do. He also believed it would be best if I were his business manager, rather than paying someone else to do the job. Right now, I am inclined to agree with him.'

'Holy crap. That man is going down.'

'Maybe. Regardless, the properties and shares are in my name. The shares are the most relevant, for the purposes of your loan. It is a simple thing to sell stock. It can be done in a day or two. And it can be done without Stephen's involvement. As Stephen's business manager, I have supervised the portfolio for decades.'

Dave let out a slow whistle. Christine realised he'd stopped work completely, and so had she. Jenny would be unhappy if she saw them lazing around. She had told Christine to keep an eye on Dave, not to sit around and chat.

'Coffin, Dave. We've got work to do.'

'Rightio. Of course.' Dave didn't object. He was cheerful now. It was almost as though five hundred thousand dollars was the solution to his problem. But it clearly wasn't.

Dave's problem was the remaining six-million-dollar debt. If his goal was financial survival, he needed to put a plan in place. This was no time to sit around and pat himself on the back.

113

Jenny wound the final clamp in place and stepped back. Floor glued. She checked her watch. Twelve nineteen. Five hours to inspection time. One advantage of the heat was that the glue would set fast. It would be safe to do careful sanding by two thirty, and they could hand-saw the final shape around four. Which meant the lid and the floor were well underway and she could turn to other tasks.

She could have if she was on her own, anyway. When Jenny turned around Dave and Chris were chatting away, though they stopped when they realised she was watching them.

Jenny walked over to Chris and Dave, now studiously measuring lengths.

'Hey, Jen!' Chris said brightly, like they'd been caught out.

'How far have you got?' Jenny asked.

'Nearly done,' Chris said. And they should have been. They'd only had to make a few measurements. Jenny looked across at Sophie. It looked as though she was flagging as well. It was probably time for a break.

'We need lunch.' Jenny was business-like. 'Chris – your turn. Sandwiches will do.'

She watched Chris leave the shed, checked the measurements, and gave Dave the go-ahead to start the power saw. Then she paid a visit to Sophie's part of the shed.

'Finally!' Sophie pulled her earmuffs off. 'Finally, someone is coming to help. I am so tired. And *so* sore. And I have been slaving away, all on my own, while everyone else is standing around and chatting.'

Jenny listened for a sentence or two, nodding, and then picked up the other orbital sander. She clamped a fresh piece of 100 grit paper into place, put on her safety gear and switched the power on. Two sentences of self-pity was about as much as Jenny could take.

Sanding was hard work, it was true. But it was also true that Sophie had been absent from the shed for hours the day before, and everyone had continued working – planing, sanding, resawing – in her absence. These were tiring jobs too.

Jenny finished her first board and examined the surface. It was a surprisingly good finish. This was fortunate, because the sanding was taking too long. Jenny didn't love the idea, but there was no way they'd get a run of 120 grit done. It was only the sides and floor. No one would know the difference except their father if he was watching.

'Soph!' Jenny beckoned to her. 'Come here and I'll change your paper.'

Sophie was wary.

'We'll use 120 grit to finish this run.' Jenny was clipping the fine paper onto Sophie's orbital sander. 'Then we have the used paper to prove we sanded to 120.' Jenny handed the tool back to Sophie. 'We'll make this the last lap. We'll finish it before lunch.'

If her father was watching he'd probably laugh. He respected rebellion when it succeeded. 'Good on you, Jen,' he'd be saying. 'That's the spirit.'

Jenny worked fast, and Sophie sped up once she got the grievances off her chest. By the time lunch was ready they were done. They took their headgear off and Sophie gave Jenny a high five. It was a ridiculous action, but Jenny gave it a try.

They joined Chris and Dave on the south side of the shed, and Chris handed Jenny a cup of iced water. She gulped it down and held the cup out for a refill.

They still had to glue the sides, headboard and toe board, and screw in the ribs to keep it all in place. While the glue was drying, they could measure and cut the lid and floor, and screw the holding rails in. Mitre cuts, joiner ribs for the sides and a touch-up sanding of glue stains and it would be ready to assemble.

It would be one thirty by the time they'd finished lunch. Four hours to go. At best. There would be no room for silly conversations or bad moods. They'd eat their sandwiches fast and get back to work. And they could obey her instructions without complaining. Otherwise, they were all going down.

114

Chris had been talking like a rational, sane person – almost like a bloke. But there had to be a catch. There was always a catch. It took Dave about thirty seconds to spot it.

'Hey, mate?'

They were gluing the sides. Jenny and Sophie were doing the long sections, and Dave and Chris were on the shoulder pieces. It was a tricky job. Glue, clamp and screw the ribs on before it was set. It was fair to say he was doing all of this while Chris held the pieces in place. It wasn't the time to comment though.

'Mate!'

Chris looked up and one of the boards slipped. She took a few minutes to get it back in place. The glue was rapid set, but Dave held his tongue and waited for her to sort it out before he spoke again.

'Why would you lend me five hundred k?'

'What?' She still wasn't totally with the program. Holding two boards together was taking all her concentration.

'I'm a seriously bad credit risk.'

Chris heaved a sigh. As though he was an idiot.

'Yes. You are. For any other creditor.'

Dave waited.

'As far as I'm concerned, you are no credit risk at all.'

Dave snorted. 'Come on, Chris, a debt of six point three mil?'

'And a five-million-dollar land inheritance, with shares on top.'

Dave sat down heavily on his plank. She didn't know. He couldn't believe he'd got his hopes up this far.

'Did you read the will?' he asked.

'Of course I read the will.'

'About how it's some kind of trust? And we can't sell our part?'

'Not unless it is to the benefit of Ellersley as a whole. And the same condition applies to the shares. It was quite clear.'

'The five mil can't be surety, mate. Not if I can't sell it.'

'Not to someone outside the family, no.'

Dave wasn't sure where Chris was going with this. He hoped the destination was on planet Earth.

'Quite frankly, David, the problem here is not my lack of knowledge, it's your lack of vision.'

'What?'

'You have a six-point-three-million-dollar debt. Your primary aim seems to be to pay off five hundred thousand – less than ten per cent of the total sum. And you have no strategy in place to deal with the other ninety per cent.'

'What would you suggest?' Dave couldn't help the sarcastic tone.

'I would suggest that you go a step further. Don't use Ellersley as surety. Sell me your share.'

'Fuck, mate, I'm telling you I *can't*.'

'Why not?'

She didn't get it. Of course she didn't. A coked-up nudist one day is not going to be a savvy businesswoman the next.

Dave was doing his best to deal with the disappointment when Chris spoke again.

'I know you can't sell it to an outsider, but why can't you sell it to me?'

Dave said nothing.

'Think about it,' Chris said. 'If I buy your share, Ellersley stays together. The sale would be to the benefit of the property.'

Dave let the idea loop in his mind. It sounded solid. He locked eyes with Chris, trying to work out if she was serious. And sane. She seemed to be both.

He felt like he'd been hit by a truck. A beautiful, big money truck. Like he'd been winded, but in reverse. The air rushed in, filling his chest.

There was Chris at the steering wheel. Her hair sticking out in all directions, a scrape of wood glue on her forehead and a shitload of real estate in her name. He grinned. He threw his head back and gave a massive whoop. Jen looked up and Sophie turned around and he gave them both a thumbs up.

Fucking oath, he gave them a thumbs up.

'For goodness' sake, David, get back to work.' Chris spoke sharply. 'If we don't have this coffin built by five thirty you won't see any of it.'

And there she was. Officious, abrasive Chris. It was concrete evidence she was back to normal, and Dave couldn't have been happier.

115

Vince shivered. The furious heat in his face had evaporated, and his wet shirt was now cold, clinging to his belly. He decided to go outside for a walk. Perhaps he would walk along the river. Why not? People could say what they liked. Vince was leaving.

He donned his Fedora and strode out of the office. Positively strode. Ben must have watched in amazement. But he couldn't waste time thinking about Ben now. The future! The choices before him! Where should he begin?

He would begin with his name. He would be pent up in the dull prison of 'Vince Barton' no longer. Oh, the richness, the dignity, the liberty of his name! *Vincenzo Bartolo*. He would shout it from the rooftop when the time came.

Next, his destination. His parents were dead. His sister had not spoken to him for twenty-three years. There was no one else with a claim on him. So why not go home? *Really* home. Napoli, Italy, the birthplace of the Bartolos. A place where he would be known and welcomed *because* of his name.

Vince tripped over a large root and steadied himself with one hand on the bank. He was hot again, sweat trickling from under his hat. Perhaps he would strip down to his underwear and jump in the river. He laughed. It was intoxicating, all this not caring.

Nonetheless, Vince scrambled back up to the road instead. He might be carefree, but he wasn't a child.

Now. What would he take?

Money, birth certificate, passport. Bank cards. A suit for the journey. An overnight bag. Everything else he would leave behind. Everything! He would sell what he could – house, car, furniture.

His investment properties. They were not grand, but every bit would count.

He would wrap up the business of Barton & Sons. He would pursue outstanding invoices and be selective about new assignments. Rapid turnaround for fast money. That was his goal now.

What would he do about Ellersley? Oh, this was hard. He would have been a millionaire. A multi-millionaire! Over the past few months Vince had dared to dream of inheriting this fortune, but he had lost. He was certain of that now.

Some people would say twenty thousand dollars was reward enough for four months of legal work. But who could deny the bitterness of losing the bigger prize?

Vince's steps quickened. A wild thought had occurred to him.

There was a brief window, between the granting of probate and the disbursement of funds, when Tom Edwards' savings would be resting in the Barton & Sons Trust Account. Two hundred and thirty-five thousand dollars, just sitting there. It was not strictly legal, to move money from this account to another, but as a one-off it would not be immediately detected. Particularly as the banking staff at Coorong were, at best, under par. If he were to transfer funds from the trust account to his office account, then it would be no problem at all to transfer this money to a personal account. Another thought whirled to the surface. What if he took the transaction one step further and moved the money *offshore*?

Vince scraped open the door of Barton & Sons and, once again, bypassed Ben without a word. He shut the door of his office and approached the desk, leaning against it while he caught his breath.

Offshore. The word was enough to make him giddy.

But why not? He planned to open an account in Vincenzo Bartolo's name in any case. It was eminently sensible to make it an Italian account.

Two transfers in quick succession. Barton & Sons Trust Account to the Barton & Sons office account, then the office account to Vincenzo Bartolo and presto!

He would have to choose his time carefully. The paperwork must be perfectly lined up. And he'd have to leave Australia the minute it was done.

Two hundred and thirty-five thousand dollars was not twenty million, but it was a far sight better than twenty thousand. And it would contribute, in some small way, to the emotional recovery of a man who had done so much for the Edwards family. Done so much yet received so little in return.

116

By three thirty Sophie wanted only one thing: a long, hot shower. She and Jenny had been working way faster than the other two. They had glued and screwed together the long sides, the headboard and the toe board in the time it took Dave and Chris to do the shoulder pieces. Jenny was getting stressed, looking at her piece of paper and then the pieces of coffin and then the paper again. Sophie got the impression they weren't matching the way she wanted them to. Jenny yelled at Dave to do some mighty joins and turned to Sophie.

'Lid and floor now, Soph. I'll measure one and you do the other.'

Sophie was proud to be asked, but also slightly concerned. Jenny smiled at her.

'It's all right, Soph, we'll do them together.'

And that's what they did. Side by side, they measured the lines and angles, and by the time they were done, Dave and Chris had finished sawing. And then they did the best thing Sophie had ever done in her life. Ever.

They laid out the pieces, exactly the way Jenny said. Then Jenny picked up the toe board, Sophie picked up one of the long side pieces and Christine the other, and the three of them held firm while Dave glued and screwed a rib in each corner. Jenny was one hundred per cent calm now, talking them through every step. Next the girls held the sides steady while Dave slid the floor along the rails, all the way into place. Then the shoulder pieces were joined to the long sections. Finally, Jenny picked up the headboard and slotted it into place. They all held firm again, and Dave screwed in the corner ribs.

Then everyone held their breath, including Sophie. Jenny picked up the lid and laid it on the coffin. It slipped into place, and everyone breathed out. It fit.

They all took a step back. And another. And looked at the coffin, and each other. Everyone was sweaty, and tired, and covered in sawdust. And one by one they started smiling, then grinning and laughing. All four of them, laughing. They were the Edwards kids, and they'd built this crazy box from scratch, and they'd done it. They'd *done it*!

And now they were standing around, laughing together. And Sophie wasn't too young, or loud, or too outrageous. None of these things. Today, Sophie was one of them, and she wanted to hang out with the big kids forever.

117

When she was a little girl, Sophie never let Tom out of her sight. No matter what he was doing, she wanted to be part of it. Cleaning the cow bail, castrating bull calves, slaughtering a sheep for the freezer – nothing put her off. She'd skip from one place to another, or run if she needed to catch up. Pick up a shovel two feet too long and scrape the cow shit off the concrete. Load rubber rings onto the expander. Hold the butcher's knife. Anything. So long as Tom was there.

She never stopped talking, either. Not even when she was asleep. Sophie had more to say than any human in history and she told him everything. Trusted him harder than the ground beneath her feet, and so she should have.

It was the sort of thing Tom could never say out loud, but he was more in love with that little girl than he had been with anyone – including Helena. Because Helena, no matter how he looked at it, was always going to be a separate person, a stranger to the end.

But Sophie was his. Bone of his bone, and flesh of his flesh. It was his smile in her dimpled face. His blue in her eyes. Sophie was his, and she was perfect.

He took her to the cattle sales, after Helena died. He took her everywhere – he had no choice. But the sales, they both loved going. Sophie knew how to get around the yards. Ducking in and out and back again, holding court from a seat on his shoulders, pointing out the prettiest cows, the biggest bulls. She told him which he should buy and which he should leave behind. Tom was so captivated by her he almost took the advice.

He wouldn't have thought it possible, that she'd let him down. Use him like the fool he was. Take his money and piss it away. Like that's what he'd taught her. That's all they shared.

He was on his deathbed now. And Sophie was nowhere in sight.

He could have done with a conversation.

Would have enjoyed seeing her smile.

They could have talked about when she was a kid, what she got up to. The things they did together. But it didn't have to be that. He'd have been happy talking about the weather.

If Sophie had come, he would have listened to anything she had to say.

118

At 5 pm the lid was on the coffin. Jenny was handing out fine sandpaper to tidy up the glue, and she realised she hadn't factored in the finish. Twenty-four hours and Danish oil was what they needed. Twenty-seven, now twenty-six, minutes and no oil was what they had. Her heart sank.

'How will they carry it?'

Chris had her head cocked to the side, looking at the coffin. No one answered immediately, so she clarified. 'The men, I mean, who take it in and out of the church. How will they pick it up?'

'Handles, obviously.' Dave gave Jenny a wink.

Handles! This had slipped Jenny's mind entirely. The tiny coffins didn't need handles – two people kneeling on the dirt were enough to lower a pet into the grave. So now she had two problems. Finish and handles. Two problems and twenty-four minutes. *Shit*.

'Where do we get the handles?' Christine asked. Dave looked at Jenny and Jenny started to sweat.

'I know!'

It was Sophie. Standing at the foot of the coffin with a glorious smile on her face.

'The boy's chest of drawers.'

Jenny didn't know what she meant, but Sophie kept going.

'He'd love it. All that family history and the five men in the hut and the handles that came off Great-great-great-granny's piano box or whatever – it's perfect!' She stood up and beamed at the other three, as delighted as if the job was already done.

The job wasn't done, but she was right. It was the perfect choice, but they'd have to move fast.

'So now we have handles, thanks, Soph,' Jenny said, 'but where will we find Danish finishing oil?'

The others looked at her blankly, so Jenny rubbed a hand on the coffin lid to demonstrate. Remarkably, Sophie chimed in again.

'Linseed oil!'

Dave, standing with his shoulders back and hands tucked into his armpits, nodded.

'You can fix anything with linseed oil,' Sophie continued. 'Dad rubbed it all over a chopping board once. Our veggies tasted like a cricket bat for a month!'

'Right,' Dave said. 'I'll get the handles.'

And Sophie said, 'I'll get the linseed oil.'

'Turps too, Soph,' Jenny called out. 'We'll need some turps to thin it out. And a rag. Lots of rags. Clean. Cotton.'

'I'll stay here and sand with Jenny,' Christine said.

And Jenny yelled out after them, 'Quick, guys, make it quick!'

It was the tightest timing she'd ever faced. As she and Christine scrubbed at the glue stains, she was convinced she could hear the seconds tick. They had twenty-one minutes to go, and it had to be done in time. Or else she'd have his voice in her head for the rest of her life.

'Speed it up, girl. The day won't wait for you to arrive.'

119

Jenny and Dave did the handles, while Sophie and Christine rubbed in the oil. They had to duck and weave around each other to get to all the surfaces. It was a fast and furious twenty minutes, but by the time the little red car came beetling down the track they had put the linseed oil back on the bench and wiped their hands on the few scraps of cotton rag that were still clean and dry.

As Mr Barton walked across the paddock in his grey pinstripe suit, Christine glanced at her siblings. She realised the four of them were standing in line, at attention. Like school children ready for the assembly to begin.

Perhaps they would each get a certificate, or a gold star, when the judging of their project was done.

120

Vince arrived at five thirty. His little pimple of a car puttered up the track at five twenty-nine, and he was at the shed bang on time. Didn't want to give them a second more to work on the coffin than he had to. Charles Briggs was around fifteen minutes late. He wasn't so fussed on punctuality. Dave had never met a doctor who was. Also, he was driving a BMW. He had to go slow to protect the duco.

Vince had a clipboard with a checklist on it. Charles had his hands in his pockets. Vince picked his way around the coffin, inspecting joins and handles and wiping a finger on the oiled surface. Charles wandered about like he was in the livestock tent at the show. Interested, sure, but not too concerned about the finer details.

Dave leaned against a post and watched them circle the coffin. He felt as relaxed as he had done for twelve months. Probably more. They'd certify the coffin. They had to. It was built. On time. By the four of them. Siren sounds, game ends, trophy to Team Edwards.

And five million dollars to Dave. How about that? Two weeks ago, before the will was read out, he would have been horrified. Now he was ecstatic. Nothing like the breadline closing in to make a man thankful.

It left him one point three mil short, but he'd sell a block or two from Eastside. Maybe he'd win the lottery. Or bargain Chris up.

Dave snorted and coughed to cover it. Bargaining with Chris was not an option. She'd have him for breakfast. And yet, something was niggling at him. A pinprick of light somewhere . . .

Vince stepped back from the coffin, writing notes with a silver pen. Charles had been standing with Jenny, talking low, but now he approached Vince, still scribbling away. He put a hand on the little bloke's shoulder and said, 'All right, Vince.'

Vince stopped writing and his shoulders slumped. He looked utterly defeated. Charles gave him a hearty slap on the back.

'That's us, I think, Vince. We're done.' He steered Vince out of the machinery shed and waved at them all. He paused as he passed Jenny. 'It's a good job,' he said, and Jenny nodded.

Sophie ran to the edge of the shed and yelled out, 'Bye! Bye, Dr Briggs, bye, Vince! Thanks for coming!' Like they were family friends, and she didn't want them to go.

Jenny watched them leave, but she didn't shout.

And then it hit Dave, what his bargaining chip was – the shares! The fucking shares.

Aiming for a casual saunter, he made his way across the shed. Chris was standing behind the coffin and he walked around it, as though he was checking it out. He was wasting his time. Chris knew he wanted something. He decided to get to the point.

'Chris?'

'Hmm?' She was onto him, all right.

'Do you want to buy my shares?'

She didn't rush to answer. Dave cast a critical eye at the toe board. It hadn't changed.

'Yes,' Chris said.

'Yes?' Dave spun around. He couldn't help the excitement in his voice.

'Yes.'

She was decisive, Dave had to give it to her. She was bloody inspiring.

Dave was encouraged enough to dive in for the hard numbers.

'Market value?'

'No,' Chris said, 'not market value.' Less promising.

'How much?'

'Ten per cent.'

'Of what?' Dave hauled up. Ten per cent wasn't part of this conversation. Ten per cent was a whole new topic.

'Of market value.'

'*What?*'

'The shares are what you bring to the table. They make it worth my while.'

'How about Ellersley? Worth your while?' Dave spluttered.

'Yes and no. Yes, for the sentiment; no, for the investment. If you sell me your shares, Ellersley becomes interesting.'

Fuck she was smart. Dave didn't know how to play it now.

'I don't need it, Dave. We can call the whole thing off.'

'Shit. No! Fuck. Fine. Ten per cent.' Dave back-pedalled so hard he was at risk of reversing through the shed wall. He kicked the dirt, defeated. 'Fuck it.'

'Fine,' Chris said, straight as a die. No victory dance, no winner's grin. She behaved as though she had been doing this kind of deal her whole adult life. She probably had.

'David?' A hint of the North Shore accent was coming back.

'Yeah?'

'From now on, no foul language at the negotiation table. Understood?'

Dave swallowed his irritation. He'd just sold his shares down the river and Chris was getting more annoying by the minute, but he resisted answering back. He wasn't an idiot. He had five million and maybe a few grand in shares riding on this. He might choke on every sentence, but from now on he'd keep it clean. He could not afford to fuck this up.

'Sure,' he said lightly. 'Fine by me.'

'Thank you.'

And that was that. He was no worse off than he had been two hours ago, so no harm done. At the end of the day, he'd given it a crack.

121

'Excellent work, Vincenzo.' Vince congratulated himself as he started the engine.

He was careful to keep a downcast expression until he was at a safe distance, but once he hit the sealed road, he permitted himself a victorious smile and sped right up. They expected disappointment and they got it. Vince wouldn't call it an Academy award-winning performance, but it was convincing enough to get a pat on the back from Charles Briggs and that was something.

Vince had done some thinking – so much thinking! – since his interview with David that morning, and one thing was clear. Until probate was granted, and Vince had that money, he must not give any person in Coorong cause to be suspicious of his behaviour.

They would expect him to attend Tom Edwards' funeral, so he would. They would expect him to look dejected, so he would do that too. And then he would continue his business about town, a man defeated by events. This would please all the residents of Coorong. It would be exactly what they had expected.

Vince flicked the indicator on and turned into Main Street. He had a substantial list of tasks to complete, and there was no reason for delay. He would get online now and put up the Notice of Intended Application for Probate.

On Monday he would contact Mindle, Seifort & Sloane. He would inform them that the condition of the will had been met and the notice of intention had been filed. Then he would turn his mind to the dull but necessary work of debt collection. He would also commence the more interesting work of multiple property sales. And then there were all the other matters he must attend to prior to his departure. Vince beamed. What a marvellous phrase – 'prior to his departure'.

He was going. He was really leaving. And to Naples! Napoli, Italy. Perhaps that should be number one on his list – research real estate in Naples. It was the perfect job for a Friday night. And well suited to an accompanying glass of wine.

Vince was humming happily as he pulled into the carport. He turned off the engine, rearranged his face into a suitable state of disappointment and walked at a dragging pace up the path to his front door. As soon as he was on the other side of it, he did a little running-on-the-spot dance. It was going to be a glorious time.

He would have to concentrate on concealing his excitement.

'Indoors, Vincenzo, only indoors. When you've made it home – *home!* – you can smile wherever you please. But you have to get there first.'

122

Christine had watched Dave saunter past the coffin, acting as casually as a desperate man could, like it was a surprise to find her there.

He wanted to talk about the shares. It was about time he asked. Christine had been thinking about it, and she had already decided to buy his quota. At a fraction of the value, which was only fair.

Dave knew nothing about their father's shares. He didn't have a clue about their value, where the stocks were invested or who was managing the portfolio. It was further evidence that David was not a man who should be trusted with money. He had no idea what to do with it.

When Christine offered her terms he responded with offensive language, as always, but he agreed to the deal. So he should have. Christine had effectively saved his life by buying his portion of Ellersley. The shares were a token of his appreciation.

The purchase of Dave's shares achieved two things. The first was to release Dave from his association with Ellersley, which should have happened decades ago. For everyone's sake. The second was to simplify and clearly demarcate the financial interest in Ellersley. Christine now had a fifty per cent share of property and assets, and Jenny and Sophie had twenty-five per cent each. Christine therefore had fifty per cent of the decision-making power and the profit, which, under her care, should be substantial. Their father was not a fool, but he was, first and foremost, a farmer. Having a financial mind at the helm would make a significant difference to the balance sheet. In the meantime, she would speak to a real solicitor about conveyancing and the terms of the will. Tristan Shanks at Marks & Worthington in North Sydney was a wills and probate man. He had an excellent reputation. Christine decided to ring him first thing on Monday morning.

'Chris?' It was Jenny.

'Yes?' Chris switched back to the present.

'We're heading down now. Did you want to come?'

'Oh.' Christine looked around, taking stock. The tools had been picked up and placed on benches. There was sawdust everywhere, and a circle of shuffling footprints with the coffin resting in the middle. She had a strange reluctance to leave the site. Did this mean it was the end? She turned to Jenny, who was waiting patiently. Sophie and Dave were already halfway to the hedge.

'Yes,' she decided. She was hardly going to stay in the shed alone. 'Absolutely. Thanks for waiting.' Jenny smiled and nodded.

They trudged down to the house and sat on the verandah. Dave brought beers out and Sophie followed with chips.

'We did it!' Sophie said and held her can up.

'We did,' Dave said. They clinked.

Christine could barely lift her arm; she was so tired and sore.

Sophie made dinner out of a jar, but Christine wasn't complaining. There was food on the table. Dave shovelled his in and jumped up when his sisters were only part way through their meals. He said he needed a shower. Everyone did, but Dave obviously felt his need was more important. Christine let it go.

When they'd finished dinner Christine wandered back out to the verandah, leaving the bathroom to Sophie and Jenny. She wasn't in a rush. The house windows were all open, including those of the porch, so Christine heard Dave pick up the phone. He dialled and waited for a moment before he spoke.

'Sharon? Love?'

A pause.

'We're good, Shaz. I've done it.' Another pause.

'Seriously, Shaz. Numbers and all. I've sorted it out.'

Christine leaned against the verandah post and smiled. *Like hell, you sorted it.* But she wouldn't say anything. She wouldn't have to. As soon as Dave told Sharon about the deal, she'd know how it had come about.

It wasn't Christine's job to manage Dave. She wasn't married to him. In fact, she wasn't married to anyone. Not for much longer. She pushed herself off the post and went inside. She was unlikely to miss it.

123

It was nine thirty, everyone was getting ready for bed, and Ben Taylor still hadn't called. At another time in Sophie's life this would have been a total downer. But tonight was different.

Sophie had turned a corner. She had come to the realisation that she was, without a doubt, the ideal farmer's wife.

She knew how to get up early.

She knew how to work hard.

She knew how to take instructions from a man – or from a woman at least. Taking instructions from Jenny wasn't a problem, but Dave's instructions were a bit dumb. Sophie hadn't told him to his face, though, and that was progress. A farmer's wife didn't need to agree with everything her husband thought, she just had to keep her mouth shut sometimes. It wasn't how Sophie usually rolled, but she'd do it if she had to.

Also, Sophie knew how to get dinner on the table at the end of a day's work. Pesto in a jar wasn't a traditional farmer's meal, maybe, but it was food. Once it was mixed with pasta. The important thing was she got it on the table. She, Sophie Edwards, had fed the family.

Her legs were clean-shaven, which was highly important, no matter what anyone said. She also had excellent hair and fabulous dress sense.

She was the one for Ben Taylor, all right. And tomorrow morning, at 6 am, she'd be standing by the Ellersley grid, looking gorgeous, ready to prove she was the woman for the job.

124

It wasn't her exhausted body that bothered Jenny; her mind wouldn't settle down, and she knew why. She'd missed a step.

They had the coffin built by close of business. It had sides and a lid and a floor. It had handles and a finish beyond Jenny's expectation of linseed oil. It had been approved by Dr Briggs and Vince Barton. Even so, the job wasn't finished. Not until Matthew had seen it.

Not one of her coffins had left the shed without Matthew's appraisal. Through his eyes she viewed the timber in a new light. When Matthew saw her work, she understood what she had made.

Jenny was bone-tired and anxious. It was a terrible combination.

The phone was bad. Terrifying, even. But this was worse. She couldn't let the coffin go if Matthew hadn't seen it. Something would break. Maybe her heart. Or maybe something else, but she needed him to see it. She had to ask Matthew to come to Ellersley.

She waited until the others were in bed and then, for the third time that week, she picked up the phone. It rang and rang, and then the answering machine spoke.

'Hello. Sorry I can't come to the phone. Please leave a message.'

Jenny's breath went shallow at the sound of his voice. When the machine beeped, she started talking and talking and she couldn't stop. It was the longest message in the world, but eventually she managed to blurt out her request.

'Please, Matthew, I don't know what else to say, we need you here, I –'

And then he picked up the phone.

'Who needs me?'

Jenny took a deep breath.

'I do.'

He said he'd come, and Jenny said thank you and hung up the phone. And then she was so nervous. She walked up the track and back and around the house and couldn't settle herself down, but just as she was about to start a lap around the front yard he arrived. He switched off the engine and got out of the cab. Long and lanky, and in no rush. He leaned on the driver's door and watched her, waiting. Jenny stood still, unsure, and then she walked over to him in her bare feet and took him by the hand. She held his hand all the way up to the shed.

Once he was standing in position, Jenny walked around and flicked the light switch. The coffin sprang into view. It was resting on two sawhorses, and the lid was leaning against the side.

Matthew did what he always did. He looked. Quietly. Gently. Walking with the softest, slowest steps around the coffin, enjoying it from every angle, appreciating the depth of the grain, the neatness of the joins, the proportions of the construction.

And Jenny could see it, too.

It was beautiful.

She imagined her father's body lying inside it. The body she had prepared, under a week ago. He wouldn't be buried in his pyjamas, though. They would dress him properly.

Matthew finished his circuit and stood beside her, taking her hand. They looked at the coffin together.

'It's good, Jen.' He gave her hand a squeeze. 'It's a beauty.'

They walked out of the shed, and Jenny said, 'Don't go. We'll watch the stars. I'll get the rug from my car.'

They lay on their backs, side by side, holding hands as they looked at the sky. As the night cooled, they pulled up the edges of the rug to cover their legs and arms, and finally they curled up, Jenny protected by Matthew's warmth, and fell asleep.

125

Tom didn't pay much attention when he was losing strength, but he wasn't a fool. He knew there was something wrong.

Without thinking, he was running the property like a man on the brink of departure. He didn't put the bull out in August. Told himself something about a rest year for the heifers, and half believed it. He let some of the old girls go in the scrub.

Something went bung in Nell's front leg. She wouldn't walk unless he called her. Just wanted to stay in her kennel. It wasn't in her paw, or an abscess, or anything he could fix. Had to be her joints. Tom went around the cattle on his own. Didn't even consider getting another dog.

Jock didn't call, Sophie didn't visit, and the other kids stayed away too. Every day Tom took his Akubra off the hook, rolled up his sleeves and went out. He put his face to the ground and tramped from one trough to the next, or along a fence line singing in the wind, and held fast to the bitter satisfaction of working hard while others neglected their post.

The resentment was like a stone in his gut, rolling around, getting heavier and heavier. It made him nauseous. He started spitting up bile. It was a month before he was ready to admit it was physical. But a man can only ignore cancer for so long. It catches up with him, sooner or later.

He went to see Charles Briggs. He visited Vince. He shot poor old Nell.

He talked to his mother, and Helena too, in the final weeks. Not that he'd admit to it. It's not normal, talking to dead people. Especially if they answer.

Both of them told him to ring Jock. To ring Sophie, before it was too late. Tom thought about it, more than he should have, but he wouldn't do it. Bloody hell, it wasn't his job. He hadn't abandoned Ellersley. He hadn't bled the family funds dry.

They knew the number. Both of them. They knew how to pick up a phone.

Tom didn't call, but he thought about it all the time. Towards the end it was the only thing on his mind.

126

Six was early, but Sophie wasn't taking any chances. She was dressed and ready and at the grid by five forty-five. She did not want to miss this ride.

The sun hadn't risen yet. Which meant she was up before dawn. It was a whole new experience. And further evidence that she was the ideal farmer's wife. It probably meant she could be a farmer in her own right.

She had gone with the denim miniskirt. It was going to be a scorcher, so jeans weren't an option, but denim was compulsory. A short-sleeved shirt with press-stud buttons, a light touch of blush and some mascara and she was sorted. And totally gorgeous, in a farm-before-dawn kind of way.

When she was putting her boots on in the laundry, Sophie noticed her dad's leather hat, sagging from a hook on the wall. The rim was dark and stained with sweat, but there were no spiders in it, which was a plus.

She thought it might help, wearing his hat. It would destroy her hair, but she could wait until they arrived before she put it on and leave it on for the rest of the day. It would remind her how to behave at the cattle sales. How to show respect. When to smile and when to hold back. She didn't want to look like a pushy outsider. She wasn't one, she knew that. She was Sophie Edwards, Tom Edwards' girl. But she'd been gone a while. Anyway, she was only there to watch. She could do that from the back. It wasn't like she was going to bid.

Sophie stood by the grid, holding the hat lightly by the rim. She had cash tucked into her bra and a big smile on her face.

Five forty-five at the wrong end of the day and she was smiling. She didn't want to get too cocky, but maybe, just maybe, she'd got it right this time around.

127

When Christine woke it dawned on her that it was Saturday morning. A day for sleeping in and reading the paper; for watching a neighbour mow their lawn; a day for lazing around and doing nothing. Wasn't that right?

For Christine it hadn't been like that for a long time. Until today.

Today, Stephen would have to be up early to get Nicholas to cricket. He'd have to watch the game for half an hour then take Claudia to ballet. He'd have an hour to kill while Claudia had her lesson. It was too far to go home, and there was nothing interesting to do in Pennant Hills, so he'd have to sit in the car.

Then he and Claudia would go to Jonathon's house to collect Nicholas, and after that he would take them both to see their nana. That should have been Stephen's job anyway. It had been months since he'd visited his mother.

Saturday afternoon was violin for Claudia and jujitsu for Nicholas, and then it was time to go home and prepare dinner. Christine would be astounded if Stephen managed to co-ordinate half of these activities. It sounded like a lot of work when she imagined someone else doing the job.

Christine reached across for the edge of the curtain and gave it a tug. It was light outside but not bright. The sun wasn't up yet. She propped herself on her elbow and scanned the room. She loved her bedroom at Ellersley. It was neat and tidy. No one came in without knocking.

She loved her single bed, with room for only one. She loved hearing doors open and close and footsteps in the hall, and not caring who it was or where they were going. Christine had heard it could be devastating for parents when their children left home, but she'd never thought of leaving home herself. She could not have imagined the freedom, the exhilaration of being on her own.

Christine could have rolled over to sleep in if she'd wanted to. But she felt like getting up. She could walk down to the creek. Maybe she'd spy a platypus. It was nearly sunrise – the perfect time. They'd be out and about, swimming around. Stirring up the weeds with their claws and leaving strings of bubbles as they paddled away.

Christine slipped on a t-shirt and shorts. She was on the track within two minutes of getting out of bed. It was so quick. So easy.

She peeled off the track and made her way through the dry grass, brushing flies from her face with a feathery stalk. Grasshoppers flicked her legs, and everything hummed and clicked and buzzed around her.

By the creek though, where the shade was deep, the insect chatter stopped. The air was still. Even the gurgling water was quiet.

Christine crouched by the water's edge and watched it flow by. She decided to walk downstream to the Bird Bath. They sometimes saw a platypus there.

The pool was more of a puddle, but there was water trickling in and wet moss below. A platypus was unlikely, but Christine took a seat anyway. She chose a flat patch on a rocky outcrop and settled back, leaning into the granite. It was cool, and comfortable enough if she found the right angle for her spine.

Christine closed her eyes, breathing in the passing air. Now dry and sweet, now silty with mud. When the sun came up the scents would shift. She could stay, if she wanted to, to smell the change. There was nobody coming to find her.

128

'Sorry to bother you, Jen, but I need your ute. The silly prick left me behind.'

Jenny rolled over and squinted up at Sophie. The rocks under the rug were jutting sharply and she winced.

'Thanks so much. I owe you one.' Sophie patted her on the shoulder. She was in the ute and turning the ignition before Jenny had a chance to tell her how it worked.

Jenny listened as Sophie turned the ignition and pumped her foot on the accelerator pedal. The ute growled briefly and then went silent. Sophie rattled the gearstick around, found neutral and tried again. Jenny listened to the ignition groaning and Sophie's foot pumping away. She'd flooded the engine.

'Damn!' Sophie's frustration emanated from the ute.

Jenny propped herself up on one elbow to watch.

'You're not going to get it started now, sister,' Jenny said under her breath. 'Have some breakfast and try again.'

She was right, the engine wouldn't start, but the ute began to move anyway. Now that it was in neutral the gentle slope allowed the wheels to roll forward.

Sophie looked flustered. She was reaching for the handbrake, Jenny guessed, but she accidentally put it in first gear again, and without realising it, achieved a clutch start. The ute bunny-hopped across the paddock to the gate and revved loudly past the house. Sophie had got it moving, which Jenny supposed was a start. Hopefully Sophie knew about changing gears. If she left it in first the whole way and revved that high, it would be a dreadful ride.

Jenny lay down again, but her eyes were wide open. There would be no going back to sleep now. Matthew rolled onto his back, squinting up at the pale blue sky and Jenny smiled at him.

'Morning, love,' she said. It was such a strange thing to say. But she ploughed on.

'Sun's up. We might have to get up too.'

Jenny couldn't imagine how she'd get used to this new situation. Time, maybe. Give it time.

129

Vince was in the office by seven thirty. He was too excited to sleep properly. He had woken at six and he decided to get up and make a start on his various tasks. Vince hadn't decided to get up early for at least twenty-five years. Perhaps he was changing. Maybe rising early would come naturally to him in Italy.

After looking at real estate in Naples the night before, Vince had a moment of real despondence. As far as he could see from the photos, Naples was an uninspiring city. Dirty, brown and completely lacking in style. It begged the question: even if it were full of his relatives, did Vincenzo Bartolo really want to live there? He ran the risk of escaping one cultural wasteland only to find another.

But his despair didn't last. Vince widened his search to include cities known for their glamour. Rome. Venice. Milan. They were glorious! It was impossible to decide which he liked best.

Vince walked with a veritable spring in his step. His sleep had been poor, his waking hour unsociable, and the task ahead was one he detested, but beyond that, there was Rome! Or Milan! Or some other place equally gorgeous and far away.

It was a relief to be at the office without Ben. Vince could breathe easily. He could hum. Maybe even sing a note or two.

Vince pulled out the pile of unpaid invoices. He had his head down, concentrating hard when the front door scraped across the lino. It gave him a nasty shock.

A voice called through to his office. 'Vince?'

Vince slipped a blank folder over the pile of invoices and prepared to look irritated and interrupted.

'Vince? You there? It's Dave Edwards.'

On a Saturday? Surely not. There must be some football or cricket match on. Vince straightened his tie. Thankfully he had worn a suit.

'Oh, there you are.' David blundered his way through to Vince's office. He appeared somewhat flustered. 'Can I ask you a couple of questions?'

'Yes, I suppose so.' Vince waved towards a chair and sat down himself. He wasn't inclined to be friendly; David's presence was not welcome. He was painful evidence of the fortune Vince had lost, and he was interrupting Vince's pre-departure work.

'Can I sell my share of Ellersley to Chris?'

Vince paused. It was an unexpected question.

'Is it in the rules?'

'Hmm,' Vince said, preparing to give David a little lecture on restriction of sale. But after scanning Tom Edwards' will in his mind – he had it well and truly memorised by now – he realised a lecture was not required.

'Well? Can I?' Dave was back to being an 'Ellersley Edwards' now they had won the inheritance.

'Yes. I believe so.'

'Chris was confident,' Dave said. 'But it never hurts to get a professional opinion.'

Vince thought fast. Perhaps there was something to be gained from this.

'You will need a solicitor to do the conveyancing – I am well placed to do this, having an intimate knowledge of the will – and I would be able to commence this work immediately if required.'

'Great, thanks, Vince. I'll let Chris know. Can I sell my shares too?'

Vince raised his eyebrows.

'To Chris, I mean.'

Vince considered this briefly. 'If they remain with the property, yes, I think so.'

The deal David had struck with his sister with respect to the shares made Vince gasp internally, but to the outward eye he barely flinched. Instead, he offered his services again.

'I could also take care of the transfer of shares. At an additional cost, naturally.'

David didn't seem too worried about the cost. He just wanted to know it could be done.

'Rightio, I'll let you know.' Dave stood to leave, and Vince stood with him. Dave reached over to shake Vince's hand, and Vince reluctantly held his out too.

'You didn't think we'd let you win, did you?' David winked. He clearly thought he was being humorous.

It took all Vince's practice at being the underdog to reply.

'Oh, no, David. Ha, ha, no. Keep it in the family, of course.'

It was a hard pill to swallow, but it was imperative he keep an even keel. He must do nothing out of the ordinary. Nothing to draw attention. That may have been a two-hundred-and-thirty-five-thousand-dollar handshake right there. Two hundred and thirty-five thousand dollars!

Vince had lost more dignity for less reward more times than he cared to remember. When Coorong was behind him, he would never do it again.

130

Dave could have kissed him. Wrapped that silly lawyer in a big old bear hug and lifted him off the ground. He didn't, which was probably a good thing. Instead he looked Vince in the eye and shook his hand, ribbed him a bit – how could he resist? They'd built a cracking coffin. They'd earned it.

Vince wasn't overly pleased, but he shook hands. He seemed to have perked up at the idea of the extra conveyancing and transfer of shares. Dave would leave that in Chris's hands. He didn't want to discourage Vince, but Chris probably knew how to do it herself. She'd had no doubt that the transaction would be legal, but Dave had to ask. He needed the reassurance. It would have been unbearable to get so close and miss out at the end.

It was all coming together. The coffin was finished, the financial deals were done, and Vince Barton was on track with probate. The funeral was going to be a piece of cake compared with what they had been through. And after the funeral he'd be going home. To his wife. And kids. In time for Christmas. Unbelievable.

Dave left Barton & Sons and wandered up Main Street. There was no rush for him to get back to Ellersley. Nothing to do now the coffin was built. He could find some Christmas presents for the kids. He'd get Shaz something too, but not until he was back in Wagga. Something special. A bit pricey, but not too much. She'd have her eye on the accounts from now on.

The mall was dead, which was no surprise. It was just after nine – Coorong locals didn't go to the shops first thing. Dave stepped into the arcade and walked down to Best and Less. The lights were out and there was a sign on the door with opening hours. Monday to

Friday, 9 am to 5 pm, Saturday and Sunday, closed. Shit a brick. What was it, the fifties?

He put his face to the glass to see what was on display and spied the box at the end of an aisle. The Action 8-in-1 Sports Set! The one time Jock came back to Ellersley, he brought this set, this exact one, with him. It was big, bright, and one hundred per cent plastic. They had to share it – it was a Christmas present for all the kids – but that was all right because there was plenty of fun to go around.

They loved the present, and they loved Jock. Their dad didn't. He was angry and quiet the whole time Jock was there, so they knew Jock had done something wrong. Nobody ever told them what. Jock was with them for three days, and then he was gone. Dave was heartbroken when he left. The girls weren't so worried. They'd moved on to Barbie dolls or whatever else they had. Dave went through the 8-in-1 set, but all the games needed two or more players. He tried one-man frisbee for an hour or so, but it wasn't much fun.

Dave decided then and there to get the Action set for his kids. They'd love it. He'd have to come back Monday to buy it, but no problem. He was nearly solvent now.

Dave unstuck his face from the glass and wandered back down the tiled passageway. He hadn't thought of that visit from Jock for decades, which was a bloody shame. Such a good bloke. Strange how he left without telling them first. It had to be their old man. Cranky bastard. Probably chased him off.

Dave exited the arcade and the sun hit him hard.

Holy shit. Had anyone told Jock? Chris would have been the one – back when she was normal – but Dave wasn't counting on it now. The funeral was Wednesday, which was something. Jock would have a few days to cross over from Perth. If Chris had his number, Dave would be happy to call him. They'd pay for the flights if they needed to. Charge it to the estate. Their old man was cranky, but he'd have wanted that, surely. His own brother. And Jock would want to make the effort, Dave was sure of it. He was terrific, Jock. Great fun. Ellersley was dull as dirt when he had gone.

131

Sophie worked out how to change the gears before she'd hit the main road. She wasn't so flash on the indicators, and the brakes felt a bit wobbly, but she made it to the sales just fine.

She put her dad's hat on, her shoulders back and her thumbs into the belt loops of her denim skirt. Then she took a good look around.

There were men wandering about, looking at cattle in their pens and scribbling in little notepads. The air was laced with anticipation, the tingling of uncertainty. Sophie knew this vibe back to front. It could have been a nightspot in the Cross before the deals have been done. Blokes with high hopes and pockets full of cash. On a Saturday morning at the cattle yards, though, it felt kind of wholesome.

A couple of men tipped their hats when they saw Sophie, and one came over to her.

'Sophie Edwards,' he said. 'It's been a long while since we saw you at the sales.'

Sophie didn't recognise him, but she answered as though she did.

'Too long,' she said.

'Sorry about your old man.'

'Yeah, well, what can you do?'

'Nothing. Nothing to be done.' He was looking at the empty yard. 'It's not right. A young fella like that.'

Sophie looked more closely at the wrinkled face. He looked seriously old.

'Thanks,' she said.

'Will you bid?' He nodded towards the yard. At that moment Ben Taylor stepped forward to get a closer look at one of the bulls and Sophie flushed.

'I might.'

'Good girl.' He smiled, patted her on the shoulder, and walked away. If that wasn't a sign, Sophie didn't know what was.

There were a few lots auctioned before Ben's bull was brought into the yard, so the crowd was nicely warmed up. Sophie watched as the bidding started on the bull. Hands going up one after the other – not fast, but a steady flow – and the auctioneer rolling along with it.

'We have a bid to my left, and up the back, on the fence, thank you, sir, and the gentleman on the left, and the lad on the right, who wants to take this bull home?' Ben's hand was among them, but he wasn't rushing. He didn't look nervous. Yet.

Sophie waited for the bidding to slow down, and when there was a pause following Ben's bid, she put her hand up.

'We have another hat in the ring, the lady on my left – thanks for joining us – who's going to bid her up now?'

Ben looked over to see Sophie and now it was his turn to blush. In the meantime, the gentleman on the fence put his hand up and the auctioneer continued.

'Who wants to make the next bid? Is there anything from the lady on my left? What about you, the young lad on my right?'

Sophie was smiling. She could wait. She didn't need to beat the gentleman on the fence. Ben looked towards the auctioneer and put his hand up. The man on the fence bowed out and it was only Ben and Sophie left.

'The bid is with the lad on my right, no, the young lady on my left. What do you think, sir? Do you want to take this bull home? Yes! To the lad on the right.' Sophie waited until the auctioneer said, 'Going once, going twice,' and put her hand up again.

'What do you think, lad, will you bid again?' Ben shook his head slightly. 'Going once, going twice, sold! To the lady in the check shirt.'

It was marvellous. There were handshakes all round, and the man she'd spoken with earlier clapped. The eyes of every farmer were turned to her, the daring bidder in the denim miniskirt.

And this, Ben Taylor, Sophie turned her head to make sure he was watching, *this is what you drove past this morning. Take a look at what you're missing.*

It was only when the auctioneer called the buyers up at the end that Sophie realised she was in deep shit. Apparently, she was meant to be 'registered' to bid. She was supposed to have an agent. She had to hand over payment details to some woman in a demountable and then she had to cart the bull home.

When she fronted up to the stone-faced lady in the office, the shit just got deeper. In her rush to get to the sales she had left a few things behind. Like her wallet, credit card and phone.

The woman, whose name was Connie, looked at her and heaved a sigh.

'ID?' she said.

'What?' Sophie knew what ID was, but she had no idea why Connie would want it.

'ID. Prove it's you. Before you take the bull.'

'Shit. No.'

'How're you planning to get this bull home?'

Sophie shrugged helplessly. 'I don't know.'

'You bid for a bull, unregistered. You've got no agent, no transport, no money and no ID.'

At this point Sophie realised the door of the demountable was wide open, and there were a bunch of men outside waiting to settle their business. They didn't seem to be in any rush though. They were listening to every word. And one of them was Ben Taylor.

'So what's your plan?' Connie asked.

Sophie had nothing. And then Ben stepped forward.

'I could help you out,' he said. He sounded serious, but Sophie saw the gleam in his eye. He was laughing so hard on the inside. If she let Ben Taylor help her now, she'd never live it down.

'No thanks, I'm fine.' Sophie would stay in the demountable with Connie all night if needed, but she was absolutely not accepting help from Ben Taylor.

'Fair enough,' he said, and turned on his heel. It was just her and Connie again.

'Well?' Connie said. She was cranky and tired and Sophie still had nothing.

'Connie – is that you in there?' It was a voice from the dirt yard, and then the old bloke who'd patted Sophie on the shoulder came across.

'What do you want, Max?'

'I'm just wanting to make sure you know this is Sophie, Tom Edwards' girl.'

Connie looked suspiciously at Sophie.

'Did you know he'd passed?' the man asked.

Connie softened slightly. Let her crossed arms loosen, relaxed her unflinching expression.

'Just last week. And here's young Sophie at the sales.'

Connie picked up a pen and wrote in her logbook.

'She's taking on the farm,' Max said. Sophie looked across quickly and he winked.

Connie scribbled a note and handed it to Sophie.

'Take this over to Powell's truck. Luke'll get you home.'

'Actually I've got my sister's ute –'

Connie rolled her eyes. 'The bull. He'll take the bull.'

'Of course.' Sophie laughed. 'That makes more sense.'

'You call me on this number when you've sorted out your payment. You've got till five thirty Monday.'

'Yes, Connie, thank you so much.'

There was so much grovelling involved with buying a bull. Sophie wasn't sure she would have done it if she'd known this in advance. But it was done now. Luke Powell would bring the bull home, and when he arrived with that enormous animal, she was sure the others would be impressed. They'd want to cough up for sure.

Sophie skipped down the steps and nearly ran into Max.

'Oh my goodness, Max, thank you so much!'

Max smiled.

'It's all right,' he said. 'Most entertaining sales I've been to for a while. You put on a show for us today. You and young Ben and your bidding war.'

Sophie flushed again.

'You did the right thing,' he said. 'Send him packing. It'll do him good.'

She smiled, ready to take a compliment, but Max turned serious.

'This, though,' he gestured over to the demountable, 'this was for your old man.' Sophie could feel the lump in her throat rising. The lump that was always there, that had never left, not even for a minute since Jenny had told her. She swallowed and kept her eyes wide open.

'You bid well,' he said. 'He would have been proud.'

132

The coffin was left in the machinery shed until Darby's picked it up on Monday morning. After all that rush and hurry. They could have worked on it over the weekend if they'd wanted to. But it was finished.

Jenny checked on it each day. She couldn't say why. It wasn't as though a coffin needed food or water. It was hardly going to be stolen. But it calmed her, knowing it was there.

Matthew left on Saturday morning. Rolled out of the blanket in the paddock, kissed her on the head and drove the old Ford down the track. It was good. Jenny knew he was coming back.

On Saturday afternoon Sophie roared down the track in Jenny's ute, still revving high in a low gear, and came into the house with a mascara-streaked face looking for Chris. Jenny was in the kitchen and heard them talking on the verandah outside.

'How much is it?' she heard Chris say.

Sophie didn't answer straight away. And then, like a small child, she whispered the answer into Chris's ear.

'Fifteen thousand or fifty thousand?' Chris wiped at her ear.

'Fifteen,' Sophie said.

'Well, that could be worse. Find out the pedigree of the bull and sale prices of bulls from the same stud and we can talk.'

Sophie agreed and went to the office, but it was already in use. Dave had decided to organise Jock's return for the funeral. Jenny couldn't say why this had become a focus, but it had, and Dave was making loud phone calls and cursing when he got nowhere.

Jenny felt like she had entered an alternate reality.

Sunday was upside down, as were the days that followed.

Chris had agreed to pay for the bull, but left the logistics in Sophie's hands, which did not seem entirely wise. Apart from that item of business, Chris was behaving like she was on holiday. She went for walks along the creek, ate when she felt like it, read in the hammock and phoned her kids. She was still arranging for them to come down, so that was something.

Dave had booked flights for Jock, who said he'd catch them, but now Dave was all antsy because he was worried Jock wouldn't show up. Jenny hoped Dave hadn't forgotten to organise Sharon and the kids.

And Sophie was erratic. Crying one minute, laughing the next. Flirting with the truck driver who delivered the bull and, after he'd gone, furious with the paddock he'd put the bull in. It was ridiculous, because obviously Sophie had asked him to unload the truck there. She tried to move the bull, but couldn't, and cried with frustration. Then she laughed and started the whole cycle again.

Jenny was the only one who was behaving normally. She got up at five every day. She had tea and toast and was out the door by five fifteen.

She drove around the stock. She took salt blocks out for the cattle and checked the water troughs. She kept an eye on the feed and noted which stock would need to be moved, and where they'd do best.

Once Jenny had done the morning round, she came back to the house. By now Sophie was usually up, crying or not, and Jenny had a cuppa with her, then took her out.

They moved the cattle together. It was much easier with two people than one. Especially given they didn't have a dog. They checked the fences. Jenny drove slowly along while Sophie looked for holes. When they found one, they stopped to plug it with a nearby rock. They fastened the ring lock with tie wire if it was loose, and jotted notes about jobs they would have to come back and do.

Sophie was surprisingly handy. And she was strong. Jenny enjoyed having her along.

Rumbling along in the ute, it dawned on Jenny that she and Sophie were running the farm. It didn't feel like it. It felt like their father had gone on holidays and they'd offered to help out for a few days.

It definitely didn't feel like Ellersley belonged to them, though Jenny supposed it did. Or maybe it was some lawyer's or bank's property, until the funeral was done. Regardless, it didn't seem real. Ellersley belonged to their father. Tom Edwards. And his predecessors. Their granny, and their grandad who died too young. The generations that came before him. Not the flawed generation to follow.

The funeral was arranged for Wednesday. It got organised, somehow. Maybe because Chris had done all that planning at the beginning. Or maybe because the CWA got involved. Jenny didn't know for sure.

The time stretched far and wide for those few days. When they came together for meals, or stopped to exchange a few words, it drew closer, but not for long.

Jenny was proud of how well they managed. They were courteous. At times they were kind. They lived with uncertainty, and they didn't blame each other.

It would never be like this again, an Edwards family gathering. It couldn't. But maybe they'd recall being here. Perhaps they would remember how to do it, this quiet talk and non-talk. Fragments might remain within and reappear when they were together.

133

'Be fair, Tom. Jock got money, but you got Ellersley.'

Tom wasn't sure if it was his mother talking or his own thoughts given voice. The night sweats and waking hours were falling into each other, and it was hard to know if he was awake or talking in his sleep.

'Be fair.'

It was his mother. He wondered about disputing the point, but then the shivering started. By the time it passed, he'd lost the urge to say something.

Besides, he'd want to think twice, before arguing with her. She might bring up the night Jock left. She probably knew about that, now she was dead.

Jock had been gathering things together for about a week. The spare razor from the bathroom, the old brush, half an inch off the bottom of the shaving stick. Blind Freddie could have seen that Jock was getting ready to leave. He snuck their father's overnight bag from the closet and hid it under his bed. One afternoon while their exhausted mother slept in the spare room, Jock raided their father's sock drawer. Tom had left the house to go around the stock, but he ducked back in for a hat, and caught Jock tiptoeing across the hall, his arms full of socks. Tom shook his head in disbelief, but Jock winked at him and laughed. 'No good letting your feet get cold, is it?' he said. It wasn't much of a hiding place, a pair of rolled-up socks. Not for large amounts of cash. Especially if it was known to everyone in the house.

Jock left at 4.30 am. It was a clear night. No moon. Tom was taking a piss around the side of the house when the door scraped open. Jock stepped out, sports jacket in one hand and their father's bag in the other. He had his Stetson dipped over one eye, as if it wasn't dark enough. He had an unlit cigarette balanced on his bottom lip, and when he'd walked down the steps, he put the bag on the gravel, lit his cigarette and slipped the lighter into the pocket of his creased trousers. With Jock, everything had to be done in style. Even running away from home. He put his jacket on, adjusted the Stetson, and set off down the track.

And Tom didn't say a thing.

He knew why Jock was leaving. If he'd had half a brain, he would have gone himself. It was a terrible time, and only going to get worse. Their father dying, their mother grieving, and Ellersley. There was enough work for ten men and Jock couldn't bear to do the work of one, so it was no surprise.

But Tom could see further than Jock. The hard spell was terrible, but it wasn't going to last forever. As he watched Jock's preparation, Tom understood what was at stake.

If Jock deserted, there would be only Tom left. And Ellersley would be his. His to run; his to farm; his to manage. He wasn't even thinking about inheritance. Tom could say that with his hand on his heart.

The sky was beginning to lighten as Jock walked away. He passed the hedge and went out of view, and the morning came closer. The stars faded to nothing, the sky turned pale blue, and a pile of clouds lit up on the horizon. Tom's chest burst wide open.

Tom liked Jock when he wasn't being a prick. Loved him, even, like a brother should. But this was more important. Tom was born to run Ellersley, and Ellersley had been biding her time, waiting for him.

It wasn't fair, that Jock got the money, no matter what his mother said. Tom was right in his rage. The estate of Ellersley had been eroded by Jock's begging and gambling and God knows what else. Nothing could make that right.

But Tom never mentioned the night Jock left. Not to his dying father, or his grieving mother, or anyone else for that matter.

Tom got Ellersley, or Ellersley got him. He still believed it worked out the way it was meant to. But Tom knew the rules. Property goes to the eldest son.

Ellersley was Jock's, until Tom watched him go.

134

Christine appreciated that it was necessary for one family member to see the deceased prior to closing the coffin lid, but did everyone have to come? Annette Darby was almost as insistent as Vince Barton had been about having all four siblings present, but Christine couldn't see it making much difference. It was fine for Jenny, who wanted to see the coffin completed, and it didn't bother Christine – she had seen a few dead bodies in her time – but she was concerned that David and Sophie might not be up to it. They agreed to come, though.

Annette Darby was a vision from Coorong in the fifties. Coiffed hair, full make-up, and a pastel pink suit with matching pumps stretched wide around her bunions.

'Good morning, everyone,' Annette said, in the singsong voice of a primary school teacher. She smiled brightly. 'How are we all this morning?'

'We're good,' Sophie said, looking around at the others. 'Are we? We good?' Jenny smiled and nodded, Dave shrugged, and Christine nodded agreement so they could get the whole thing over and done with.

'Here's the suit,' Christine said and offered it to Annette.

'Well, that's fantastic,' Annette said, but like it wasn't the main item of business.

'I'll take it now and I can dress your father, if that would be agreeable to you all?'

'Absolutely agreeable,' Sophie said, her voice barely holding back a giggle. Christine shot her a warning glance. The last thing they needed right now was for Sophie to get hysterical.

'Wonderful. While I'm doing that, I have a little job for you too.' Annette took the suit and backed through a frosted swinging door, re-emerging with paper, pens and envelopes.

'Now it's time for each of you to write a letter to put in the coffin.'

'What?' Dave looked at Annette in disbelief. 'You can't make us do that!'

'No, David, it's not compulsory.' Annette handed pen and paper to Jenny, who took it without fuss. 'However, it is the way we do things at Darby's Funeral Home. You will find it beneficial I assure you.'

Dave stared at her for a minute and then he gave in. He chose wisely. If this was the way they did things at Darby's Funeral Home, it wasn't likely to change today.

Annette gave Christine and Sophie their stationery and turned to the coffin display room.

'There is a desk on each wall. Take your paper, pen and envelope with you.'

'Are you going to mark this?' Dave asked suspiciously.

'Of course not, David!' Annette smiled indulgently. 'No one else will read your letter. That's why you have the envelope too. When you've finished, we will simply pop the letters in the coffin with your father.' She made it sound like a mail service. It was absurd. Still, Christine decided, better get it over and done with. There were other things she needed to do today.

She sat at the tiny desk, which was a school desk as it turned out, and made a start.

Dad,

It was a ridiculous will. I can't believe you were going to give Ellersley to Vince Barton. On the bright side you had the foresight to divide the property equally and put in the condition of no sale. Strange that insanity and sound judgement should sit alongside each other like that. Maybe they did in your life too.

I've never thought of that. You didn't pay me much attention. Even though I was doing all the work. You laughed at me a lot. You despised my husband. You were right about him, by the way. I am out of there and couldn't be happier about it.

I've been thinking, while working on this coffin, why you laughed at me. I've come to the conclusion that you laughed because the things I was doing worked. My cooking, the cleaning, the rosters – they weren't perfect, but they worked. And you had to watch me, an eleven-year-old girl, succeed in this while you failed in everything else. The drought, the dust storms, the starving stock; and Mum's depression, too. In a way that was your fault.

It can't have been easy, but it's no excuse. I've spent my life making sure no one will laugh at me. It's been a terrible waste of time. I've taught my children to abide by every social norm and what kind of lesson is that? I'm done. With all of it.

You taught me some things. Honesty. Courage. How to carry on when there is no relief in sight. You taught me that family is everything. I don't buy that, but I'll admit it's worth something.

Anyway, Jenny and Sophie think they're going to run Ellersley. Let me assure you, they're not. They'll be doing the farming and so forth, but I will run the business. It will be in safe hands.

Take care,

Christine

135

Jenny listened to Annette Darby's instructions, took her pen and paper and walked to the desk most private on the other side of the coffin showroom. Jenny was grateful it was a letter, and not the phone.

Dear Dad,

Well, it seems like you knew about my business. I've been wondering for a while.

We did a good job. You'll like it. We did it together. Like you wanted. We got on with each other. Mostly. So I guess the plan worked.

I'm going to run Ellersley, I've decided. I think maybe Sophie will help. Maybe Christine, too, but we'll see. Dave says he's done with it. He might visit at Christmas though.

I have a man in my life. His name is Matthew. Maybe you knew that too. He's different to you. He's gentle. And encouraging. I'm not meaning to put you down, they're just the things that Matthew is. He's strong. That's like you. He doesn't get upset. He is patient and kind, and he is my man.

You weren't patient or kind, but maybe you did your best. I don't know. One thing I do know is that you were honest. And you never left us. Not until now.

Take care. We won't be far behind.
Jenny

136

It was bloody ludicrous. Worse than building a coffin. All right, maybe not worse. Just one more abnormal coffin-related activity. Annette Darby said it wasn't compulsory, but she wasn't fooling Dave. If he'd said no Annette would have held him in that coffin room until he gave in.

'Fine.' Dave snatched the paper and identified the only empty desk. Right in the corner near the sliding doors.

He sat down, flattened his paper and made a start.

See you later, Dad. Four words in and he already had an ink splodge on the page. Dave reminded himself this wasn't a test. And that his father was dead. He wiped his pen lower down on the page and continued:

See you later, Dad, you old prick.

He leaned back in his chair, balancing on the rear legs, and chewed the pen.

You screwed me up bad. I've never gotten over it.

Dave looked around at the girls, all of them hard at work.

You made me a better dad, though. Taught me what not to do.

He was starting to enjoy himself. If it wasn't being marked, he could say what he liked.

> *You could have come to my games. You could have taken an interest in my trade. You could have loved my kids. You could have laughed, sometimes, at my jokes.*
>
> *You could have been kind to your wife. You could have respected mine.*

Dave was writing fast, words pouring onto the page.

You could have taught me something, anything, without showing me first how hopeless I was. You could have treated me like I was worth the time.

Now there were tears running, snot dripping. He wiped his nose on the back of his hand and kept writing.

Footy. Trade. Construction business. Hell, even the debt. Who did you think I was doing it for? I was aiming high because that's what Edwards men do.

You never forgave me, for being second rate. I don't know if I'll ever forgive you.

The Edwards men don't do forgiveness.

We don't do love either. Not for each other. But I did. I loved you. There was no one like you and there never will be.

Dave
PS. I'm leaving Ellersley.

137

It was hilarious. Annette Darby with her big hair, flapping heels and lipstick leaking into the wrinkles around her mouth. A room full of coffins with no prices on them, so they were definitely expensive. Sophie went across to the third desk. She sat with her back to the coffins, so it was just her, the blank paper, a pen and her dad.

Hi Dad,

You've got to see this place to believe it. Padded coffins! I mean really padded. It's crazy. Puts our building effort to shame. It's been crazy at home too. Love, drugs, fights, whatever you can imagine, we've had it at Ellersley this week.

Sophie paused. It's what she would have said if they were catching up after a couple of weeks. But they weren't. It was years since Sophie had a conversation like that with her dad. Mostly she made up rubbish stories about her life and avoided questions. Maybe this letter was her last chance to say something real. She scratched out what she had written and started again.

Hi Dad, she began. It was as good a start as any. She'd never written a letter like this. She was resisting the temptation to make him laugh.

Last chance, Sophie, last chance.

Her hand was sweaty, and she was holding the pen tightly to stop it from slipping.

Hi Dad,

She had to make it about him. About how great he was.

You are the best dad a girl could want. I have fabulous memories of when I was a kid, and you always believed in me.

It was like a Father's Day card written by a primary school child. *Last chance, Sophie, make it real.*

Her heart was thumping and she wondered if she was going to pass out.

She took a deep breath and started again.

Hi Dad,

I've done a terrible thing. So many terrible things. Or maybe it's only one thing, but so many times. You knew. I knew you did. I couldn't call when I realised. I couldn't call.

Hi Dad,

I took your money.

Hi Dad,

Hi Dad,

It's me, Sophie. I wanted to say goodbye. That's not true. It's the opposite of true. I want to say hi. And I'm sorry.

I'm sorry. I'm sorry. I'm sorry I let you down. I didn't know. That's not true. I knew. I'm sorry, Dad, I'm so sorry.

I'm still your Sophie. It's going to be good from now on. I promise. I swear, Dad. I've met this guy. You'd like him – you know him! It's Ben Taylor. I've come home now. Maybe it's for good. I'm sorry, Dad. I love you. Please don't go.

Xxxxxxxxxxxxxxxxxxxxxxxxx

138

Tom Edwards' funeral was, in the end, just as everyone expected it to be.

It was held at St Marks, Coorong, on Wednesday morning, a proper eleven days following his death. The service was followed by the burial, and a wake held at the Coorong Community Hall with light refreshments served by the CWA.

The Reverend Allen did a good job, everyone thought. A few personal touches, not too religious.

The pallbearers were the family men. David and Stephen Minehan – Christine's husband – at the front, Jock and a man named Matthew Blake in the middle, and two of Darby's men at the back.

It was good that Jock came. In the end the family paid for him to fly over, which was the right thing to do. He was an old man now, but he wanted to walk with the coffin and people respected that. Matthew, the bloke from Albury, was about a foot taller than Jock, but he stooped low enough for the coffin to touch Jock's shoulder, so it worked out all right. No one quite knew how Matthew fit into the picture, but he had some connection with Jenny. A boyfriend, maybe. She was an odd one, Jenny Edwards.

There was a bit of nudging to begin with: people craning their necks to get a look at the coffin. You had to give them credit, they'd done a good job. Nice timber. It didn't look home spun. It looked like a real coffin.

There were flowers, and service booklets, and a guest attendance list. The funeral director did all that these days. Too much stress on the family, they said, just give us a photo or two, we'll sort out the rest.

There was a decent gathering of mourners. Not like you'd see for a young one, not right up the street, but the church was full and there was overflow into the yard. The lucky ones stood in the shade of the building, where it was nice and cool, and not too close to the preaching.

The family chose not to make speeches, which was a shame. Maybe they felt like building the coffin was enough. You can't overdo respect, though. Not when it comes to a family member passing. It doesn't hurt to say a few words.

They waited out the front to greet the congregation, though, they got that right. Stood at the church gate as people filed past, shaking hands, and kissing cheeks of those they knew.

Christine and Sophie stayed there until the church was empty. Jenny left early. She was a bit distracted. She followed the coffin to the hearse, watched the men put it in the back and checked it was stable and steady before she'd let them drive off. The cemetery gates were only about a hundred metres away, but Jenny had always been a nervous sort of a girl.

Dave was looking out for her, which was kind of him. He was a good bloke. Once the coffin was loaded in the hearse, he took Jenny by the arm and steered her towards the cemetery.

It was only a short walk, but not everyone chose to go. A smaller group, close friends and family, gathered by the graveside.

The women went to the hall to lay out the food. The CWA had done it all. Sandwiches, slices, cakes; anything you could think of. The men headed to the hotel to get a cold one before the wake. They were worth their weight in gold, the CWA ladies, but they tended to cater more to hunger than to thirst.

By the time the graveside mourners came across, the hall was ready, the men had returned, and women were handing around plates of finger food. It was just as it should be.

All in all, it was a good funeral. Dignified. Respectful. Tom Edwards would have been pleased.

139

It performed beautifully on the day. Jenny didn't have any particular doubts, but she was never completely at ease until a coffin was in the ground. She watched the straps unwind, slowly. They rubbed against the soil of the grave, and the edges of the coffin too, and the smells of linseed oil and earth mixed together and lingered in the air. The broad daylight revealed the grain of the timber. Reds and orange-browns and long threads of black. Jenny wanted to halt proceedings, so they could all enjoy it, but the coffin touched the bottom before she found the words.

Just as the Reverend Allen began the burial rites, Jenny felt a touch on her shoulder. It was Dr Briggs, with an envelope in his hand. Jenny took it, and glanced at the spidery handwriting, unmistakably their father's. Her name was first, then the others. She slipped it into her pocket and tried to concentrate on the burial.

'We therefore commit this body to the ground,' Reverend Allen continued. It was so dignified. Compared to the average pet funeral, anyway.

One of the Darby's men got a little trowel and dug into the pile of soil behind her, then handed the trowel to Jenny.

'Earth to earth.'

Strangely she had never been the one throwing dirt in. Maybe they didn't do it at their mum's funeral.

The dirt slipped off the trowel and made a dull thud when it hit the coffin. It scattered out, some making it to the edge of the coffin and falling over.

'Ashes to ashes.'

She handed the trowel back and put her hand in her pocket.

The letter was red hot. They should read it before they left the graveside. As soon as the service was done.

'Dust to dust.'

Jenny watched her siblings throw clods of dirt into the hole, then various mourners tossed in roses and carnations. Whatever was available at the Coorong Florist Shop yesterday.

'In sure and certain hope of the Resurrection to eternal life.'

The mourners peeled off for the final words, heading across the yard to the hall.

Jenny caught the eye of each of her siblings in turn, and they directed their families to the hall before they came around the coffin to Jenny, and she pulled the envelope from her pocket.

'Will I read it out loud?' she said, and realised she didn't want to. 'No, I'll read it then pass it on. Me, then Dave, then Chris, then Sophie. All right?' The others nodded.

Jenny slipped her thumb under the flap of the envelope and pulled the letter out. It was on embossed paper, with the Ellersley address in block print. Jenny had never seen this stationery. The address didn't include road names or numbers. It must have been decades old.

"Ellersley"
Coorong
NSW 2640

Kids,

Jenny – You did it. I thought you would. You're determined. Slow, but you get the job done. First class. You think Charles Briggs didn't show me the little ones?

I met Matthew a while back. Liked him. You could bring him home sometime.

It's not a bad thing, being slow, if you're on a property. Ellersley might enjoy a change of pace.

Dave – You're not the victim, you never were. Do everyone a favour and give it up. You've got a good brain. Use it. You're handy. Your kids love you; you're a good father. Don't let that hairdresser go, whatever you do. You lose her, you'll lose everything.

Christine – You're smart. Too smart for St Ives. You ran a household when you were eleven, you've done enough of that. You do something worth your while. Like running Ellersley. Don't let that old bore hold you back.

Sophie – You stuffed up. Stole my money, broke my trust. You took your old man for a fool. Don't waste your time thinking about it. You're not the first to do it, you won't be the last. You've spent a lot of years running away. Try staying home for a bit, you might like it. I love you.

Kids, Ellersley's in your hands now.

Make me proud.

Dad

Jenny didn't know how to take it. She handed the letter to Dave, and the others watched on, wanting him to hurry up so they could read it too.

The big shovels were out now. The Darby's men had their jackets off and their shirts were soaking wet as they filled the hole. It was ridiculous to be working so hard in the heat. Someone should have hired a bobcat.

Jenny realised they were standing in the sun too, but they wouldn't be long. There wasn't much shade to be found in the cemetery.

Dave handed the letter to Christine, dazed. She read it quickly and handed it to Sophie and then they were done. What kind of 'done' they were was another question. Maybe the others weren't sure what to make of it either. Except Sophie. She was sobbing so hard she could hardly breathe. Dave absently put an arm around her shoulder. 'You right, mate?' he said, and gave her a squeeze. 'You'll be right.'

'Right,' Christine said, brushing the wrinkles out of her skirt, 'time for us to get to that wake.'

They walked across the stubble to the road, then across the hot asphalt to the hall. Jenny put on her best public face, and they walked up the steps to re-enter the fray.

140

The letter was a bit of a shock. Maybe Annette Darby had got her hooks into their old man as well. Started with a barb for Dave, which was no surprise. On another day it would have destroyed him. Today, though, it skated right past. Maybe there was such a thing as 'funeral immunity', and maybe Dave had it. Who knew? There'd be plenty of time to stew on it when this was all over. Anyway, turns out the old bloke had a couple of positives to say. Didn't say Sharon's name, Dave noticed, but he did give her the time of day.

Sharon wasn't all that keen on coming to the funeral. More to the point, she wasn't keen on seeing him. But Dave had the numbers now. Five hundred thousand was a number. And so was five million. Sharon was sceptical, but when he told her Chris was lending him the money, she said she'd give him the benefit of the doubt. For now.

The truth was, Sharon would have come, regardless, for his old man. Dave was sure of it. But it was better to be on speaking terms when she arrived. She brought the kids. Put them in their best outfits and drove them up. They sat in the second pew, just behind him. He spent the whole service wanting to turn around.

Jock came, too. It took more effort than Dave expected, tracking him down. He didn't want to come, had plenty of reasons, but Dave told him the ticket was paid for and that was that. When Dave saw him, he was shocked. Jock was shaky and whingy and frail and nothing like the man Dave remembered. He regretted suggesting to Darby's that Jock could be a pallbearer.

Carrying the coffin was tricky. Dave was at the front, with Stephen, the poor bastard. Then Matthew and Jock. Matthew had to be over six four, and Jock had shrivelled to nothing much.

The Darby blokes were at the back. It was tricky, but nothing on being a pallbearer for his mum. He walked alongside his old man that day, and every step was taken in fury and despair. Today was totally different.

They moved slowly. With dignity. Dave stood straight, with his shoulders back and took small steps, like he'd been told. He fixed his eyes on the stone wall at the back. He had a serious expression on his face, but he had to concentrate to keep it there. What he wanted to do was grin. Throw his head back and laugh.

There were Sharon and the kids, close enough to touch, dressed in their funeral clothes and looking so smart. And tomorrow they were going home. Dave Edwards and his wife and kids, going back to Wagga to make a fresh start.

Dave wasn't mourning; not today. He wasn't grieving the loss of his old man. He was carrying the coffin with a serious face, and he'd go to the graveside and the wake. He knew what was expected of him, and he'd do it. But he wasn't sad.

From the moment he realised he could sell Ellersley, he had felt lighter. It was partly the money – Dave wasn't going to brush over that. But there was something else at play.

He had never realised how heavy it was, the weight of Ellersley. It had never occurred to him that getting out of Ellersley might be the start of something. A life of his own choosing – not tied, not waiting on the judgement of his old man.

Strange, that letter. No guilt. No pressure. Keep the hairdresser, his father said, but he didn't tell Dave to devote his life to Ellersley. Use your brains, look after your kids, keep your wife. That's what he said.

Typical of his old man. He had to die before he'd admit Dave was doing something right.

141

Stephen and the children arrived, as instructed, on the day of the funeral. It was an eight-thirty flight, arriving in Albury at nine twenty-five. Christine met them at the airport. She was wearing her funeral clothes – black pin-skirt and jacket, with a cream chemise underneath – so she was looking smart, at least.

It was strange to be in a suit again. To put on her stilettos. But she was grateful for the armour. The thought of seeing Stephen unnerved her. She would need every scrap of self-respect an outfit could give her.

The heels were problematic. They tipped her forward and propelled her awkwardly across the threshold of the arrivals lounge. She was out of practice. But the suit did its job. It helped her remember who she was a week and a half ago; what her family might expect of her now.

As it turned out she barely noticed Stephen. He could have been any middle-aged man, in any airport, on any day of the week.

What Christine saw was an awkward boy in a suit, with self-conscious hair and angry red blotches on his neck, and a dumpy girl in a black dress, her foundation and mascara too thickly applied.

The loneliest longing of Christine's life welled up in her, and she kicked off the stupid heels to run for those bodies. She ran at them hard and reached out, burying their heads in her chest, clutching their shoulders, their wrists, touching their hands to her face and crying, sobbing like the most embarrassing, emotional mother would.

She handed Stephen the car keys and put one arm around each ungainly adolescent. She was laughing and crying, while Nicholas and Claudia stood straight, uncertain about how to behave in this strange time and place.

Christine had stopped crying by the time they got to Coorong, which was clearly a relief to all concerned. But when they got out of the car, she kept her children close, a hand on each of their shoulders, alternately kneading and gripping as they walked down the aisle.

The last time Christine had attended this church was for her mother's funeral. She was not much older than her children were now. The thought was a crying fit in the making, so Christine brought her mind back to the present.

There were hymns and a sermon and prayers, as one would expect, and her son and daughter sat either side of her. Stephen carried the coffin and he didn't trip over, worse luck, but Christine supposed it was better for the event as a whole that he stayed upright.

She greeted people at the gates, then gathered her children to walk to the graveside.

They didn't know what to make of her, Christine could tell. She didn't know either. Every time she went to speak, she cried, or laughed. It didn't seem so out of the ordinary by a graveside, but she had no confidence that the end of the day would mean the end of her volatile state.

When the burying was done, Jenny beckoned to them all.

It was a letter from their father. Christine's part said she was smart, and to ditch Stephen and that maybe she could run Ellersley. But the thing she mostly noticed, and surely the others had seen the same, was that he said, 'I love you,' at the end, but it wasn't clear if he meant it for all of them or only Sophie. It was a jab, either way. He didn't say it to Christine. Again.

Christine got ready to weep, to fall apart, but she didn't do either. Maybe it was the fact that she'd already left Stephen and decided she'd be running Ellersley, and her father was barely keeping up. She'd try not to be too hard on him. He was a dying man. Well, dead man now.

It was thanks to him, and his appalling will, that Christine had a new life direction. Ellersley was only the start of it. There was a whole continent of farmers who needed someone to tell them how to make a succession plan. It would have to be someone smart. Savvy. Strong enough to take them in hand and make them do what they were told.

142

Sophie had decided she wasn't going to stick around. Up until she wrote that letter. She'd told her dad now. Told him she'd come home. Even said she'd met a bloke! In that *'I think he's a keeper'* kind of way. What did she want to go and do that for? She'd never told him she'd 'met someone' like that when he was alive.

At least she hadn't specified anything. Hadn't mentioned the grid episode. Or buying the bull. She could see her dad laughing at her. With her. They both knew she was interested, even if she was furious.

Ben came to the funeral. Wearing a shirt and tie, and a suit jacket. He came to pay his respects and he did it properly. No smiling, no hint of laughter. He gave her a polite nod as he walked through the church gate at the end of the service. Sophie lost sight of him when they walked to the cemetery. It wasn't far, but the ground was hard and rocky, and she had to watch every step.

The graveside part was the worst. Actually, the worst was walking into the church and seeing that coffin, which was so beautiful, but now it had her father's body in it. It was horrible, seeing his body. Annette Darby suggested it, and Sophie did what she was told, but she wished she hadn't. It wasn't him at all. It was some other waxy, cold, staring person.

So the graveside was the second worst. Or third if she counted seeing the body. Anyway, it was bad. Watching those men let the straps get long enough to lower the coffin into the hole, and knowing once it was filled in there was no way out. Worse, there was nothing left. Just a piece of marble with his name on it, next to a piece of marble with her mother's name on it, with a whole mouthful of marble teeth that had 'someone Edwards' carved on them scattered all around. Which wasn't nothing, exactly. But it was near enough. It was a dead body surrounded by dead bodies, though probably a load of them weren't bodies at all by now.

Someone handed Sophie a trowel, which brought her back to the present. She had no idea what it was for, so she held onto it until a person near her whispered, 'Throw it into the grave, dear.' Sophie did. The metal rang out when it hit the coffin. The Reverend Allen stopped speaking and everyone looked into the hole. One of Darby's men came quickly to the graveside with some enormously long grabbing-thing and pulled the trowel out. Apparently she was only meant to throw the dirt.

Jenny beckoned them over after the service was done. The kids and partners had been sent to the hall, so Sophie knew it was serious. She was the last one to read the letter, so she'd seen the others' reactions first. They weren't all that dramatic. Maybe a bit shocked. When Sophie read it she could see why. The letter was meant for her. He wanted her to come home. He loved her. Even though he understood what she had done. 'I love you' was what he wrote. In his paragraph to her.

Sophie started to sob. She couldn't stop. None of the others were crying, only Sophie. Weeping, heaving, choking on her words, crying like a lost child. Then Dave put his arm around her.

'You'll be right, mate,' he said.

They walked across to the hall together, and Dave made a couple of jokes on the way. The others thought it was a scream that she threw the trowel in. It helped her to right herself. By the time they got to the hall she climbed the steps without help, and by the time she walked through the door she was ready to greet the mourners.

She didn't expect the first one to be Ben Taylor. She realised immediately that she wasn't ready. Her face was red and blotchy. Her eyes were puffed up. She hadn't done her lipstick and her dress was hanging crooked, and it suddenly occurred to her that Ben was probably at the graveside and, if he was, he would have seen the trowel-throwing incident.

'Hi,' she said. It was the best she could manage.

'Hey,' he said. 'Curried egg sandwich?' He held out three white bread triangles. Sophie accepted one and took a bite.

'Bit greedy?' she said.

'Self-defence,' he replied. Sophie laughed.

'I'm serious. They're unstoppable, those CWA women.' He held out another one and Sophie took it. She wasn't hungry, but it was a whole lot easier than talking.

'I'm sorry about your dad,' Ben said. Sophie teared up again and nodded. The white bread went to clay in her mouth, and she reached into her pocket for a tissue. While she was scrounging around Ben offered her a napkin.

'Thanks,' Sophie said and blew her nose. So much snot. Such a loud snort.

'Classy,' Ben said, and she laughed again.

'Thanks. I like to think so.'

'River red was a good pick,' he said. Sophie looked at him blankly. 'For the coffin.'

'Oh, right. Of course.'

'Did you ever see one fall?'

'What?'

'They do that, red gums. One minute tall and strong, the next crashed to the ground. Dead. No warning.'

'Really?' Sophie couldn't tell if he was being serious.

'True fact.' They stood silently for a minute, then Ben changed the subject.

'I'm sorry about the bull, too,' he said.

Sophie could feel the flush rising to her cheeks again. 'Oh?'

'You didn't deserve to win him.' He still looked serious but not so convincing.

Sophie smiled. She couldn't help herself. 'Why not?'

'I've had my eye on him for months.'

Sophie smiled big, dimples and all, and accidentally winked. At her father's wake. She didn't mean to, of course she didn't. It was just the flirting instinct was very strong in her. Sophie looked around the room quickly but didn't see any disapproving siblings.

'If you behave yourself,' she said quietly, 'I might lend him to you.' Somehow saying it quietly made it more suggestive. Sophie's blush was now radiating heat, probably to the other side of the room. It only worsened when she realised she had effectively just said, *I've decided to stay at Ellersley and I want our cows to have sex with each other.* It was her father's wake!

'Deal,' he said and offered her another sandwich. Her safest option now was to take the sandwich and avoid eye contact. She wasn't about to eat it, though. Curried egg sandwiches were the worst. She couldn't believe she'd already had two. Ben had caught her in a weakened state. She wouldn't let it happen again.

143

There was nothing to be done. If David had been in charge Vince would have stood a fighting chance of getting the lot. His payment, the bank deposit, legal fees for conveyancing and transfer of shares – Vince could easily have added these sums to his Italian bank account if David was in control.

But he wasn't. Evidently Christine had completely recovered from her drug experiment and was more in charge than ever. She wore a pinstripe suit and patent black stilettos to the funeral. Her hair was a little wild, though Vince had some sympathy for her on that. It was very hard to find a hairstylist in Albury – forget Coorong – who knew how to deal with a natural wave.

Vince had not wanted to rock the boat prior to the funeral, so he had said nothing about Christine's attempted bribe, and by the day of the funeral he realised the opportunity was lost. It was a great shame, because he could have used that leverage to negotiate terms to do the conveyancing work.

The moment Christine entered his office – without embarrassment, Vince noted – to discuss the outstanding legal and financial details, he knew there would be nothing in it for him. Less than nothing.

She had employed a Sydney solicitor to do the conveyancing of David's sale of assets to her. She had discussed the terms of the will with this appalling person, who had advised her to ensure Vince Barton notify her the moment the money from the bank deposit was transferred to the Barton & Sons trust account, and as soon as the funds were cleared to have them transferred to the Ellersley Trust. She instructed Vince to provide her with a receipt proving he had done so, and went further still, saying, 'Mr Barton, you have done very well for yourself in this matter. Yet I can see you would not be above trying to push your advantage further. Let me warn you that if you try to appropriate any part of the Ellersley trust it will be detected and you will suffer the consequences.'

She was terrifying. There was no way Vince could come up against a force like Christine Minehan and achieve victory.

Once again, Tom Edwards had his laugh and came out on top. The scraps under the table; that's what he'd left for Vince Barton. A measly twenty thousand dollars, which Vince would not receive until probate was granted. Which meant Vince had at least four months more of living in the desert-lands of Coorong.

It was humiliating. And inevitable. He realised that Vince Barton of Barton & Sons was always going to come to this end.

Maybe he had to.

Maybe Vince Barton needed to die an irrevocable death for Vincenzo Bartolo to rise.

It was a long and drawn-out death, but eventually it was completed. And from the ashes – or petty, rural town politics, as the case may be – Vincenzo Bartolo did rise.

He found his birth certificate. He obtained a passport. He acquired bank cards and cash and a jaunty overnight bag. He booked flights and a pensione in Rome and bought a brand-new suit for the journey. He put oil in his hair, a silk handkerchief in his pocket and his grandfather's gold ring on his pinky finger.

He sold what he could and did better than he expected.

Everything else, Vincenzo Bartolo left behind.

144

It was pitiful, to write a letter from his deathbed. But Tom couldn't give the idea up. The nearer he came to the end, the closer it clung to him.

It was Charles Briggs' suggestion. He didn't bother with advice or medicines – Tom wouldn't have taken either – but he mentioned a patient who'd written a letter. Tom didn't much go for that sort of thing, but if his kids succeeded, he had a word or two he'd like to pass on.

When he'd first had the coffin idea, he was pissed off. That was all. He imagined them coming home in dribs and drabs. Jenny was the slow one, but she'd get there first. Dave would be last. Chris would come belting down the highway. And Sophie – he couldn't think about that or he'd come undone.

He wrote the letter. It wasn't much. Gave it to Charles to pass on if they built the coffin. It could go in the rubbish if they didn't.

He was strangely hopeful in his final days. He found himself smiling. Often. He woke early. Watched the pre-dawn pink turn blue and the sun rise over the ridge. 'Look at that,' he'd say and shake his head, his heart so light he barely knew it was there. Later in the day he'd be leaning on the gate, looking out at the paddock, and he'd come over all emotional. Smiling, but tears too.

What a season to die. The grass knee-high and bright green. The cattle fat and sleek. Water in the troughs and the sun glinting off the wire. God, it was beautiful. If only they could see it. If they could get a glimpse of this glory.

He didn't want them to fail, was the truth. Never had.

He only wanted to open their eyes.

ACKNOWLEDGEMENTS

Thanks to Phil Power, who taught me about building coffins, and Glenda Bloomfield who taught me about wills. You were both generous with your time, and your advice was sound. Any veering away from fact has been mine.

To Irma Gold, who awarded me the Editor's Pick for 'Fly to Meet You', and years later edited the manuscript that was to become *The Deed*. Your positivity kept me writing and your criticism made this book readable.

To Jane Novak, my agent, whose books were full but read my manuscript anyway. Thank you for taking a punt on this unknown writer.

To Hachette, the Richell family and Emerging Writers' Festival – the Richell Prize is a gift to the writing community of Australia, and submitting to this prize changed the landscape of my writing life.

To all the team at Hachette who have worked on *The Deed* – it has been a pleasure to work with every one of you. An especial thank you to Vanessa Radnidge who has seen me through from longlisting to publication. Your combination of expertise and good humour have made it a delightful ride.

To my parents, Richard and Carla, who taught me the pleasure of reading and writing, surrounded me with books and encouraged me every step of the way; my brother Tim, whose legal advice at the end steered me back on course; my sister-in-law Kim, whose joy in all things novel related is a gift; and my beautiful sister Em, who was there at the beginning and knew I'd get there in the end. Thank you, though thanks can hardly cover it.

To all the friends, aunties, uncles, cousins and kids whose optimism buoyed me up, I'm grateful for your support. Even if I didn't let you read the manuscript. (I stand by my position though. Reading it in finished form is definitely better.)

The Deed was written on Ngunnawal and Ngambri land, and is set in Wiradjuri country.

Susannah Begbie grew up in rural New South Wales on a sheep farm. She is now a GP, and has worked all over Australia. In 2006, Susannah started a Graduate Diploma in Professional Writing at Canberra University and was awarded the Editor's Pick for her short story 'Fly to Meet You' in the university's anthology, *FIRST*. She was also awarded the best-written text for her children's book *Don't You Dare!* in The Get Real Project. *The Deed* is her first novel.

About the Richell Prize and logo

In 2014, Hachette Australia's CEO, Matt Richell, died suddenly in a surfing accident. To honour Matt and his passion for nurturing and celebrating emerging Australia writers, Hachette, together with the Richell family, established The Richell Prize for Emerging Writers, in partnership with The Emerging Writers' Festival (EWF). The Prize was launched in 2015 and the community of writers it is building and the incredible talent it has unearthed over the past ten years is something everyone at Hachette Australia is extremely proud of. The Prize is unique in the Australian literary landscape because it is open to unpublished writers of adult fiction and adult narrative non-fiction and writers don't need to have a full manuscript at the time of submission, though they must intend to complete one. The Richell Prize gives writers the chance to chase their dream of completing a work, and offers them money and a mentorship to help make that happen.

Each winner receives $10,000 in prize money, a year's mentoring with one of Hachette Australia's publishers and a stunning trophy based on a swallow motif Matt Richell had tattooed on his arm. This is also the logo for the prize. The Emerging Writers' Festival's involvement in this Prize is sponsored by Simpsons Solicitors.

To date, Hachette Australia has published or contracted twelve debut authors who have been discovered through this annual prize, including Sally Abbott (2015 winner), Brodie Lancaster (2015 shortlist), Susie Greenhill (2016 winner), Sam Coley (2017 winner), Julie Keys (2017 shortlist), Ruth McIver (2018 winner), Mandy Beaumont (2018 shortlist), Zaheda Ghani (2018 shortlist) Allee Richards (2019 shortlist), Aisling Smith (2020 winner) and Simone Amelia Jordan (2021 winner). In the tenth year we are publishing *The Deed* by Susannah Begbie (2022 winner) with more news to come.

So, to all writers out there, be brave, be bold, back yourself and enter the 2024 Richell Prize.

emergingwritersfestival.com.au
hachette.com.au